ENVOY OF THE LORD

Missi Dominici

S. W. O'CONNELL

Lanyard Press
Leesburg Virginia

Envoy of the Lord

Lanyard Press
Leesburg, Virginia 20176

ISBN: 978-1-7376636-4-5

Cover art by Jennifer Gibson http://www.jennifergibson.ca/

Map by Bryon Line

Printed in the United States of America

For Pietro Giampietro

Acknowledgments

Some talented people helped me in the development of the story. Paul Harpin, Frank Capuano, Susan Harrison, Frederick W. Abel, L.J. Litton, John Molino, and Thomas J. Howley provided many thoughtful suggestions. Bryon Line, whose map will help orient the reader to the setting, and Jennifer Gibson, whose fabulous cover art captured the feel of this tale.

"Everything is the sum of the past."

—   Pierre Teilhard de Chardin

Contents

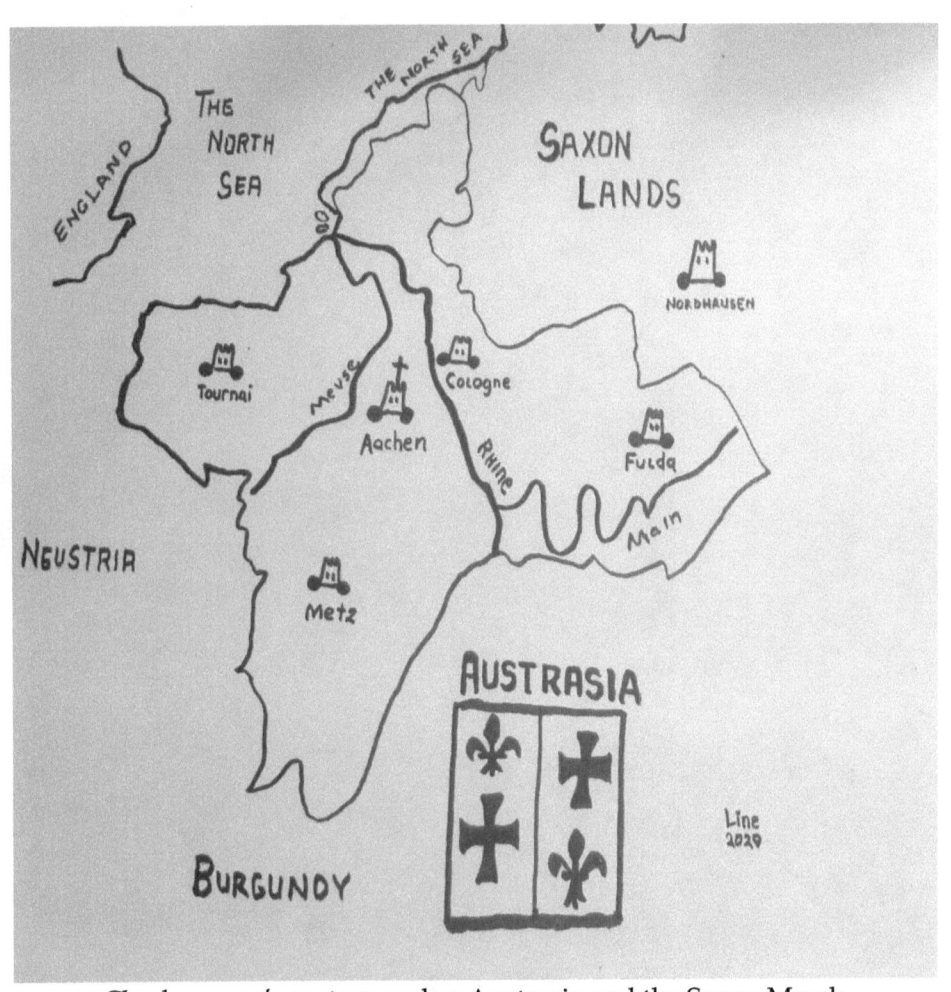

Charlemagne's eastern realm: Austrasia and the Saxon March

Prologue

Aachen, Germany, October 1944

Artillery and mortar shells pounded the earth, flinging shards of hot metal in a hundred directions. The almost constant boom of high-explosive shells made bones shudder. The incessant rattle of machine guns scratched out a cacophony that dimmed the senses, especially sound and smell. *To think that the war has returned me to the city that provided my family's legacy.*

Hauptmann Matthaeus Melchior reflected on his lot as he gazed through the plumes of thick black smoke rising before him. So, it has come to this, commanding a battalion of 200 *Volksturm* to defend the first German city to be attacked by the Allies. And this time against the once laughable Americans – the *Amis*!

After joining the Wehrmacht in 1942, Melchior had seen action in campaigns from North Africa and Italy to the steppes of Russia. His sojourn in the green fields of France completed what he always joked was his *Kriegsurlaub*...vacation in war. A medical student in his final year at university in *Koeln*, he stunned his professors and classmates when he quit to join the *Wehrmacht* as a sergeant in the *Sanitaetstruppen*, the medical corps, just weeks shy of receiving his medical degree, the coveted *Diplom Medicinarzt*.

Now, he was hunkered down amid some Roman ruins, a replica of the famed gate of Rome. No longer a gate, just a shattered pillar with the image of the Roman god Janus, faded and worn from over a thousand years of wear. He wondered if the god would survive this. Hitler and the *Amis* will do what a thousand years and the climate could not.

"Why are you doing this?" everyone asked. The truth was, he did not know. The necessities of war quickly overcame him and he soon was transferred to the *Infantrie Offiziersschule* at Hammelburg. A natural leader, he rose to the head of his class and soon graduated a *Leutnant der Infantrie*. After two years in almost continuous combat, he was promoted to *Hauptmann*. Soon after, he received the first of his wounds. He now had scars on both hands and feet. The former, from British artillery during the retreat from El Alamein in late '42, the latter shrapnel from Russian mortars near Smolensk in '43. Then there was the scar on his chest, courtesy of a Canadian sniper at Normandy, the place the Allies called Juno. Fortunately, the round was spent and the flesh torn, but the bullet lodged in his breastbone, stopping further penetration.

An ear-shattering barrage behind him roared like a midsummer thunderstorm. A geyser of earth and stone shot into the air and scattered across the defenders, who hugged the ground like moles seeking shelter. Around him, desperate men dove for cover. But Melchior did not flinch. Why should he? He knew by now that God chooses how, where, and when a man dies. A safe bunker could be a tomb given the right circumstances. A stray bullet from a raw recruit was just as deadly as a well-aimed shot from the most experienced sniper. It was all a matter of timing.

Melchior looked down at his dirt-spattered tunic. *Feldgrau* – field gray. He thought bitterly, *Scheissegrau*, shit gray, would be a better term for it.

A tarnished silver oblong badge was the only decoration he wore. His three Iron Crosses he had long cast aside. By this time, the Reich was handing them out like cigarettes… no… cigarettes were more precious and rarer… more like bonbons.

He received the silver medal from the division commander himself just before they shipped to the front with the 12th Division. A big ceremony…the *Infanterie Sturmabzeichen* was awarded only to soldiers who had survived over a dozen infantry close assaults, recons, and counterattacks. The Knight's Cross, presented by Hitler, was a farewell gift he had hoped to buy for Kristel. *Kristel*. The thought of her sent a chill down his spine.

But it has come to this: leading exhausted old men and sniveling boys to their deaths just to support a hated regime in an unworthy cause. Long live the Vaterland – *Sieg Heil!*

A gaunt runner braved the spitting lead and threw himself into his position. The boy's eyes had that deadened look Melchior knew all too well. "Sir, First Company cannot hold the right much longer…the *Ami* infantry and tanks are everywhere!"

A young boy of about fifteen, Melchior thought. He nodded wearily. "How many men do they have left?"

"I don't know, sir. Less than twenty I think."

"Less than twenty? Where are the rest?"

"Dead or fled, sir. Most fled. *Faernerich* Weber says the ones with him are firm but low on ammunition. One machine gun left and two *Panzerfausts*. *Herr Hauptmann*, the *Amis* have over a dozen tanks."

"Weber is a good man," Melchior said, calmly puffing on a cigarette.

Melchior glanced at his map. Made by the French firm Michelin, it was a city map, the type a tourist would use. *So, now we Germans rely on the French for our maps?* He searched for a street that offered more defensible ground while providing an escape route. Then he saw it, just up the road. He glanced down the rubble-strewn *Allee*. It was still there!

"*Nah gut so*, have him bring his men to the cathedral up on that hill. That is where we are going to defend – the *Dom*. I am moving the other companies now."

"*Ja, Herr Hauptmann!*" The boy was off before Melchior could point out the safest route to the ancient cathedral. Matthaeus Melchior had decided that his last stand for the Reich would take place at the sacred seat of the first German Reich.

He quickly settled the battalion in four defensive points at either wing of the *Dom*. The famous cathedral of Charlemagne was not as large as later palaces of worship, but its sturdy stone walls and turrets made it a strong defensive point. Melchior suddenly wondered why the division commander had not thought to occupy it with troops. He quickly put such musings away. He had more practical problems to occupy him.

Leutnant Norbert von und zu Zelinsky rushed toward him, bent over and running at full speed, wide-eyed, and without his helmet. A rare breach of military decorum for his usually meticulous lieutenant.

"What's our status, Zet?"

Zelinsky bristled just a bit.

Even at this moment, the proud Prussian disdains the nickname.

Zelinsky scratched his three-day growth of stubble. "Not good, Matthaeus. We are down to just over 100 effectives. Less than twenty rounds per man and a total of one machine gun."

"Nothing heavier?"

"A few or so *Panzerfausts* to stop an untold number of tanks."

"Do you have a spotter in the belfry?"

Zelinsky shook his head. "The upper belfry and cupola were damaged so I could not put a spotter there. And why bother? Their artillery had few shells left to waste supporting a hapless *Volksturm* unit."

"Most of the division has pulled back to the east and south," Melchior said. "Our battalion of boys and pensioners is cut off. And I think it was intentional."

"Intentional! Why?"

"We are *Ami*-fodder to them, Zet. We are nothing but the scum of the Reich, fit only as a sacrifice to the *Fuehrer's* insanity."

Zelinsky nodded slowly. "Perhaps you're right."

Weber scrambled into their position. "The *Amis* have stopped to resupply, *Herr Hauptmann*. We still have time to break out and join the regiment by the river."

"I should try to save the lads at least," Melchior mumbled. He suddenly felt guilty about his decision.

"Matthaeus, why did you choose this place of all to defend?" Zelinsky asked.

"I don't know. This was the first German emperor, Karl's, seat of power. Where the Franks created the first non-Roman empire in Europe. My father made me study medicine. I preferred the study of antiquity... and history."

"Is that why you quit medical school?"

Melchior looked into his friend's bloodshot eyes. "I am no longer sure why I did anything. From here, Karl the Great ruled Europe, defended Europe, attended to Europe. And what have we done? Nazis! They have turned the German people into pigs following the swineherd. Well, now the wolves are here to devour the pigs."

Weber lit a cigarette and took a desperate drag. "We should go now, *Herr Hauptmann*. Otherwise, surrender. They say the *Amis* give good cigarettes to prisoners."

Melchior grabbed his wrist. "No! I am against this regime, and I hate this war, but I have served too long to run. Not without dishonoring the fallen. He looked around the cathedral...or Karl."

He drew a flask from his pocket and took a long chug of cheap brandy. More firing began to plaster the rubble around them. First, the boom of cannons, then the blast of mortars and the rattle of machine guns, followed by the crack, crack of the *Amis'* deadly M1 rifles.

He looked up at Weber. "Too late. No, we fight until the ammunition is gone. Then, I shall surrender. Go to your company, now."

"We should surrender now! Further resistance is madness," Weber pleaded.

"Resistance is madness? Weber, war is madness. This war is madness. Look around you. A place dedicated to God caught up in this. Once the seat of a true German Reich, it has become a place for tourists and now, a death place. At least in *Karl der Grosse's*, Charlemagne's time, men fought honorably and for a just cause."

"What cause was that?" Weber asked with eyes wide in disbelief.

"Christendom..."

Melchior's words were all but drowned out by the rumble of cannon fire coming ever closer. A blast struck near them, spitting dirt and rubble fragments into their faces.

"Never mind this *Scheisse* talk! We must do something!" Zelinsky said. "Matthaeus, I'll take a company forward. We'll slow them down. Give them something to think about."

Melchior wiped dirt from his face. "Okay, Zet. Take the First Company. It's our best. But cover the right flank."

"*Heil* Hitler!" Zelinsky's hand flapped weakly.

Melchior knew he was joking. "*Geh mitt Gott.*" Go with God.

When his friend disappeared into the gray smoke and rubble, Melchior turned to Weber. "Get me the last of our *Fausts*. I plan on smoking at least one more Ronson before I die."

The rumble of tanks was masked by the harrowing din of the bombardment. Machine guns hummed like bees. Suddenly, the dull bursts of tank main guns began exploding around them.

"Get me the *Faust*, now!" Melchior growled.

A young trooper handed him the long, ungainly grenade launcher.

Melchior slid his hand along the narrow tube and flicked open the primitive sight. "They arm us with *Scheisse* from the last war..."

A dark hulk edged slowly out of the smoke. The Sherman M-4 turned its turret-like the head of some prehistoric beast. And it seemed to stare at Melchior.

He sighted in on it... Steady...

The co-axial machine gun spat bullets that rolled along like a lead wave. Then the long barrel of the main gun lowered in on him. He knew a 76mm shell would soon end his war.

But one last shot! He aimed where he knew it would cause the most damage. Whoosh... the Sherman exploded in a burst of flames.

Melchior managed a grim smile. *The first Ronson!*

His men fired wildly as the crew spilled from the stricken behemoth like ants from a plowed anthill.

Melchior noticed a second tank backing its way down the avenue. *Ronsons fear the Faust!* He grabbed the last *Panzerfaust* and fired into the Sherman tank's tail, but the round clanked harmlessly against the metal. "*Scheisse* – a dud!"

Their ammunition was almost gone. The firing started to drop off, and now only the stray Mauser round cracked in response to hundreds of American bullets.

"We've done our duty here. Get to your company, Weber," Melchior ordered. "They can flee or surrender as they like. I will die here."

"Most of my boys are probably dead or dying, Melchior. I'll die with you."

Melchior looked up. The roar of fighter planes suddenly filled the sky, challenging the artillery and mortars for supremacy in the cacophony of hell.

A flight of P-47 Thunderbolts creased the cold autumn air above Aachen. The flight was just minutes out from its objective – a bridge from which the Nazis were trying to reinforce the city's defenders.

Amid the buzzing of engines and the sound of combat, Melchior could almost imagine the signals crackle across the airwaves.

This is Bunko. Target at two o'clock. Going in. Stay with me.

Wilco! I'm at your seven.

Melchior watched the flight leader begin to dive. The river was now to their rear, and in moments, they would be blasting German tanks and trucks to smithereens, effectively trapping the last defenders.

Suddenly, 20mm cannon rounds stitched the flight leader's plane like a hammer gun.

Messies on my six! Messerschmitts on my six! The flight leader's plane began a mournful drone and tumbled out of control.

Kraut fighters! Leader's down!

Melchior watched the second plane break left in a spiral dive. From out of nowhere, a second Messerschmitt swept in. The next burst sliced through the remaining Thunderbolt, blasting it apart.

As the Thunderbolt plummeted toward the river, Melchior saw two dark objects tumble through the gray sky. *Its bombs are tumbling off target!*

One of the objects plunged through the cathedral roof and exploded directly over Melchior and Weber. The blast shook the earth and sucked the air out of everyone and everything. A numbing sensation pierced his ears, making every sound dull. His eyes were singed and stung bitterly. His nose and throat choked with smoke and dust. He wanted to scream, but nothing came out.

In a mind-numbing haze, Melchior dreamed the building survived the bomb. Most of his men lay dead or dying. The survivors of the battalion raced out with their hands in the air, where the advancing American infantry greeted them with bayonets fixed.

Melchior could not move. His last thought was that because of him, the first German city, the ancient capital of the first German empire, had fallen to the Americans. A voice that was not quite a voice seemed to whisper – *Be not Afraid.*

***

Aachen, 803 A.D.

Melchior saw only darkness. And he heard noises only faintly, like distant echoes at first, but then slowly closer... louder. Was this a *Wehrmacht* field hospital, and was he under the influence of a surgeon's ether? But he felt no mask on his face.

Melchior's mind slowly cleared. He began to recall things. *MacKay's great experiment failed. Fools trifling with science. Or was the whole affair in Canada a dream? I must have had a dream – a dream of a future in the Americas... But dreams are of the past… or are they?*

He blinked his eyes. A dim light burned in an otherwise dark room. *Is this some sort of Ami hospital or an Ami prison?*

The sounds got louder, but the echo chamber effect resonated, and gradually the sounds became clearer. Someone was chanting in Latin. His confusion grew.

Have I been dragged off to some church… to die? Is this my funeral Mass? Am I dead? Yes, I must be – dead…

He lay motionless for what seemed hours. He tried to recollect what happened, but only brief snippets flashed before him. He vaguely recalled a great war and the strange journey he agreed to take. *But a journey to where? From where?*

The door opened, and a voice spoke in Latin. At first, he did not comprehend it, but his boyhood Latin studies began to prove their worth. *But I've never heard Latin spoken except at Mass. How do I understand this?*

"It is time, *Dominus*," a voice said.

Melchior sat upright.

"Time for what? Where is this?" he replied in fluent Latin. *I don't speak Latin.*

His head throbbed. He felt like he had spent a week at *Fasching* or a night in *Sankt Pauli*. It was hard to focus in the dim light. It seemed like a dungeon. The smells overwhelmed him—a mix of sweet candle wax, damp cloth, and smoke.

"Incense," Melchior said. "That's incense! We are in a church. What church is this?" His voice seemed an echo.

"*Dominus*, we are in the chapel of the palace cathedral, of course," the voice answered in a form of German. It seemed a strange German – a strange Germanic language. But somehow, he understood it.

So…he was still in the cathedral. *What the deuce had happened?*

"Are you with the *Amis*? Where are my *Volksgrenadieren*? Are we all prisoners?"

The voice laughed. "You are no prisoner, *Dominus*."

"What language are you speaking?" Melchior barked. He needed time to clear his head. It ached like no headache he had ever experienced. Like the insides of his head had been scraped on a long rug. It burned.

"Whatever language you prefer, *Dominus*. Latin or Frankish. My Saxon is not very good, as you know."

"As I know? How would I know? And how would you know what I know?"

"I am My Lord's servant," he replied, this time in Arabic.

"What language did you speak? Was that Arabic?"

"That was the tongue of the Muhammedans, *Dominus*." He was a shadowy-looking figure.

How do I know he spoke in Arabic? Or Latin or Frankish or Saxon? How is any of this possible?

"Are you one of Weber's men?" Melchior asked. It was then he realized the figure wore a robe.

"I am sorry, no. I know nobody named Weber. And *Dominus*, you know well that I am Udo, a deacon of the chapel. I serve the lord, and the bishop, Angilram."

"Well, all clerics serve the Lord, don't they now?" Melchior said. "Are you a chaplain?"

"I don't know what you mean by a chaplain, *Dominus*. I serve the Lord our God too, but I meant the lord, the king...Karl. As we all do," Udo replied calmly.

"Rubbish! We serve Adolf Hitler...at least until the *Amis* overrun us." Matthaeus could see this was a prank. *I'm a prisoner. The Amis aren't clever enough for something like this. The British must be behind this trick... or the Gestapo. Am I to be executed for failing to stop the Amis' onslaught?*

"I know of no Hitler. Karolus is our lord and master. And you should know that better than I."

If this was a dream, it was high time to wake up, Melchior thought. "Why so?"

"Because you are Lord Melchior, his most able warrior. You are the best of his *Missi Dominici*."

His memory was spotty. *I must bide my time until I can piece things together.*

"Melchior jumped off the bed onto his feet. He looked down and saw that he was wearing a blue tunic that ended halfway down his legs, leather breeches, and knee-length boots.

"What is this?"

"I took the liberty of dressing you. You were sleeping without any covering."

"That can't be..." Melchior had a sense he should have been wearing something. *But what?*

He ignored the question. "I will help you into your *brunia*, *Dominus*."

"My what?"

The deacon went to the nearby sofa and picked up a leather jacket covered with iron rings that overlapped. He pulled it over Melchior's head and tightened the leather side straps. He then handed him a set of heavy leather gloves. "Detleff has your weapons, *Dominus*. He is waiting."

"Who is Detleff? Waiting for what?"

"Detleff is your squire. You and the abbot are leaving for the Thuringian March this morning. The bishop has blessed us, and Mass is celebrated. You told the bishop you wanted to travel at least six leagues before nightfall."

Mein Gott, I have crossed time! Melchior realized something impossible... implausible had occurred with him. But he could recall only fragments from either century or the events surrounding his journey.

"And why am I going to Thuringia?" Melchior suddenly remembered that he had gone to the German Army infantry school not far from there. He grabbed his head. It hurts like the blow of a Sankt Pauli pimp.

"To bring Lord Karolus's justice to the heathens. To convert those who will hear the word of God. To kill those who will not. And of course, to burn their witch."

Melchior laughed. "Their witch?"

"Why yes. A band of pagan Saxons has seized part of Thuringia, and their witch-queen has drunk the blood of many good Christians. You are charged with converting her or burning her and all of her followers and..."

"And what?" Melchior's mind was beginning to race with flashes of things he once knew or thought he once knew.

"Our Lord Karolus wants their gold and treasure as payment for his troubles."

"Gold, is it?" Melchior threw back his head in laughter. "Ah-ha, ha, ha!"

The deacon looked askance. "*Dominus,* have you been drinking?"

Melchior pondered the question. Of course, he felt hungover. Yes, once he sobered up, he would be back to normal.

"I should hope so, Udo. I should hope so. Fetch me some wine and bread. Unconsecrated, of course."

"But your journey, *Dominus,*" Udo protested.

"I changed my mind. I need more time to..." He looked up at the simple wooden cross hanging on the bare wall. To reflect and to pray. Fetch me a prayer book and rosary as well."

"A rosary?"

"You know, prayer beads."

Udo smiled. "Why yes. Beads. *Paternosters.* Prayer and reflection are always a good idea, *Dominus.*"

Udo returned with a servant bearing a large platter of food and a flagon of wine. He handed Melchior a worn, leather-bound book and some carved wooden beads on a string with a roughhewn cross. "Physical and spiritual sustenance, Lord."

Melchior sipped his wine and chewed chunks of the heavy black bread. The cheese and sausage were a surprise. Better than he had ever eaten. *Pretty good Metzgers wherever the hell I am.*

"Sit, Udo. I like company when I eat. Have some wine." He would try to piece together things by extracting information from the cleric.

Udo poured the deep red liquid from a heavy brown earthen jug into a pewter goblet.

"I took the liberty of informing the bishop of the delay," Udo said finally.

"Good. What did he say?"

"He said, as the *Dominus* wishes. God has more time than the devil."

Melchior smiled. "I like that!"

"The bishop is most learned and wise, My Lord."

"And what of you, Udo? What do you know of things? Of me, for instance?" Melchior was stalling to have time to recall this strange world he was in... or had been in. *It would be useful for this monk to help me remember.*

"*Dominus?*"

"Imagine I am a stranger. Tell me what you can of me, our Lord Karolus's favorite?"

"Favorite *missus,*" Udo corrected. "His favorite among men is Alcuin of York. His adviser."

"And his favorite among women?"

-8-

Udo blushed red. "His daughters share that honor."

"Go on now. Tell me about Melchior, this *missus Dominus*."

"Very well… As you know, our Lord Karolus, King of the Franks and Lombards, was crowned Emperor of the Romans, that is, of all Christendom, the previous year during Christmastide. Our Holy Father Pope Leo crowned him in Rome. Karolus is now emperor and ruler from the western sea to the Eastern March, from the northern sea to the middle sea."

"The *Fuehrer* would not be satisfied with that…" Melchior said. He suddenly had vague recollections of the Nazi era.

"I beg your pardon?"

"Nothing. Continue Udo. Tell me more about him."

"But you know…"

"Do as I ask," Melchior said. *If I am a lord, I should get used to giving commands.*

Udo bowed his head and spread his hands in supplication. The hood had fallen to his shoulders. Melchior could see he was in his mid-twenties with curly brown hair and a short-trimmed beard of the same color.

"As you know, our Lord Karolus has led numerous campaigns to protect Frankland and bring pagans to Christianity. You were with him in his last two, and that is where you saved him."

"I saved, King Karolus? And how did I manage that?" he munched loudly as he spoke.

Udo flushed in disbelief. "Yes, *Dominus*. You… you saved him twice, in truth. Surely you remember. The first time was on the Eastern March when Lord Karolus defeated Tassilo, the Duke of Bavaria. He then divided the western portion of the duchy into counties, each controlled by a count loyal to the king."

"But how did I save him?" Melchior struggled to remember any of this.

Udo gave a puzzled look. "I was not there but you. They say it was after the battle. Our Lord Karolus went to pray in a nearby chapel. To give thanks to God for the great victory over an implacable enemy. He insisted on riding alone. No retainers."

"That does not sound too wise of our great lord," Melchior said sardonically.

Udo shrugged. "It is his way. As you know, he is a head taller than a normal man and stronger than most. While he knelt in prayer before the crucifix, a band of escaping Lombards decided to stop and loot the church's gold."

"Always gold, nah? How many in this band?"

"About a score," Udo said. "Their leader was Lord Samo, a cousin of Tassilo."

"Lombards are not to be trusted," Melchior quipped, although he had no idea where the thought came from.

Udo smiled faintly. "Indeed, *Dominus*. Our Lord Karolus heard their horses' hooves and exited the chapel as they rushed him on foot. These men were fit and strong as they had not entered the battle."

"That would also make them cowards… or wise."

"Indeed, *Dominus*. But it was not wise to attack the emperor who had vanquished foes from the Pyrenees to the Elbe, was it?"

"No."

"Our lord let his broad sword fly in all directions. He struck down five. But his arm was growing weary, and it was a matter of time before the pack of wolves would take even his mighty majesty to the ground. Then you arrived on horseback and ran your lance through two of them and decapitated several others before the survivors fled."

"Did I kill Samo?"

Udo looked at him intently. "Why no, *Dominus*. Samo was, of course, the first to flee when you arrived."

"And the other time?" Melchior took a sip of the wine. It was rich and very potent.

"*Dominus*?"

"The other time I saved Karolus."

"Against the Avars," Udo replied. His placid face formed a scowl. "Those spawn of Satan. You killed their general, Tuldila, who was about to strike a sword blow to our king. In doing so, you took Tuldila's sword point into your breast. Even with your blood staining your armor, you sliced the spawn of the devil's square head from his corrupt torso. Some called it a miracle."

Melchior clutched at his breast and felt the scar. "They were correct. It was a miracle."

"And so, our lord and ruler granted you vast *demesnes* in Pannonia and eastern Frankland. He wanted to build you a new manor house, but you insisted on living in the one your grandfather built. Not that you are there much. Our Lord Karolus has you nearby whenever you are not out on a journey."

"What do you mean... a journey?"

"As I said, you are a *missus dominicus*. As such, you must travel to the reaches of the empire to keep watch on the counts, dukes, and bishops."

"Ah, a *Sendgraf*! Why?"

"To see the emperor's laws are enforced. A *missus dominicus*, or *Sendgraf* as you say, is an envoy."

"Envoy for what?"

"An envoy of our lord and master, Karolus. With authority to act for Karolus. To ensure that Christianity is taught unblemished by heresy or paganism. To ensure that proper taxes are assessed and that these lords do not mistreat the emperor's subjects. You act in his name. It is the greatest honor to be in such esteem by the emperor that he grants you his authority. And there were only three of you. It makes his paladins jealous, of course. And he has given each of you his greatest of possessions. That is, greatest except his daughters."

Melchior thought he saw Udo smile.

"And what are they?"

"A bible – the word of God; an ancient Frankish amulet – the iron disc of Charles Martel, and a map."

"I understand the bible. Is the amulet magic?"

Udo smiled. "We are Christian, *Dominus*. But these iron discs belonged to Frankish chieftains when we were a lost band of pagans. Before baptism saved us from the fire of hell and brought us the love of God."

"Of course. And the map?"

"Some consider *mappae* to be a form of sorcery. But they were drawn by the Romans and cover most of the realm. The only other copies are in the possession of our Lord Karolus himself and the Abbot Baugulf in Fulda."

"Where are these?"

"With your servants, *Dominus*."

"I should like to visit my manor house. Is it far?"

"Perhaps thirty leagues."

"And do I have a family there?"

Udo gave a puzzled look. "'Tis too far afield, *Dominus*. I can see from the look on your face the memory of this saddens you. Perhaps that is why you ask me to recall all these things you already know?"

Melchior hesitated for a second. "Of course. And thank you for your patience. There is much I would like you to remember for me. But please, on your word as a cleric, make no one aware of this."

"Of course, *Dominus*," Udo said.

"Now tell me the truth. How do people regard me? How do they regard, Lord Melchior?"

Udo gave a very puzzled look.

"Please humor a… *missus dominicus*," Melchior said. "It amuses me." He hoped to get a sense as to who he was… or rather who they expected him to be.

"Well… You, that is, Lord Melchior is considered a kind nobleman. Retainers, servants, and clerics all like you for your unpretentious, although sometimes reckless, ways. Our Lord Karolus likes that in you as well. The court has grown in power and has become full of courtiers and sycophants. You, My Lord, are of the few who behave like Franks of old while embracing Karolus's new role for his people."

Melchior sipped his wine and thought about what Udo just told him.

"Are we finished, *Dominus*? I'm afraid any more of this, and I will have to be defrocked and serve as your bard."

Melchior smiled. "Is that so bad an idea? Even bards serve God in their own way."

"I am going to be missed at prayers," Udo said. "I'll have a servant standing by to attend you. I must report to Abbot Jurchen."

With that, Udo left. Melchior reflected on his lot. The savage battle he had just fought and the soldiers who fought with him seemed to be fading in his mind. *Have I woken from some futuristic dream?* He wondered. He closed his eyes, and a vision of the battle passed before him. Then it faded. He thought he saw a different vision. Very different. But it too faded before he could focus enough to gather it in. *This is like grasping at smoke.*

He looked down at the wine jug. *Could the wine be so potent?* He took another taste. He tried in vain to recall what had happened and why he was there. He touched the damp, stone wall. It was real to the touch. As were the draperies and the stained-glass window.

"Can you help me with this?" he called to the servant waiting outside the doorway.

"As you command, *Dominus.*" A gaunt man of indeterminate age with scaly skin entered. Despite his appearance, he was dressed in quite nice clothing. Melchior smiled. *Good to serve the king of the Franks.*

The servant knew exactly how to loosen the rods that held the window and push it open to let in some fresh air. Melchior took a breath. It smelled like early spring. He looked down at a large courtyard. Several armed retainers lined the walls. He saw people walking about and, strangely, a gaggle of children. Several carts drawn by donkeys were in line. Stocking the larder of the lord, Melchior thought.

"Is this a normal day here? Who are those children?"

"My Lord Karolus has many children, *Dominus.* Some are even from his wives," the servant replied.

Melchior nodded in amusement. *Good to be king of the Franks.*

Several of the children started crying and fussing. It looked like they were fighting over a toy. One of the matrons watching them smacked one, and the crying grew more intense. *Not so good, maybe.*

"The lords and ladies at court are at Mass right now. The Archbishop, Lord Angilram, is officiating. The servant spoke as if that were a special thing.

Melchior nodded. "A special day."

The servant's eyes widened. "Indeed, *Dominus.* The anniversary of the day our Lord Karolus's life was saved… by you, *Dominus.*"

"Which time? I saved My Lord Karolus's life twice. Which one is this?"

The servant looked incredulous.

"Never mind. When the Mass is ended, I want to meet my retainers."

"Yes, *Dominus.* But the bishop wants to meet you as well. As soon as he is done saying Mass."

Melchior nodded. "In the meantime, I could use more of this wine. And that cheese and sausage, too."

***

An hour later, Udo returned. "*Dominus*, the bishop awaits your company."

Udo led him through the palace. Melchior absorbed the sights and sounds as if he had never seen them before. The archways were decorated with ornately painted wooden beams, and all sorts of tapestries lined the whitewashed walls. Thick carpets lined most of the stone floors. Where no carpets covered stone, the floors were oak, but finely cut, not rough. There were few windows, but these were open, allowing light and air to fill the hallway. Solid brass torches lit the darkened areas.

Many clerics passed them. All nodded or bowed their heads as Melchior passed. *They all seem to know me.*

"The chancery is right up these stairs, *Dominus*," Udo said.

They walked up a wide stone staircase covered with finely woven ruby-red carpeting. Udo turned the highly polished brass handles of a large wooden door. He led Melchior into a surprisingly large chamber.

The bishop was a dour-looking man of medium height. His skin was darker than most Franks'. He was clean-shaven and had finely cut hair. He was fat.

"Ah, *Dominus*, I hope you are feeling better. Udo tells me you were... not yourself."

Melchior shot a burning glance at Udo, who stared blankly.

"I assure My Lord Bishop that my recovery seems to be underway."

"Excellent. Come, let us eat. The fast before Mass is the only thing about our beloved Christian faith that I would change were it in my power."

He led Melchior to a large table covered with fine cloth and lined with plates of food and several jugs of wine. "There's a washing tub in the corner if you are one of those who clean their hands before food. I do not as a rule, but today I shall."

"Why not as a rule?" Melchior asked as he scrubbed his hands and dried them.

"It is a Muslim practice. Ever since *Roncevaux* Pass, I stopped washing. You were but a lad then—a brave lad. You tried to save your father from a pack of the curs. I still remember when they found you and brought you to our Lord King Karolus. You were crying that you did not kill the one who skewered your father. But you killed three others before they left you for dead. We knew you were marked for greatness from that day on. You were not yet ten years of age."

Melchior tried to recall. He thought he saw a glimpse of a steep mountainside covered with thick stands of trees. He thought he heard cries in Arabic and some other languages. He could not bring back a vision of his father – just the taunts and grunts of men locked in mortal combat and the constant swirl of blades at close quarters. He felt a tremor roll quickly through his body.

"Are you all right, *Dominus*? You seem a little weak. Have some wine."

Melchior sipped the wine. It tasted lighter than the other wine. *Am I used to it already?*

"Do you have any ale?" Melchior asked.

The bishop clapped his hands, and a servant took Melchior's wine while another brought him a mug of ale.

"Thank you." Melchior sipped the brew. His eyes widened. It was thick and dark and heavy. And it tasted a bit sour. "It is excellent.".

"You always preferred wine, *Dominus*," the bishop said with a more than amused look.

Melchior had no recollection of that. "Well, I am trying to adjust my tastes. Besides, some of the places our Lord Karolus sends me have indifferent wine."

"So true. And there are journeys in your future. The emperor and I have long talked of this."

"And I plan on an audience as well. I want to make sure I am completely understanding of his wishes."

He waved his hand at Melchior. "*Dominus*, there is no need. I have placed his requests in writing for you. So fortunate that you can read, *Dominus*. The other *missi* were

-13-

completely illiterate. Of course, my clerics were always here to read the commands and see that things were done properly."

"What do you mean *were* illiterate? Are they now knowledgeable of letters and numbers?"

The bishop gave a pained look. "Surely you are joking? The *missus* Ansegisel recently came down with stomach cramps and the flux. He died a miserable death, poor soul."

Melchior could not bring up a face to match the name. "Had he been ill before? This sounds horrible."

"No. But he would eat anything. Perhaps something he ate disagreed with him. But we should pray for his soul, which I am sure will depart the pains of purgatory before long and enter into heaven."

Melchior racked his brain to remember the subtleties of his religion. "Why is that, Your Grace?"

"Well, before he died, he willed his entire estate to the church."

"What of his progeny? Did he have children?"

"Of course. Six bastards who are entered into the military service of our Lord Karolus. Oh yes, and one girl by his wife. She has entered a convent. And of course, his wife died some years ago."

The bishop winked. "Rumor had it that you fancied her while her husband was on a journey for the Lord Karolus."

Melchior hesitated. "Well, only my confessor knows for certain. And God."

The bishop made the sign of the cross. "Your confessor is dead."

"I have a new one, I meant."

"Who?" The archbishop asked.

"Jurchen." Melchior remembered the name that Udo mentioned. It was the best he could do.

"Jurchen? I had not been told."

"Never mind that. What of the other *missus*?" Melchior asked.

"Chlodowig? The fool, besotted with wine and mead, fell from his horse. Broke his neck instantly. And after twelve pitched battles and a score of skirmishes and fights... Such a shame."

"I always found him unlucky," Melchior said. It amazed him how quickly he was thinking of responses to things he had no recollection of.

"Not like you, *Dominus*. You are the best of the best. Our Lord Karolus holds you above his paladins in esteem. Pity you can never be raised to their actual ranking in the realm."

Melchior sensed a little discomfort. *He's lying. He's a tricky swine of a cleric. There is treachery here.*

Melchior could still not fully grasp his lack of memory.

"Is something wrong, *Dominus*?"

"No. I just think I need to meet personally with our king-and-emperor, Karolus."

"Eat some of this food with me. Then we will talk more about it."

They ate fresh fish, duck, and venison, all stewed. Roasted ox and a mix of root vegetables and apples followed. Melchior drank the ale while the bishop drank the wine. When they were done, the servants removed all but the drinks.

The bishop opened the lambskin parchment and spread it on the table. "So here are My Lord Karolus's requests."

"You call them requests. But they are, in fact, commands," Melchior said.

Angilram ignored his comment and read the words.

Count Melchior

You, my last Missus, must do the work of three. For that, I am sorry but also glad that my best and most loyal continues in my service. For in you, Lord Melchior, I have full faith and trust. As your king-and-emperor, I request you Journey to the Thuringian March – beyond Fulda.

Your journey is not to exceed six turnings of the moon. In this short time, you are to ascertain the faithfulness of Count Lothar and the Bishop Willehad of Fulda. I have correspondence suggesting these nobles have secreted a significant portion of the great trove of the Avars. Lothar is a fearless Frank warrior but is known for his greed, even among men of greed. As for Willehad, he is suspected of having knowledge of this and there are also suggestions he is less than energetic in his pastoral duties – allowing the faithful to fall in the knowledge and the practice of our Christian faith.

Now, I come to the most troubling problem you may face. Some thirty leagues to the east of the Fulda lay lands now occupied by a tribe of Saxons. These Saxons have fallen under the rule of a mysterious pagan queen by the name of Udela. This same Udela is said to spread her pagan beliefs to the faithful and is also suspected of witchcraft. My Lord Melchior must find this witch and convert her and her tribe to the true faith. If she resists, she must suffer the penalty of death by fire. If she and her tribes convert, they may keep their possessions and forfeit merely one-tenth of their gold. If they refuse the one true faith, they must forfeit all.

I wish you all the blessings of God on this journey. For it is not only my will but God's will."

Karolus
Rex et Imperator

Melchior swallowed his ale in thought. Memories flashed through his mind. He began to remember things, but not everything. Recollection came slowly.

"Quite a task our king-and-emperor has entrusted to you, *Dominus*. I can think of no other who could achieve this in the time allotted," Angilram said.

Melchior rubbed his chin. "How many men do I have for these... requests?"

"As you know, in a typical 'Journey', a *missus* takes a squire, retainers, and three men-at-arms, plus his spiritual men-at-arms."

Melchior was confused. "What do you mean by that?"

"Why surely you know you must bring clerics to ascertain the spiritual side of the journey. For this one, you shall bring the Abbot Jurchen and the monk, Father Thomas. They are prepared for the journey. But because of the complication of witchcraft, I am sending one of my best priests. One expert at identifying and excising demons. His name is Vulmar. He will join you at a hamlet deep in the western forest. He lives in a small cave, like a hermit. Some say he worships the ancient Gods."

"So, he is a pagan?"

"He excises demons for me. I care little of his methods," Angilram growled. "Surely you know many of our people still worship the ancient gods, as well as our Lord and Savior."

Melchior nodded. But he did not like the idea.

"You seem displeased."

"I do not believe I know enough to be displeased, Your Grace. Perplexed is a better word."

The bishop laughed. "Then you are about to be even more perplexed. Our king-and-emperor has ordered Audeon to ride with you."

Who the hell is Audeon? Melchior took a deep breath. "Why Audeon?"

"It seems our king-and-emperor wants his bastard to learn a warrior's ways and a leader's ways from his best *missus Dominus*. Oh, he'll never rule. But he can do much to prop up his half-brothers. And you are proof enough that bastards make the best warriors."

"What do you mean?"

Angilram gave a devious smile but did not respond.

"What scullery maid did our king-and-emperor shaft to produce such a likely lad?" Melchior asked.

Angilram gave a strange look. "That is the curious part of it. No one knows but Karolus himself. Many rumors abound, of course: the wife of one of his lords, an abbess, another huntress. For some reason, he will not say. And the lad does not know. He was brought to the court when he was four by two maids with a note for the king."

Melchior rubbed his chin. "What happened?"

"He immediately took the boy Audeon under his wing and had him baptized. And he had religious and some other learning, so he is literate. But our Lord Karolus does not want him to take Holy Orders. At least not yet. And he insists that Audeon may be of the greatest help to you on the journey."

"How old is he now?"

"Fifteen."

"Then he's old enough to wield a sword."

The bishop nodded approvingly, running his plump fingers across his belly. "Our Lord Karolus will want you to leave immediately. And I almost forgot the most important of his requests."

"What is that, Your Grace?"

"Deliver this to the Abbot Baugulf of Fulda. Our king-and-emperor had it sealed. Its contents are most secret. I am not even privy to them. Neither Count Lothar nor anyone else may see its contents."

"This command is not in the manuscript you just read."

"It is the spoken request of our king-and-emperor." Angilram played with the gold cross and chain that hung from his neck.

"You know, Your Grace, that a spoken request is only valid when it is given among four eyes – from the requestor to the requested." Melchior had no idea how he knew that.

"But I am a prince of the church and a lord of the realm. You cannot doubt my word."

Melchior smiled. "Your Grace, I would never doubt your word. I would just never obey it."

***

Later that day, Melchior gave orders that his entourage would be ready to depart after morning Mass. He returned to his chamber and sank onto the bed. He glanced over at the wall and saw that his armor, tunic, and weapons were laid out.

He lost the train of thought as an image of different weapons crossed his mind. Then he recalled, only briefly, the events in different places and times. He shook his head. *Devil's work...* He wondered if he was mad or possessed. So, true to his calling as a warrior of Christendom, he prayed.

And as he did, visions, voices, and thoughts, both familiar and strange, swirled in his mind. Voices in German – then in English – familiar and strange. *What is in the drink in this forsaken place?* His head pounded, and he reached for his temples. His mind seemed to travel – his body twisting and turning to the sound of explosions. *Be not afraid...*

S.W. O'Connell

Part 1

NORAD

"The universe as we know it is a joint product of the observer and the observed."

- Pierre Teilhard de Chardin

Chapter 1

Ottawa, Canada, November 1959

Matthaeus Melchior blinked. His eyes felt heavy and his head banged like he had spent the night at a local *Gasthaus*. After all the years in Canada, he still used the German term for taverns. But beer had not touched his lips in a week. He pushed away the covers and pulled on an old pair of corduroy pants. He threw open the curtains and gazed from the window of his two-room flat. The morning rain pelted the glass pane with a steady drumming he found somehow soothing. Outside, the misty rain cast a curtain across the nearly bare trees and soaked what shriveled brown leaves remained.

The Canadian maple season is over, he thought grimly. *Soon winter's freeze will put this country into a long sleep.* Melchior sipped a mug of hot tea and recalled the German skies of his youth. Almost ten years since he emigrated from the war-torn country to his new homeland. Suddenly, his mind raced with the pounding of heavy guns, the rattle of machine guns, the crack of rifles, frantic men barking orders, and desperate men screaming as their bloody guts poured onto the ankle-deep mud.

Heavy fingers pressed his temple, and he slowly sucked in the sulfur-tasting air. *Will it ever end?*

An old Motorola radio hummed a concerto from the corner of the room. *Mozart? Bach?* There was a time when he knew such things. But his life in Germany and beyond had become a blur. He struggled to remember the war that brought him and his countrymen to a hell richly deserved. But he recalled even less of his pre-war life, other than it was an idyllic period of study, fun, and family. Melchior grunted. Now he was down to one of three. Melchior laughed to himself, self-defense of the mind. He took another sip of the tea. *These Canadians brew good tea, even if they poison it with milk and sugar*

He glanced out at the rain. More sounds and images swirled in his mind. Large horses panting and straining as they galloped across a rain-soaked field, war cries in strange tongues he could almost understand, the clashing of blades and the pounding of war hammers and the crack of bones. More desperate cries of anguish. Fields strewn with corpses. He grabbed his head in pain. But he had no pain. The images and sounds faded. *Will I ever be left in peace?*

He took another sip of tea. A dark sedan rolled along the rain-splattered street. Melchior watched the wiper blades swishing slowly, almost in tempo with the music in the background. The car, it looked like a Ford, suddenly turned up the driveway of his building and stopped. A moment later, it turned around and slowly drove away. He thought little of it and went back to work at the small table he used as a desk. Piles of job announcements cluttered it. He picked up the latest edition of his *Curriculum Vitae*. Despite his German *Abitur* and high grades at University, Matthaeus Melchior was on his tenth job search in as many years. He worked in research, mostly for industry. A stint as a secondary teacher ended badly… more than once. Despite flawless and accent-free English and French, he could not fit in.

Among the detritus of his desk lay his last letter to Kristel… *Kristel*. His one-and-ever love waited for him throughout the war. But when he immigrated to Canada in 1949, she broke her pledge to follow him within the year. At first, she wrote that there were things to clear up before she could come. Family things, she wrote. He thought little of it, but of course, her family was wiped out in the last series of air attacks on her home. Melchior lit up a cigarette. He gazed at the picture every day since he came to Canada, but never tired of it: Kristel at the *Bodensee,* Lake Constance, in a white bathing suit. It was not her perfect form that called him back. Nor the long, heavy blonde braids that gave her the look of a Norse goddess. It was her face. Not just beautiful, not just interesting, but somehow mysterious. Corn blue eyes that were large and deep…. He put it down.

***

The rain drifted off by the next morning. In its place was a surprisingly bright sun framed in a blue sky. He opened the window and took a deep breath. The crisp autumn air tugged at him. *No need for cigarettes today*, he thought. He would enjoy the fresh air instead. He could not stand another breakfast of stale toast and tea. Instead, Melchior decided on a walk. He cleaned, shaved, and put on one of his two suits with a white shirt and a blue tie. He glanced down at his worn black shoes. *Perhaps I'll find an industrious shine-boy out and about early.*

The streets were empty. He strode briskly to the boulevard and turned right. He glanced at his watch, an old nickel-faced affair with a weathered leather wrist band. It had survived hard years of wear, but still never missed a second. Melchior noted it was the only dependable thing in his life. It read half-eight. Most of the shops along the street were not yet open. Colorful shutters and brightly painted wooden doors gave an otherwise nondescript street a pleasant appearance. Canada's capital was not a crown jewel like London or Paris, nor even as picturesque as sleepy Bonn, the new West German seat of government.

As quiet as the shops appeared now, Melchior knew that in another half-hour they would be open for business and the street abuzz with shoppers and clerks engaging in the daily routine called commerce. He spotted a newspaper stand just rolling up its front shutters.

He stopped and gestured to the worn-looking man taking morning inventory. "Excuse me. Do you carry any foreign papers?"

The vendor did not look up at him. "I have this morning's *New York Times.*"

Melchior smiled. "I'm sorry. I meant from Europe."

The vendor looked up and nodded impatiently. "Of course. I have all the London papers. And I carry *Match* and *Le Figaro* from Paris. *Parle vous Francais, Monsieur?*"

"*Oui,* but I prefer something in German… *Je préfère Allemande. Frankfurter Zeitung, peut-être?*"

The vendor rubbed his bulbous red nose. "Occasionally, I get some German rags, *Monsieur*. But quite by mistake. I usually save them for the bottom of my bird's cage. The university book store is probably a better bet."

The vendor lifted his left pant leg, revealing his prosthesis. "*Normandie, Juno Beach.*"

Melchior nodded grimly. He opened his shirt to display a wicked three-inch scar on his chest. "*Aussi Normandie, Monsieur. Aussi Juno Beach.*"

The vendor gave a knowing look.

"Now, if you don't mind, I'll take *The New York Times*," Melchior said.

The vendor passed him the paper, neatly rolled tight with a bright pink rubber band. Melchior handed a coin to the vendor and tucked the paper under his arm like a swagger stick and continued on his way. With luck, he would still make it to "Charley's" before the morning rush.

The small coffee shop had only a few stools scattered along the window and a half dozen cramped tables in the back. Melchior entered "Charley's" to a curiously pleasing mix of smells, sights, and sounds. Smoke from a dozen cheap cigarettes hit him first, followed by the heady aroma of good, strong coffee on the stove.

He sniffed again. *Canadian bacon and eggs sizzling on the grill.* The jukebox played a popular hit from America, "It's All in the Game." Melchior was not interested in pop music, but Tommy Edwards' tune did catch his attention more than others had.

The hushed murmur of the early-morning customers blended into a constant buzzing sound that reminded him of an artillery barrage in the distance. *Why does everything remind me of war?* But Melchior enjoyed the break from the dearth of human voices in his flat. By good fortune, he saw the last empty stool by the window. He rushed to grab it and then opened his paper slowly and deliberately.

"I'll have coffee to you in a jiff, Matt," said a plump blonde waitress as she went whisking by with two trays wobbling in her hands. He disliked the Anglo corruption of his name but had gotten used to it.

"All right, Lilly. No rush." He held up the front page of the paper. "It is The New York Times, after all."

Her face showed she did not read much.

As soon as the coffee and buttered toast arrived, he paid his bill. He did not like to linger when he was done. The war had taught him always to stay prepared for a quick exit. He began the ritual of one small bite and one small sip with each page. That got him through eight pages of news and commentary. Lilly poured him a complimentary second cup while he perused the jobs section and classifieds. Once done, he began to fold the paper. Then he noticed an article that gripped him. It was an Op-Ed piece, and the author, someone named Buckley, chastised the Canadian government for its "low energy level" regarding the new NORAD partnership with America.

Melchior found himself nodding in agreement. "North American Air Defense," he said out loud and shook his head. He had filled out a ream of paperwork, plus fingerprints, but never heard back from them. That was a year ago, when the organization was forming, and he thought his skills could help his new country contribute to the eternal fight against Bolshevism. *Made sense, though,* he thought. *I wouldn't hire me.* Although now a Canadian citizen, he was still foreign, if no longer an alien. And not that long before, he had fought savagely against the Canadians and the Americans, as well as many others.... *Many...*

A short time later, he was strolling full-tilt towards the park. He liked a long walk after breakfast. It helped him digest and build up his strength and stamina. A world-class fencer and rider before the war, life in Canada had made him too sedentary. He decided, should he ever gain full-time employment, to take up the blade and join a fencing school. As soon as he shed his part-time evening job, tutoring.

Melchior needed to be part of something bigger than himself. While a student, he had left the church of his youth as retaliation for the horrors of the war he thought it did too little to prevent. And of course, *Der Vaterland, Das Reich,* was no more. Even the army, *Das Heer,* which thrust him among a band of brothers who fought for each other if not the state, had soured him. *Good riddance to them all,* he thought. But he felt a void. He was alone, without friends, family, or even colleagues. And he was without purpose.

The park was nearly empty, but he did not notice the dark sedan as it slowly pulled to a halt next to him. The front and rear windows rolled down, and a pair of strange faces looked at him. He paused. Melchior had lived long enough in a police state to know when he encountered "the bulls."

"Are you Matthaeus Melchior, sir?" the bull in the front seat asked politely.

Well, these aren't German bulls. They're too polite.

He grunted, "I am Melchior. What is this?"

The figure in the back seat slowly stepped from the sedan. Melchior could see now that he was thin but muscular. He had a pale, slightly ruddy face and a military cut to his hair. His gray suit looked cheap, but it fitted him well. He wore a regimental-style tie. He flashed a dull, tinny badge and credentials.

"I am Roger Doolan. These lads are with the RCMP. We'd like to ask you a few questions, Mister Melchior. That's all."

"Very well... ask." Melchior was not used to polite bulls.

"Not here, Mister Melchior. In private. Better that way," the man in the front seat said.

Doolan pointed towards the car door.

"Am I under arrest? What's the charge?"

"Not arrest, sir," one of the Mounties said from the car.

"It's best you come with us. I'll explain what I can later," Doolan said. He motioned towards the sedan with his eyes.

This is bullshit. But he got in without another word. The sedan pulled out of the park and drove around for the better part of an hour.

Finally, Melchior spoke, "Where are we going anyway? We drove by at least three police stations."

The Mounties did not answer right away. Doolan, who sat next to Melchior, said nothing. Then the beefy one in the front seat whispered, "We are taking you to the School."

***

The sedan turned down an alley. Melchior glanced at his watch. "I didn't believe it possible to drive for an hour and still be five miles from my flat."

The Mounties laughed.

What the hell? Melchior tensed. His fight-or-flight instinct, dormant since the war, suddenly arose. He figured he could probably coldcock the bull next to him and grab his revolver. He was sure he could plug at least one of the two bulls upfront. *But then what?*

"I'm a bad driver," the Mountie at the wheel chuckled.

Melchior decided to play along and shrugged. "Well, we could have walked there on our hands and beaten you by at least ten minutes."

The Mounties laughed again.

A security officer in a dark blue tunic opened the narrow gate as though he were expecting them. Above it, a simple sign read, "Carleton University, Northgate."

"I applied for a teaching position at Carleton University some two years ago. Did I finally get the job?"

None of them laughed this time. Doolan turned to him. "Mister Melchior, it's probably better to save the banter for another time. If that's all right with you, sir."

"That's fine with me."

The sedan pulled up to a remote two-story building at the edge of the campus. The road was lined with bare maple trees, and the grass had the straw color of winter. Melchior noticed then that he hadn't seen any students.

"Interesting school you have here. No students," Melchior said. "Not banter, just a statement."

"It's a satellite campus, sir," Doolan said.

Melchior, for the first time in a long time, grew anxious.

Doolan stepped out and held the door for Melchior. He glanced at the Mountie in the passenger seat. "Stay with Billy and the car, Sergeant Tremblay."

"Sure thing, captain. How long should we wait?"

Doolan checked his watch. "I'd get some lunch if I were you. Pick me up around three."

Billy nodded. "We'll be here by two-thirty. Will we need to return Mister Melchior to his flat?"

Doolan looked at Melchior. "I don't know just yet."

Melchior startled. *What shit is this? Did they mean to arrest me?*

"Come along, sir." Doolan headed into the building with Melchior strutting behind.

The inside of the building was surprisingly pleasant. Fresh paint and tasteful furnishings gave it the look of a law office or a high-end research center.

"Nice looking place," Melchior said.

Doolan nodded. "Don't worry. You're not in any trouble."

Melchior smiled.

But Doolan kept a straight face. "That I know of, at least."

They stopped in front of a double door of highly polished oak.

"I didn't think they sent Mounties to fetch people, not in trouble," Melchior said.

Doolan smiled sheepishly. "I'm not a Mountie. My colleagues are, however. I'm with the Special Investigative Unit, MOD."

"Ministry of Defense?"

"Yes. I'm actually an Air Force officer assigned to MOD's special investigative arm. You know, vetting our chaps, detecting spies and subversives among the forces."

Melchior gave a puzzled look.

"We are a new unit. Created when NORAD was formed. Most of the public knows nothing of us. We prefer it that way, so we use the Mounties as a sort of cover."

"But..."

"I've already told you more than I should. Don't worry, Mister Melchior. It'll all be explained soon enough." Doolan paused a moment. "Well, maybe not all."

Chapter 2

The School

Doolan opened the wooden door revealing a large reception room. Several clerks rapped away at typewriters that looked like World War II surplus. A very pretty receptionist rose and smiled warmly.

"So nice to see you, captain." She looked at Melchior. "Is this our guest?"

Melchior could see she had a crush on the dapper Air Force officer.

"Yes, Brooke. Mister Melchior, meet Miss Brooke Costain. She's the one who makes this place run. So be nice to her."

"Who wouldn't be nice to her?" Melchior noted Doolan looking at her long legs and trim waist.

Brooke stretched out her hand and Melchior took it. It felt soft, but not weak.

She lowered her dark lashes and then turned to Doolan. "I'm merely a secretary, Mister Melchior. But it's a real pleasure to meet you."

Melchior let go of her hand.

"Are they ready?" Doolan asked.

Brooke walked to another door and went inside. A moment later, she returned and flashed a warm smile at him. "They'll see you now."

Doolan led Melchior into a large, well-appointed room with an impressive stone fireplace and high, wood-beamed ceilings. The drapes were closed, but a large chandelier of blackened iron and several lamps provided more than ample light. Several large Persian rugs covered the tile floor. An eight-foot-long table with several large captain's chairs was set off to the left. The center of the room had an expansive desk. Like a governor-general of Canada might have used in the last century. A small sofa sat opposite it.

The desk fascinated him with its dark wood and fine workmanship. Two large green lamps adorned each side, and the center was blanketed with a large black ink blotter. The massive wooden bookcase along the wall contained a set of embossed leather-bound books – the classics.

A fortyish man of medium height greeted him with a handshake that belied his slight stature. "My name is Evan MacKay, Mister Melchior. I'm a psychiatrist."

"Well, for years, people said I needed to have my head examined. Now's as good a time as any, I suppose," Melchior said.

"It's nothing like that, I assure you," MacKay said with an impish smile.

Melchior nodded. *I'll bet.*

MacKay had graying black hair and a mustache of the same. He wore a dark blue jacket with gray fine-wool slacks and a bow tie and plaid vest.

These Canadians like their plaid.

"Doctor MacKay is the Director," Doolan announced.

"Director? Director of what?" It occurred to Melchior that the answer to that would play a role in what happened next.

MacKay smiled pleasantly. "For now, let's just say I'm Director of Research, here. I understand you have expressed some research interest, Mister Melchior."

Melchior eyed MacKay carefully, trying to understand his meaning. MacKay was a man of nuance. Melchior knew himself to be a man of bluntness. But his senses now alerted him to some hidden danger. *But from what?*

"I studied Biology and Medicine before the war. In that sense, I have an interest in doing research, so yes."

"And here? Here in Canada?" MacKay's eyes revealed this as more than an innocent query.

"I applied to several research firms over the years. I worked on and off at them. But nothing very interesting. Or permanent."

"Well, please take a seat here, and we can have a chat about research that might prove not only interesting but fascinating."

MacKay walked to his desk and picked up the phone. "Brooke, please send us some coffee."

Doolan pointed to one of the swivel chairs, and Melchior took a seat. He liked the fit and the feel of the soft leather upholstery.

Doolan slid a stack of forms in front of Melchior. "Before we begin, I must ask you to sign some papers. Merely a routine formality."

"Papers for what?"

"Security, Mister Melchior. I told you I am with the Special Investigative Unit. These are non-disclosure forms. Bureaucracy, I'm afraid. How do they call it back home? *Beamten Gesellschaft?*"

Melchior winced. *He knows some German. Perhaps he's not just the lover-boy...*

MacKay took his seat at the table with a large Cambridge notebook. "Captain, does Mister Melchior know why he is here?"

"I'm afraid not, sir. He needs to execute these papers first. I don't make the rules. MOD does. And those are my orders from MOD."

MacKay nodded. "Please look them over, Mister Melchior. If you don't feel comfortable signing, Captain Doolan will drive you home."

They know where I live, Melchior thought. *What else do they know? Maybe I should have bolted when the bulls pulled up.*

Melchior read the papers. "What is this... uhm... U.M.?"

"The code name for the School here." Doolan slapped a new Reynolds ballpoint pen in front of Melchior. "Once you agree to the non-disclosure and other security terms, we can tell you more. But not prior."

Doolan had finessed more than one bird into the nest in his day. Melchior waved the pen. "Am I signing away my freedom with a Reynolds?"

"In a way. But we must have assurances before we can say any more. You Germans are pretty good at signing papers, as I recall."

Melchior's face flushed. He felt he was being railroaded. "I'd normally shove this pen up the nose of someone like you, Doolan." He hesitated for a second but then began to scrawl his signature.

The door opened, and Brooke entered with a tray of coffee. She poured each a cup with neatness and finesse that caught Melchior's attention.

"Cream and sugar, Mister Melchior?" she asked.

"No, thank you."

She batted her long lashes. "I'll be right outside if you need anything at all."

"Thank you, Brooke," MacKay said.

Melchior noticed Doolan eyeing her as she left. He sipped his coffee. MacKay stirred his cream. Doolan placed the papers in a dark brown accordion portfolio. It had a white cover sheet with deep fuchsia letters that read, "TOP SECRET//UM."

"I'll let Captain Doolan begin if you don't mind." MacKay struck a match to his pipe.

The smoke drifted in a slow, upward spiral. Melchior's eyes followed the smoke, but his eyes were suddenly drawn to a white carving in the corner of McKay's bookcase. It looked familiar. The head of a man with two faces, each looking in the opposite direction.

"What is that carving?" Melchior motioned upward. "I feel like I have seen it before."

McKay eyed Doolan. "It's a carving of Janus, a Roman god. Said to guard the gates of Rome."

Melchior nodded. "I vaguely recall such a thing. I always wondered why the Romans regarded a two-faced man as a god. The ancient Romans abhorred treachery. Or so I thought."

"Very good, Mister Melchior. You are quite right. But the two faces of Janus signify the ability to look forward and backward. That is, towards the future and into the past."

Melchior noticed Doolan's lips tighten as McKay said the words.

***

Doolan's eyes bored into Melchior's. "You applied some time ago for a position with MOD, with NORAD to be specific."

Melchior blinked. For the first time, this cop was getting to him. "Yes. Yes, I did."

"What does someone like you want with a position at NORAD?"

"I asked myself that very thing when I applied."

"And your answer... to yourself?"

Doolan's tone hinted he knew the answer better than Melchior.

MacKay blew some smoke and leaned forward.

A hint of red flushed Melchior's face. "I explained it all in my application. It took you *Bullen* this long to come to this?"

"*Bullen?*" Doolan's eyes widened.

"*Bulls* – You know, cops. It's German slang."

Doolan smiled. "Everyone writes the same drivel on those application forms. You know, the desire to serve the monarch, Canada, etc. So, I must ask you, Mister Melchior, exactly why? Our investigation shows you were just two months from becoming a physician in 1942. But you quit. We find that strange."

Melchior raised his chin. "I wanted to do my patriotic duty to Germany, as stupid as it sounds now."

"You could have received your diploma and served as a military doctor at the front. God knows Germany needed them."

"The fact of the matter is - I wanted to kill our enemies more than heal our soldiers."

MacKay and Doolan looked at each other.

"Interesting response," MacKay said. "Your demeanor changed when you said it, Mister Melchior."

Melchior felt uncomfortable. "In what way?"

"A seemingly broken man had for a moment the posture and demeanor of a warrior."

"Can't I be both?"

"Of course," MacKay said soothingly.

Doolan scribbled a few notes. "Very well, Mister Melchior. But after the war, first in Germany and then here, you could have finished your degree and settled into a comfortable medical practice. Why didn't you?"

"I don't know. For the first year, I just wanted to make some quick money and send for Kristel."

"Kristel?" MacKay asked.

"If you read my application, you know she was my fiancée. We were engaged."

"And why didn't you marry?" Doolan asked.

"You'll have to ask her."

Doolan put down his pen. "We tried, Mister Melchior. Our SIU lads in Lahr tried to interview her, but they couldn't."

Melchior felt his heart sink. "Don't tell me – she's dead!"

"She's gone, Mister Melchior. And all trace of her. And of course, her family died in the war."

"But the police should know…"

"I am afraid there is no record of her at all with the police or anyone else," Doolan said.

Melchior's eyes widened. "Anyone else? What do you mean, anyone else?"

"I mean the Americans, the British, the French, and even the Soviets. Of course, we don't expect the truth from them. We believe she has defected."

"Kristel? She's not a Red. She's a pharmacist."

"No record of her attending any German pharmacy school."

"But she was at university with me!'

Doolan fondled the two-inch dossier on the desk with his thumb. "That's another problem, Mister Melchior. There's no record of you at the university. Other than you attended. All of your grades have been eradicated. But we suspect you knew that. And that was why you never finished your studies and became a simple laboratory assistant for some third-rate research labs."

"The Gestapo had nothing on you fellows," Melchior said. Their thoroughness surprised him. Somehow, the notion appealed to him.

"I'll take that as a compliment, Mister Melchior. Now tell me what happened to her."

Melchior gripped the armrest. "I never learned why she didn't come. She put me off for two long years. Then refused to come. Then I stopped getting replies to my letters."

"And you stopped writing to her?" Doolan asked.

Melchior hung his head. "I have written once a month since. But never mailed them."

"Why not?"

Melchior looked into Doolan's eyes. He could see from Doolan's face that he had read the letters.

"I don't know."

"Something tells me you know."

Melchior did not reply.

"Tell me about the jobs you held," Doolan said.

"Not much to tell."

"Then this shouldn't take long. Please begin with." Doolan glanced at the papers. "Begin with Cavendish Laboratories."

After four hours of back-and-forth, Melchior had exhausted himself by revealing the high and low points of his work life in Canada. In the end, he realized Doolan was always one step ahead of him. *Canada has some good Bulls, damn good.*

MacKay looked up at the clock. "It's four thirty-five."

Melchior glanced at Doolan. "Your car has been waiting for over two hours."

Doolan smiled sheepishly. "No. No, it hasn't as a matter of fact."

"How will I get home? I don't have enough money for a taxi."

Doolan twirled his fingers together. "I have taken the liberty of having the boys pack a few of your things, Mister Melchior. The doctor has a room for you right here."

MacKay smiled. "Just for a few days."

"What the hell is the meaning of all this? Am I arrested? What's the charge?"

"Your voice reveals that this wasn't entirely unexpected, Mister Melchior," Doolan said. "But no, this is still voluntary."

"*Still* voluntary? I don't like the sound of that either."

MacKay took the pipe from his mouth and waved it. "No, Matthaeus. Do you mind if I call you that? You are free to go if you like. But I hope you'll consider the offer to stay here as part of the team. We want to get answers to some of these blank areas. For that, we need your help. Just a few days."

Melchior's lips tightened. "Why should I help you? Why should I stay?"

MacKay tapped the still-warm tobacco into his hand. "You applied for a position with NORAD. If things here work out and we can resolve some questions, you'll likely have a job with NORAD. Perhaps the most interesting job in NORAD. But first, we have some tests to perform."

"Are you the Doctor Mengele of Canada?" Melchior sputtered.

MacKay laughed. "Goodness no. But we'll need a flight surgeon to assess your physical state. As for the rest, well, my team is more than equipped for that."

"There's a small gymnasium on the compound. We know of your pre-war exploits. We took the liberty of acquiring some *epees* and fencing sabers. And some horses," Doolan said.

"If you need a fencing partner, I used to duel a bit at McGill," MacKay said.

"You said you had horses? Is there a stable here?" Melchior asked.

"Yes, this was a cavalry barracks once," MacKay said.

"And as for a riding partner, it so happens that Brooke was a junior Olympian," Doolan said with a lewd grin.

Melchior hesitated for only a moment. These men troubled him. But he had little love for his flat and certainly not for the life he led. "Very well. I suppose it was time I went back to school."

***

Melchior liked the old Canadian army horse they had procured for him. It was his first venture out of the paddock and as importantly, out of the School. Brooke rode alongside him, content to let him maintain the rhythm. They did not speak much during those paddock rides, but now, out of the compound, their conversation became more expansive... more personal.

"How do you find Corporal as a mount?" she asked.

"Corporal?"

"That's his name."

Melchior patted the bay on the neck, running his fingers through the shiny black mane. "He's a fine old fellow. A real gentleman. Unlike many of the horses I rode back in Germany."

Brooke's dark eyes were wide with interest. He tried to gauge just what kind of interest it was.

He grew silent for a moment. What the highly skilled psychiatrist could not coax from him, this attractive young woman did. Melchior spurred Corporal towards the riverbank ahead. Brooke, although riding a much younger and fitter horse, could barely keep up the pace.

They halted on a low bluff overlooking the Rideau River.

"What are you looking at?" she asked.

"Those islands. I've got a mind to swim over there."

"I don't think Corporal would appreciate you dipping him in the icy water."

"I didn't mean with him."

"How are you holding up? We have had several students here over the past year. None lasted more than a week. It's been almost three fortnights now. What makes you so extraordinary, Mister Melchior?" She placed her leather-gloved hand on his. "May I call you Matt?"

Melchior's eyes met hers. "Maybe it's as simple as I have no place else to go. May I call you Brooke, Miss Costain?"

She smiled. "Yes, of course... Matt."

Melchior was confused by a strange mix of suspicion and infatuation. *Was she really my friend? Did Doolan or MacKay tell her to be nice to me?*

"Let's head back," he said.

The cold November wind cut through them like an ancient scythe. Still, the horses ambled along as though it were spring.

"You still love her, don't you?" Brooke said after a few minutes.

Melchior stared ahead. "I'm not sure I ever did love her, now. Love must be reciprocated. Returned… for it to be true love. I see now that it was not so true."

"But you were…" Brooke did not finish.

Melchior glared at her. "You have been reading copies of my conversations. They told me, assured me, my words would remain strictly confidential. Not open to…"

"A secretary?" Brooke asked dolefully.

"I am sorry but…"

"I know Matt. In Germany, non-university types are on a second tier. And clerical types…well… "

"I didn't mean to insult you, Brooke."

She put her hand on his arm. "It's all right, Matt. It's all right."

They rode silently until they returned to the stable. After a thorough wipe down, they watered and fed the horses.

"I usually eat alone, Brooke. Would you like to have supper with me?"

She looked at her watch. "I'd love to, but I can't. I have to be somewhere at seven. Can I see you at another time?"

He put his hand on her smooth olive cheek. "Of course, as long as it is soon."

She smiled brightly. "Very soon, Matt."

***

Melchior had no idea she meant that same night. But at nine, just as he was finishing a book, his door opened, and Brooke Costain appeared in high heels, a black skirt, and a low-cut sweater of the same color. A tight cord of pearls adorned her neck, and her hair was up in a simple style. She came up to him silently and put her arms around his neck. They kissed with a passion fueled by the shared knowledge that it was wrong.

Hours later, Melchior rolled over and kicked aside the covers. "I never asked, but how did you get in here? I always lock my door."

"There are some benefits to being a clerical type."

Before he could respond, she kissed him deeply. They embraced once more. Then suddenly, Brooke jumped out of the bed. "My gosh, it's nearly six am!"

Even in the dim morning light, Melchior could make out her lean, elegant limbs and the toss of her long dark hair.

"You have the body of an athlete, Brooke."

"I hope that's a good thing, Matt."

"I think so."

She pulled her sweater over her head and straightened it out, revealing her bosom to him in a way as inviting as without.

She bent over and kissed his cheek. "Well, you have the body of..."

"Of what? An athlete?"

"No. Of a warrior. I've never seen muscles like that..."

"On another man... men?"

She blushed but did not contradict him. "Get a few hours of rest, Matt. You'll be meeting a new member of the team today."

"Who?"

"I can't say. But I think it will please you."

Melchior could not sleep. Instead, he rose from his bed and went to the window. He watched the lithe form of Brooke leave his building and turn up the walkway. The bright salmon pink and azure glow of morning twilight caught his attention for a moment. Dawn was upon them. He heard a *slam* and glimpsed Brooke closing the door of a dark sedan, which sped off.

Who would know she was here at this hour? Who would pick her up? Was this a planned visit?

Melchior was scheduled to have coffee and toast with Doctor MacKay at nine-thirty. He spent the time before at the gym and in a long, hot shower, where he mused over the recent events.

What was Brooke about? Who was she meeting? Another bull, he finally settled on. This was all an elaborate pretext to pin some ridiculous rap on him, a German war vet turned immigrant. *But maybe the new person was just another analyst? Maybe they thought him insane? If they did, they would not be too far from the truth,* Melchior thought. Physically, he felt good. He managed to bench press his weight ten times without straining very much. He could deadlift more than double his weight now. At this rate, he soon would be in the best physical shape since 1942.

***

"More marmalade, Mister Melchior?" Brooke asked. She presented him with a platter of crisped bread with butter and various jams, without a hint that they had made passionate love just hours before.

"No, thank you. I am watching my weight," Melchior said.

MacKay laughed. "I think we put twenty pounds on you, Matthaeus. And it's all muscle. What do you think, Brooke?"

She tossed her dark hair back fetchingly and smiled. "From what I can see, it's all very powerful looking. The weight he has gained, I mean."

For a fleeting moment, Melchior's eyes met hers.

"Yes. Yes, you are correct," MacKay bit into a slice of toast smothered in butter.

She spun about and strolled out the door, her high heels clicking her goodbye.

Melchior noted an informality in MacKay he had not seen before. But he was anxious to get on with whatever it was. "I have taken all your tests, Doctor. About all I can stand, that is. Am I ever going to learn what this is all about? I've signed all your forms."

"Of course, you will. We were waiting for your medical results, and they are finally in. Including your X-rays. And you passed all the routine psychological exams."

"Do you mean that there are non-routine exams too? What the devil are they?"

MacKay sipped his coffee. "As a matter of fact, there *are* non-routine exams. They don't measure your stability or sanity."

"Then what do they measure?"

MacKay took a bite of his toast and slowly, deliberately, chewed at the bits in his mouth. Finally, he swallowed the last morsel. "They measure your inner strength... your psychological stamina...your mental... resiliency. Those are much more important to us than physical strength."

Melchior's face darkened along with his mood. "My mental resiliency? My inner strength? Psychological stamina? What poppycock! *Mist*! Or as you here might say, *Merde*!"

"My dear fellow, don't take this as..."

"Hear me out, *Herr Doktor*. I lived through the machinations of an insane regime, the Third Reich. I fought in an insane war under insane and inhuman conditions. Conditions so terrible, I still feel the effects. Conditions that sent men into asylums or drove them to self-mutilation and suicide. And I led others through that hell. I failed at times, but I gave them my all. I watched them suffer and die for an evil regime. Why, I *helped* them suffer and die for an evil regime! For that, I paid a heavy price. I returned to see my world shattered. Family wiped out. And my loved one is a different person."

"I understand the hardship. But maybe you were that different person. Maybe your world needed to be shattered to move to a better world. We know you didn't succumb to the barbarism so many Germans did. We know how you suffered, Matthaeus. But what we are planning will test you even more. What you will have to do will surely test your physical, mental, and psychological resilience like nothing experienced by anyone."

Melchior's eyes suddenly flashed. "My God! Am I going into space? Am I to be a human Sputnik?"

MacKay's eyes darted into his cup. "In a manner of speaking..."

***

At ten that morning, Melchior was summoned to a small conference room on the second floor of the School. Doolan escorted him. The room was painted in an institutional shade of green. Its scarce furnishings consisted of a metal table and four straight-back chairs, painted almost the same colors as the walls. The floor was a simple black-and-white checkered linoleum. There were no windows. A long fluorescent light suspended from the ceiling hissed like a punctured steam pipe. The room smelled freshly scrubbed with ammonia.

"Is this my place of execution? I didn't see a 220-volt plug anywhere for the chair," Melchior said as he took his seat.

Doolan rolled his eyes. "We leave such things to the Americans. Canadians prefer a more genteel approach."

Doolan crossed his hands together. "Don't worry, Mister Melchior. Before this is over, you may think execution the wiser choice. Today, you learn what it is all really about. We are peeling back an inner layer of the onion. But first, you must sign these forms."

Melchior stared at the sheaf of paper Doolan suddenly thrust at him. "Haven't I signed enough papers?" He scribbled his name.

"Some might say so," Doolan said. "Some not..."

The door opened, and Doctor MacKay entered the room. "Are the formalities done with?"

Doolan's eyes met Mackay's, and he nodded.

MacKay took a seat. "All right, Matt. As you know, we are a Top Secret, actually more than a Top Secret, unit of the MOD. That's the Ministry of Defense to you civilians. What you don't know is...We have been around since the war. The war against the Axis, that is. Our mission is very focused operational research and development."

"Of what?" Melchior asked. "I read the Avro Arrow program was suddenly and mysteriously shut down. Any connection?"

He saw MacKay look at Doolan with narrow eyes. Doolan nodded.

MacKay smiled weakly. "Of many things... all centered on non-kinetic approaches to warfare. Non-material approaches to warfare."

"Non-kinetic? Non-material?"

"Yes, Matt, warfare that does not directly involve explosions, blunt trauma, etc. No missiles, bombs, planes, or rockets. We have pursued several lines of research along the way. These included things you may or may not have heard of."

"Such as?"

"Telekinesis, telepathy, hypnosis, and remote mental manipulation. You see, where the Brits and the Americans focused on bigger and better traditional weapons, we Canadians took a "softer" approach. In part, for economic reasons, but mostly because we are simply better at it."

"You left out galvanic chemistry and electro-biology," Melchior said with a laugh.

"Left out what?"

"Just a joke, *Herr Doktor.*"

"Quite funny," MacKay said, adjusting his bow tie.

"I assure you this is all quite serious, Mister Melchior," Doolan said. "This is a national security matter of the utmost importance."

"I get it," Melchior said. "I thought I was meeting someone new."

MacKay nodded. "In good time. I thought it would be better if you met Doctor Noble this afternoon. We are meeting for drinks at five-thirty. In the meantime, we want to discuss more of your past."

"My past? Haven't we discussed that enough? I'd like to discuss the future."

"That's quite the point, Matt," MacKay said. He opened a beige notebook and read through the text.

"What the doctor means is we learned quite a bit about you during your vetting," Doolan explained. "That's why it took so long. Not pure bureaucracy. Anyway, we learned things of interest to national security."

Melchior's face darkened. "What kind of things? We all know I fought against your country. You brought me here to talk about the war?"

"We only want to discuss one small aspect of it," Doolan said.

"And that would be?" Melchior grew agitated.

"Aachen."

Melchior swallowed hard. His eyes smoldered. "Not very much to say. My last battle. I led a forlorn defense and was wounded and captured along with those of my men who weren't killed."

Doolan smiled, a smile that showed he was out of patience. "Let's try the longer version, Mister Melchior. Or should I say, *Hauptmann* Melchior?"

Melchior felt boxed in. He did not know what they knew. He did not know what they wanted.

"Please continue, Matt," MacKay said politely.

"We shall be recording this," Doolan said.

Melchior lowered his head and placed his hands to his temples. Then he sat bolt upright and looked squarely at Doolan.

"I commanded the 481st *Volksgrenadier Battalion*. As you know, I was a captain. Normally, a major would command a battalion. But of course, this wasn't a battalion. Just in the dreams of Hitler and Himmler. Company strength. Barely over two hundred men. Did I say, men? I meant old men and boys, *Opas und Naseborer!*" Melchior paused a moment as he recalled them in a burst of memory that startled him. He had tried so hard to forget.

"Go on. There are drinks at five-thirty," Doolan coaxed.

"We lacked everything necessary for a sane defense. Ammunition and grenades were low… very low. Maybe two magazines per grenadier. We had just one MG 42, our best machine gun, and a few old *Panzerfausts.*"

"What?"

"Primitive anti-tank rockets. I think we had three left. No mortars. No *Schmeissers*. The automatic pistols went to the SS and some of the regular troops. The boys had the old M98s with a few clips each."

"The what?"

The Mauser. Bolt action. Still powerful but pre-Great War vintage. Antiques. Essentially, the same rifle the Boers of South Africa used against the Tommies in the 19th century."

"Your dossier said you were wounded at Normandy some months previously? On our Juno Beach."

"You mean *our* Juno Beach?" Melchior smiled grimly. "Yes. A sniper, maybe .50 caliber. Lucky for me it was a glancing round, a ricochet. Still tore into me but a direct shot would have cut me in two like last week's salami."

Doolan's eyes rose. "Except *we* Canadians owned that beach and our snipers didn't use that caliber."

"Your doctors have seen my scar! So has…" Melchior paused. He now thought he understood the purpose of Brooke's visit. He placed his face into his hands. "So long ago. I have tried only to forget."

"Tell us more about Aachen," MacKay coaxed.

Melchior nodded. "We were cut off from the rest of our division. They had pulled back across the river, the Rhine. We never got the word. The bridges were to be blown before the *Amis* took them. The Americans, that is."

"We know," MacKay said soothingly. "What went wrong?"

"At first, I thought the telephone wire was cut by enemy artillery. But I later discovered that wasn't true. They deliberately left us there. To fight to the end just to slow the enemy. *Ein Witz*…A joke."

"Happens in war," Doolan said.

"Jokes?"

"No, self-sacrifice. Suicide missions. Cannon fodder. Looks like you were all three for *Herr* Hitler's generals."

Melchior's eyes narrowed. "Of course. I should have known. The *Ami* guns were at close range, pounding everything in the open and crushing it. It rained steel. Plumes of black smoke and balls of fire were everywhere. Then I saw it."

"Saw what?"

"The old *Burg*! The old castle from the Dark Ages. I remembered Aachen was Charlemagne's capital near the end of his reign. I decided to make our last stand there. I thought it fitting, from one *Reich* to another."

"Clever enough. Do you know much about him?" MacKay asked.

"Who?" Melchior asked.

"Charlemagne."

Melchior shook his head. "Not really. Great lord of the Franks. Built a European empire of a kind, I guess. Fought pagans and Muhammedans. That's all."

"And built a castle that might have saved you," Doolan opined.

"Ironic," Melchior said sullenly.

"When did you realize something was wrong?"

"I never knew for certain. But after years of combat a special instinct sets in, or you die."

"A sixth sense?" MacKay asked.

"Or maybe a seventh," Doolan said.

Melchior smiled grimly. "You know, then. By the afternoon, we had fended off three infantry attacks. Their infantry was bad. Well-armed, but they didn't know how to fight in a city. They were easy pickings for my lads. But then, Klaus, my number two, *Leutnant* Klaus von Zelinsky." Melchior smiled again. *von und zu Zelinsky*, he called himself."

"What did he do?"

"He commanded the forward outpost. Suddenly, he appeared without his helmet or his men. I asked him what was wrong and gave him a drag on my cigarette. His eyes bulged with fear. He said a pack of Ronsons was coming up the road. And the lead three had overrun their position, killing all who had not deserted but him with their machine guns and ground them under their tracks."

"Ronsons?" Doolan asked.

"Tanks."

"Tanks in a city?"

"*Ja. Dummheit, na?*"

"Without infantry?"

"I told you, we had dealt with their infantry. Now our only protection against the tanks was the shattered walls of a shattered empire. An unlikely place for a last stand," Melchior said softly. "But we stood."

Doolan handed him a lit cigarette. "What happened next?"

"You know, I tried to quit smoking after the war." He took a puff and blew a cloud of smoke.

"As I said, we held off the infantry with Mausers, no problem. By then, the MG 42 had overheated."

"MG 42... Best weapon of the war, some say," Doolan noted dryly.

"Most say the atomic bomb." Melchior blew a large cloud of smoke. "It didn't matter. The MG 42 was out of ammo. I drew the boys in close to me. A tight perimeter using the line of rubble."

"Like a shield wall of ancient times," MacKay noted.

Melchior ignored the comment. "I told Klaus to bring up the *Faust*. The clanking, grinding sound of tracks crushing rubble grew close. Too close. Suddenly, two Ronsons appeared thirty meters to our front. Thirty meters!" Melchior choked.

"Why did you call the Sherman tanks Ronsons? That's a cigarette lighter." Doolan whipped out his smooth nickel-finished lighter and flicked open the top, and a blue-yellow flame shot up.

Melchior smiled. He took a drag on his cigarette. "I prefer 'Lucky Strikes,' by the way. We used to take them from the dead *Amis*. Better than the shit "Galois" we took from the French. But yes, Ronsons. It's what we called the American Sherman tanks. Our anti-tank gunners coined the name: one shot, and the gasoline engines exploded in a ball of flame. How stupid to send tanks into combat with gasoline engines! One good hit from a *Faust* or well-tossed grenade and they lit up like a Ronson cigarette lighter."

"Indeed," Doolan said. "But those stupid *Amis* managed to crush your army, destroy your cities, and may I say, save your life."

Melchior took a puff. "You are... correct. And we brought the carnage on ourselves. As for crushing our armies, that was done on the snowy steppes of Russia, not the green fields of France."

"What do you think of the Russians, now that you bring them up?' Doolan asked.

Melchior's eyes narrowed. "The Bolsheviks were a menace. The only thing the Nazis got right. But to invade them was insanity. And they continue to menace us all. That is why I submitted my application as a researcher. I was hoping to help develop new weapons for NORAD."

"Have you or any member of your family ever met a Russian... been to Russia?" Doolan asked.

Melchior shook his head. He dabbed his cigarette into the ashtray. "No. We were staunch Catholics. Rhinelander... Christian Democrats."

"Do you know or have you ever known anyone who has been there?"

Melchior shook his head. "I don't believe so. Certainly, no one I was close to. Or I would have known."

Doolan glanced at MacKay, who nodded.

"Tell me more about Aachen, then."

"I planned on one last gambit before I'd throw up the white flag. Klaus wanted to surrender right then. But I told him, no."

"What was his reaction?"

"He nodded and picked up a Mauser. *I'll cover the right flank, then*, he said. I told him to take the First Company. It was our best unit."

"You said you knew no one who ever went to Russia. Wasn't this Klaus a close friend of yours?"

Melchior took a breath. *These boys have done some homework.*

"I am impressed at your research, Captain Doolan. Yes, Klaus was my closest friend throughout the war. When I agreed to command the *Volksgrenadier* battalion, it was on the condition that he be assigned there with me."

"Assigned from where?"

Melchior's mouth formed a cynical smile. "You are good... the Russian front."

"Pretty handy to have such influence. *Droit du Seignior?*"

"No. *Droit du* Knights Cross with crossed swords and diamonds. I led a rescue party behind British lines in North Africa and saved the son-in-law of a very high-ranking party member."

"A *Gauleiter?*"

"I never knew. But some weeks later, I was whisked to Berlin for a secret ceremony with the Führer. It lasted all of three minutes, but because of it I escaped the *Kessel* at Tobruk."

"Do you feel guilty about that?" MacKay asked.

"No."

"You met Hitler?" MacKay the behavioral scientist, was intrigued. "What was he like?"

"Hardly met him, really. He thanked me for my gallantry and asked where I would like to fight for the *Reich*."

"And you chose?"

"I said I would fight wherever the enemies of the nation were. Hitler smiled faintly and tapped my shoulder. Within forty-eight hours, I was in Italy with a *Sonderkommando*."

'That's how you wound up in the SS?"

"*Waffen* SS. Not political. But yes. Although I never actually joined."

"And that's how you avoided de-Nazification?" Doolan asked.

Melchior nodded. "And where I met Klaus. He was a specialist of sorts and attached to the support group." Melchior grew melancholy. "And that is how I met Kristel."

"I thought you said you were engaged before the war," Doolan said.

Melchior stared silently.

"Mister Melchior, are you all right?"

"Did I say that? I don't know. Part of me says I knew her before the war, but part of me says I met her later through Klaus. She was his sister, and he told me I'd be perfect for her. When he showed me her picture, I thought her the most beautiful of women. Woman... she was all of nineteen."

"You were all of twenty-five?"

"I began to write to her, and she wrote back. We became engaged via the *Reichspost*. But it was pure love, unspoiled by the physical. I think somehow that made it all the better. All the more special." Melchior blushed and then grew stern. "What has this to do with anything?"

"Quite a lot, possibly. Where were they from... the *von und zu* Zelinski family? "

"Koenigsberg..."

"Which is now part of Russia."

"Yes."

"Tell us more about Aachen, please."

"Klaus and his *Kompanie* disappeared as the last phase of our defense commenced. I should have surrendered the lads, but something made me want to make a statement. The first Ronson, a Sherman, turned its turret on us like a lion that catches the scent of an antelope."

"But unlike the antelope, you had no place to run," MacKay said.

Melchior shook his head. "There is always someplace to run. What is it you psychiatrists call it, fight or flight? I decided to fight. I grabbed the *Faust* from the gunner, a boy named Mueller. Find a Mauser and shoot the crew if they try to escape, I told him."

"Why did you take the weapon from its gunner?"

"Because he had never actually fired one! I can shoot them in my sleep. And we only had two rockets left. More like long grenades, really. But at fifty meters, a direct hit can be deadly, especially against Ronsons. And so, it was. I snapped the warhead into place and aimed, knowing if I missed, the tank's 76 mm gun would blow me into the Fourth Reich." Melchior laughed grimly. "I placed the sight at the point between the turret and the chassis of the tank and squeezed the lever. The warhead launched with a woosh and struck, blowing the turret off its ring and sending smoke and flame, spewing from every hatch. So goes the Ronson."

"You said there was a second tank?"

Melchior shook his head. "It backed off in a hurry. Good thing too. I fired our last rocket into its ass – it proved a dud."

"Bad luck, trumped by good luck," Doolan said."

"Our arms workers were cutting corners to meet *Herr* Speer's ridiculous production demands. The result was bad weapons and munitions that were an enemy equal to the

Allies. No matter. The American machine guns began spraying us, and their small mortars pounded us like the fists of a middleweight. No knockout blow. But lots of punches that hurt the body and wear down the opponent. The machine guns were so numerous it was like one continuous stream of fire. They rang in our ears like a sawmill buzzing up lumber. I saw three of my boys cut to pieces trying to carry back a wounded soldier. I ordered a retreat to the inner works of the *Burg*."

"What happened next?"

"I think you know."

"I called for my next most experienced *Landser*. A *Faehnrich* named Weber. He was just over fifty. A *Metzger*, that is, a butcher by trade, before he was called up at the end to do his duty. Well, he never saw a *Schlachterei* like Aachen. We shared a last cigarette. Then we heard it."

"Heard what?"

"We heard planes overhead, a dogfight. Our Messerschmitts finally managed a *Schwarm* to try to stem the flocks of *Ami* bombers and fighters." Melchior adjusted himself in his chair. He was tired of sitting. "In such cases, our fighters almost always win."

"And did they?"

"I don't know. We heard a high-pitched whistle, and the ceiling of the *burg* exploded, killing my last boys and blasting me into the next Reich."

Chapter 3

Melchior sat in silence while Doolan went back through his notes, drawing more details on his subject. Melchior was tired of the questioning, and the questions For he knew he contradicted himself on occasions, yet on each occasion, he knew he was being quite precise. *Am I going mad?*

"I am finished answering any more questions unless you answer one," Melchior abruptly demanded.

"That's not how it works," Doolan said.

"I think I can say something without compromising your questioning, captain," MacKay said. His voice was calm and soothing.

Doolan's eyes narrowed. "Okay, professor."

"Why focus on Kristel?" Melchior asked.

"It's quite simple, Matt," MacKay explained. "Despite your evasions, evasions to yourself, that is. It seems clear that you harbor a great love for her, despite her abandoning you after the war. Despite your cognitive attempts to, say, divorce yourself from her. Not divorce in the legal sense but…"

"What does that have to do with anything?"

"For our program to succeed, we must know you better than you know yourself."

"That shouldn't be too hard, professor," Melchior said. "I hardly know myself. I know things… yet I don't know things. I remember things… that I can't remember. I think you should have me put away, don't you?"

"No, Matt. No, I don't. Admitting your doubts is the clearest signal of sanity."

Doolan put down his notes. "Now, just when was the last time you saw Kristel?"

"I thought you wanted a war story. Suddenly, this is a love story," Melchior said.

"I think you know there's hardly a difference," MacKay said.

Melchior bristled, and his voice rose. "I told you, *Herr Doktor*. On the day I left Germany. We rode the night train to Hamburg, where I boarded a tramp steamer named *Frankland*.

Doolan gave MacKay a glance Melchior found unsettling.

"What did she say?" Doolan asked.

"We were lovers by then. We knew it would be our last night together for some time. We didn't talk all that much." Melchior was biting his lip and began gripping the table.

"Did you speak of Klaus at all? I understand she lost her father on the Eastern Front. Did she speak of him?" Doolan asked.

"I suspect she blamed me for Klaus's death. I believe that was one of the reasons she wouldn't join me. She said she wanted to find him. I told her he was missing in action. That the *Amis* would have released him by then."

"Why do you think she felt otherwise? After all, you were her betrothed."

"I... I don't know. Maybe she... And of course, she hoped to be in Germany when her father returned from prison in Russia."

"Prison in Russia? So, there is a bit of a Russian connection. But Kristel's home was in Konigsberg. By 1949, Konigsberg was Russian territory." Doolan said. "Was she going to return to the east to await her father?"

"There was one letter from him."

"What did it say?" Doolan prodded.

"She would never let me read it. She said it was her only bond with him. Her mother and sister were lost in the east too, you know."

"Bombing?"

"We never knew. They just disappeared. Probably shot by the Russians like most of the nobility."

"How did Kristel escape that?"

"She was in the west. Came to see me in the *Lazarett,* the military hospital, when I recovered from my wound at Normandy. Kristel had studied chemistry and physics and found employment at an arms factory of some sort near Siegen. That's all I knew."

"And if I told you that we found that the arms factory was building secret weapons for the Reich? Weapons so secret that both the Americans and Russians waged a clandestine war to find everyone involved."

Melchior slumped in his chair. "I don't know. I was just a simple soldier."

MacKay slowly shook his head. "A soldier, yes, Matt. But simple, no."

***

Melchior stared silently into the nightfall. The smattering of lights on the river twinkled like stars. Clouds darkened the sky – casting an early winter gloom that at once comforted and disturbed. He glanced down into his whisky and soda. He longed for a good German beer and a *Schnapps.* The Canadian party had just started, but already he found it dull.

A soft hand touched his shoulder, and an even softer voice whispered in his ear, "Mind some company, Mister Melchior?"

Her breath tickled, and a chill shot through him. But he straightened himself abruptly and turned to her. "Did Evan MacKay send you to check on his specimen?"

"Evan doesn't view you like that at all. Besides, he just left. One of his boys has a birthday tonight. He's quite the family man." She gave a smile that tore at even Melchior's stone edifice. He found her very beautiful. And that disturbed him. *Was she another honey trap?*

Melchior grunted. "I see." He looked across the room. Brooke was deeply engaged in a raucous conversation with some of the staff. Young scientists and technicians mostly, but Melchior suspected a few more SIU men among them.

Melchior sipped at his drink. "Looks like Brooke is having fun anyway."

"She seems so nice."

"Who are you?"

She smiled warmly. "I was wondering when you were going to ask. Patricia Noble. Doctor Patricia Noble. Evan thought it would be good for us to meet. To get to know each other."

Melchior barely heard what she said. He suddenly felt drawn to this strange woman. Her soft, arching eyes intrigued him. She was tall and statuesque with lustrous black hair. *She looks like Ava Gardner.* She seemed refined and elegant. He was beginning to think she was not another honey trap. He had not felt this way in many years. Even thoughts of Kristel seemed to fade as he looked at her. This tore him, but it also warmed him.

Melchior motioned at Brooke. "So, you are not friends with her?"

"Goodness, no. Today is my first day here," she said.

"Really? The doctor sends for reinforcements. How many behavioral scientists does he need? I count at least eight so far. They all had a turn with me."

"I'm neither a psychiatrist nor a psychologist."

Her long lashes fluttered. He swallowed.

"What the? Wait, let me guess – a physicist! Better yet, a radiologist! They have been talking about X-rays and things. God, haven't they taken enough? I don't want to end up like Madame Curie."

Patricia smiled and put her hand on his arm. He liked her touch. "No, I'm a historian and an expert in ancient artifacts."

"That explains it then. I am certainly an ancient artifact."

Patricia slapped his chest playfully. Soft as her touch was, the scar hurt.

"Don't say that, Mister Melchior. May I call you Matt?"

"Call me what you like, Doctor Noble, but I prefer my actual name, Matthaeus."

"Very well, Matthaeus. Please call me Patricia, then. But you can't be more than ten years my senior."

"And how old are you, Patricia?"

"In Canada, we never ask a lady's age."

"In Germany, we always demanded it," he said with a grin.

She smiled. "Besides, age is mostly a matter of mind."

"That's what Doctor MacKay has told me, several times. I wonder why?"

"I am sure he was just making conversation."

"You don't know him then. He rarely makes conversation."

"I understand. But you look like a twenty-something, Matthaeus. I haven't seen anyone as fit since I finished at university."

"Carleton?"

"No, McGill. I'm from Montreal."

"Well, the regimen here is killing me. Four hours of conditioning and drills each weekday. They even brought in a Canadian Olympic instructor for the saber. Truth is, I'm teaching him, but the workouts are good."

"They certainly seem to do you well, Matthaeus."

Melchior lowered his voice. "Is this really a secret Olympic training center?"

Patricia laughed. Her laugh made him feel good for the first time in a long time.
"They say you are doing very well."
"For a patient," he muttered into his glass.
"No. The way I understand it, you are more of a…"
"Of what?"
"More of a weapon…"
"Let me get us both a fresh drink."

***

The following morning, Noble met with MacKay for coffee in his office.
"How did you hit it off with our subject?" McKay asked.
"Seriously? I look forward to working with him," she said.
"He's a very rare man. We assess maybe only five or so like him in the world. We are lucky to have stumbled upon him through our vetting process. Have you read the UM folder marked 'JANUS'?"
"Yes, but it's all so confusing to me. But also fascinating." She cocked her head. "If it is true."
"It's true. The question is whether we can harness him properly. That's where you come in."
"I've been waiting to learn how I fit into all this," Noble said.
"Well, your role isn't an exact science, but pivotal, nonetheless. You will help vett his story for us, and more importantly, arm him with knowledge of where we hope to send him."
"If things work as planned, Evan. This is all such a stretch of the mind if you'll excuse my pun."
"*Touche'*!"
"After meeting him last night and despite what I said of him, I feel he is very vulnerable."
MacKay frowned. "Leave the mental and psychological assessments to us." He took a sip of his coffee.
"I am speaking as a woman, not as a scientist."
MacKay glanced at his watch. "It's almost eight. He's due at radiology at nine, sharp. While we wait, let me show you his X-rays.

***

Melchior followed Doolan into the X-Ray room.
A short man in a dirty lab jacket greeted them. "Mister Melchior?"
"Not me, this is Mister Melchior," Doolan said.
"I see," he said. "I'm Bill Coats. Doctor Bill Coats. I'm a radiologist. Doctor MacKay and Doctor Field should be here shortly.
"Why are we here?" Melchior asked. "And now who the hell is Doctor Field?"
"Didn't they tell you?"
Melchior shook his head. "They tell me as little as possible." He glanced at Doolan. "Security."

-46-

Coats nodded. "Of course. Well, we have a very interesting chest X-ray."

"I'm not sure an 'interesting' chest X-ray is anything one should want, doctor," Melchior said.

The door opened. MacKay stepped into the room with Patricia Noble and a balding man of medium height with a dark mustache that matched his black horned-rimmed glasses.

"Glad to see we are all here," MacKay said cheerfully.

"Can we start, sir?" Doolan asked.

"Are we ready, Bill?" MacKay asked.

"Yes. But I think Mister Melchior has some questions."

"What questions, Matt?" MacKay asked.

Melchior frowned. "Why the hell am I here? And who is this new doctor? Another shrink?"

"We are here to discuss your physical and metaphysical state," MacKay said pleasantly.

Melchior could tell he had struck a chord. But he had had enough. "I'm tired of the bullshit. Explain all this, or I'm leaving, even if I have to fight my way through every doctor, shrink, and bull from here to Montreal!"

Mackay reddened slightly but stayed calm. "Relax, Matt. Simon Field is a professor of Philosophy at Carleton with a concentration in Metaphysics. He is also a trained psychiatrist. He's an expert on the intersection of mind, body, and things we have yet to comprehend."

This was a new twist. Melchior crossed his arms. "What sort of things?"

"You'll understand soon enough, Matt," MacKay said.

Coats darkened the room and flipped on the X-ray table lights. To the layman, it made no sense.

"What we have here, Mister Melchior, are your X-rays taken in a series. The three on the left are inconclusive. But look at the one on the right. It's different. See that?"

He pointed to a small triangular-shaped form. "This displays a shard of metal in your chest. Just under the scar indicated in your medical records. Do you feel any pain?"

Melchior reflexively touched his chest. "Not normally. Maybe a twinge now and then."

"You *should* feel a twinge now and then," Coats said.

Melchior glanced at MacKay. "The shrapnel, I told you, is a bullet I took from one of your Canadian sharpshooters. Fortunately for me, it was a ricochet. Your marksman wasn't even aiming at me."

"No," Doolan said. "Wehrmacht surgeons removed your bullet. Our investigators found one of the doctors who assisted. Lives in the Black Forest now. But you knew that."

Melchior's mind raced. *How could they know?*

Coats stood up. "Mister Melchior, the X-ray shows a triangular-shaped shard of metal. More like a spear point than a bullet."

Melchior stared straight ahead, not wanting to hear what they had to say. Even though he knew they were right. The military *Arzt* told him the other metal could not be removed. But it posed no immediate danger. They just wanted him back at the front.

Patricia Noble spoke in a soft voice, "No, Doctor Coats. It is more likely a sword point. The X-ray appears to date to the late Merovingian or early Carolingian period. But I could be off by as many as one hundred years. I'd have to examine it to be sure."

All eyes turned to Melchior.

"This is absurd," Melchior said.

"Is it?" Doolan replied calmly.

MacKay tried to calm things. "Matt, I know this is upsetting. But we'd like to confirm all this. We need to confirm all this."

"Confirm what?"

"We'd like to remove it. So Patricia can examine it properly. In part, that's why she's here."

"Cut me open? To test a theory? Is Doctor Mengele in the next room? What other shit are you pulling on me?"

"Yes, Matt, we do want to cut you open," said MacKay in an offhand way.

Melchior's face darkened. "This is *Scheisse*… bullshit! I won't allow it!"

"But you already did allow it," Doolan said. "Included in the papers you signed was authorization for the unit to perform whatever medical procedures were necessary to further our study."

Melchior felt duped. *But of course, these Canadians had been duping him all along. Their politeness is a shroud for duplicity.*

"Very well," he said. "But I must know why you need to do this."

Doolan looked at MacKay, who nodded.

Coats stood up again. This time, he stepped towards the door. "I'll leave the discussion at this point."

Chapter 4

Melchior was glancing at the wall clock as if it would provide him with some relief. "I think you people are mad," he growled.

"Listen, Melchior, our boys turned over every stone searching for people with the phenomena of the universal mind," Doolan said. "All leads point to you alone. At least in Canada."

"I ramble… have nightmares… I drink too much. That's all," Melchior stammered. *They are not convinced.*

Doolan shook his head. "Your stories about life in the Dark Ages were too detailed to be just drunk ramblings. I've statements from almost a dozen people."

MacKay's chair squeaked. He slowly leaned back, and his usual genteel face bore in on Melchior in a way that chilled. "As you know, Matt, we have been working hard on the soft science approach to the Cold War. Since the thirties, at least, the theory of a highly select group of humans having extraordinary mental capacity… a capacity to go well beyond mere thinking, reasoning, or even imagining, has intrigued a small circle of scientists. Mostly in my field. But a few physical scientists and biological researchers as well. Some theologians, too."

MacKay turned to Simon Field. "And of course, those chaps who study metaphysics like Simon are all over it."

Field pulled his pipe from his mouth. "The hard scientists have denigrated us in the field of metaphysics. But now we believe the theory of the intersection of mind, space, and time – of the physical and the non-physical- can be proven by this program. The theory is quite advanced. Take the Jesuit Teilhard and his writings on the idea of radial energy."

"Take what? Who? Some priest?"

"Yes, Matt. Pierre Teilhard de Chardin is a French philosopher and Jesuit priest," MacKay said.

Field nodded. "But Teilhard is also a scientist – he studied paleontology and geology. He suggests, among many things, that all energy is psychic in nature. But divided into two distinct components: tangential energy, which links the element with all others of the same order, and radial energy, which draws it towards ever greater complexity and centricity. In other words, forward."

"Teilhard infers that the act of the individualization of our planet, a certain mass of elementary consciousness was originally imprisoned in the earth's matter," Mackay said. "To Teilhard, evolution is a constant move toward the sacred. As a priest, that means towards God. In our case, we are not so sure where it is heading, but the idea behind it is intriguing and offers possibilities."

"I don't understand," Melchior said.

Field waved his pipe like a pointer. "Well, we believe he refers to an underlying spiritual energy or intelligence that propels the outer world. Combine that with spiritual energy or intelligence lodged within each soul. This could be the key to moving across time and space if we can understand it better."

"How? This can't be true. I was a medical student. The physical and the mental are separate. I won't even address the idea of the spiritual. *Quatsch!* Hogwash."

"Well, we have a dusting of evidence," Field said.

"What evidence? Me? I'm your evidence?" Melchior mocked.

Doolan looked up from his notepad. "Let's just say nuclear theory preceded nuclear weapons and leave it at that."

MacKay shot him a look. "World War II ended before anyone with the skill, which is what I'll call it, for now, could be identified."

"At least at the extreme end of the spectrum," Field said.

"But with you, we now have at least one," Doolan said. "Who would have guessed we'd find it in Germany?"

"Is that supposed to be an insult?" Melchior spat. "Or something else?"

"What do you mean by something else, Matt?" MacKay asked.

"I'm not sure. But I have the feeling that I am not the only one. And maybe that other one is also from Germany. But which Germany?"

MacKay's eyes widened slightly, and he glanced at Doolan. "No, it was not an insult, Matt. It's just that we always thought we'd find who we were looking for, someone with those unique skills, in Asia. Based purely on the statistical odds. There are at most five people whose minds are wired this way. I'm sorry to use that expression, but I can't think of a better word."

"Wired to what? Wired for what?" Melchior asked.

MacKay paused a moment. "You can explain it better, Simon."

Field slowly drew on his pipe. "Wired to not merely process thoughts and ideas, but *to actually experience them.* For people with universal minds, thoughts, and memories are in the same spectrum as physical reality. Your random, or not so random recollections, are actual experiences."

"You mean you think they happened? Or is this just some more $E=mc2$ psychobabble?"

MacKay burst into laughter. The others joined in.

"Did I say something funny?" Melchior asked.

"Excuse me, Matt. It's just that I never heard those terms used that way before. But yes, I suppose it is psychobabble… until we prove otherwise. That, you see, is what we are about."

"Mister Melchior, we think these things happened and are happening. We aren't sure yet. This is an ongoing process. We hope that you will help us find out more," Field said.

"How do I help?" Melchior asked. He was suspicious but also curious.

"Step one: let us find out what is in your chest," MacKay said.

"And step two?"

"Trying to unite you with the blade that pierced your chest. Getting you back to that state of your mind, which we believe is also a state of reality," Field said, fumbling in his jacket pocket for his pipe tool.

Melchior blew a large puff of smoke across the table. "What does any of this have to do with NORAD and beating the Russians?"

"A fair question. Quite a bit, as it turns out," MacKay said.

"The Soviets have been exploring the practical application of metaphysics since the mid-1930s. But they thought anyone could be used. It is believed that hundreds, if not thousands, of men and women died in various experiments, mostly using mind-altering drugs and shock therapies to advance the theory," Field said.

"We have reason to believe, based on our investigation into you, that the Soviets are now on to this idea that only very select persons have the possibility of transcending," MacKay said.

"We also believe they are on to you," Doolan said.

"To me?" Melchior was confused, but somehow not surprised.

Doolan nodded. "That's why we picked you up when we did and where we did. It was a matter of days, if not hours, before they'd be in your apartment. You don't think we'd pick a Canadian citizen up in broad daylight, do you?"

Melchior eyed him skeptically.

Doolan continued. "Our friends down south tipped us off that an illegal had been dispatched to Canada a year ago. The mission was to locate a former German officer."

"Why would the Bolsheviks be interested in me?"

"For the same reason, we are interested in you. We identified pre-operational surveillance of your flat. That means they were closing in."

"Closing? To do what? You don't think the Bolsheviks sent a Russian agent to kill me?"

"Oh, he's a Russian agent, but not a Russian."

"What?"

"German...more exactly, East German," Doolan said. "As to what the game was, we don't know. Some think to lure you back, not kill you. Any Russian could kill you. But only another German could lure you back."

"Do you have any proof of this?" Melchior asked.

Doolan laid three black and white eight-by-ten glossies on the table. "Here you go. Three different teams of two. Three different days. Three different times of the day. We found they had rented a room within eyeshot, or gunshot, of your place. When we raided it after we picked you up, it was clean."

"Clean?" Melchior asked.

"Wiped clean. They paid cash, and the lease ended that day. So if you back out of this now, we release you to who knows what."

Melchior's mouth tightened. *Damned Bolsheviks!* "Don't worry about that. I'm in."

MacKay smiled. "Excellent, Matt."

"Thank you, Mister Melchior," Field said.

Doolan looked skeptical. "Why the change of heart?"

"I fought the Bolsheviks. Don't like the Russian variety. But I loathe the East German version even more. What do you people say? Fuck them."

Doolan stifled a smile. "Why do you loathe your *Landsmen*? They only had the misfortune of geography."

Melchior stared a moment. "I don't know. Perhaps geography, the earth, is as important as our minds. Somehow shaping them. I really don't know. But the idea crosses my, as you say, universal mind."

Doolan shoved a folder in front of him. "Before we can discuss more of that, you need to read this sub-compartment and sign. It's your final ticket."

Melchior startled. In bold block letters at the top and bottom were stamped, JANUS.

"Janus? The carving on your bookshelf? What is Janus?"

"You are Janus, Melchior," Doolan said. "All along."

MacKay smiled sheepishly. "A bit of humor, eh Matt? Janus, the guardian of the Roman gates, has the power to look to the past or the future. Now we hope you can do the same. We are counting on it. As is the free world. And the not-so-free world."

***

MacKay looked up at the clock. "It's after five. We have been at this for some time, Matt. I think you earned a break." He glanced at Patricia. "We all need a break. I am scheduling the surgery for the day after tomorrow. Seven, sharp."

"So soon?" Patricia asked.

"We are in a race with the Soviets now," Doolan said.

"*Wunderschoen*. You want to use me, weaponize me before the Bolsheviks kill me."

"No. Before the Soviets figure out how to exploit the universal mind, we want to beat them to the draw," Doolan said.

"I don't understand, Doctor MacKay, if there are only five or so of us... assuming I'm one of them... who can they be using?"

MacKay smiled. "We were hoping you might help us find out. Perhaps you already know... but don't know you know. Or possibly can't remember that you know."

Patricia placed her hand on Melchior's wrist. "You see, Matt, the answer might have been learned, or lost a millennium ago. I hope to help you with that. As soon as we verify our theory, I'll be working with you on studying and learning more about the Carolingian world."

Melchior shrugged. "How soon will we..."

"I'd say we give you a month to recover from the surgery. During that period, Doctor Noble and you will explore the time of Charlemagne. She'll do her best to equip your mind as well as draw any subconscious knowledge of the period from you. After all, if we are correct. You have been there."

"A month of mental gymnastics, eh?" Melchior replied.

"Physical, too," Doolan said. "As soon as you are able, you'll be able to train on horse and sword again,"

"And you'll spend some quality time with Doctor Field. He'll have his own set of tests and questions. All to prep you for the big journey," MacKay said.

Melchior grimaced. "So, I'm simply going on a journey, eh?" He well knew it would be no simple journey.

***

"He seems to be doing swimmingly," the surgeon said to MacKay.

MacKay smiled. "That's great news, Doctor. How big is the cut?"

"Small and neat, if I don't say so myself. The shard of metal wasn't so deep."

"I'm right here, gentlemen," Melchior said.

MacKay flashed a wide grin. "And so you are, Matt."

"What next?" Melchior instinctively reached for the scar.

"Patricia is examining the specimen right now. She's meeting with some colleagues at McGill University. Of course, they aren't privy to its source. Once she has reached her conclusions, we'll decide on the way forward. Or backward."

"How long will I be laid up?"

"Three days. Then two weeks of light activity," the surgeon said.

"Then a month of intense training and study. You'll have the fortune of having one-on-one sessions with Doctor Noble," Mackay said.

"I'd pay extra for that. And the misfortune of one-on-one with your Doctor Field?"

"He's not such a bad chap," Mackay said.

"I'll be back later to check on you, Mister Melchior." The surgeon stepped out.

MacKay closed the door behind him. "You agreed to all this, Matt. I hope you are still up to it. A lot is riding on your complete cooperation."

"You mean a lot is riding on your reputation. And your Doctor Field's metaphysics. I went to medical school for a few years, and everything I know about this tells me it's crap."

"No. It's not crap. These are some of the most interesting ideas to come out of the Cold War, and a very elite group of people have been working hard to advance this. Less than forty people are aware of it. Of those, a mere dozen are fully briefed. There's no glory in this."

"Am I one of those... fully briefed?" He knew the answer.

MacKay ignored the question. "If the Soviets learn how to exploit this before we do, who knows what the result will be?"

"You sound like Captain Doolan, now."

"Maybe so. But this is important to science as well as national security. This may prove that the universal mind is one of the universe's transcending phenomena. Possibly transformational. If the mind can leap time, what else can it do? And if its workings can be harnessed, the power of it will be worth a million hydrogen bombs. Can you imagine that?"

"Honestly, no," Melchior said. "It's as though you expect me to enter some twilight zone of past and present, as well as the future."

"Just imagine if we could secure the world without a nuclear holocaust."

"You are quite the dreamer. Not good for a scientist. Stick to data, not dreams. My recollections were real. But only to me." Even as he said it, Melchior was not so sure.

"I aim to prove you wrong, Matt. But I'll use data to do it, not dreams."

***

"I'm quite impressed with your grasp of these things, Matthaeus," Patricia said at the close of a particularly grueling session.

The weeks that followed enabled Melchior to recover. But his light activity proved anything but light. In the mornings, the trainers pushed him to his limits, physically. In the afternoons, Doctor Noble immersed him in the Carolingian world.

"I studied medicine for years. This is nothing like that."

"You're a quick learner," she said warmly.

"You're a remarkable teacher. None of my professors in Germany were like you." He could not take his eyes off her.

"Matthaeus, are you flirting?"

"Harmlessly, I hope. You are blushing like a schoolgirl. I'm not used to that in a professor."

"I'm sorry."

"About the material – as you go through it, I sometimes do feel like I know it already... hints of it... not all of it."

"Well, even if you lived in that period or experienced that period, your knowledge would be limited to your personal experiences and vague telling. There were no books or other media."

"The church played that role." His eyes widened. "Why did I just say that?"

"Because it's true. The clergy were somewhat literate, but even that was wrapped in vague superstition."

"So you say."

"What do you mean?"

"I don't know. I don't know why I said that."

Her sympathetic eyes gazed at him. "We believe, or should I say Evan believes, you have experienced much of this. Our sessions are meant to draw them out. I hope to learn more, or shall I say glean more information from an eyewitness of the period? But..."

"But what?"

"You seem so tentative in your knowledge."

"That's because I am tentative in my knowledge."

"I'm sorry. I should have told you. "She put her hand on his. "But Evan didn't want you to know. He and his team decided we'd learn more from you and about your phenomena that way. I'm not so sure now."

Melchior placed his hand over hers. "So I'm a phenomenon. Well, if anyone but you said that I'd be mad as hell."

"You're not mad at me?"

"No. But you must promise to have dinner with me when our formal sessions are over."

"I promise, Matthaeus."

***

A heavy fist pounded on the door to Doctor Field's office.

"Come in."

Melchior found Field shrouded in smoke and sitting at a desk strewn with piles of paper.

"Glad you agreed to come to have this chat, Matt. It's an important component of what we're about."

"Why do all you professors smoke pipes?" Melchior eased into the leather seat across from Field. The office had cheap faux maple wallpaper, and the obligatory bookshelves were a beige metal, not the solid wood Melchior had come to expect.

"Why do non-professors smoke cigarettes?" Field flashed a smile that revealed brown, stained teeth that looked like the treads of a King Tiger tank.

"It gives us a reason to carry a Ronson. Ronsons are useful tools."

"I read the report on your exploits, Matt."

"My efforts to defend the *Vaterland*?"

"Yes – but not just Hitler's Reich. Charlemagne's as well."

Melchior scoffed. "You must be joking!"

Field shook his head. "I'm sure Evan and the others mentioned the reports on your vetting. Well, we pieced them together. Patricia helped a bit. Helped us fill in some blanks. But we have learned some interesting things you told people over the years."

"Yes, but I think I was a little off when I brought such things up. Drunk most of the time... other times in a mood... I can't explain..."

"A mood. Indeed. It's precisely that mood that we are here to discuss."

"I don't understand this thing you call metaphysics."

Field slid an open pack of Lucky Strikes across to Melchior.

Melchior flipped out his lighter and lit a cigarette. "Go ahead."

"As we tried to explain before, Matt, metaphysical ideas, because they are not based on direct experience with material reality, are often in conflict with the modern sciences. Beginning with the Enlightenment and the scientific revolution, experiments with and observations of the world became the yardsticks for measuring truth and reality. Thus, our valuation of scientific knowledge over other forms of knowledge today. It's that valuation of pure science that brings controversy and skepticism to metaphysical claims, which modern science considers unverifiable. You may be our first verification, Matt."

"That was an earful. But I'm still listening." Melchior took a drag on his smoke.

Field gazed at the smoke wafting above. "There is a spiritual dimension to this, Matt."

The comment intrigued Melchior, but he wasn't sure why. "What do you mean?"

"In matters of religion, the problem of validating metaphysical claims is most readily seen in some of the "proofs" theologians give for the existence of a God. Trying to prove the existence of a "soul" or "spirit" in the human, mirrors attempts to scientifically prove the existence of God and other nonobjective, nonhuman realities is seemingly impossible."

Melchior laughed. "You mean like spirits, angels, and witches?"

Field nodded. "Perhaps. But we feel metaphysics may be the link, or part of it, between the sacred and the profane. The difficulty is establishing that connection. It is no easy task to scientifically study and objectify something that cannot become an object of scientific study by its very nature. The scientist in me insists that everything be explained scientifically, connected to natural causes we can verify and evaluate. So, our challenge, the metaphysician's challenge, is to overcome the notion that only the seen or sensed… only what can be hypothesized and tested, can be true. Can be reality."

"Reality is the only thing meaningful to us as humans. All this other stuff is *Mist*."

"Yes, we are grasping at 'mist'. Now you get it, Matt."

Melchior laughed. "You don't get it, *Herr Professor*. *Mist* is a German word. It means shit. That is, manure."

"And many naturalists would say exactly that."

"Then I am a naturalist."

"No, Matt. We believe you are the link we've been seeking. In our world, consciousness and action are often assumed to be importantly related. You are a unique opportunity for us to examine different aspects of this purported relationship. Was there a flash of light when the '*Ami*' bomb exploded over you?"

Melchior nodded. "It was like no other I had ever seen in years of combat."

"Yet you failed to mention this before. Why not?"

"I don't know." Melchior's eyes widened and rolled about a bit. "I didn't want to appear more of a madman than I do already. Maybe I was in denial. Or trying to forget."

"Was there heat?"

"What do you mean?" Melchior asked.

"Was there heat – like in a blast from a bomb?"

"No. That's the strange thing. Just the sound of the bomb and a flash of light like I had never known of until…"

"Until what?"

"Until I read about, and later watched films of, the Bikini Island atomic tests. It was that bright. Maybe brighter. I closed my eyes, but it burned right through like I had no eyelids."

Field's face brightened. "That is precisely what I thought! Honestly, when Evan asked me aboard, I wasn't too keen. This just made me very keen."

"How so?" Melchior asked.

"Ever hear of the Shroud of Turin?"

"Yes, "Melchior said. "It is believed the outline of Christ's body was imprinted on his shroud."

"Well, some scholars believe the markings were caused by heat, not by blood or other phenomena, but heat so intense and so sudden that there was not enough time to burn. Only enough to leave a trace."

"I don't see what…"

Field waved his pipe in the air. "You have read of transfiguration?"

"I was raised in Catholic Germany. Before the Nazis putrefied everything, it is a complete change of form or appearance into a more beautiful or spiritual state."

"Exactly," Field said. "In the New Testament, there is a reference to it in several encounters. Theology teaches that giving the disciples a glimpse into the reality of Jesus as God. In such cases, a burning, bright light is seen."

"So?"

"To me, as a metaphysics person, the light may prove the key to the connection between the sacred and the profane."

"You mean..."

"Yes, I am using this test to prove that relationship."

"What about going back to develop a way to get the Bolsheviks?"

"Yes, of course, that's important. And it was the only way to secure government funding to try this. But my interest is more theoretical, philosophical, and scientific. I want your exploit, this test, to show a scientific connection between the sacred and the profane."

"And MacKay?"

"He's a Cold Warrior like you. Like the rest of them."

"And you aren't?"

Field puffed his pipe but did not reply.

"I'll bring you back a witch then. Will that prove the case?"

"It's a start, Matt. Look, I am among the few who consider metaphysics a science. We know thought affects matter."

"You do?"

"Of course – for years, scientists have proven that with laboratory observations."

"I did read after the war some speculation that the Nazis had a certain cult that..."

"Precisely, but what if they were more than a cult and there was a connection?"

Melchior took a long drag on his Lucky and crushed it in an ashtray, as if he were trying to crush an idea.

"Your body language shows skepticism. But for this test to work, you must have some confidence in it, and some faith. Your confidence affects the physical, as it sends signals to your body through the endocrine system and the metabolic system."

"I was a few months short of being a medical doctor. I know these things," Melchior said. His mind now raced back to recall classes that touched on this.

"Your faith is the spiritual component. We are seeking the intersection... the amalgamation... looking for patterns. Why, to their astonishment, doctors have also observed this phenomenon in their terminally ill patients. You know – the hopeless cases where the patient suddenly recovers simply by reforming their attitude or thought-forms about themselves, others, or the world in general."

Melchior nodded. "Of course, I learned of this in medical school. But we usually were told these were purely random events of no account."

"What if they were wrong? The conventional doctors, I mean. What if the profane, simple physical matter can affect the sacred, the spiritual non-physical, and vice versa? For this to work, you must at some level believe it can."

"I'd like to help you. But there is no way." Melchior suddenly sat erect with eyes wide. "Wait!"

"What is it, Matt?"

Melchior thought a moment, then it dawned on him. "I remember now!"

"Remember what?"

"When we were in our final defenses in Aachen. In the palace and cathedral near the city. I heard the planes. I was desperate to end the nightmare of the war. When I heard the planes' droning... I willed... I prayed... my every fiber bristled as I willed... prayed..."

"Willed what? Prayed for what?"

"That one of those *verdammt Ami* planes would place a bomb on us and take us away from the hell we suffered. Crazy, no?"

"Why do you say it was crazy?"

"Because I took us there precisely to avoid that. Hoping the *Amis'* sense of justice would spare an ancient relic from its onslaught."

Field smiled and quickly scribbled notes on his pad. "And it did do it, Matt. It took you to the 9th century in a blaze of light. In a sense, you were not transported but transfigured. Ironically, into a century you may never really have left."

"It took me to an *Ami* hospital..." Melchior's eyes narrowed and he slowly nodded. "No. Not just to the hospital but another world... Maybe, I think yes, to another time."

Melchior buried his head in his hands. He was both confident and confused.

***

A special agent closed the door with a firm snap of the handle. MacKay looked up at Noble, Field, Doolan, and three other team members. MacKay sensed their concern. Melchior had been in training for only a few weeks. But MacKay was the one concerned. He cleared his throat. "You are probably wondering why I called this meeting."

"From the look on your face, doctor, can we assume this will not be a conversation about hockey?" Doolan quipped.

MacKay waved a sheet of shiny yellow paper. "This TELEX just came in from MOD. The chaps at the Ministry want the operation moved up."

"You can't be serious," said one of the scientists, a physicist named Luc Martin.

"What's the reason?" Doolan asked.

"They didn't give one. But they gave us a week or it's to be shut down. I'm afraid Doctor Noble's reports have had an unanticipated consequence." MacKay could not reveal the complete truth.

"What do you mean?" Patricia asked. "How could that be?"

"I suspect the first one, confirming the shard as the point of an eighth-century blade, got them going. But your last two have several deputies at the Ministry quite excited. In fact, nervous. I believe the decision is wrong. But we have no choice."

Doolan looked at Noble. "What did your reports say?"

Patricia swallowed hard. "Just that... he always seemed one step ahead of me. I'd begin, say, a discussion of the primitive castles built in Europe during the Dark Ages, and he'd fill in the blanks with rich detail, the likes of which no one has seen in any books or manuscripts."

"Wasn't something like that expected?" Doolan asked.

"Hoped for," MacKay said. "Reality is different. They are panicked at the Ministry."

Patricia nodded. "I'd say something we knew, and he either refuted it or completely confirmed it with much more detail than any of our current batch of scholars could. He revealed things that are found only in unpublished documents."

"Did he say how he knew?" Doolan asked.

"He denied he knew some of these things. Yet I have every session recorded."

"Excellent," Doolan said. "I'll have our voice experts analyze them for deception."

"You'll do no such thing," Patricia said.

Field interrupted. "Let's assume it is what it is. And remember, Matt was not inclined to cooperate much at first. But as you know, I met him several times alone to prepare him metaphysically. He resisted at first. Yet once things moved along it was as though he couldn't help himself."

Patricia nodded. "It was as though he really couldn't restrain his knowledge."

"That's because he couldn't," Field said. "This universal mind phenomenon, at least in our theorizing, often causes unintentional streams of facts. But he may be our first case of intentional metaphysical manipulation. We are definitely on to something."

"Is the facility ready?" MacKay asked.

"No. But we'll work around the clock to get it ready. I'll leave tonight," Martin said.

"Excellent, Luc," MacKay replied.

"Should I tell Melchior he has a week to practice his sword arm and equestrian skills?" Doolan asked.

"I'd like to be the one to tell him," Patricia said.

"Very well," MacKay said. He knew that Patricia and Melchior had become involved. He turned to Doolan. "I'd rather have you focus on security at the facility anyway."

Doolan snapped a two-fingered salute. "Righto."

"I must confess, I'm nervous," MacKay said.

"We shouldn't be afraid of failure, Evan. We are scientists. After all, most of what we do fails," Martin said.

"It's not a failure I fear, but success. This could prove a boon to mankind or..."

"Or what, Evan?" Patricia asked.

"Or deviate all history from the time of Charlemagne onward," MacKay answered.

Field scoffed. "What does it matter? We need to make this connection between the profane and the sacred. We must send him on this journey."

MacKay's eyes widened. He knew Field was right.

Chapter 5

The morning sky was a vibrant blue, but the waxing rays of the March sun could not soften the wind's bite. It sliced through them like a deluge of razor blades. Melchior leaned forward and urged his horse along the bridle path. Chunks of gray snow mixed with ice and dirt flew from the horse's hooves as it broke into a canter. Brooke was right behind him. Try as he could, he could not shake her. And he had been trying all week.

Why did I even allow her to ride with me? Melchior had several theories but the one he settled on was primal. Facing an unknown fate, perhaps a bizarre death or worse, insanity, he craved the company of the female. He had Brooke for his morning rides and Patricia for his afternoon studies. At night, he prayed and went through his bible. Never very religious, the approaching "journey," as MacKay called it, had nudged him in the direction of God. Melchior was not so sure.

Melchior brought his horse to a walk and swung effortlessly from the saddle. Brooke pulled up beside him, her horse snorting spurts of steam. "What's up?"

"Nothing. I decided Corporal and I would both walk back."

"Are you kidding? It's a good four miles."

"That's the idea, Brooke," Melchior said. "You can ride back without me."

"You know I can't!" She slid down and walked beside him. "Damn you, Matt, my boots will be a mess by the time I'm back."

Melchior noted she cut a trim figure in her riding habit. He finally figured out she had been Doolan's girlfriend. The idea bothered him in ways he could not understand.

They walked silently along the tree-lined path. The wind was beginning to die down, making it a crisp morning. After a mile, Brooke broke the quiet. "Are you afraid, Matt? I'm worried for you, you know."

"Save your sweet talk for Doolan."

"What? No way. He's my boss. Okay - yes, we've had a certain level of intimacy. I shouldn't have, I know. But it's over. And if this operation succeeds, I'd earn a slot at the academy and become a credentialed investigator. The first woman to do so."

He looked at her. "Is that so important to you?"

"Yes."

He smiled. "Then give it your all."

She grabbed his arm and stroked it gently. "I want to spend tonight with you, Matt. I mean it."

"Don't bother. I'll be spending my last night in thought and prayer."

She laughed. "You? Religious?"

Melchior lowered his head. "I haven't been. I'm agnostic bordering on atheist. But if this goes as MacKay thinks…" He wasn't sure what he felt. "Just don't come creeping by my room. Go study for the bull academy with Doolan."

'You don't like him, do you?" Brooke asked.

"No."

"Don't like rivals, huh?" Brooke said playfully.

"No, I don't like bulls."

***

"This is our final session, Matthaeus. I admire your ability to absorb things. You probably know as much about the time of Charlemagne as I do," Patricia said. "Think of it. If all this plays out, you might be the man who began the process that led to what we call Europe. The transition of Christendom began with this pious ruler and brutal warrior."

"You're gushing. Maybe you should go. I hear he likes brunettes."

She gave him a playful shove. "Back to work, you."

Melchior shrugged. "What is the most important thing I should know about them?"

Patricia paused for a long moment. "That is such a good question. So like you. Me? I never thought about it."

They sat side by side on the sofa. Each engaged in the chaste intimacy of their last week together.

"So?"

"I should say they are not like us. They are very pious, but also very violent people."

"Then I'd say they are exactly like us. Well, us Germans of course." He took her hand. "Not the nice Canadians."

"Oh, you…. You are a Canadian now or this wouldn't be happening. But yes, the world they live in is not unlike ours. A sort of Cold War between Christendom and Islam – as well as a not-so-cold war with the pagan world."

He grunted. "Sounds like a world I can come to understand."

"Are you fearful?"

"Not of death. I'm more fearful that whatever MacKay has in store might destroy my sanity. Despite my so-called universal mind."

"Truth be told, Matthaeus, that's exactly my fear."

"Then I believe you are the only one in this place who has been truthful with me."

Patricia let go of his hand and looked intently at him. "You dear man. You have been treated awfully. Like a specimen."

"That sums it up. I wish I knew how any of this can help us with the Bolsheviks."

Patricia hesitated. "I shouldn't tell you this, but since I overheard it, I can assume it is not from a confidential document."

"Tell me what?"

"If this is successful, it won't be your last journey…"

Melchior blinked incredulously. "Are you serious? Am I to commute into the Dark Ages? For what purpose?"

"No. No, Matthaeus. If this works as they hope…. They want you to go… forward. To learn the future."

"What? *Wahnsinn!*"

She lowered her eyes. To me, this has always been an endeavor to learn more about the past. But to Evan and those at the Ministry, this is an intelligence operation. They want to use you to peer into the future. Not just bring us clarity on the past."

Melchior laughed. "They are all mad!" A hundred thoughts and sensations suddenly flooded his mind. His eyes narrowed into thin slits.

"Are you all right?" she stroked his arm gently.

He pulled it away, firmly, but not roughly, and took a slow breath. He liked this woman. Melchior's eyes widened, and he stared for a moment, beads of sweat bubbling across his forehead. "I…I think so. But I saw, I felt."

She put her hand on his forehead. "Saw what?"

"Nothing. It was nothing. I think I need a drink." He fumbled for his cigarettes and flicked open his Ronson.

Patricia glanced at her watch. "Oh my gosh! It's almost five. Our dinner is at seven. I have to go and get dressed."

He gripped her hand tightly. "You look just fine to me."

***

Melchior flipped his last slice of beef back and forth across the gravy-splattered plate. Despite the sumptuous array of food, he ate very little. He didn't try the wine but downed two scotches and helped himself when coffee and brandy made the rounds. He splashed some brandy into the coffee and took a long sip.

A spoon clinked against a wine goblet. The room grew quiet. MacKay stood. Melchior glanced at Patricia. She looked stunning.

MacKay cleared his throat. "I want to say a few words of thanks to the entire team for all the hard work to get us to this point. As you know, there were many skeptics when we began."

A voice at the table mumbled, "And still are."

Muffled laughs erupted.

MacKay ignored them. "But I think our theoretical models were sound and our test and evaluation, well done. Our testing has given this program legs. Now we must give it wings. Tomorrow, our real trial begins. Our calendar is, unfortunately, out the window, and we must move more swiftly. Captain Doolan will have those who are moving to the operational base execute another secrecy affirmation…"

Groans erupted.

Always bureaucracy. The dinner party was coming to an uneventful end. Melchior stared into the heavy glass ashtray in front of him. Some of the ashes had spilled, smearing the white tablecloth a sickly gray. The pile of butts attested to the depth of his nicotine habit. He smiled to himself. *I'll quit when I arrive in the 9th century.*

Brooke sidled over to him and kissed him on the cheek. She put her lips to his ear. "I have come by to wish you luck and to proposition you. The ladies' room here locks from the inside. Why don't we powder our noses?" She tried to kiss him on the lips, but he pulled back.

"I have other plans for my last night here," he said.

"I was just teasing, Matt." Brooke cast a jealous eye at Patricia. "You've spent quite a bit of time with her – why not spend your last night with me?"

She tried to nibble on his ear. He grabbed her wrist and held it tightly.

"Doctor Noble and I aren't lovers."

Brooke frowned. "Neither were we. But I'm driving you back to your room. A car will pick you up at six a.m., sharp."

"Sorry, Brooke, but Doctor Nobel offered to drive me back, and I accepted. Thanks anyway."

"This is a security matter, Matt. I'm also your bodyguard until the car comes tomorrow. I've been ordered to stay close to you."

"I think you meant my guard, not my bodyguard. That damned Doolan is way too mistrustful."

"It's routine, Matt. But look at it from our viewpoint. If you were to bolt now, the program would be compromised beyond repair."

He let go of her wrist. It occurred to him that most women would have winced or even cried.

"I'm riding with Patricia. You can follow us in your car if you like."

Brooke frowned. "I suppose I can. But make sure she drives slowly. My orders are to keep an eye on you until you are back at the School."

Melchior met Patricia in the cloakroom. He took her soft fur jacket from the clerk and gently snuggled it over her elegant shoulders.

"It's a shame to cover up such lovely skin," Melchior said.

Patricia turned and looked at him. "You are so gallant. Most men aren't."

"Neither am I. Unless the lady is special."

She kissed him on the cheek. "Thank you for that."

"Thank you for driving me back." He motioned towards Brooke. "That one wanted to take me. I think she's jealous."

Patricia smiled. "She's such a beautiful girl. I'm flattered she'd be jealous of me."

They strolled silently. The night was cold. But there was no wind, and the air was dry.

"Such a refreshing night, Matt," Patricia said, gazing at the sky. "Look at that. Inky-black from horizon to horizon and millions of stars."

A shooting star suddenly snapped across the sky and faded.

"Did you see that shooting star, Matt?"

"Yes."

"So pretty. They're special. In the past, they were considered an omen."

"Reminds me of the flares on the Eastern Front at night. And in the desert of North Africa."

"Flares?"

"Flare guns. A signal."

"Signal for what?"

"Usually nothing good. Often death for many."

"The war was difficult on you, dear."

"Difficult for many more than me. I'm just lucky to be alive. And in your company."

"Now I am flattered again."

They embraced and kissed passionately.

They continued toward the parking lot. Melchior walked slowly. He did it deliberately to savor each moment with Patricia. When they reached her car, he grabbed her gloved hands and pulled her to him again. Her mild perfume enveloped him in a sensation long forgotten. Again, they kissed passionately, but also tenderly.

***

Brooke watched Melchior and Patricia Noble from the cold sedan. She flushed with jealousy and maybe a little shame. *They think I'm just a secretary.* Then she saw the movement – a figure in the shadows. Brooke stepped out of her car and slipped a .38 revolver from her bag. She had trained for this moment but never thought it would come.

The figure stepped back into the shadows, and Brooke relaxed a moment. *Just a stranger giving the lovers privacy.* Then she saw the flashes in the darkness.

A pair of shots erupted. Low, spurting sounds – a silencer. She saw Melchior clutch Patricia just as she was hit, turning his body between her and the assassin.

The deep bang of Brooke's .38 exploded in the cold night air. Hands shaking, she fired three more rounds in the direction of the flashes. Then she crouched and sprang to where Melchior was kneeling over Patricia.

"You all right?" Brooke panted.

"Patricia's hit! I think we're losing her! Call an ambulance, now!" Melchior responded with alarm but not fear or panic. He then calmly opened her fur jacket and began to search for the wound.

"I asked if you're all right, Matt?" Brooke said, her eyes scanning the darkness for a sign of the shooter.

"I'm not shot. Patricia's shot!"

Brooke was already gone, her heels clattering into the darkness. When she was convinced the shooter had fled, she ran to her car to get on the radio.

"I'm calling for help, Matt!" She clicked the Motorola's handset. "Code White! Code White!"

The signal for help accomplished, she rushed to Melchior's side. What she saw made her stomach turn.

"Don't bother." Melchior held Patricia's limp body. A small hole in her temple oozed blood that was already hardening in the cold night air.

"Let's get her into my car," Brooke said.

"Shouldn't we call the police?"

"The police aren't cleared for what happened here," Brooke's mind raced with a hundred thoughts.

"Police not cleared for murder?"

She saw tears well in his eyes. "This was much more than murder, Matt."

***

A thick blanket of cigarette smoke smothered the room. On the table, three oversized ashtrays lay buried under a mountain of fine gray powder.

"The recovery team searched the area. They found two brass casings," said Sergeant Jean-Pierre Hanley of the SIU forensics squad.

"What caliber?" MacKay asked.

".38."

"Traceable?"

"Hardly. No markings."

"What about Brooke's rounds?"

"We found all but one. But the fact that we found no blood means Brooke missed. Her shot went wild."

Brooke turned red in the face, and her fists clenched up into balls. "That can't be. I fired right at the place the flashes came from, not a second after the shots rang out."

"A blind shot, Brooke. Face the facts," Hanley retorted.

"Four shots, dammit! A tight shot group too..." These men were going to pin this on her if they could, she thought. *Maybe they're right.*

"We'll continue to look for the third round when it's light enough, and we can do it discreetly. Now, I'll need to examine the victim. Where is she?"

"In the dispensary." MacKay barely choked out the words.

"Why would someone kill her?" Melchior was resting his head in his hands, a cigarette dangling from his fingers.

"They weren't trying to kill her, Matt," MacKay said.

"What do you mean?"

"They were trying to kill you, Mister Melchior," Hanley said.

Melchior bolted upright. "Me?"

"Of course," Hanley said. "They had you staked out, as you may recall. We mucked it up. They must have tailed our boys when they brought you in."

"The whole compound is compromised," Mackay said. "The whole damn mission!"

The outrage and anger in MacKay's voice startled Brooke. She wasn't used to such emotion in the normally polished and calm doctor.

Melchior slammed his large hands onto the table, sending ashes everywhere. "I wish you'd feel as angry over Patricia's death as you do over the compromise. She's dead thanks to Doolan's bare-knuckled bull behavior."

Brooke interrupted, "There will be time for anger later. I'm sorry I couldn't protect you...er, her. But now we need to know what the compromise means. We're dealing with killers now. And they aren't done."

Everyone looked at Brooke. The office flirt seemed transformed before their eyes.

MacKay nodded. "Of course, you are right, Brooke. We'll have to tighten security until we move to location Alpha. Doolan is already there. We'll move all UM activities there once I have the cover story out."

"What cover story?" Brooke asked.

"That a research assistant and his fiancée were the victims of a botched robbery. Both were killed in the heinous attempted armed robbery. Just another random crime in our nation's grimy capital."

"You must be kidding," Melchior said. "What will Patricia's family say?"

"Sadly for her, but fortunately for us, she has no family," MacKay replied.

"Then I will bury her," Melchior said. "She saved my life and died for it."

Tears welled up in Melchior's eyes. Brooke's eyes also teared at the sight. She suddenly felt bad for both of them and regretted her jealousy almost as much as she regretted failing in her job.

MacKay shook his head. "No time, Matt. Besides, you were killed too. We'll arrange a double funeral at the right time. You'll be buried together."

"This is madness," Melchior said.

"The sedan is picking you up at six am, as planned. That's in two hours. But I assure you, a thankful Canadian government will see you both properly buried, and in our own way, honored. Remember, Patricia was a colleague and friend to me. I am heartbroken. But I have my job. So do you, as well."

Brooke saw Melchior's eyes widen.

"We can't be going forward with this mission?" he asked.

"Matt, if we don't move forward, your would-be assassin wins," MacKay said. "Patricia's killer wins. The Bolsheviks win. Do you want that?"

"We'll do our best to find these guys, Matt," Hanley said. "I have some off-duty Mounties and local police who'll scour the city."

"Patricia would want you to continue with this, Matt," Brooke said, although she was not so sure herself. She wanted him to continue.

Melchior straightened up and crushed his cigarette into the ashtray. More ashes were scattered across the table.

"*Nah gut*...Very well. I have done my duty in the past in support of an evil cause. I shouldn't back away from supporting a noble cause."

Brooke caught the wry play on words – his noble cause included avenging Doctor Noble. If others did, they did not show it. Gloom had dulled their senses.

***

Near Goose Bay, Labrador

"We have been driving for over twenty hours. Where are we going?" Melchior remarked sleepily. He dozed off right after the car picked them up. Stress and fatigue had taken their toll.

"The journey hasn't begun yet," MacKay said. He sat in the front seat next to the driver, a Warrant Officer named Gregory Coale.

"We're almost there, though," Coale said. He looked back through the rear-view mirror to make sure no one was following them. The long, flat terrain and straight highway made it easy in daylight, but it had grown dark.

"It's dark out, Greg," Brooke said. "How are you able to clear the rear?"

"I'll give you a lesson someday, Brooke," Coale replied.

"In your dreams."

"Done that," Coale replied.

She sat in the back seat next to Melchior. In the distant horizon, they saw lights flickering dimly. It had begun to snow. An hour later, they drove inside a gated compound, and a heavily armed soldier wearing a military parka and hood closed it behind them.

"What is this place?" Melchior said.

"It's a top-secret airfield," MacKay explained. "You did want to work for NORAD after all, didn't you?"

Brooke snuggled against him playfully. "Welcome to Kingsmill Farm, Matt."

"So we took a trip to the country, I take it?" Melchior sniffed.

"The farm is so top secret, Matt," MacKay said. "Not even our government knows of it... officially. It's an undeclared site."

"Where are we then?" Melchior asked. "Or do I need another read-on to know?"

"Let's just say we are closer to Hudson's Bay than Ottawa and leave it at that," MacKay replied.

"Shit. You've taken me to Canadian Siberia," Melchior said as they exited the car.

"We'll have a quick bite of food and some sleep now," MacKay said as they entered a hangar-like structure.

"This is an airfield?" Melchior asked.

"Among other things," MacKay replied. "But there are living quarters here."

"I suppose we are having moose meat pie and some moose milk?"

MacKay looked at Costain. "He spoiled our surprise, eh, Brooke?"

The dinner was moose meat, but the milk was a creamy alcohol concoction that appealed to Melchior. They ate in silence. After the dishes were cleared, MacKay lit his pipe. Brooke offered Melchior a cigarette.

"No, thank you. I decided to quit now rather than a thousand years from now."

They all laughed.

"We must be up at 2 am," MacKay said. "An orderly will wake us. I'm afraid breakfast will be coffee and leftover moose meat."

"I think they can find an egg or two for you, Matt," Brooke said.

"Why so early? More training?" Matt asked.

"Our flight is at 3 am," MacKay said.

"Flight? To where?"

"Matt, if we manage to take you back a thousand years here, you'll do us no good. Even the natives hadn't discovered this place's charms by then," MacKay said. "We are taking a secret flight to a Canadian airfield in Germany. Then we go to Aachen. Captain Doolan has everything arranged."

"I can't go!" Melchior insisted.

"Why not?" Brooke asked.

"I don't have a passport, for one thing."

"Charlemagne will surely get you one if you ask nicely," she quipped.

"We are traveling under secret military orders with cover names. No need for a passport. Why, we've made you a major in the Canadian Army – the Princess Patricia Regiment. Maybe our best outfit. How does that sound to you?"

"Can I give orders to Doolan?" Melchior groused.

"You can give orders to me," Brooke said suggestively.

Melchior's mouth turned down into a frown. "Interesting coincidence that this regiment would have the name... Patricia."

"I am sorry, Matt. But the name was picked out for specific reasons. It is a coincidence. We are all heartbroken at Patricia's demise. She was a valued team member," MacKay said.

Melchior raised his cup of moose milk. "To Patricia Noble. I dedicate my efforts to her memory."

They all raised their cups. "To Patricia."

Later that night, Melchior was aroused from a deep sleep by the movement of Brooke's leg over his. He thought he was dreaming. Then he felt her hand running across the hairs on his chest.

"What the hell are you doing here?"

"I thought I might help you fight off the cold arctic air." Her hand wandered.

"You need to stop and leave or..."

"Or what?" Her hand moved with a certain tempo. "I know I'm not Patricia, but..."

Melchior suddenly threw the covers off and pulled her under him, taking her wrist in his hands. "Patricia would never enter a man's room in the middle of the night and..."

He drew himself to her and, despite himself, gave her the love he was hoping to give Patricia.

He woke to the rapping on his door. "It's time, Major."

Melchior sat bolt upright and looked at his watch. "*Scheisse!*"

His head throbbed from the moose milk. He flicked on the light. Brooke was gone. *Did I just dream that she was here? Nein! Doch, I must have dreamed it.*

***

The German Federal Republic

The twin-engine Caribou bounced down the runway at Canadian Forces Base Baden-Söllingen and came to a smooth halt.

"Impressive aircraft, eh?" MacKay said. "Hardly a bump."

Melchior nodded. "If you say so."

"This is a special prototype. The stock versions will be out within a year. Even the Americans are impressed with it," MacKay said.

"Didn't you once tell me that Canadians focused on the 'soft sciences' and left the big kit to the *Amis* and Tommies?"

"A little Universal Minds marketing hype, I'm afraid. But look. We made it here with only three stops for fuel."

"I didn't even know we had a base in France," Brooke said.

"Handy, eh?" MacKay quipped. "We are scheduled to meet Captain Doolan in the briefing room. It's been swept by the SIU Tech boys."

"Swept? You Canadians are almost as keen on cleaning things as the Germans," Melchior said. "I need to get out and have a smoke."

A half-hour later, they were drinking coffee and eating fresh donuts as Doolan briefed them on the situation.

"We have a special car arranged with the *Bundesbahn*. It will not be disturbed. Our liaison officer with the German rail police has seen to that."

"How did you get the bulls to agree to that?" Melchior asked.

"There's not much that a case of good Canadian whisky can't get you in this country," Doolan said.

"Thank God for thirsty police officials," Brooke quipped.

Doolan looked at her. "We could swap your charms for a whole train."

"I'll take that as a compliment," she said. "Can we be armed?"

"Yes, the NATO agreements allow Allied law enforcement to be armed. We have a squad of The Pats – the Princess Patricia Regiment, along for backup. Up from Lahr. One sniper and six hand-picked riflemen."

Melchior reflexively rubbed his chest. "I'd rather not meet another of your snipers."

"Are they cleared?" MacKay asked. "Fully, I mean? They are an infantry outfit, after all."

Doolan smiled. "Just for what they need to know. Even at that, their hands nearly fell off - I had them sign so much paper. The Pats were not happy."

"Are the others here? The technicians and doctors?" MacKay asked.

"They are on station, as they say. Local German authorities have been suitably liaised with. There will be nobody around. And no police patrols for kilometers." Doolan feigned a German accent. "*Vee* have arranged it so they'll arrest anyone who comes in that close and doesn't have *zee proper papers*."

Melchior flashed an annoyed look. "I hope I have *zee proper papers*."

Doolan slapped a Canadian military ID in front of him. "Yes. You are in command, Major." He feigned a salute at Melchior.

"When do we depart?" MacKay asked.

"The train leaves at dawn, tomorrow. It will arrive at its destination by dusk," Doolan said.

"The trip isn't that far," Melchior said.

Doolan smiled sheepishly. "We booked the cattle train, I'm afraid. A local. It stops in every *Burg* and *Dorf* along the way. We'll have a lad at each stop, though."

"Why's that?" MacKay asked.

Doolan frowned. "I was saving the bad news for last, Doctor."

"What... bad... news?"

"Intel now indicates this was a level 3 operation for the Russkies."

"I see," MacKay said without expression.

Melchior stiffened. "What the hell does that mean?"

MacKay looked sternly across the table. "It means the team that went after you is dead. They killed the assassins they hired for maximum security."

"Why is that bad?" Brooke asked.

"That means a fresh team... or teams are on the hunt. But we don't think they are aware of our presence in Germany this soon." Doolan replied.

"What makes you so sure?" Melchior asked. He did not like the way things were shaping up.

Doolan lowered his eyes.

"I don't think you are so sure, are you, Roger?" Brooke asked.

"Well, we are moving as quickly as possible. They'd have to know we are in Germany and what we are about," Doolan said. "I'll have weapons for each of you, just in case."

Brooke lifted her sweater to her waist, revealing a new pistol – an automatic. "They asked for the Colt Cobra snub nose to put it through more forensics. So I had them issue me this 9 mm Browning Hi-Power in its place. I know I won't miss with this weapon."

"Jeez, Brooke, that's too much for a woman. Especially one of your size. Have you ever fired the thing?" Doolan said.

"No."

"Take this." Doolan handed her a Smith and Wesson Model 36. "Give the Browning to the new major."

She handed her pistol to Melchior and then retrieved a second magazine from her handbag. "There are thirteen rounds per magazine, Matt. That should be enough, right?"

Melchior removed the magazine, pulled back the receiver, and checked the barrel. It was empty. He reinserted the magazine and put the safety on. It smelled freshly cleaned and oiled somehow, which made him feel good.

"Feels enough like a Walther for me," Melchior said finally. "I was hoping to use the battle sword on this mission, though."

"That's waiting for you," MacKay said. "We have a waterproof bag with all kinds of kit for you. Go fetch it, Brooke."

A few minutes later, two airmen carried a large duffel sack into the room.

MacKay opened it for Melchior to inspect.

"What the hell is all this?"

"Based on Patricia's recommendations, we assembled some interesting kits for you to take," MacKay said. "Take a look."

Melchior removed items one by one. "Is this armor?"

"Chain mail. But instead of iron links on leather, Patricia had the boys use milled steel. Lighter and stronger. There's your battle sword. Again, the latest top-quality steel. This will give you an advantage in any fight."

"Fight?" Melchior asked.

"What else?" MacKay replied. "You are a sort of knight, remember?"

"No shield?"

"Sorry, not enough space for one of those huge Frankish things. But a nice, albeit small, shield of polished steel. Keep it polished, and you can use it as a mirror or to light a fire."

"A backup Ronson?"

"Exactly, although we included a pair of those. Also, some basic medicines to keep you healthy. We aren't sure how your system will react to the food at first. So, there are plenty of stomach things."

"Anything else?"

"Some penicillin. It may spoil, but it's the best we can do. Syringes, too."

"I hear Charlemagne himself had the clap," Doolan said.

Melchior rolled his eyes. "Anything else? I might get a hernia dragging this stuff around."

"Various sundries. Plus, a radio."

"A radio?"

"The technical boys insisted. On the odd chance, radio waves transcend as well. You might be able to get some Marlene Dietrich," MacKay said.

"Or Frank Sinatra," Brooke quipped.

"I'm taking the Browning," Melchior said. "Let's hope I still have 26 rounds by the time we get there."

"It might not be wise to brandish such a weapon. Someone could accuse you of sorcery," Brooke said.

"If they do, I'll put a round between their eyes," Melchior said. "And that's not magic."

***

The train rolled slowly north. Melchior took in familiar sights. But instead of nostalgia for *die Heimat,* he felt a churning in his stomach. Thoughts of battles, as well as love, won and lost drifted in and out of his mind. They passed the numerous enchanting castles along the Rhine River – those gray and brown edifices of stone that stirred the senses.

"I hope these scenes help prepare you, although most of these castles were built long after Charlemagne's time. The condition of your mind is the key to any chance of success." MacKay puffed at his pipe. "Try not to fight things. Just let them occur."

"I am ready for anything at this point. But tell me what you think the Russkies are really up to."

Doolan shook his head.

MacKay waved him off. "It's all right. He has a right to know, if not a need. You see, Matt, we think the Soviets and East Germans have done this already."

"The hell…Why do you think that?" Melchior asked.

"We know they see the merit in it. And we now know they will do anything to stop us and to stop you."

Melchior nodded. The train rumbled along. The group grew silent, each in their thoughts. To Melchior, it felt like a troop train rolling towards the eastern front. Only they were rolling west. He closed his eyes, hoping to sleep. Thoughts of the war plagued his sleep as they too often did. Men engulfed in fire and smoke; men so scared their bowels stained their pants. Men so fierce they rushed streams of machine-gun fire or bounded through minefields under a hail of mortar shells.

After an hour, Melchior's eyes opened. He glanced out the window. "We'll be near Cologne in an hour. Aachen isn't far from there. So they'll need to show themselves soon."

Doolan nodded. "That's what I am thinking."

"Well, if the Soviets have someone there? You'll need to be on your guard. Trust no one," Mackay said.

"No problem with that." Melchior glanced over at Brooke and saw her cheeks blush.

"This is such a beautiful country, Matt." Brooke was gazing out the window. "And it's amazing how it's recovering from the war."

"Most of the cities were completely destroyed by Allied bombs and artillery. But the worst of it was the soul of the people. Germany may never recover its soul as a nation. We need a Germany that is good and strong. Strong in character. Not Nazis or Commies. But good Christian Democrats."

MacKay puffed his pipe. "The world you describe is sort of what Charlemagne might have envisioned, eh? A Christian Europe protected by its secular power. You are a likely *Missus Dominicus*, Matt."

The words made Melchior think of Patricia... then of Kristel. *Why are some women so hard to love... and others so easy?*

He looked over at Brooke. He suddenly felt ashamed. She saved his life, and he treated her rudely. But for some reason, he did not understand why he could not bring himself to thank her.

The whistle blew, and the train began to slow. A knock on the cabin door brought one of the SIU agents. "We are pulling into a little-used siding outside of Cologne, captain. We'll be decoupled, and a special engine will tow us to our destination."

Melchior's ears pricked. He did not like the plan. It seemed ponderous. He started to remark and then shrugged. *They are in charge of this mission, not me.*

Instinctively, they all checked their weapons. A half-hour later, the special engine was pulling them along at a fast pace. The train's horn did not sound as it made its way through crossings, around verdant curves, and through tiny villages. It was almost dark, and clouds obscured the glimmer of the evening twilight on the horizon.

An orderly brought sandwiches and coffee. They ate once more in silence.

"We'll be there soon," Melchior said.

"You have been here before?" Brooke asked.

Melchior nodded.

"The war?" Doolan asked. He glanced at his watch with a look of boredom.

Melchior nodded again. "And as a youth. I used to play here when we visited. My family originally came from this area hundreds of years earlier and… "

"And what, Matt?" Brooke asked.

"And… and I now get a feeling that I know it in other ways… other times."

MacKay nodded. "I was hoping something like that would click. This is a good sign."

The train's brakes suddenly screeched like some primeval bird of prey descending on its victim. They all jolted forward. MacKay slammed his head against the cabinet, smacking it with a nauseating thump. Melchior's war instincts saved him from the same. When he heard the screeching, he grabbed Brooke, shielding her from the impact with his body. A loud thump followed by a rumble struck the engine, and it exploded, sending metal shards searing through the air and filling the chamber with smoke. The screams of the crew could be heard from the engine cabin, which had burst into flames on impact.

The crack of rifle fire erupted.

"The sniper has found the perps," Doolan said. "Are you okay, Doctor?"

MacKay picked himself off the floor and pulled out his pistol. Blood trickled down his forehead.

"I am… We need to get our things and make our way to the site. It shouldn't be far."

Melchior let go of Brooke and charged his Browning. "It would take us hours to reach Aachen in the dark. And the *Polizei* will soon be swarming here." He looked at Doolan. "I don't care how much whisky you gave them."

A second thump and explosion jolted the train. One of the Pats opened the door, "Captain, we need to decide – bug out or fight."

"I'll stay with you boys and fight. We'll try and hold them long enough for the doctor to get away," Doolan said.

"Better we fight them here," Melchior said. "Those were anti-tank rockets. They sound Russian-made. Whoever they are, they mean business. Get your men under the railcar. They'd need a lucky shot to hit you."

"Matt, we must go. Let Captain Doolan and the Pats sort this out. We have only a little time before the whole operation is finished," MacKay said.

"You have less time than that," Melchior said. "Look!"

Up the embankment, a machine gun barrel could be seen protruding from pine trees clinging to the mountainside like moss. With a heavy ratatat…ratatat… ratatat… the machine gun sprayed the car, shattering the windows and spitting shards of glass everywhere. They hugged the floor and crawled towards the other side with the heavy rounds buzzing not a foot over their heads.

One of the Pats called out, "Our sniper's been hit, sir! But he got the men with the rockets."

"How bad is he?" Doolan asked.

"He needs medical help soon."

The machine-gun fire continued but was now reduced to methodical and crisp three-round bursts. *Ratatat…ratatat… ratatat…* sent heavy bullets thumping into the soft panels as the gunner worked the train.

"*This Kerl knows his business.* Melchior knew they had to act quickly or they would die.

"Take me to him," Melchior said. 'Come on, Brooke,"

They found the sniper lying on the floor at the rear of the train.

"Move him undercover. Brooke, use some of this stuff in my kit. The medicine and bandages. Keep him from bleeding."

"Right, Matt."

Melchior picked up the sniper's Macmillan TAC 50 rifle and ammunition. *They lied to me about the caliber of their sniper rifles.*

"Where are you going, Matt?" MacKay asked.

Melchior saw the doctor's head still drizzled with fresh blood.

"I've taken out a few machine guns in my time. Why not one more? Have Brooke flip you a bandage to stop the blood."

Melchior rolled off the train and slithered under the car, taking a position behind one of the large steel wheels. The machine gun was still firing short, disciplined bursts: Ratatat…ratatat… ratatat…

These Jungs are good. Really good. He locked a round into the chamber and waited on the next burst. He did not have to wait long. A ripping sound erupted from the woodline one hundred meters away. He calculated exactly where the gunner would be in relation to the muzzle blast that lit the darkness and squeezed. The rifle kick-back jarred his shoulder. It was strangely pleasant to feel the jolt.

"*Punkt,*" he whispered.

The night went silent. The gunner was dead. He just knew it. He thought he heard voices. *Russian voices… Yes, the machine gun would have rifles protecting it.*

"I got the gunner! But he has friends. Be watching."

Doolan signaled to the Pat, who lay prone along the rails under the carriage.

A searchlight suddenly lit the night, its beam painting the cars as it scanned along the train for targets.

"Don't fire! It's what they want. Be patient. Time is on our side!" Melchior did not believe what he said, but it sounded good. The searchlight slid back and forth, and then finally stopped on Melchior's location. He fired a .50 round into it, and the sky went pitch dark.

As their eyes adjusted, they could make out forms slithering from the pine trees. In the shadows, they resembled a wolf pack closing in on its victims. There were only six, but he reckoned they were six of the Soviet KGB's best operatives – trained and, more importantly, experienced killers. In such things, experience trumped training. *Can these poor Canadian boys face men such as these?*

Melchior did not know it, but all but one of the Princess Patricia men were hardened veterans of the *Kapyong* Valley in Korea, where they had fought off thousands of fanatic Chinese Communist soldiers.

"Like old times, boys, eh? Killing Commies," the sergeant said. "Let 'em get close... then we each take a wrist-shot."

But the one inexperienced private let loose too soon. Melchior cursed. The attackers, as one took a knee and unleashed a murderous fire that laced the private with bullets, sending his body jumping for more than a meter before the shredded corpse finally lay still. His mates coolly returned fire, and Melchior saw two of the attackers go down. Then the others stood in unison with their hands brandishing grenades.

Crack! Melchior placed a round into the eye of one. His body lurched backward, and his grenade exploded, sending chunks of metal in all directions.

The attackers began screaming as the hot shrapnel cut through them.

The Pats unleashed a curtain of fire with their Belgian FN battle rifles. The night air was heavy with 7.62 caliber bullets that peppered the woodline and embankment. The last attackers were cut to pieces in less than a minute.

"Police them up, sergeant. I need to get our cargo to its destination," Doolan ordered.

They walked along the north side of the railroad tracks. Melchior carried the sniper rifle across his shoulder. He had a feeling he would need it.

They soon reached an abandoned side-station. Doolan picked the lock, and inside they found an old manual wagon, used by repair crews.

"Well, what d'ya know, a hand-wagon," Doolan said to Brooke with a lewd smile. "If we pump the handles in tandem, we should be there in no time."

"I think I can pump harder than Brooke," Melchior said.

"We'll all take turns," MacKay said.

The trundle car glided noiselessly along the tracks. The night air was cold, but none of them minded. It meant they lived. An hour later, they arrived at a spur. The switch had been set, so they shifted over to the spur that ended near an immense forested hill.

"What is this?" Brooke asked as they tramped up a *Foerster Weg,* a typical German woodsman's trail covered in pine needles.

"I know this place," Melchior said. "There was once an *Oppidum* at the top of this hill – a Celtic walled city. Then a Roman town, and finally a Frankish village and stronghold. The *Wehrmacht* made it a defense point until the Americans bombed it out."

"How do you know this?" Doolan asked.

"I was here."

"With the *Wehrmacht*?" Doolan asked.

"I told you. I never joined the SS. Just forced to serve with them... once."

"Just once?"

Melchior did not reply.

They moved up the hill in silence. They reached the top, huffing for breath and muscles aching. But Melchior sensed the common feeling of accomplishment. They had made it despite the odds.

"There it is," Doolan said.

They could see dim lights inside what looked like a pile of rubble. The sound of generators hummed from somewhere off in the darkness.

"It looks like they are ready," MacKay said.

"Who goes?" a voice from the darkness challenged.

"Champlain," Doolan responded with the password. He whispered to MacKay and the others, "I have two more squads of The Pats as security for the place. We passed one of them at the foot of the trail."

"Good," MacKay said. "Let's get right to it before we have any more surprises."

***

An hour later, they were inside the rubble, and Melchior was wearing the mail shirt and clutching his sack. MacKay was consulting with his team.

"His blood pressure and heart are fine. His lungs are clear. I also checked his ears and reflexes. Fastest exam I've ever given, Evan," said a tall, thin physician in military uniform.

MacKay nodded. "They told me you were the best internist in the Canadian Forces. That's why you are along, Mac."

Dr. Captain Leander "Mac" MacConnell smiled a boyish grin. "Anything to get out of the stuffy dispensary in Lahr."

MacKay turned to a thin man with a mustache that looked like a milk stain. "Doctor Norton, I'm afraid we won't have time for the best psychologist in MOD to assess his mental state. But I was just with him in a very...uhm, taxing situation, and he's in total control. It seems high-stress situations bring out the best in him. Quite impressive. My assessment is not scientific but nonetheless correct."

Doctor Charles Norton nodded. "I'll take your professional word for it, Evan."

A technician approached. "Everything is set, Doctor MacKay."

"The explosives are ready?"

"Yes, sir. You'll get one good blast. It will be more flash and bang than an explosion. We've specially designed the device. It will sound and feel like a five-hundred-pound bomb without the destruction."

"It's a good thing we leaned on the film industry. It would have taken the program five years just to get approval to develop this," MacKay said.

MacKay walked over to Doolan. "Is security set?"

"All set. And the transport-lorries are ready. We need to leave as soon as possible. We have the border crossing set for us. We'll be out of Germany within an hour once you give the order."

"Very well."

MacKay walked over to Melchior. Brooke was sitting next to him, trying to make small talk.

"How are you two getting along?"

"I'm ready to get on with it," Melchior said.

S.W. O'Connell

"We are, too. Here's what we'll do. You'll clutch the kit bag tightly. We want to test the theory that this is not purely metaphysical. You'll likely hear vague sounds of fighting. We have recordings. Authentic sounds recorded by the US Army Signal Corps during the assault on Aachen. It would have been ideal to do this at Charlemagne's castle in Aachen, but that would cause complications." MacKay chuckled.

"More complicated than this?" Melchior asked.

"I'll be nearby, Matt. As will Captain Doolan," Brooke said.

"As will I," Field said, stepping out of the shadows.

"How comforting," Melchior said. "What are you doing here?"

"Did you think I'd miss the most important event in my professional life, Matt? I have ensured the correct stimuli is recorded as you go through this. But get him out of that mail shirt so we can get the sensors placed correctly."

A pair of technicians removed the mail shirt from Melchior. Then they began attaching electrodes to various points on his body and head. Clips were placed on one of his fingers.

"What the hell is this for?" Melchior asked.

"These will measure pulse, metabolic rate, perspiration, etc. Profane to sacred, as we spoke of Matt," Field said.

"You could have just kissed me goodbye," Melchior said.

Brooke wrapped her arms around his neck and kissed his lips. "Goodbye, Matt."

Melchior did not respond. He wondered if he should get up, thank them for the free trip to the *Vaterland*, and leave. He smiled grimly at the thought. But it was too late.

"We are going to inject a special solution into you. Then, Doctor John Golden, Canada's finest psychologist, will put you into a hypnotic state. Things will seem dream-like," MacKay said.

"Maybe you'll dream of me, Matt," Brooke said.

"I hope not," Melchior replied. Then he noticed the blood that stained her hands and clothes. The result of her work saving the sniper. "I am sorry, Brooke. Perhaps I will dream of you."

"I hope you dream of nothing but actually making the journey," Field said.

"One thing we never cleared up. Is this a round-trip journey?"

"We hope so, Matt," MacKay said.

Melchior smiled grimly. He was not so sure he cared. The point of the hypodermic needle pierced his skin. A strange fluid evacuated and immediately flowed through his veins. Melchior felt woozy.

"This should take only a few moments, Matt. Any last comments?" Melchior heard MacKay ask.

"Yes. But for you alone."

MacKay signaled Doolan and Brooke to leave.

"Be careful. If the Russians knew our route, they may have a spy in your team."

MacKay gently patted his hand. "I've thought of that, Matt."

MacKay signaled for Golden to approach. "Follow Doctor Golden's instructions."

Golden spoke in a soft, strangely calm yet authoritative voice, "Okay, Matt. I want you to think about Aachen. It's 1944, and you are defending the ruins with your battalion."

The machines began to churn out the sounds of battle. It seemed real to all.

Golden droned on in his flat monotone, "The bombs are dropping. Shells and mortars falling. You hear tanks approaching…"

"Ronsons…" Melchior nodded and then lost the trail of Golden's voice in a misty mix of memory and reality… His mind transported him back to a time and place of battle… and of transition… of journeys… near and far…

His senses suddenly rocked with a mad combination of light and noise. His mind swirled into a state of darkness… he sensed and experienced total quiet and total darkness… then light so bright he knew he was being scorched by the sun or… He thought he heard a voice… but the voice came deep from within… *Be not afraid*…

Part 2

Frankland

"Matter is spirit moving slowly enough to be seen."

-   Pierre Teilhard de Chardin

Chapter 6

Aachen, 803 A.D.

The rays of dawn lit the stained glass in a palette that seemed to mesh with the voices of the choir. A bishop coadjutor of the palace officiated the Mass. *Where is that fat bishop Angilram? Fast asleep in bed? Or concocting another plot?*

His mind was even more confused when they woke him from his nightmares. The look in the eye of the deacon revealed his own suspicions. *Was it bad drink? A demon? Or something else.*

Melchior put such thoughts from his mind when the priest intoned: *Introibo Ad Altare Dei.*

Melchior knelt on the bare stone floor and with the other faithful and responded: *Ad Deum qui laetificat, juventutem meum.*

When the Mass ended, Melchior remained kneeling. As he prayed, flashes of memory flew before him. Each flash grew in intensity. First came the rumble of thunder. Then he realized he was hearing artillery, mortars, and bombs. Now, he felt the sights and sounds of his last great battle. The memory and trauma of years of combat suddenly returned.

He suddenly recalled MacKay... but the rest seemed a blur. He took a deep breath and glanced around the darkly lit cathedral, and saw the last Franks filing out. *I have been here before fighting Amis, or maybe I will be here again. What matter?*

Jurchen tapped him on the shoulder. "*Dominus*, it is time to go. The bishop wishes to see us off."

Melchior nodded weakly. He questioned his very being. Tears began to sting his eyes. Tears he had not shed since a poor *Landser* from Essen left his vitals to drip all over him somewhere in Russia. Tears he had not shed since the day he realized Kristel would not come to him in... Canada.

His eyes widened as flashes of his life and work there returned to memory. His mind flashed with thoughts of the experiment gone awry: the SIU, Canadian doctors... Canadian soldiers... the name MacKay... *Doctor MacKay! Have I really crossed time? Am I dreaming? Or am I – mad?*

Jurchen led him to the narthex of the great chapel, where Angilram gave them a last blessing. They all knelt. Angilram stood before them in full regalia, miter, and scepter, and raised his hand. "May Our Lord and the saints guide you on this most important journey for our great and noble king-and-emperor, *In Nomine Patris et Filii et Spiritus Sancti, Amen.*"

Then, the squire Detleff ceremoniously handed Melchior his conical iron helmet, followed by his broad leather belt and leather scabbards containing his long sword and his *Seaxe*, a wicked-looking long knife favored by the Saxons and adopted by the Franks. Melchior's *Seaxe* had a twenty-inch blade and a maple handle with polished brass bands.

He then handed him his shield, large and circular, made of wood covered with hardened leather, painted a deep blue with a white cross, and embossed with brass fittings.

Melchior slung the shield over his left shoulder and drew the long sword from the scabbard. He examined the blade. It was long and heavy – the length of a man's arm. The hilt was banded brass, gold, and leather with a polished nob. The blade was inscribed *Missus Dominicus et Fidelis,* Envoy of the Lord and Faithful Servant.

A groom led a large gray charger with a coal-black mane and tail. A high wooden saddle on a deep blue blanket, trimmed in silver, hid the horse's long black dorsal line.

"Timbo awaits you, *Dominus,*" the groom said.

Melchior patted the horse's neck and talked soothingly to it. The horse behaved skittishly.

"Strange for Timbo to act so, *Dominus,*" Detleff said. "He has carried you through many a battle without a whimper."

Melchior stroked the horse again. "He will soon remember my touch."

When he mounted, Detleff handed him his *Francisca,* a throwing ax favored by the ancient Frankish tribes. The S-shaped blade was five inches wide and stretched back some four inches to the polished wood shaft sixteen inches long. Melchior thrust it into its leather belt socket.

"I will carry your lance, as always, *Dominus,*" Detleff said.

Bishop Angilram stepped up and took Melchior's hand. "I wish you well, Lord Melchior, *Missus Dominicus.*" He handed Melchior a leather tube twelve inches long. "Remember, no one but the Abbott Baugulf of Fulda must possess this or see its contents."

Melchior nodded and hung his helmet from the pommel of his saddle. Before he put on his heavy leather gloves, he ran a hand through his hair. Strangely, this began to seem normal. "Are all prepared for this journey?"

"They are all ready, *Dominus.*" Detleff pointed at the men sitting quietly on horseback. There were six. But the Abbot Jurchen and Monk Thomas wore simple robes of cheap gray cloth and ropes tied at their waists.

"They are unarmed?"

"We are men of God, *Dominus,*" Jurchen said.

Melchior turned to Detleff. "Find them each a *Seaxe* and *Francisca*. We all ride as Franks. The Saxons will not respect the cloth."

"Who are they?" Melchior asked, gesturing at four mounted men-at-arms. They were older than Melchior, with fierce-looking faces and muscular limbs. Melchior noted Detleff's surprise at the question.

"Why, *Dominus,* the men with battle lances are Cassyon and Hartmutt. They once served your father and rode with us on seven journeys. Each has slain a well over a score of enemies."

"And the other two?"

"*Dominus*, they are your retainers. Fromm, a Danish warrior who can cut six men across with his two-handed battleax. The other is Gaetano, an Apulian once enslaved by the Muhammedans and spent eight years serving in their armies."

Melchior pointed at Gaetano. "He looks like a rodent. Can he fight?"

Detleff fought the urge to chuckle. "Gaetano? Why, as you well know, *Dominus*, he excels with his scimitar but is second to none with that light but powerful Arabian bow he carries."

"Can we trust their loyalty? To me, I mean," Melchior said. He knew that this journey would require loyal men.

"*Dominus*, you freed them both from bondage. They are sworn to guard you to the death. All four of these men are *Fideles*. They are faithful to you even before the king... even before God."

"I was told our Lord Karolus's bastard would join us. Did he decide to attend a second Mass? Or is he chasing village girls?"

A young man walked up to Melchior, leading a large warhorse. He was long-limbed and stood almost a head taller than even Melchior. Melchior suddenly recalled from somewhere that Karolus was of almost giant proportions. *He is certainly Karolus's bastard.*

"Here I am, *Dominus*. Before mounting, I wanted to ask *Dominus's* leave to accompany you on this journey."

"Your presence is our Lord Karolus's wish," Melchior said.

"But you are *Missus Dominicus*. I could not accompany you without your leave, despite my father's wishes."

I have an honorable boy here. Melchior had little recollection of his boyhood.

Melchior nodded with a smile. "Well said, Audeon. Mount your fine horse and join us."

***

Their horses trod slowly in the cold, misty rain, covering only a few leagues per day. Fog seemed to envelop everything. He knew he was riding deeper into what would be the heart of Germany. He wore a heavy woolen mantel and hood as did his riding companion, the abbot they called Jurchen.

Melchior wiped the rain from his face. "How many leagues left, abbot? That is, how much longer do we ride?"

It still surprised him that he understood their language, which was somewhat akin to German but had aspects of French and Latin. It also surprised him that he could take to a horse so easily. Then he had a new memory. He had joined the fencing club, *Fechtverein*, at the university and felt comfortable when they handed him his sword. He caught a glimmer of his riding and sword training in Ottawa. *What are these thoughts, and where do they come from?*

"Perhaps some fifteen days to Fulda, *Dominus*. Then, on to the march, perhaps another five."

"We will take our time. I have much to consider. And I want time to develop a plan. And to teach the young bastard a thing or two about fighting."

"He is a good lad. He'd make an excellent man of God," Jurchen said.

"It seems his father has other ideas."

"Perhaps God has others."

Detleff rode up. "*Dominus*, your cousin's *demesne* is not far from here. It might be good to ride a few leagues out of our way to have shelter for the men and horses tonight."

Melchior reined his horse and thought silently as the rain pelted them.

"*Dominus*?" Detleff asked.

Melchior was trying to remember this cousin. His mind struggled to retrieve an image or thought. "He's a small man? But powerful? With light hair and fair skin?"

"He is, *Dominus*," Detleff said. "But they say his hair is graying and fading."

"He has a limp?"

"When it rains, *Dominus*. A horse fell on him in battle."

"Was he riding towards the enemy? Or away?"

Detleff lowered his head. "It was *Dominus's* order not to report this to the king."

"Then he owes me hospitality. Let's get out of the rain." He looked up at the dark clouds that stretched across the sky. "If only for one night."

Chapter 7

Mallobaudes's Manor

Through the heavy rain, Lord Mallobaudes could make out horsemen riding from the village. They turned up the road toward his manor house, their horses pounding through the heavy mud.

He called to his wife, "Gudrun, we have visitors,"

"Send them away, My Lord," Gudrun replied casually. She lay leisurely in their bed.

"Nonsense! If these aren't enemies, we'll have to feed them. Now that you performed your wifely duty, get dressed, and perform your manorial duty."

Gudrun rose from the large square post oak bed and slowly ambled towards her wardrobe. Mallobaudes eyed her naked form. Despite the heat of the fireplace, he could see her skin was cold, almost as cold as her heart. *If she were not so comely, I'd have replaced her by now.*

"Move quickly," he barked. "Make sure we have some meat. And ale. Visitors like ale."

He slipped on his tunic and fastened a leather belt to his waist. He picked up his *Seaxe* and yanked it from the scabbard. At twenty inches, it was on the long side. He slid the blade back into the scabbard and hooked it to his belt.

Just in case the strangers are less than friendly. He threw a bright blue tabard over his tunic, cloaking the weapon. Mallobaudes knew from experience that a surprise cut was the best cut. He heard shouts from the gate.

"Visitors, Lord," the sergeant of the guard barked from the tower across the courtyard.

Mallobaudes cupped his hands. "How many?"

"Around six, Lord."

"Are they wearing colors?"

"Yes, Lord. Their *seigneur* is wearing the colors of your house."

Mallobaudes rubbed his hands together in anguish. *My house? What mischief...* *Melchior!*

***

The manor had a modest banquet room, fit for no more than twenty guests. Mallobaudes sat at the head with Melchior on his right. Next to Melchior sat Gudrun. The abbot sat to Mallobaudes's left. The rest of Melchior's entourage sat at the far end, below the salt. Several of Mallobaudes's retainers sat nearby as well. They ate quietly. No music or bard entertained

"Your table is well-appointed, Lord," Jurchen said to Mallobaudes.

"The farms here produce well. My manor is not large, but it is productive. Would that I had a wife so productive."

All looked at Gudrun. Her face turned red.

Mallobaudes frowned. "Married six years and now, it is clear there might not be issue."

"Such things happen, Lord. Issue is God's will alone," Jurchen said.

"Under Frank law, it will be my right before long to send her to a convent and take a mistress."

"I shall pray that God's will makes such a move unnecessary," Jurchen said.

Melchior raised his cup in a toast. "To my cousin's issue! May it be soon and may it be male!"

They all raised their cups to the host. Melchior kept a sideways glance at Mallobaudes, who went on bantering with some of his men. They fawned and gulped ale at his every word. With only a vague recollection of his past, Melchior decided to use the meal to pick Gudrun's brain about her husband. She clearly thought it was a game.

Gudrun stroked Melchior's powerful forearm and whispered, "One more night with you, and I would have had a son. You know I did not want to marry him. But my father wished otherwise. He hated you. So he gave me in marriage to someone who hated you equally."

Melchior gazed straight ahead. He was slowly learning about this world even as he was slowly recalling the world he had left. He now knew he was a man between two worlds.

Gudrun lightly tapped his wrist. "You sit there like a rock, My Lord. Am I so boring?"

"Love always triumphs over hate," Melchior said. Gudrun had large, light brown eyes and soft brown hair plaited down her back. Her ample cleavage pressed against him from under her fine woolen dress. He pulled back and glanced at his cousin, who was now deep into a religious discussion with Jurchen.

Gudrun put her mouth to his ear. "Your cousin is not possessive of me. He wants me gone. Perhaps I should ride off with you. Now that Rotrudis is dead."

"Rotrudis? Dead?" Melchior asked. He had no idea who that could be.

Gudrun slapped his forearm with her soft, plump hand. "How quickly men forget their late wives! Well, I hope you did not forget Pair as well—the poor sweet boy. Sickness can strike any of us so quickly. And the stomach fever... so painful." Tears welled up in her eyes.

Melchior took her hand. "Do not cry, Gudrun. As the priests tell me, they are with God."

Melchior could not think of what else to say. *So I have had a family...as well as a lover.*

Mallobaudes turned to Melchior. "Well, cousin, I seem to have neglected you. How long will you stay?"

"Until the rain lessens, but no longer than three days. I am on a journey for his majesty."

"What kind of journey is our Lord Karolus's favorite *missus* headed? Do not tell me. Let me guess – to slay a giant, no, a dragon. Perhaps a giant dragon."

Mallobaudes's men guffawed.

"Perhaps a witch," Melchior retorted. He could tell his cousin did not like him.

Mallobaudes's face reddened just a little. Several at the table made the sign of the cross.

Melchior laughed. "You seem afraid of witches. We are headed to the Thuringian March, is all I can say, Mallobaudes."

"Then you shall visit My Lord, Count Lothar?"

"Perhaps," Melchior said. *My Lord?*

"And the bishop, of course."

"I am on his majesty's business." Melchior sipped at the thick ale in his mug.

"And his business brings you to my *desmesne*. Some would say that makes it my business as well. There are rumors of Lothar and..."

"I do not listen to rumors."

Mallobaudes's eyes took on a crafty, demonic look. "Maybe you should, Melchior. Maybe you should."

***

The wind and rain rattled against the window shutters. Melchior lay restless in bed. He could not sleep. He was awake, yet he dreamed — dreams of a land like this one, but not like this one. People dressed differently and acted differently. *Or did they?* He was not sure. Faces and events glimmered like wraiths before him. Just as the thoughts came, they evaporated. In his dreams, he was called Matthaeus by some... Matt by others... He heard sounds like thunder and saw men die horribly. Yet no sword or lance cut them open. For a moment, he thought he sailed across a large sea. Then he thought he had flown over it on a giant bird of prey.

Noises... strange noises... and sights.

Suddenly, he heard something real. The rain continued rattling the shutters. But he heard another noise – footsteps in the dark. He reached for his *Seaxe*. Slowly, gently, he drew the long knife from the sheath and rolled out of bed and into a crouch. He held the wicked blade before him, ready to parry or slash the intruder. The embers in the fireplace gave off enough light for him to make out a form just feet away. He braced himself to spring forward and drive the blade home. Closer...

"Melchior," the shadow whispered.

Melchior exhaled and relaxed his grip on the *Seaxe*. "Gudrun? One more step and I would have split you in two... what are you doing here?"

"What do you think I am doing here? My husband and lord fell asleep, drunk. I want to comfort you... In your loss. We haven't spoken since you were widowed." She undid her hair and took his hand.

He tried to resist, but her charms and sweet breath drew him in. They made love like they had done so for the first time, but with the certainty of a hundred times. She whispered things both familiar and strange, like memories that were not memories. When they had finished, Melchior lay staring into the dark recesses of the ceiling.

"I missed you, Lord Melchior, *missus dominicus*," Gudrun said. "But it is obvious you did not miss me."

"What do you mean?" Melchior's voice was gruff but wary. "Am I some Gallo-Roman runt who cannot satisfy a woman?"

"I could sense there was someone else… is someone else. Not to worry. Frankland's finest warrior should have many concubines and lovers. I just hoped I would be first among them… I know now that I am not."

"Now you have me confused. I don't know who …"

Gudrun stroked his chest lightly. "Ah, but you do know. You just don't know that you know."

She slid over him and kissed him. Mindlessly, Melchior slid her form from his.

A kind of panic overcame him. His mind had the glimpse of a face… a form… It receded as quickly as it embraced him. He felt a shudder.

"Is she a noblewoman or low-born? Not that it matters, Lord."

Gudrun tried to remain controlled. But Melchior realized she was hurt. He could tell she hoped she could be with him someday.

Melchior said nothing for a long while, then, "Neither… just a woman."

But who? His mind fought to retrieve the face, but he had a thought. "I was betrothed. That's all. But no more."

"What is her name?" Gudrun asked.

"I can't say." Melchior could not tell her the truth. He did not know the name, just the sensation. He felt the sensation of a great love that slipped through his fingers like the morning mist of Frankland. He felt a sensation that both charged and drained him at one moment.

"I see. Her family disapproves. This tells me she is not of Frankland but a foreigner. I will be your mistress in any case, Lord Melchior," Gudrun said. "You need comfort to ease your obvious discomfort."

Anxious to drive off the feelings of a woman he could not recall, he reached for Gudrun. He turned and pulled her to him in the hope her willing body would drive away a sensation that he hoped to lose but knew deep inside would burn eternal.

When Melchior rose at dawn, Gudrun was gone. He stared into the cold, dark fireplace. *Was this just another wicked dream?*

***

They breakfasted on day-old bread and cheese washed down with a heavy red wine. Each man was given a skin of ale and a loaf of bread for the journey. Melchior's party left to get their horses. Hoping to talk to Mallobaudes, he lingered, nibbling a piece of fruit. Gudrun entered the hall. She was wearing a finely spun white gown. Her brown hair was once more plaited with a single glistening braid delicately placed over her left shoulder.

She smiled. "When I awoke and saw the rain was easing, I knew you would leave. I wanted to make sure you and your men had a good breakfast."

"Where is your lord-and-husband? I want to thank him for all his hospitality."

"He rode out before dawn. He took a few men-at-arms and his squire."

"Likely gone hunting while the rain is weak," Melchior said.

She lowered her eyes. "Yes, I suppose."

"Mallobaudes has not gone hunting for game, has he?"

Gudrun shook her head.

"Another woman?"

She shrugged.

"I am sorry I disturbed you last night," she said.

"I was not sleeping. You..."

She grabbed his wrist. "I hope I have a baby from you."

Melchior stared with widened eyes.

"He'll soon put me aside if I don't. I don't want to live in a convent."

"There are worse things." Melchior waved his arm in a circle.

"He would send me far away to punish me. Some say there are convents near the southern marches that are mere way stations. That after a suitable time passes, the nuns are sold to the sultan to be used as concubines or sold into slavery."

"I see." Melchior gazed at the village below and the forests and fields beyond. He wondered if his cousin waited in ambush somewhere up ahead. "Do you know which direction he rode?"

"One of the grooms said he was riding east."

Melchior took her in his arms. She smelled good. He stroked her hair. "I will ride through here when my journey is finished. It may take months."

"He hates you."

"Because I had you first?"

"No. He is not that sort of man. Because he blames you for his limp, he said you injured him in a childhood game."

"I do not remember... wait... perhaps I do... I remember two boys fighting... playful. I was the large one...he the smaller. He jumped my back, and I tumbled him onto the ground. Angered, he ran and fetched a spear, mounted his horse, and tried to run me through."

"What happened? He never said anything about..."

"A Frank would never reveal something like that to his wife," Melchior said. He wondered why he had said that... how he had known that. "I avoided the spear point and pulled him from the horse. His foot tangled in the stirrups. The horse spooked and rode off with him under its hooves. He's lucky only his hip was crushed."

"I understand My Lord well enough to know he is capable of carrying his hatred forever. Even over a childish prank," Gudrun said.

"You are very wise, Gudrun. I also saved him in battle. He was less than... a warrior. But I gave him credit for a gallant act."

"Why would you do that for him?"

"I don't know... I suppose to make up for the childhood injury."

Melchior could not believe he recalled so much at once. His mind swirled with images... thoughts... memories. Other memories began to come clearly into his mind.

Memories of his life in Frankland… and his life in a time and place he had almost forgotten.

Gudrun stroked his face. "Are you feeling sick, Melchior?"

He shook his head. "It is time to go."

"Take me with you."

"There are laws against that."

"And you are the king-and-emperor's official envoy. His last *missus*." Gudrun's moist lips caressed his cheek. "Stay well, *Missus Dominicus*. And remember, a Frankish woman in your bed is more certain, safer, than a foreign woman in your mind, and much safer than one who is in your heart."

Melchior pulled her to him and stroked her chin. "Unless she is carrying my child."

Gudrun stood on her toes and kissed him passionately. "Especially if she is carrying his child."

***

The rain grew heavy again. Melchior and his band moved slowly, heads lowered so their sodden hoods provided some protection from the sting of the drops. They rode sullenly across fields of mud, on roads that ran like rivulets, and through heavy woods that did little to slow the downpour. The gray sky and mist blurred their vision to no more than a quarter-furlong. But the rain and fog did not cloak them from eyes that spied on them.

Melchior reflected on all that had occurred since he awoke in the palace. He had begun to recall his life as a Frankish warrior. Not all of it, but enough to know he had lived a hard life full of violence, but also of service to his king and now his emperor. But he had yet to recollect his personal life fully.

"Detleff, how long have you been in my service?" Melchior asked as they rode along.

"Oh, let me think, *Dominus*. I am not good at numbers, as you know. We were both young. You may be fifteen summers. I was, maybe twenty?"

"So we have served twenty years together?"

"As you say, *Dominus*."

"What do you remember of my family? My earlier life?"

Detleff gave him a strange, almost mournful look.

"What? You think me mad, don't you?"

"I have considered that perhaps My Lord has some sort of illness."

"You are not being truthful. Being truthful is your first duty to your lord."

"I am faithful. I thought that was my first duty, *Dominus*."

"The two are intertwined like vines around an oak tree. Tell me what you think. For if you think something, the others must think it as well, or worse."

"The last *missus dominicus* was possessed. They said only his service to Karolus prevented him from an accusation of sorcery or worse, possession by the devil."

"So, you think I am possessed?" It occurred to Melchior that Detleff might be right.

"No, *Dominus*, but I am concerned for your well-being."

Melchior paused a minute. "I realize I'm acting difficult. I simply need help with my memories – some of which are fleeting. My mind is like a fortress wall. Now and then a brick falls loose, leaving a gap. Sometimes more than one. As long as they are repaired and replaced quickly, the wall remains strong. Just help with that."

"Well, *Dominus*, you know of your feats against the Saracens. That brought you under Karolus's special protection. You became a member of his *Scara* – the *Schola*. You were one of a hundred men of blood who protect the king and live at the palace. When of age, twenty I think it was, you were sent to your father's *desmesne* to restore it to prosperity and to raise a band of warriors of your own."

"Warriors, you say? And where are they now?"

Detleff paused. "Well, they are all dead, *Dominus*. Surely you knew that. Perhaps that has afflicted you?"

Melchior weakly whispered, "Dead."

"They died as good Franks – in the service of their lord and their king. And God."

"How many?"

"All of them, *Dominus*. Except for those who are with you. We, here with you now." He pointed back at Melchior's other retainers, riding silently.

"What number?"

"Oh, I think your battle was six-score mounted men and another four-score or so on foot. All professional men-at-arms. Not the local levees. The horsemen all wore full mail *brunia* over their tunics and iron helmets. The footmen wore leather. Our band... your band was the elite of the army, *Dominus*. Well trained and equipped."

"Where did it happen?"

"You don't remember any of this, *Dominus*?"

Melchior raised his head and gazed out into the gray mist. "Let us just say I want to hear it all from you."

"It happened in the Hunewald. King Karolus sent your force to cover the flank of his planned attack against Widukind, his brother Albion, and their Saxon army. They had broken the truce. Destroyed churches and convents. Ravaged nuns and killed priests. Took Christians as slaves."

"How many warriors did Karolus go to war with?"

"He marched with five thousand men-at-arms and five thousand of the *Landwerei* – the peasant levee. The Saxons were said to number ten thousand. And the main force under Widukind had seven thousand, with another three thousand as a diversion under Albion, sent to destroy farms, villages, and churches. They hoped to divert our lord Karolus from marching to them."

"The Saxons are crafty as well as vicious," Melchior said. He was beginning to remember some.

"And luckily, our king was given false information. We never learned from whom, and split his army, sending you with your band plus an extra sixty mounted men-at-arms to screen his army while he marched against Widukind. But a Saxon trick..."

"Tell me."

"As it transpired, our Lord Karolus was pursuing Albion's smaller force. You were sent headlong into the main Saxon army led by that spawn of the devil, Widukind himself."

Melchior began to see flashes of the battle grow clearer in his memory. He halted his horse to gather his thoughts. "I remember some of it now. A narrow valley with plowed fields in the shadows of the forested mountainsides. The valley seemed so peaceful, but village after village lay charred and smoking."

"Yes, *Dominus*, you remarked that it didn't seem right. No dead. No buzzards circling for carrion. But when a band of Saxon infantry appeared before us, your horsemen spurred into action before you could give a command."

Another memory flashed. "I remember. I ordered the trumpet recall."

"You did, *Dominus*. But it came too late. The horsemen, blood boiling, pursued the Saxons right into a trap."

Melchior looked at Jurchen. "Your loyalty must be to me and this journey now. Not Willehad and not Lothar."

Jurchen's jaw tightened.

"And not Angilram."

"Certainly, *Dominus*."

After they rode on for some time, Melchior turned to Jurchen and asked, "You are not a Frank, are you?"

"No *Dominus*. I am Saxon. By birth, that is. My parents would not accept the true faith, and when they... died... I was baptized by Willehad and raised to be a cleric."

Melchior knew that meant his parents had been killed for not converting. This was contrary to Karolus's current edict on the matter but typical of an earlier time. His eyes and his mind were opening to the world to which he had returned.

"Baptized... by a bishop who is no bishop and who takes liberties with church teaching?"

"Yes, *Dominus*."

Jurchen's voice had weakened. Melchior knew he had touched a chord.

They rode on for longer until finally, Jurchen broke the silence. "*Dominus*, there is something I should probably tell you."

"I have been waiting for you to reach that conclusion, abbot."

"I do not think Willehad is a true man of God."

"So our false bishop is also a false priest?"

"I believe he worships something else."

"A pagan?"

"In a way... I'm not sure."

"That would mean you are not a Christian and therefore not a priest. Your life is a sham."

Jurchen hung his head.

"Why are you revealing all this to me?"

"I am not exactly sure, *Dominus*. But I believe there are more like me. That means many, many people have received sacraments from Willehad's falsely ordained priests... have been confessing to priests who were not properly ordained, like me."

Melchior's ears pricked up. "And if they gave away their transgressions to such men those secrets might be valuable to a certain bishop..."

"Yes, *Dominus*. I was recently approached to break the confessional. I refused."

"What happened?"

"An attempt was made on my life. There will be more."

"What happened to your assassin?"

"I killed him. God forgive me."

"God forgive him." The admission impressed Melchior. "How did it happen?"

"They sent an assassin. But there are more about."

"An assassin? Why?"

"I am not sure. Perhaps I grew too close to Angilram. To the Franks."

"Who was the assassin? More importantly, who sent the assassin?"

Jurchen did not answer. Melchior could see he knew something but would not say it. Melchior sighed. "What happened?"

"He came at me with a *Seaxe*. I had learned to use one as a boy. I disarmed him, and we struggled. Finally, I buried the blade in his throat."

"Who knows of this?"

"No one. It all happened quickly and without a sound. I buried his body in the chancery garden."

"And the weapon?"

Jurchen opened his robe and exposed a long, slightly curved *Seaxe* with a blade on one side.

"Keep it hidden. You might need it."

"But I am a man of God," Jurchen said dolefully.

"Maybe not. If this false bishop is your anointer."

"What should I do?"

"Your secret is safe with me, Abbot Jurchen. We'll settle this when the journey is finished."

Chapter 8

Bavo's Farmstead

They spent the night at the farmstead of an old Frankish warrior turned farmer. The modest estate was nestled along the bank of a small stream. The farmer, Bavo, had his wife make them a soup and served them ale. When they had all eaten their fill, Melchior's men retired to the barn. Melchior remained with Bavo, along with Jurchen.

"I remember you, *Dominus*," Bavo said. "I was with the *exercitus*, the levee, in the second Saxon campaign. You were just a lad. But already we in the levee knew your mettle."

"Kind words from a good and loyal Frank, Bavo," Melchior said.

"I should have stayed on after the *exercitus* went home and spent my life as *milites*, as a professional warrior, instead of coming home to work my father's fields."

"Well, now you are the owner. Frankland needs good men tending good farms. We are no longer wandering savages."

"No, but there are savages about, *Dominus*."

"What do you mean?" Melchior noticed Jurchen stiffen slightly.

The old man put a finger to his lips and looked about hesitantly. "Paganism is returning, *Dominus*. And not just the Saxons, I'm talking of Avars and Franks."

"Avars? Their lands are hundreds of leagues from here. And they were supposed to convert after..." Melchior could not fathom how he knew of this.

Bavo's face reddened. "An Avar can't be trusted! But I'd rather have good pagans than bad Christians anyway. You know?"

Melchior glanced at Jurchen. "Perhaps. Go on."

"A band of them was spotted a month ago. Hiding in the forest a day's ride from here."

"But you said Franks... have returned to the old ways..." Jurchen said. The priest in him was evident in his demeanor.

Bavo's leathered face creased, and he gave a withering frown. "Some have returned. And some never gave them up."

Jurchen's eyes widened. "But Bishop Willehad..."

"The bishop is quite aware." Bavo turned his head away.

"And the abbot at Fulda?" Melchior asked.

"Rumors abound. The abbot has taken sick. That he has not left his chambers for months, some say he has died. Others that he, too, has gone over to the devils."

"Where is your local priest?" Jurchen asked.

"Our church has been empty of priests since Father John rode off one night."

"Where did he ride?" Melchior asked. He was tired of the questions without answers.

"Well, truth is, no one saw him ride off."

"Did anyone inspect the church after he left?"

Bavo's eyes widened in fear. "Oh no, *Dominus*. The word was, the church had been taken possession by evil spirits, strange gods, and sorcery."

"There's no such thing as sorcery, evil spirits, and all that," Melchior said.

"You have been in the shadow of our king Karolus, *Dominus*. But the further one is from him and his religious advisors, the less protected are poor Christians from the evil that walks the earth."

"But the abbot and the monastery at Fulda should offer protection from spiritual depredation," Jurchen said.

Bavo did not reply.

Melchior wondered if Jurchen believed what he said. "Pour us some ale, Bavo. Perhaps we can drink these evil spirits from your home if not from the land."

***

While Melchior was with the farmer, his men tried to turn the barn into a fit place to sleep. They took what clean straw was available and placed their blankets on it. The rain had soaked cloaks and mantels. They hung these from the rafters.

Cassyon and Hartmutt sat rubbing their bare feet while stockings dried. Audeon helped Detleff clean and sharpen blades.

"It's a rare lord that works alongside the likes of us," Cassyon said.

"Aye, I have been told he's the king's bastard," Hartmutt replied.

"He's big enough. Our king is the largest man in Frankland," Cassyon said.

"The largest man in Christendom, in the world," Hartmutt declared. He felt proud of his ruler and his race.

"Lord Audeon, let Detleff sharpen and oil your blades," Cassyon said.

"I'm doing a bastard's work," Audeon quipped. "Besides, a warrior should know how to care for his weapons."

"Wise advice, Lord," Fromm said. "I sharpen my iron maiden every day."

"And I grease my bow strings almost every day. Especially when your foul Frankish weather spits upon us like it is now," Gaetano said.

"I'm not from Frankland, I'm a Dane," Fromm said.

"You have better weather in Daneland, Norseman?" Gaetano asked.

Fromm stroked his long beard. "No. Worse in truth."

They all laughed at the powerful man's dilemma. A horrifying shriek broke up the banter.

"What in Odin's name was that?" Fromm exclaimed.

A second shriek had them scrambling for their weapons and shields.

Hartmutt did not bother. He grabbed his *Francisca* and ran out of the door. He heard the third cry. It sounded like a stuck pig. His heart now beating for action, Hartmutt raced towards the sound, which came from the farmer's field. He wiped the rain from his eyes and ran ankle-deep in the mud towards the sound.

Hartmutt had run no more than fifty paces when something struck him. He tried to call out a warning, but nothing came out of his mouth. His eyes widened, and his lungs coughed up a river of blood. He clutched desperately at the javelin that transfixed his chest and tried to pull it free. Each tug sent explosions of pain radiating from his core. His third try wrenched it free, but more blood erupted. Hartmutt took a step backward and fell into the sodden furrows with the night rain pelting his quivering body.

***

Melchior and Jurchen heard the shrieking and bolted from the farmer's house. Each was armed only with his *Seaxe*. Melchior scanned the dark field.

He heard Audeon organizing the rest of the band. "Form a line. Stay within sword reach of each other. We'll march towards the sound." Audeon and the others emerged from the barn.

"Where is Hartmutt?" Melchior asked.

"He ran off with only his *Francisca*," Audeon said.

"I see something," Gaetano said. "Twenty paces to our left front.'

"I don't see anything," Fromm said.

"You're no archer, Norseman," Gaetano said.

Melchior raced over to the form, barely noticeable between the furrows.

"The work of a demon, *Dominus*. As I warned you."

Melchior turned to see Bavo standing behind him in full battle: leather *brunia*, conical helmet, shield, and spear.

Melchior pried the shaft loose from Hartmut's cold hand.

"This is an Avar short javelin – a dart. See the shape of the blade. Removing it causes more damage than the original wound," Bavo said.

"Avars killed him," Melchior intoned.

"Your man killed himself, *Dominus*," Bavo said grimly. "Rushing out alone and with no shield."

"I'll search for the assassin," Audeon said.

Melchior raised his hand. "No. They did this to entice us."

Bavo shook his spear. "They are waiting with another dart or even a javelin."

"If it is an Avar, *Dominus*, they see almost as well at night as in daylight. They hurl these darts fifty paces with accuracy, javelins twice that," Cassyon said.

"What should we do *Dominus*?" Audeon asked.

Melchior motioned toward the buildings. "Get his body inside the barn. We'll give him a Christian burial in the morning and move on. I won't be lured from my mission by a random killing."

"I don't believe this is at all random, *Dominus*," Bavo said.

"What mischief are you talking about, old man?" Cassyon barked.

"Never mind that. Get him inside," Melchior said.

The men raised their comrade from the sod and carried him back.

Jurchen scanned the darkness. "I saw a spark of light."

"Where?" Melchior asked.

"In that direction. But it is gone."

"Let me mount and ride towards it. Who knows what I'll find?" said Audeon, with boyish enthusiasm.

"And have My Lord Karolus's bastard fall into the hands of a demon? Or worse, the Avars? No, Audeon. This is a diversion only. If you are ever to be a count or a great general, you must learn that warfare is won by craft as much as strength. By stealth as much as numbers. By speed and surprise as much as weapons. A little power at the right place in time is much more effective than a lot of power used randomly."

"Then we should pursue the assassins now!" said Audeon.

Melchior smiled. "We'll not pursue them at all. For that is what they want. Set up a guard in turns. Everyone must get some rest."

"I'll be ready to ride at dawn, *Dominus*," Bavo said.

Melchior eyed the grizzled warrior. "Your weapons are older than your body."

Bavo raised his shield menacingly. "I can still wield a sword and spear. I have never been unhorsed or disarmed. And I have killed many enemies, *Dominus*. Can this bastard son of our great ruler say as much?"

"I cannot," Audeon said. "*Dominus*, I think this fellow should be given a chance to serve our Lord-and-King Karolus one last time."

"Very well, Bavo," Melchior said. "You show the spirit of times past. Perhaps that is needed for us to succeed. Since you know these lands, you will lead the way."

"As you say, *Dominus*."

"Now go make love to your wife. It is no telling when you will return to your home."

Bavo shook his head. "My true home is with Frankish *milites*. This place is only a dreary interlude."

***

Dawn broke with a filmy rain and the sky a dull gray. They had wrapped Hartmut's body and buried it in a pit of mud near Bavo's home. The monk, Father Thomas, gave a small prayer service. Few understood Latin but all kept their heads bowed in reverence as he said the words.

"My wife will have the peasants come and fasten him a Christian cross, *Dominus*. When the rain lets up," Bavo said.

Melchior looked up at the cloud-covered sky and scanned the mist-shrouded fields. "When the rain lets up? The devil will have him before then."

"I think he has already, *Dominus*," Bavo said.

"Sacrilege," Father Thomas said, making the sign of the cross.

Melchior rubbed his chin. "Father Thomas, this may or may not be the devil's work. In either case, one of my men is dead. So, whoever did it is a devil to me."

Melchior's band rode silently, with the rain spitting in their faces while the wind whipped their ears and noses. They rode through dark, dense woods of pine trees. They crossed countless hills, leading weary horses up trails seeping in mud and soaked by the rain.

They passed through numerous tiny villages of oak-hewn buildings with thatched roofs. Despite the rain, the peasants and yeoman farmers were seen hewing wood, tending fields, and herding small flocks of barnyard animals. Melchior noted the people's sturdiness. They seemed unaware of their situation: *a life of back-breaking work.* They were all well-clothed in simple wool of basic colors.

He and his men made the obligatory sign of the cross as they passed the numerous small chapels. Each hamlet had one, no matter how small. It was clear to Melchior that the villagers invested whatever "extra" they had in the chapels. All were well-appointed with a quite attractive design and artwork. Some stemmed from the Roman era, with their simple design and dome-like terra cotta roofs. Others were of hewn wood and stone with a more Germanic appearance. At nightfall, they came to a village on the great river – the Rheine.

"Do you know this village, Bavo?" Melchior asked.

I did, *Dominus*," Bavo replied. "But it has been many years."

"It's only a day's ride from your *demesne*. I find that strange."

"I send my goods west, not east. Besides, this was the site of a Saxon ambush some ten summers ago. I rode through with the *exercitus*. The sight and smell of death... the stink of burnt flesh... I swore I'd never return."

"Yet you led me to this crossing. Why?"

"It is the easiest crossing for leagues in either direction. That's why the Saxons struck it. Anywhere else, the rocks and cliffs make crossing dangerous. Why, not ten leagues from here, the maiden of lore summons boatmen to their death. They say some twenty a year perish on those rocks alone. Other than passing through Koeln itself, this is the best place."

"I have specific orders to avoid Koeln and its bishop. So this is it," Melchior said.

"Koeln would have offered dry beds and good food, *Dominus*," Audeon said.

"And a place of worship. I have not celebrated Mass once since our departure," Father Thomas said.

"Nor I," Jurchen said.

Melchior eyed him and laughed. "Well, now. Better let our good monk, Father Thomas, do the honors."

The others looked askance, but Jurchen flushed. He whispered to Melchior. "My status is yet to be proven, *Dominus*."

"So you say. But on this journey, I need your handiness with a blade as much as with the cross."

Jurchen nodded. Melchior saw him reflexively grasping the *Seaxe* under his robes.

Melchior scanned the silhouettes of thatched buildings along the water and saw the faint glow of the hearths warming the homes. "Who lives here now?"

"Like Koeln, this place is a crossroad with a mix of folk: from Frankland, Lombardland, Pannonia, Bavaria, and lands I care not to think of," Bavo said.

"Maybe you should have stayed home and fed your cattle, old man," Fromm said.

"I'll lay you low like an ox, you fat spawn of Daneland," Bavo replied.

"Enough chatter! Lead us on, Bavo," Melchior said. "By the way, what do they call this place?"

"This town was said to be a Roman camp many years ago. Until we, the Franks, took it from them. They call it merely, The Crossing. Count Weid controls the territory and has a small castle near the bluffs. But he is almost always in Koblenz, downriver. He prefers a city with all its attractions."

"A town with no name, then? How fitting," Melchior said. "Let's get out of this cursed rain."

***

Some hours later, they had their horses safely stabled. They were given accommodation with a Frank, a ferry master named Morloch, who once served with Bavo in the *exercitus*.

Melchior and his retinue ate supper with Morloch and his sons in the great room of his large half-timbered house. A fire roared from a great two-story stone fireplace, spitting sparks in all directions. A balustrade of dark wood lined one wall. Melchior could see several doors along it.

"What have we for supper this damp evening, Morloch?" Bavo asked.

"Had I known a former member of the great *exercitus* was coming, I would have slaughtered a swine. Alas, all we have is fish. But the fish is fresh and good."

"It is also the food our lord Jesus multiplies," Father Thomas said.

"So it is, priest," Bavo said. "And it is grilled perfectly. I like grilled whiting. And the bread is fresh too."

"I wish I had ale. But all I have right now is wine. The grapes grow like weeds along this river," Morloch said.

"It is crisp and dry to the tongue, Lord Morloch," Audeon said. He held his cup up as if to admire it.

Melchior sipped his wine and gnawed a piece of bread. "So, Bavo, how is it you maintain a connection to our host after all these years? I thought you did not travel east?"

Bavo shrugged.

"I have traveled to Bavo's farm on occasion, *Dominus*," Morloch said, "Most recently in the last year."

"What do you trade?" Melchior grew suspicious.

"I often send dried fish and other goods from across the Rheine with my crops. And I charge him a fee of course."

"But only a small one, as he saved my life more than once," Bavo said.

"I'll save your life one more time, Bavo," Morloch said.

"And how will you do that?" Bavo was running his tongue along the bones of a fish he had just picked bare.

"Cross here. Do not go to Koeln," Morloch said grimly.

"I had not planned on going through the great city," Melchior said, "But why should we avoid it?"

"I believe… it to be… cursed!" Morloch sputtered the words.

"I told you, *Dominus*," Bavo said. "There are evil spirits at work here. The devil's work."

"The bishop would drive off any devils. There are ways," Jurchen said complacently.

"The bishop is taken with a strange malady. As are many of the clerics at the cathedral. Many of the town leaders as well. Babes have been murdered. Young women, too. After unspeakable things were done…"

"I don't believe in devils," Melchior said. "And if I do, they are men like we." His mind had a sudden flash of insight. He recalled Hitler and the Nazis. He recalled the millions slaughtered by the Bolsheviks. His memories of the war and pre-war flashed through his consciousness and then quickly faded. *Maybe there are devils that walk the earth.*

"Do you believe in God, the Father Almighty?" Father Thomas asked.

Everyone at the table made the sign of the cross.

"Of course," Melchior said.

"Then you can believe, must believe, in Satan and his host of fallen angels."

"I believe in Odin and Thor," Fromm roared and clutched his pagan amulet.

"Why did we bring a pagan with us?" Jurchen asked.

"It will give you someone to convert, abbot," Melchior said. "I admit that with God, can come devils. But it is man who allows the devils to walk among us."

"We must pray to Saint Michael the Archangel to help us battle them," Audeon said suddenly.

They all looked at the youth in surprise.

"Indeed," Melchior said. "He'll be our patron saint for this journey."

"You'll need him, *Dominus,*" Morloch said. "For unspeakable evil lurks in the east."

"We are going to Fulda, the seat of the church's spiritual center among the Germans. I find it hard to believe evil can touch such a place." Jurchen played nervously with the silver cross around his neck.

"I'm afraid you'll find that the abbey is afflicted too," Morloch said, "In its own way."

"What way is that?" Melchior asked.

Morloch hesitated.

"Answer the *missus's* question," Audeon said.

"Many priests are being pressured to leave their flocks. The people are beginning to return to the old ways," Morloch said.

"As I told you, *Dominus,*" Bavo said.

"Old ways are the best ways," Fromm said.

"Enough, you heathen," Jurchen said.

"Fromm is a pagan. But he is not evil," Melchior said.

"However, this new paganism is evil," Bavo said. "I sense it. Men doing the bidding of the devil."

"That, I have seen." Melchior was not sure why he even said it.

"In dreams, *Dominus?*" Audeon asked innocently.

Melchior did not reply. His mind heard the booming of artillery and tanks. Bombs falling and the shriek of Stuka dive bombers falling from the sky to wreak death. He saw smoke rising from camps. Hundreds and thousands of dead, numbers these men could never understand. And these were but a snapshot of the evil he had seen. But then it faded from memory.

Melchior pointed along the balustrade. "What is behind those doors, Morloch?"

"Bed chambers, *Dominus*. My family sleeps there—my two sons and my daughter. My wife is long gone. May she rest with God."

Everyone made a sign of the cross except Fromm, who grabbed his amulet.

"Indeed. Well, we'll leave you to your peace. I should like breakfast before dawn and cross over at first light. Audeon will see you about supplies. We'll need salted fish and bread. Some fruit and a few skins of that wine."

"As you will, *Dominus*," Morloch said.

***

Audeon was up before the others, except Fromm, who had the last watch. He was to meet Morloch and gather the victuals for the trip.

"Did you see any devils or demons, Fromm?" Audeon asked.

"I saw many. But none that you Christians would recognize. We Norse have our special gods and demons. More powerful than yours. That I can say."

"Ours has a power that does not constitute pure might," Audeon said. "Being raised as a Christian in a very Christian part of Frankland, I think little of pagans. My father thinks of them more as misguided children than savages."

Fromm gave him a curious look. "I have seen your king-and-emperor's power and might. You Christians are not so different in that regard."

"In what regard are we different?"

Fromm scratched his head. "Well, I find your fasting strange. A warrior should eat as much as he can take, whenever he can take it. And your views on women are well..."

They heard a rustling from one of the doors along the balustrade.

"Go get some sleep, Fromm. I have my broadsword and *Francisca* to guard against demons of the dawn."

When Fromm returned to the others, the door opened and a figure wafted across the balustrade with the flow and grace of a spirit. In the early morning darkness, it gave Audeon an eerie feeling. *Did I send Fromm away too soon? Could this indeed be a...*

Before he could think of what to do, the figure had virtually glided down the staircase and was next to him.

"You are up early, Lord."

Instead of a demon, the early morning moonlight revealed the face of a young girl with icy beauty. She was lithe, not plump like so many Frankish girls. She had sparkling blue eyes, finely chiseled cheekbones, a small beak-like nose, and black hair, which contrasted perfectly with her fine white skin. Audeon fell in love.

"I...I expected a devil sent by Satan, and instead I see an angel before me," Audeon blurted out. He had never been so forward with a woman.

"I am Genofeva. Morloch's daughter. My father asked me to rise early and gather the food and drink for your journey."

"I am... Audeon." He barely got his name out.

"I know. I spied on your supper. Father does not want me around men. Especially soldiers."

"But we are the retinue of Melchior, the last of our king-and-emperor's *Missi Dominici*."

"I know that. The last *missus* to come through here was an older man-at-arms. He had more priests than soldiers with him. That was five years ago. I was but nine."

"And now you are a grown woman of fourteen?" She looked older, wiser than a girl of fourteen, he thought.

She nodded. "Soon enough, fifteen."

Audeon smiled. "I remember well my fourteenth year."

"And how long ago was it?" Genofeva asked.

"Almost two years now," Audeon said proudly.

"Well, can an old man be trusted with a young daughter of a ferryman?"

"No Frankish woman or girl need ever fear Audeon,"

"But I am only half-Frank." Genofeva smiled. "Should I half fear you?"

Audeon did not want to frighten or disturb her. "No... never."

"My mother was from Pannonia. The Avars killed her family. Their farm burned to the ground. I was only five. An Avar warrior carried me off to be raised by his wife until I was old enough to... become his concubine or be sold off."

Audeon took her hands in his. "I would have saved you first."

"I watched my mother die, but I cannot recall her face, only her cries as the Avars took their turns. Then one of them cut her throat like a butcher cutting a pig." Tears began to streak her cheeks.

Audeon drew her to him and held her gently. He whispered, "Avars are devils on horses. Thank God my father and my brother punished them."

Genofeva pushed back softly and threw back her head. "Father says I look more and more like her."

"Then she must have been the most beautiful woman on this side of the Rheine."

Genofeva blushed.

"How did he know her?"

"He served with a column of Franks who marched through Pannonia on an expedition. His band stayed at her family's farm to fatten their horses for a few days before the long ride back. They fell in love. When he left, he said he'd return for her in the spring. But he did not come back until after the Avars pillaged us five years later."

"I am sorry." Audeon could imagine her shame. He understood bastardy well.

"He had no choice. His lord would not permit him to return. Then, he married a local."

"How did the Avars treat you?" Audeon shivered at the thought of her in the hands of the eastern savages.

"Like a slave. I worked at everything, but mostly caring for Dgno's horses."

"Dgno?"

"The Avar chieftain whose mistress I would be. They often joked about it. At the time, I had no idea what it all meant."

"How did you return?"

"Our Lord and Emperor Karolus sent another army east. This time to punish the Avars for their unceasing attacks. When my father rode to find my mother, he learned of my fate. The Avars met the Franks in a great battle, and they were scattered. Risking the wrath of his liege, he took his band of twenty and found me at Dgno's camp."

Audeon knew well his father had punished the Avars some years back, subduing the great khanate except for some renegade tribes. "What happened to Dgno? Was he killed in the fighting?"

"I don't know. I was caring for the foals and ponies when this band of warriors rode up. I could tell at once they weren't Avars. Their horses were large and they rode slowly and carried heavy lances and shields."

"How did your father know it was you?"

"He never said. But I understood his language, although much of it sounded strange. I was with the Avars for almost two years, you see. He saw I was not an Avar and spoke to me. Then, on a hunch, he said my mother's name. When I said it back, he put me on an Avar horse, and we departed."

"How did your father become the ferry master here?"

This time she had no reply. After a short pause, she said, "Let us go and gather the food before the others rise."

They worked quickly and silently, gathering food from the larder and placing it in sacks.

"I think this will do us," Audeon said finally. He was feeling upset at the thought that they had but a few minutes together. But he knew he had his duty.

"The plums are just now ripening. Let me pick some fresh ones from the orchard," Genofeva said. Her voice was like honey to his ears.

"It is still dark. We can do without the plums."

They suddenly embraced and kissed tenderly. As one, they lay their head on the other's shoulder.

"I must leave within the hour, Genofeva. But I would like permission from your father to return when the journey is finished."

"Am I so uninteresting that you must seek my father's permission?"

He stroked her hair gently. "Why, no. It is because I..."

"The morning twilight is upon us." Genofeva smiled mischievously and ran off into the dark.

Audeon waited for her return and was about to run after her when a cry as horrifying as any he had heard ripped open the quiet dark of morning.

"Genofeva! Noooo, Genofeva!"

The girl's name came from a man's throat. However, a gurgling sound gave it a demonic timbre.

Audeon drew his broadsword and raced into the darkness. He bent into a crouch, changing his direction. The morning twilight broke suddenly, and in the glimmer of dawn, he saw several figures on horseback. He thought he saw what appeared to be Genofeva struggling across the saddle of one of the ponies.

A javelin creased his shoulder.

"Avars!" He shouted. "Avars!"

Three horsemen spurred their ponies at him. They wore long black cloaks and had their heads wrapped in gray cloth caps that spiked.

Lucifer's army could not look as menacing. Audeon ducked behind one of the orchard's plum trees as the riders swept in on him. Audeon twisted to his right and severed the leg of a pony with his broadsword, sending the rider tumbling to the ground with the horse shrieking and wildly kicking its three legs. To his astonishment, the horseman landed on his feet and rushed him with what looked like a rope.

His heart pounding, Audeon raised his broadsword, but the rope, a Hunnish lasso, caught his wrist. Audeon dropped the broadsword and met the Avar. Their bodies slammed together. The smaller man hit hard. The blow winded Audeon. The Avar merely grunted and reached for his curved dagger. His chest exploding but with a desperate fury, Audeon buried his *Francisca* into the Avar's shoulder, killing him instantly.

Before he could draw his blade free, another horseman lassoed him about the neck and dragged him to the ground. Another dart flew by. He could hear the Avars chattering. They were mocking him in their language, which sounded like a swarm of starlings. He then realized they were deciding who would get to kill him. But they had not reckoned on Audeon's size and strength.

Audeon pulled the rider and horse towards him. Enraged, the Avar turned his pony and tried to drag Audeon instead of riding into him. With shoulders and arms heaving, Audeon ripped the Avar from the pony. He quickly tore his *Francisca* free and hurled it into the chest of the onrushing warrior. *That's for Hartmutt!* The blade made a sweet crunching sound as it cut through the Avar's armor and breastbone and turned organs to butter. The warrior tumbled backward into the cold, wet morning grass.

But Audeon did not reckon on the third rider. Who bore down on him at full speed, waving a long, curved dagger. He could smell the horse's sweat and almost feel its snout blowing. Audeon turned. Rider and beast came as one. At the last moment, Audeon leaped up and grabbed desperately at the limb of a tree. Drawing his boots together, he slammed them hard into the chest of the onrushing pony.

The impact sounded like the grunt of a primeval beast. Audeon fell from the tree, his arms nearly torn from their sockets and his bare hands ripped red. The horse collapsed and rolled left. Audeon could hear the snap of the rider's leg, now pinned under the thrashing pony.

Audeon stood and retrieved his broadsword in time to see the last rider, with Genofeva trussed across his saddle, riding up with a dart held high. As the pony trotted within twenty paces of Audeon, the young Frank knew he could not outrun or dodge this last missile.

Desperate to save her, he wildly rushed the rider, bellowing a Frankish war cry. The Avar's face twisted into a crooked scar of a smile. He turned away from the Frank as if he posed no threat. Instead, he calmly launched his dart with perfect accuracy into the heart of the Avar struggling to break free from his pony. The rider laughed and snapped his pony's head around, galloped into the gray morning mist.

Audeon staggered forward and fell face down into the wet grass in tears, pounding and tearing at it in frustration. "Genofeva... Genofeva..."

***

Melchior grasped Audeon's shoulders and lifted him to his feet. "The men are searching the field and orchard. Is this a way for the son of Karolus to act?"

"A bastard son." Audeon wiped the wet dew and tears from his face. "We must ride, *Dominus*! They took Genofeva. I think they were Avars."

"I know they were Avars. But we'll do no such thing." Melchior saw the despair in the boy's eyes but remained unmoved.

"You are a Christian warrior of the Franks. You are obligated to save Christian women from pagan depredations," Audeon said.

"I am obligated to serve My Lord Karolus. Nothing else. This is another distraction. They want to draw us away from our journey. There could be hundreds of Avars out there lying in wait."

"Does the great *missus dominicus* fear a fight with heathens from the east?"

Melchior's mind flashed with the image of a field full of smoking hulks and the explosions of hundreds of shells. "I have fought men from the east. They are not to be taken lightly. They are crafty and brutal men, who fear little."

"*Dominus!*" Gaetano called. He was kneeling over the dead Avar after he slit the struggling pony's throat. "These are the same darts that killed Hartmutt."

Melchior approached him and examined the dart. "The same length and feathers. But the point is different. Hartmutt's point was meant to inflict pain before death. This one was designed to kill swiftly. To kill a fellow Avar out of necessity."

"I have seen such things when I served under the Mohammedans. They fought the Avars, but also hired them when convenient," Gaetano said.

Melchior drew his longsword from its scabbard and showed the blade to Gaetano. "The Saracens appreciate quality weapons. They made this one from forged steel. Our steel is not nearly the quality of theirs."

"*Dominus!* Over here," Cassyon said.

Lying under a plum tree lay one of Morloch's sons, an Avar dart squarely in his chest. The bulging eyes and twist of the mouth had the look of someone who had stared into hell. Jurchen made the sign of the cross while Bavo closed his eyes.

"It was his cry, *Dominus*," Cassyon said. "He died trying to save the girl."

"Where is Morloch?"

"I am here, *Dominus*," Morloch said. "What have... Chrodegang!"

"I am sorry for your loss, Morloch. He was killed trying to save his sister from the Avars," Melchior said.

"I wish I could have done as well as he," Audeon said.

"A dead Frank can no longer be of service to his lord," Melchior said. "No more talk of senseless death."

"What, what happened?" Morloch asked.

Audeon hung his head in shame. "Genofeva wanted to pick us some fresh plums and ran into the orchard. I lost her in the morning twilight and the mist. I heard her name called… I realize now by Chrodegang."

"What was your son doing out here at this hour?" Melchior asked.

"I suppose he was going to prepare the barge for crossing, *Dominus*. He is… he was a very eager lad. Always did his father's bidding without question."

Melchior crossed his arms and stared at the body. He was suspicious of this boy but he did not know why.

"We should be going, *Dominus*. Before more Avars are upon us," Jurchen said.

"I suspect the Avars are already upon us," Melchior said. "Make ready, Morloch. I want to be across the river as soon as possible."

"But I must bury my son, *Dominus*."

"You'll have time enough when we are gone. Unless you plan to join us," Melchior said.

"No *Dominus*. My son must receive a proper burial. And I'll have to hire a new man."

"New men, you mean," Melchior said. He needed to replace Hartmutt.

"*Dominus*?"

"Your second son will join us. Give him your arms and horse and tend to your ferry, old man."

"Werinbert is no warrior."

"We may have other rivers to cross. He will be of value. He will come with us."

They crossed the river Rheine just after the sun was high overhead. Werinbert looked forlornly as his father took the barge over the last time. Melchior saw his despair. The boy needed a purpose.

"You will serve Audeon," Melchior said. "Carry his arms and obey his orders."

"I should stay with my father, *Dominus*," Werinbert said. "I must search for my sister."

Melchior scanned the east bank until Morloch's barge arrived at the far side quay. "I find it curious that your father made no mention of the same."

***

Wilineburch

The horses plodded along the valley of a river that Melchior knew as the Lahn. His companions called it the Laugona. The remnants of a Roman road that once supplied the outposts guarding Germania now offered only an overgrown trail. Melchior raised his gaze. The steep mountains on both sides and the dark stands of trees put the valley in a gray shade even on the few days with sun. The appearance of hamlets dating back to the

Romans provided this forested land with tiny pockets of civilization. Small toll stations offered food to wayfarers, and a cross or chapel every few leagues offered spiritual sustenance.

"As we ride east, more of these hamlets seem empty," Melchior said.

"I have noticed, *Dominus*," Jurchen replied.

Melchior barely heard the clop of the horse's hooves along the muddy trails. He was deep in thought about his predicament. He realized he had not fully gone from one time to another or even from one world to another. Instead, he felt he was in a strange blend of two worlds that would somehow collide and crush him. *What of Kristel? Of Zet? Weber? Patricia?*

Melchior pulled up on the reins. His hand trembled slightly as he touched his forehead. Something caused him to look up into the gray sky. He gazed for a few moments that seemed like hours. "Not a sign of any bird or beast the past five leagues."

"Aye, *Dominus*," Detleff said. "I noticed. Very curious."

Melchior grunted and spurred his horse forward.

The rain came in the late afternoon, just as they reached a stretch of the river that bent into a bow around a high wooded stretch of land dominating a valley.

"It will be dark soon, *Dominus*," Jurchen said. "There is a village at the summit. I traveled through it once. They should have warm food and shelter."

They turned up a trail that wrapped around the island in a spiral climb. They passed the ruins of a Roman watchtower. Most of the stone had been picked at by the locals to build their hovels.

"Great Karolus must restore the greatness the Romans left us," Jurchen said suddenly.

Melchior halted Timbo and threw back his hood. "He will, abbot. But I am not sure things can end differently for the new Christian Empire."

"What do you mean?"

Melchior pointed to a small promontory that stood some forty feet above them. A beam stretched another twenty feet in the air. It was blackened by fire.

"The omens of evil are around us," Bavo exclaimed. "Just as I said!"

"That surely was a cross!" Father Thomas said as he made the sign of the cross. "But who would destroy the cross beam and burn a sacred site?"

"I can think of many," Melchior said tersely.

"Like who?" The young monk asked.

"Never mind." Melchior spurred his horse up the hill.

A pack of dogs appeared suddenly, barking and baring their fangs. Gaetano drew an arrow and aimed it at the lead animal.

"Put away your weapons," Melchior said.

A pair of hunters emerged from the woods. They wore leather and carried spears and axes.

"Who rides in our land?" the older hunter challenged.

"This is *Dominus* Melchior, representative of our King-and-Emperor, Karolus," Jurchen said.

The hunters bared their heads, accepting the pelting rain on their necks as a price for their servility.

"Cover yourselves," Melchior said.

The hunters pulled up their hoods and stood waiting expectantly.

"We need shelter for the night. I recall a nice village called Wilineburch near the top of the ridge," Jurchen said.

"The place you call Wilineburch is gone," the hunter said.

"Gone? How could it be gone?" Jurchen asked. "It had maybe five hundred dwellers?"

"A band of raiders came through over a month ago. They killed all but those few of the girls whom they took as slaves."

Melchior saw the hollow look in the hunters' eyes—the eyes of men with no hope. Melchior had seen it too often before. "What kind of raiders?"

"Does it matter, *Dominus*?" the older hunter replied.

"Did your priest bury the dead properly?" Father Thomas asked.

"Our priest was nowhere to be found. He left the village the day before the attack."

"Did he know of the attack?" Melchior asked.

"How could their priest know of such a thing, *Dominus*?" Jurchen said.

"Father Mannix was a new priest. Sent from Fulda, he said. He was only here a month himself," the hunter said.

"Fulda? Not Koblenz?" Melchior asked.

"Fulda is what I said, *Dominus*."

"Take me to where they are buried, and I can say the prayers for the dead," Father Thomas offered.

"Too late for that, priest," the hunter said. "We buried them in the old Frankish ways."

"What! A heathen ceremony? That is apostasy," Father Thomas said.

"When our priests and bishops abandon us, where should we turn?"

"What is your name, hunter?" Melchior asked.

"Spad. The boy is called Wala. He is my nephew. We have a camp with shelter, *Dominus*. And a freshly killed boar sizzling in the cauldron. You and your men are welcome to share what we have."

Melchior nodded. "Show us the way, Spad."

"This could be a trap, *Dominus*. These men are apostate now," Jurchen hissed.

"Apostate? This coming from a false priest spawned by a false bishop?"

"Our Christian god abandons us," Spad said defiantly.

Melchior raised his hand. "You were not abandoned by God. Just by his servants. If they ever were indeed his servants."

"What do you mean, *Dominus*?" Jurchen asked.

"I mean, Lucifer exists. Evil exists. It does not mean God has abandoned us. He may be testing us," Melchior said.

"Why would he do that, *Dominus*?" Jurchen asked.

"To prepare us for the greater tests that lie ahead?" Father Thomas said.

"Yes, Father Thomas," Melchior replied. He realized that Thomas was a very pious man. *This land needs priests like him.*

The large black cauldron bubbled with a thick, coarse concoction of roots and grains mixed with the grizzled flesh of an old boar. Melchior's men scooped cups into the stew and slopped the thick gravy and morsels into their mouths.

"By Thor's hammer! This is the best pig I've ever eaten," Fromm said, wiping grease and gravy from his beard. "Shame you have no ale. But the wine we brought will do us."

Fromm took a deep gulp from the wineskin and offered some to Spad and the boy, Wala. They both signaled no. Fromm shrugged and laughed. "I'll drink your share."

The rain had stopped, and the men went to turn in. Cassyon had the first watch. Father Thomas and Jurchen remained with Melchior in the hut, along with Bavo and Spad.

"How long do you plan to remain here?" Melchior asked.

"This is our land. We'll hunt here until we die," Spad said flatly.

"More people will come. A new village will grow," Jurchen said.

"Not while the evil we now see walks this land," Bavo said. "I already sensed it far to the west. But I sense it is stronger here in the east."

"It's true," Thomas said. "I sense it." He made the sign of the cross.

"You will come with me on this journey, Spad. And Wala too. I need strong men who know the land. I need hunters," Melchior said.

"To hunt what, *Dominus*? We can take boar, wolf, lynx, bear, or stag."

"To hunt men. To hunt what is hunting us. The valley will narrow for many leagues. I want you and Wala to leave a half-day ahead of us and secure the way."

"As you say, *Dominus*," Spad said. "I should like the privilege of meeting the priest Mannix once more."

"Mannix is no priest," Jurchen said in a low voice.

They all looked at him.

"What do you mean, abbot?" Thomas asked.

"He was 'ordained' by Bishop Willehad. But he is a Saxon. A pagan. And a killer."

"You see, *Dominus*," Bavo said. "These are evil tidings. Frankland is in peril."

Chapter 9

The Land between the Waters

For two dreary days, horses and men struggled along the narrow, twisting road along the Laugona river. Heavy hooves sunk deep into loamy mud, making each furlong a journey. Just when Melchior thought the dark trail would never end, the road entered a large open valley where the river turned north. They followed the tree-lined waterway for several hours.

A familiar whistling broke the strange quiet around them. Melchior's hand signaled halt and they all looked up into the face of Wala peering from branches high above them. With his shock of brown hair, leathered face, and dark clothing he looked like an extension of the tree itself. Wala pointed across the road where Spad suddenly appeared as if from the woods.

"Hail, *Dominus*," Spad said.

Melchior raised his hand. "Where are we, Spad?"

"This is area is called Giezzen, *Dominus*. The land between the waters. There is a village they call Wiesek just around the next bend. But a band of Saxons raided it as well."

"Saxons," Bovo growled. "We should kill all Saxons."

"And Avars," Audeon said.

Melchior frowned. The impulse to combat among these men was noteworthy. "Has the town been burned?"

Spad extended his hands, palms up. "No, *Dominus*. For some reason, it was spared. But the chapel was burned and the priest died in the flames, they say. The folk were robbed of their goods, but not their young women. Although the raiders had their will with all they fancied."

Father Thomas made the sign of the cross.

Melchior's eyes smoldered. Yet he expected nothing less of the Saxons. His mind drifted to images of burning villages on the eastern steppes – the work of any marauding bands. "You have seen us through the forest, Spad. You and your nephew are free to return."

Spad shook his head slowly. "No *Dominus*. We have decided to serve you. If you will have us."

"Do you agree to accept baptism at the first opportunity? I want but one pagan on this journey and that is Fromm," Melchior demanded. He remembered that as *Missus Dominicus*, he had spiritual as well as temporal roles.

Father Thomas smiled.

"Yes, *Dominus*," Spad said.

"Very well. Lead us to this Wiesek, then," Melchior ordered. He glanced at Father Thomas. "You will take baptism from Father Thomas later."

***

They rode through light rain, moving slowly north along the river until it twisted once more, uncoiling to the north and east like a dark serpent. They halted at Wiesek. The dozen or so stone and timbered homes smelled of chicken, pig, and cow droppings. The muddy ruts that served as the main street were strewn with straw. The rain had stopped late that afternoon, and rays of pale gray sunshine now warmed the air.

The town elder, a solid-looking farmer of indeterminate age, was brought to Melchior.

"Spad the hunter told us of your misfortunes," Melchior said. "I am sorry our Lord Karolus's peace could not protect you from the rape of the Saxons. But in the name of God and our Lord Karolus, I intend to remedy that."

The elder looked incredulous. "But *Dominus*, the Saxon band that robbed us numbered some fifty warriors. And packs of Avars numbering twenty, have been seen riding across the fields. Your men number but eight, perhaps. How can you do anything? Even with God's help."

Fromm grabbed the elder with his paw-like grip and shook him. "You talk to Lord Melchior that way? Why, I'll break you in two."

"Enough, Fromm. His remark was truthful, not insulting," Melchior said. "Hear well. Our journey is on behalf of our Lord King-and-Emperor Karolus. It is God's will that we attend to his business. Can a pack of Avars or a band of Saxons thwart God's will?"

"They had their way with us, *Dominus*," the elder said. "How can…"

A shrill whistling sound cut through their ears.

"*Dominus*, this is a trap!" Wala cried out from a rooftop.

The doors of the squalid homes suddenly burst open. More than a score of Saxons erupted from within. They wore wolf-skins and brandished large *Seaxes* with 22-inch blades. The leaders carried heavy leather shields. Their heads were bare, displaying their long, greasy locks, encrusted in rancid fat, and pointing in all directions. They looked and sounded like something more sinister than rabid animals. They sounded like demons.

With a rapid snap of the wrist, Wala threw a hunting spear into the first pack, the short blade tore open the chest of the lead warrior, sending him to the ground and blocking the rush of the others. He quickly hurled his second spear and killed another. Spad, angered at the trickery he had enabled, drew his hunting knife and buried it in the side of the village elder.

They could hear the screams of the other townsfolk. They sounded more like wild pigs than people.

"*Wehrt euch!*" Melchior bellowed in German. He repeated it in Frankish, "To arms!"

Detleff handed him his lance. Balancing it level with the ground, he spurred Timbo through the crowd. Anxious for combat, he charged the screaming pack of Saxons. "Steady, Timbo," he whispered. The gray charger's ears went back, and he snorted in reply.

Melchior strained forward in the saddle. His heart pounded, and his blood raced with a mix of fervor and fear. This was at once a new and familiar experience. The wind rushed past his face. Timbo snorted in anticipation, hooves pounding a rhythm bred from centuries of war. He could smell its sweat mixed with his own. Melchior shivered and then readjusted his spear tip to strike the lead Saxon.

A short but sturdy warrior with a bare chest and an oversized shield stood at the head of the pack. Melchior felt something slam into his shield but bounce off harmlessly into the mud. A spear! Suddenly, his spear point drove through the great leather shield and pinned the Saxon. With a powerful move, he wrenched the spear from the impaled body, sending the Saxon flopping into the mud like a useless piece of meat.

Around him, his men ran their spears through the bodies of the screaming Saxons. The *whish* of broad swords flying from scabbards filled the air. Now the cleaving of Saxon limbs, shoulders, and heads began. Still, the Saxons came at them, snarling like a pack of mad wolves. The Franks stabbed and cut. They sliced open arms and hacked legs. Audeon drew his *Francisca* and chopped his way through the swarm. In minutes, more than half the Saxons were dead or dying.

The remainder formed a circle around their leader. Wala had recovered one of his spears and hurled it from another rooftop, but he hit one of the warriors, not the chief. Then Gaetano launched an arrow into the chieftain's eye. The large, blubbery Saxon pulled it out, along with half his brains and gore. His body plopped into the muddy ruts.

"Form up behind me, quickly," Melchior commanded. He held Timbo steady as the horse pawed the mud with angry snorts.

He could see confusion among the Saxons, who seemed to be deciding who the new chief was. *Strike when the enemy is confused. Hit the Schwerpunkt.* He could not recall how he remembered that edict.

"Now!" Melchior ordered.

Leading Detleff, Bavo, Cassyon, and Audeon, Melchior charged the leaderless circle and broke it apart, once brave warriors scattering through the alleys of the town and escaping like rabbits into the woods. Fromm, Werinbert, and Gaetano fell upon the last organized pack. The archer launched shaft after shaft, each taking down a Saxon. Half-naked bodies were sprawled in the mud, some thrashed about trying to extract the arrows, only opening greater wounds.

Fromm bellowed his Nordic cry, "Odin!" This halted the Saxons, for they worshiped the same God. While they hesitated, Fromm stepped up with his two-handed battleax and sliced through rows of legs. Barking like mad dogs, the last Saxons fell like chaff.

Moments later, the village grew silent. The narrow, muddy streets were strewn with clumps of dead and dying. None cried for mercy. Instead, they clutched for their weapons, eager for a passage to Valhalla.

"Count the dead and strip them down," Melchior said. "Gaetano, take a position and watch for more. Audeon, scout the western edge of the village."

Audeon spurred his horse up the muddy lane. The Apulian scrambled up a ladder and climbed onto a roof. He notched another arrow and scanned the valley for signs of more Saxons.

"Find me a live one," Melchior shouted.

"Over here, *Dominus*," Jurchen cried.

Melchior looked down at a Saxon of some worth, based on his weapons and the quality of his shield, lay twitching and grabbing at his entrails.

"You have just a little longer to live, Saxon. Who sent you and why?" Melchior was surprised by how fluently the Saxon words rolled off his tongue.

"I'll be with Odin soon enough, Frank," the Saxon spat.

Melchior stepped on his hand and separated the *Seaxe* from his bloody fingers. "Not without a weapon. Now talk, or I'll have this priest speak the holy words a pagan as you should never want to hear."

"Deny me Valhalla?"

Father Thomas pulled out his psalter, his prayer book, and began to pray in Latin.

"Who sent you? And why?" Melchior demanded.

"Eberger … never said. He told us… drive the Christians from the land that our queen had magical powers… from the gods that the Avars were now… allied with us. Even now… more Saxons are marching west. More Avars are riding west. The time of the Frank is over."

"It cannot be that simple. Why now? Why here?" Melchior asked.

The Saxon did not respond. His eyes stared upward in a glaze.

"This is a monstrosity!" Bavo said. "Pagan Avars and Saxons united against us. Disturbing news, *Dominus*."

Melchior turned to Jurchen. "This is nothing to be surprised at, is it, abbot?"

"I don't understand, *Dominus*," Jurchen stammered.

"These are your people, the Saxons. As you know, we may have to kill the lot of them before they submit to Frankish rule. But what is disturbing is that these Frankish villagers went over to them. Why?"

"Perhaps they were not as sure in their faith as our Lord Karolus would like," Jurchen said.

Melchior stroked the stubble on his chin. "There is much in what you say, abbot. I am glad you are on this journey."

Audeon rode up, followed by Werinbert. "*Dominus*, the villagers who were not killed are gone."

"*Dominus*, I see something on the horizon," Gaetano called out.

"Avars," Audeon said. "I shall ride out and see what they are up to."

"No," Melchior said. "The Avars are a diversion to lure us from our task. They ride and burn and pillage. But they will not occupy. The Saxons are the threat right now. And apostate Franks, of whom I suspect this land is awash."

"What shall we do, *Dominus*?" Audeon asked.

"What do you think we should do?"

"I think we should seek the Avars and find Genofeva before…"

Melchior cut him short. He knew what was on the boy's mind. "No. We are here to fulfill Karolus's wishes, not rescue some poor farm girl. We shall continue the journey. Only now we must avoid the towns from here to Fulda. The land has turned on us."

"What good can we do in Fulda, *Dominus*?" Audeon asked.

Melchior did not answer. For in truth, he did not yet know.

"We have gathered all the dead, *Dominus*," Bavo said. "I say we burn this place. Treasonous Franks have no right to it."

"No. If they return, I want them to see more than a burned village. Pile the Saxons and burn them. Bury the ashes near the river, but pile their skulls in the village center for all to see."

"But *Dominus*, to burn them deprives them of the resurrection of the body," Father Thomas said.

"Spoken like a monk," spat Bavo. "These are heathens."

Melchior could not explain that the burning was as much to avoid disease as to send a message. *They would never understand the concept of bacteria.*

"It will… purify things… to burn them," Melchior said at last.

"Spoken like a true Frank of old, *Dominus*," Bavo guffawed. "We'll get right to it."

"Father Thomas will say a benediction and prayers for the dead first," Melchior said.

"Thank you, *Dominus*," Thomas said.

Jurchen stood watching, hands folded under his robe.

"What are you thinking, abbot?" Audeon whispered.

"I am beginning to think there is something quite unusual about this, *missus dominicus*."

"What do you mean?" Audeon asked.

"I'm not sure," Jurchen replied.

***

The journey continued east. Now they rode more carefully to avoid ambush from Saxon footmen and Avar horsemen. Spirals of smoke from burning dwellings occasionally drifted across the horizon. The stench of burned wood and roasted flesh assaulted their nostrils. But they saw no signs of any living creature: animal or human.

"We have entered a world of death and despair. Can this be Frankland?" Audeon remarked.

"It is. But I have seen worse."

"Worse?"

"You too shall see worse before this journey is through. Be strong of arm and of spirit."

"Yes, *Dominus*," Audeon replied.

Melchior's men swore more than once they had spotted Avars, or at least the dust from Avar ponies. Melchior dismissed them with a wave of his hand. He had no time for distractions.

Melchior glanced up. The weather had become surprisingly dry, although iron-gray clouds still dominated the skies above them. He needed to press forward before the grounds once more turned to a quagmire. An hour later, they came to a fork in the road.

"*Dominus*, I think I know a route that will keep us from the sight of the pagans," Jurchen said.

Melchior scanned the area as if he knew it. "The Romans planned this ancient road for a campaign against the old Chatti tribes. Although they never used it, we will. The way is straight and somewhat flat."

He remembered studying how the Chatti were the first tribe to stand up to the Romans. *Standhafte Chatten*. The steadfast Chatti fought the Romans and Germanic rivals with equal ferocity. Melchior vaguely recalled from Patricia that a branch of the Chatti merged with other Germanic groups, forming the proto-Franks. He grimaced as thoughts of Patricia quickly evaded his mind.

"I believe I know a better way, *Dominus*," Jurchen said again. "Slower, but more secure."

"I think the abbot is correct, *Dominus*," Audeon said. "We should avoid the most obvious approach."

Melchior looked at Jurchen. *Could he trust him?* "Very well. Do you propose we take the other fork?"

Jurchen nodded. "For a distance of a few leagues. Before the ground begins rising, there is a forested swamp. Not deep. We can leave our spoor behind us and emerge where neither Saxons nor Avars will go."

Melchior eyed the fork. He reached into his sack and pulled out a plum. He bit at it while he regarded the land ahead. *Should he trust the Saxon?* "A good plan, abbot. You and Thomas carry Spad and Walla on your mounts. Ride a quarter-league ahead. Audeon and Werinbert will accompany you."

***

Fulda, The Fortress and Castle of Count Lothar

Willehad bit heartily into the fat-soaked goose leg. He gnawed slowly at the dark meat, both succulent and spare. Then he tossed the naked bone into a sack and reached for another.

"Eat slowly, bishop. There are only so many geese in the yard," Count Lothar said with a laugh. He enjoyed teasing the cleric.

"Then I'll wash it down with this fine ale," Willehad said as he slurped his tankard.

"For a man of the spirit, you place no small stock in your body," Lothar said.

"That is what separates us from the angels, isn't it, My Lord?"

"And the devils." A shudder went through Lothar as he said it, and they both made a sign of the cross.

"Indeed," Willehad sniffed. He took another quaff of his ale.

"Have you heard from Vulmar, speaking of devils?"

The bishop's eyes widened. "Father Vulmar is an exorcist. He is trained to walk among devils."

"Does he stroll with them like a lover?"

"My Lord Lothar, Vulmar is our key agent for change. He has influenced the Saxons to our way of thinking. He has brought the Avars to our cause. And he has established the basis for teaching our new catechumens."

"You mean for your heretical new church." Lothar had no illusions about the unholy alliance he had made.

Willehad rolled his eyes. "Speak not of heresy. We shall establish a new orthodoxy that will enable us to create a larger Christendom incorporating some of the better aspects of the pagans' way of life and thought. And you, My Lord Lothar, shall be the first Frankish lord to benefit from this new world order."

Lothar nodded. He enjoyed baiting the fat bishop, but he had to admit Willehad's mad scheme was now showing promise.

"Soon you will no longer be a mere count. Soon you will step from the shadow of Karolus and his paladins as the new master of Christendom and beyond."

"Your ideas have merit, My Lord Bishop. But know well, I take great risks here. I risk much."

"As do I, Count Lothar."

"Do you really? A false bishop spreading a false faith? No, you gain more than you lose. The king-and-emperor suspects you, if not your scheme. I am sure he has sent Melchior this way to depose you. With my help, of course."

"I have an agent among his party, Count Lothar. I have Saxon and Avar bands searching the way my agent is instructed to guide them. We will have his head soon if the savages spare his corpse."

"Let us hope so, Willehad." But Lothar was not so sure.

A servant entered and whispered in the bishop's ear. Willehad nodded. "It seems we have a visitor, Count Lothar."

A few minutes later, Father Vulmar was escorted into the room.

Willehad smiled. "Welcome, Father Vul..."

"Have you brought the head of the *missus*?" Lothar asked without introduction.

"It shall not be long, Count Lothar. I have taken a score of villages and converted or killed the peasants there. Saxons and Avars roam freely between here and the Rheine. Sometimes beyond."

Vulmar remained cool. Too cool for Lothar's liking. "You failed to answer me, priest."

Vulmar looked at the bishop. Willehad nodded at him.

"Not yet, Count Lothar."

Lothar turned to the bishop, who was now playing with his cross.

"You assured me you had an agent among them. Leading them to destruction."

"I did. That is, I do, My Lord. But something has happened to him. To them."

"What do you mean?" Lothar's face reddened.

"They have disappeared," Vulmar said. "They were to take a certain road – the old Roman road. But suddenly they have vanished."

"Vanished? With the land controlled by your Saxons and Avars? I suspect treachery."

Vulmar remained calm. "Oh, there is treachery, My Lord. I suspect someone gave up my man. The question is who and how?"

"What does it matter? We must stop the *missus* before he arrives," Lothar said.

"I think not, My Lord. I think we must now prepare for his arrival," Vulmar said.

"Oh, he'll turn back to Karolus like the lapdog he is once he realizes what this is about."

"No, he won't, Count Lothar,' Vulmar said. "I know the man. I rode with the man. I even served with him on two of his journeys. The two *missi* we have disposed of are not of his ilk. We made the mistake of killing the weak ones. Now we face the strong one. He fears nothing. Sometimes I think he does not fear God."

Lothar spat. "Do you fear God? You, who call on devils to do your work?"

Vulmar lowered his head. But then slowly raised it in proud defiance.

Willehad let go of his cross. "Do not chastise my exorcist. He fears God. That is why he is doing this work. To expand the reach of God."

"To expand the reach of man is more like it. And I am fine with that," Lothar said. "You may grease your plots with spiritual underpinnings. But make no mistake. This is about power. About building a religious and corporal force that we can control, to expand east and west, north and south. Karolus moves too slowly against his enemies. He plays too much with bishops and monks. He thinks and prays now when a true Frankish chieftain should smash and take."

"Did the Avars find the girl?" Willehad asked.

Vulmar nodded. "Yes, Your Grace.

"And she is unharmed?"

"So they say."

"So the Avars say? When did an Avar ever touch a Frankish maiden without inflicting harm?" Lothar asked.

"Half-Frankish maiden," Willehad corrected.

"By Satan's breath! Lothar fumed. "She has Karolus's blood. When we eliminate the rest of his progeny, legitimate or not, she will be our living talisman to control unrepentant Franks."

"That was my plan, Count Lothar," Willehad said.

"And a good one, bishop. I just don't favor reliance on Avars in such matters."

"I understand," Willehad said. "You must trust in God's will."

Lothar laughed. "Don't speak of God's will to me. This scheme is man's will. That's the only reason I agreed to it."

"As you say, Lord Lothar," Vulmar said. "But I have met with the priests of the Saxons and the Avars. They agree we can find common ground. If we accept some of their ways, they can adopt a Christianity of sorts. They agree it can help us conquer new lands for the 'new' Christendom."

Lothar grinned as he twisted the ring on his finger. "Why, that's the longest speech I have heard from you, exorcist. I believe that is a good sign."

Envoy of the Lord

Willehad smiled. "Of course, it is, Count Lothar. In the 'new' Christendom, you shall be emperor, and I shall be…"

"Be what, Willehad? Tell me your secret desire. Will you be my archbishop?"

"No, your pope," Willehad said in a low voice as if the pope in Rome might hear him.

"Well, that will make the Lombards happy once more," Lothar said. "But what of the Byzantine emperor?"

"The Avars are anxious to take him and his city. Once the treasure stolen by Karolus's son is returned to their secret trove, they can buy the support of the eastern tribes and perhaps the Caliphate too."

"So, we are to treat and ally with infidels?" Lothar asked.

"Is that no more than our own lord, Karolus, had us do in Andalusia?"

"In the end, they are no more dangerous than the Arians or the followers of Pelagius," Vulmar said.

"So they would have us think," Lothar said. "I am not so sure. But it doesn't matter now. Like Caesar, we have cast the die. Have you heard from the Saxon queen? The witch they call Udela?"

"Why, I have met with her myself, Lord Lothar," Willehad said.

Lothar looked startled. "You have met with her? And why didn't you tell me this?"

"I was going to tell you in good time, Lord. She is more beautiful than any woman I have ever seen, if a humble priest's opinion matters in such things," Willehad said.

"You are no priest, Willehad, nor humble. When did you meet her?"

"Why, she came to the abbey, Count Lothar."

"What? Have you profaned the abbey with the presence of a pagan witch? That is sacrilege, is it not, Bishop?" Lothar's sarcasm was not veiled.

"We will now be the deciders on what is sacrilege and what is orthodox, Count Lothar. In any case, if this plan unfolds as envisioned, I propose you marry her and seal the alliance."

"But I have a wife."

"Things can be arranged, Count Lothar. Queen Udela is most intelligent and wily. And she does have great powers," Willehad said.

"Powers? Such as?"

"Powers that cannot be explained just yet, Count Lothar," Vulmar said. "I have observed them. I am trying to understand them. As of yet, I cannot."

"What have you seen?" Lothar looked nervous.

"She can summon thunder from heaven with her fingers. The burst of the sun and the crack of lightning," Vulmar said.

"My God, she really is a witch, or the devil's consort," Lothar said.

Willehad laughed. "As her king, that will only make people fear you the more, Count Lothar."

"I have sent Father Mannix off to seduce new villages," Vulmar said.

"Mannix? He failed to trap the *missus*," Lothar said.

"Yes, but his skills in recruiting Christians who are weak in their faith are remarkable," Willehad explained.

Lothar sulked. "Would that he had taken Melchior."

"True. But now we can make a better example of him."

"Unless he turns the tables on us," Lothar said.

"My agent knows almost nothing of our grand plan. So I think Melchior will be sufficiently in the dark so to stumble his way to our purpose," Willehad said.

"Do you have something particular in mind, Lord Bishop?" Lothar asked.

"Why yes, Lord Lothar. I thought it fitting to invite him to your wedding to Queen Udela. Perhaps we will celebrate it at the abbey itself."

"What of the Abbot of Fulda? What does Baugulf know of this? Does he approve?" Lothar was concerned.

"Our dear abbot is turned to things spiritual, not elemental. I have succeeded in cutting him off from contact outside the abbey."

"Is he a fool?"

"No, Lord. Truth is, he is rather ill. As are his closest retainers." Willehad looked at Vulmar, who nodded.

"What mischief is this?" Lothar asked.

"Queen Udela instructed me in some potions, My Lord," Vulmar said. "They dim the senses enough to control most thought beyond simple things. The abbot and his entourage are in prayer and fasting – much fasting. They are confined to a small part of the abbey."

"And the other monks?" Lothar asked. The twists in Willehad's schemes made him nervous.

"They go about their business. Unsuspecting for now," Vulmar said.

"How much longer will this trick go on?"

"Not much longer, Count Lothar," Willehad said.

Lothar tugged his beard and regarded the situation. "Very well. When do I meet my bride?"

"She will meet with you at the full moon. That is their way," Vulmar said.

"Their way? This is about our way!" Lothar said.

"It is about a new way, My Lord," Willehad said. "In all, it will be a better way. Our king-and-emperor would want mass conversions to Christianity for these simple folk. We propose accommodation and nuance in our approach."

Lothar gulped his ale and drummed his fingers on the oak table. "You realize that I may be the only paladin who could turn his cheek at such things."

"That is why I approached you, after all. You are a man of wisdom and vision."

Lothar nodded.

"But I do have other nobles," Willehad said.

"Others? You never mentioned others."

"One has recently been lured to our side. He will be invaluable when we begin the new baptisms."

"What do you mean?"

"I mean, a new type of religion needs new customs. He, and you, will be among the first to receive such baptism. A mix of the old and the new, shall we say. Just a ritual. For the masses of Christians and pagans."

"And who is this nobleman?"

"Why you can meet him yourself, Count Lothar."

"He will be here tomorrow. He is returning from a meeting with Dgno."

"Dgno? The Avar khagan? That spawn of Satan? I thought him dead," Lothar said.

Willehad laughed and patted his belly. "He prefers it that way. But our good exorcist also resurrected him for us. And well for us he has returned from the dead. After all, he has Karolus's daughter."

***

The stench from the putrid swamps still clung to them when they reached the drier ground. Jurchen led them up a steep, heavily wooded path. Audeon rode beside him. "How much longer to Fulda, abbot?"

"Oh, it depends, Lord Audeon. If we recklessly make our way in a couple of days. But I plan an indirect route to ensure we have no more surprises."

Their evening camp lay in a small valley surrounded by dark fir trees. The slopes were steep with large rocks that spread like veins. The place looked oddly familiar to Melchior. As the men made camp, he decided to walk about. He sensed he had once fought there. But the fighting was with fire and thunder. He closed his eyes and envisioned himself with gray-clad men... shooting... rifles and other weapons... He heard voices... commands in German. He saw plumes of smoke everywhere and the sound of something... some things that moved but were neither men nor horses... nor ancient pachyderms. *What hell do I imagine?*

"What hell do I imagine?" he said out loud in German. Melchior dropped to his knees and began praying with his prayer beads, a special set blessed by the pope and presented in a ceremony by Karolus. It had a heavy chain and semi-precious jewels for beads.

"*Dominus*?" Father Thomas's voice spoke to him in Frankish. "What language do you speak?"

Melchior turned. "It is from a distant place and time, Father Thomas." His mind once more flooded with thoughts of his life in a different millennium. He remembered the war and his youth. He was beginning to recall more of the period after the war. But it faded as he tried to draw it in.

"Let me pray with you, *Dominus*," Thomas said. "It is better to pray with more than one voice."

Melchior gazed thoughtfully at the young monk. He saw a certain element in him he had thought forgotten in men: pure humility, devotion, and love. "Yes, Father Thomas. Let's pray together."

Their prayer was broken by the arrival of Jurchen. "Here you are, *Dominus*. And Father Thomas. We feared you lost, Thomas. The *Dominus* is an experienced traveler and warrior, but a poor monk like you from Britain would be a babe in these woods."

"I thought you said the woods are free of Saxons," Melchior said.

"Indeed, *Dominus*. The way is safe here. But one can't be too sure of anything, as you know."

"That is true, Jurchen. But I am praying. Send Detleff for me when the food is prepared."

Later, they supped on rabbit and quail Spad and Wala snared in the forest.

"Our hunters bagged a modest feast," Melchior said.

"This high up there is little else. The wild goats are almost all killed off here and the deer cannot feed themselves enough," Jurchen said as they sipped wine around a small fire. The rest of the band slept, except for Gaetano, who stood watch.

"Tell me about Thomas," Melchior said. "He's Irish?"

"Yes, he is from Ireland. However, he trained under Alcuin of Britain, who brought him to our Lord Karolus's court. When Alcuin returned to Britain some years ago, Thomas stayed on and served as a teacher at court under the new master, Clement. Clement is also from Ireland, so they got on very well. He is a brilliant but quiet fellow. Like both his masters."

"I see. Well, Britons and Irish are quiet and clever folk," Melchior said.

"Have you traveled there, *Dominus*?"

Melchior hesitated. He had a vision of traveling sailing past the British Isles on board a large ship that spat smoke, a vessel larger than any village he had seen in Frankland. His journey across the sea. He began to recall more before things slipped away.

"On a boat once," was all he said. "Not much to say of it."

They sat listening to the others' snores. Fromm had cut loose a stench as well. Melchior recalled other campfires. Both with men-at-arms and men armed with modern weapons. Weapons he was beginning to once more understand.

Suddenly, he sat upright. "Walk with me, Jurchen."

Melchior pulled on his leather boots and thrust his *Francisca* into his belt. He marched off into the forest with Jurchen trailing behind him.

They walked for more than an hour. Jurchen stumbled in the dark, tripping over roots and stones. Melchior stalked along as if he knew where he was going. They halted at a high promontory over a wide, bending river.

Melchior quickly turned and grabbed Jurchen by the throat. He drew his *Francisca*. "When were you going to tell me, Jurchen? When the slopes were covered with Saxons? Or the valleys flush with Avars? Or maybe both?"

"*Dominus*, I assure you I intend to avoid…"

Melchior rubbed the sharp ax blade against Jurchen's ear. "I can filet snails with this or cut open the heavy skull of an ox. I can take down a bear or a stag with one blow. I can make you cry for your mother's womb before you die. I can arrange it so you can watch yourself die. You'll hold your balls and your entrails and cry for whatever mother spawned you!"

"*Dominus*, no!" Jurchen struggled, but Melchior tightened his grip.

"I'll do all those things if you don't speak truthfully, false priest. I know Fulda is one day down that river. Why did you lie of it to Audeon?"

"Because it is no lie, *Dominus*."

Blood oozed from Jurchen's ear. Melchior sliced the thinnest slice but knew just where to draw the most blood for effect.

"Arrgh…"

"Tell me…"

"I… I was to lead you to Vulmar. In the forest. That was my command from the bishop."

"Yes. The archbishop mentioned he had a man. An exorcist named Vulmar I was to meet. He had connections to the evil Saxon queen."

"I said the bishop. Not the archbishop. There are connections one should not have, *Dominus*. The so-called Father Mannix is Vulmar's acolyte. They hoped to trap and kill you. Or worse."

"Worse?"

"Are there not worse things than death?"

Melchior relaxed his grip and lowered his blade. "Talk."

"My bishop… Willehad… has turned to evil ways. I don't know his scheme exactly, but I overheard him discussing a new Rome."

"Well, that is what our Lord Karolus has created," Melchior said.

"That is not what he meant—his new Rome. I heard the words distinctly. Christendom of pagans and Christians united in an accommodation."

"What sort of accommodation?"

"I don't know. I don't know," Jurchen began to sob. He buried his head in his hands and fell to his knees.

"Stand up and look me in the eye."

Melchior grabbed his shoulders and roughly yanked him to his feet.

"I don't know much more than that. But I know the Abbot of Fulda is not part of it and may well be in danger. I hoped at first to find a way to say more. You are a good man, *Dominus*. While I am not. I realize now I have sinned against everything. My blood may be Saxon, but I am a true Christian if no true priest."

"Why did you lead us here? This close to Fulda, then?"

"Because this place is inaccessible to them, yet close. I thought I would avoid Fulda, but I now know the solution is at Fulda. Here, you have a sanctuary until you decide on a course of action. Thirty leagues beyond are the Saxon lands of the queen they call Udela."

"Meaning what?"

"I don't know. But she must play a role. They say she has magical powers. Perhaps she has bewitched them."

"I don't believe in witchcraft."

"But you must surely know evil powers walk the earth and are seeking to upend all that is good," Jurchen said.

"That, I do believe. And they always will. All we can do as Christians and men is to seek God's grace. And pray he provides us the means and will to resist evil." Melchior could not comprehend why he said such a thing.

"You sound like our Lord and Emperor Karolus," Jurchen said.

"King-and-emperor," Melchior said.

"You forget, *Dominus*, I am Saxon by birth. Karolus is my emperor, but not my king."

Melchior scratched his face as he considered what Jurchen meant. "So, your loyalties are divided?"

"I did not say that. But as a Saxon, my loyalty is limited. That is why I did not reveal my role in Bishop Willehad's plot. For that, I beg forgiveness from God and mercy from you. I pledge my love to God and my loyalty to you. I should like to shed this clerical garb and wear the *brunia* as a warrior, under you."

Melchior rubbed his chin. "I will consider the idea, Abbot Jurchen. But not until this journey is completed. Until then, I find it useful for you to wear the robe of a priest."

Jurchen dropped to his knees and clutched his hands. "As you say, *Dominus*."

"You may rise, Jurchen."

Jurchen stood, and Melchior placed a hand on his shoulder. "I will stand no more deceptions or tricks. Against me, that is. But I must send you into danger. The devil's work is about us. I'll need my own priest, even a false one, to stop it."

"You have Father Thomas. He's a true monk and priest."

"You're more the sort of priest I need for this work. Now tell me, how many men does Lothar have at his disposal?"

"I do not know, *Dominus*. A few hundred footmen. Maybe fifty mounted men-at-arms."

"How loyal are they to Lothar?"

"I don't know."

"I must know. If I can entreat enough men to abandon their count, it could make all the difference."

"Why are you saying this to me?"

"Because you will go among them and seek out a certain Frankish warrior, named Stilicho. He rode with me in two campaigns. He has at least a band of fifty men pledged to him—all mounted men-at-arms. I will dictate a message for you to bring to him. You must memorize it."

"But what pretext can I use to go back without you? They will want to know where you went."

"You can tell them what I am about to tell you."

"What is that, *Dominus*?"

"That I am awaiting reinforcements from Karolus before arriving. That I have orders from our king-and-emperor to ride against the evil Saxon queen. That I expect Count Lothar's full support in this journey. Tell them I sent you because, although you are a Saxon, I trust you as a priest and abbot."

"And why would they believe all of this, *Dominus*?"

Melchior smiled grimly. "Because it is all true."

It was not all true. But Melchior needed to confuse his foes with possibilities, real or imagined.

Chapter 10

The Thuringian March

The black mare trotted, spraying clumps of dark earth with a steady clop-clop of her large hooves. As Udela rode she eyed her people. *My Saxons!* They were built strongly and rough. She liked that in them. She needed a strong and rough people. The wooden village, her capital, sprawled along the Zorge river plain (today's Nordhausen) between the flat and fertile area of *Goldene Aue* in the south and the foothills of the Harz Mountains.

This once ramshackle collection of log cabins had slowly grown as word of the great queen's powers, temporal and otherwise, spread across the Saxon tribes. Although most of the dwellings were neatly thatched huts with steep roofs, many larger buildings had sprung up about the queen and her entourage. The largest of these wooden structures had brazen doors and a red dragon's head pendant billowing high above it. The pendant marked it as the great hall of Queen Udela.

She lifted her face and let the gentle rain spray it. She drew a breath. The rain had not driven many of her Saxons indoors. They were a forest people at heart and thrived in nature's embrace. Forced to restrict hunting, they had begun to adjust to a less nomadic life. Still, many hoped her power would clear the land of Franks, and they could go back to their old ways.

"Bow down, when our queen rides past your hut," cried her acolytes, who ran ahead, swatting at tribesmen with special clubs, carved and marked to ward off evil spirits.

Hajo, an older Saxon, did not move quickly enough and was struck on the back. He fell forward into the muddy ruts with a grunt. Few looked askance. Most Saxons welcomed a leader who demanded full obedience.

"That old turd is one less mouth to feed when the *Volk* move west," said Eberger, chief of Udela's most powerful Saxon tribe, the Nabo. He was short but powerfully built and had a temper as ugly as his face, horribly scarred by a fight with a bear. "Frankland will soon regret its depredations on our tribes."

Udela smiled teasingly. "More than Frankland, Eberger."

Eberger gave a puzzled look.

She realized he was a simple, brutish warrior and hunter, nothing more. "There is wealth beyond Karolus's realm, Eberger. Why not have it all?"

"I know, My Queen. But do we have enough warriors to expand beyond the Frankish domains? The Nabo number but five thousand warriors — he Simi and the Thuringians as many. Karolus, if he summons the levy, can bring more than five times the number."

"Dgno brings us well over one thousand mounted Avars. They are angry and hungry for revenge on Karolus. But what matter? I plan to bring Frankland down from within."

Eberger tugged his beard. "What do you mean, My Queen?"

"We are destroying the moral fiber of Karolus's people. I begin with his leaders and scare the peasants into leaving their false religion and return to the ways of old."

"Just tell me when and where I can strike. Sending small bands is fine for spoils and sport. But my warriors ache for battle with their hated enemy."

She could tell he did not understand. Udela would not reveal to the chieftain that she hoped for the opposite. She wanted to subjugate with minimal bloodshed. Not from any goodness of heart but from pure strategy and the need to expand the fight beyond Frankland. "I assure you they will have many opportunities to slake their thirst for blood and plunder."

Eberger's eyes lit. "Which is why my men will die for you, My Queen."

Around them, the clash of blades could be heard. She insisted the Saxons trained in scores of mock battles. Curses and shouts filled the air. Men both bloodied and muddied slipped and slid as they struggled on the sodden earth. Women and children cheered and offered mugs of ale to quench the dry throats of the youngbloods.

"Your warriors are impressive," Udela said. They had ridden to a small mound built up expressly for the queen to observe the mock battles and address the tribes. Despite the rain and clouds, more than half the Nabo warriors could be seen thrusting spears, swords, and *Seaxes*.

Eberger crossed his arms proudly. "We are the last real Saxons. Our cousins across the sea left Saxonland as much from fear as the plunder of Britain. The Nabo stayed to fight for their ancient lands."

Udela gave him a sly glance. "Under me, the Nabo will take other people's ancestral lands. And not just the Franks. Those who convert will provide us masses of warriors to follow in the dust of your noble Nabo."

"And those who do not?"

Her face tightened. "Those not fit as slaves shall slake the thirst of the gods."

Eberger raised his *Seaxe* in salute. "You are great, My Queen!"

She raised her long arm in a movement that made the five silver bangles adorning it clang. Immediately, a young muscular Saxon in leather and fur approached and bowed his head. "At your command, My Queen."

"Order the horns blown, Alager."

The powerful young warrior began barking commands to a dozen equally powerful warriors. Two of them raised long ox horns and drawing powerful breaths, blew into them, sending a deep and hollow sound across the field. The warriors began to put aside their weapons and the bands, clans, and tribes assembled before the queen.

"The chief of your guards is smitten with his queen," Eberger said with a laugh. "You should rut with him, My Queen. Alager is our most powerful fighter."

Udela stifled a frown and threw back her long, golden hair. "How do you know I haven't, Eberger. Do not mistake our alliance for friendship, or familiarity.

He lowered his gaze from her smoldering blue eyes. "Accept my humble apology, My Queen. I only meant that Alager is…"

"I know who the chief of my guardians is! A powerful and fearless warrior who will cut down a wild bear at my command. Don't tempt me, Eberger."

Udela knew her power came in no small part from hiding her feelings from those she would rule.

Before all the warriors could assemble a commotion erupted in one of the warbands. Yells and shouts, threats, and curses were heard above the din of the multitude.

"What's that noise? What are they doing?" Udela asked. She knew the answer, of course. She knew her Saxons.

"I'll send some men to find out," Eberger said.

"No, let Tilo bring them to me."

Eberger's face showed anger and disappointment. "He is chief of the Eucii. Not pure Saxon."

"You mean, not Nabo," Udela said. "I need *all* the tribes if we are to rule the world. Besides, some say these Eucii are the original Saxons. The first to move down from Nordland."

"They should not be trusted, My Queen," Eberger said.

"The decision is mine. They may be few, but I need these warriors."

Tilo arrived with a band of men who looked savage, even among the savages.

"Find out what the disturbance is and bring me the violators of my peace," Udela commanded.

Tilo bowed and left without a word.

"I favor quiet obedience," Udela said.

Eberger swallowed. "As you wish, My Queen."

The fifty warriors Tilo led were the best of his diminished sub-tribe, which numbered only a few hundred. Among the first to migrate from their Nordic homeland centuries before, the Eucii had been reduced by fighting the Celts, Allemani, Chatti, Romans, and Huns. Though now few remained, they were the most ferocious fighters, especially against mounted warriors like the Huns.

From her mound, Udela saw them locate the source of the disturbance, a dozen warriors beating each other with the flat of swords and axes. The crowd parted at the arrival of the Eucii.

Tilo grabbed one of the warriors by his long hair and lifted him like a doll. "He who disturbs the queen's peace is guilty of treason!"

"True Saxons don't take orders from Eucii," the offender spat. His phlegm caught Tilo in the face. Despite his gray hair, Tilo had the strength of a young man. His fist crushed the man's stomach with a blow that reached his spine.

"Oooh…" The warrior reached for his *Seaxe* but Tilo grabbed his wrist and snapped it.

"Aaargh…. Arrrgh…

The Euci yanked spears and *Seaxes* from the others and shoved them through the throng of Saxons. Some cheered the Euci. But most cursed them as outsiders and interlopers.

"Pigs!"

"Devils!"

"Sons of Hunnish whores!"

Tilo's warriors ignored the insults and marched stoically toward the mound where the queen waited.

"We found the men who dared ignore your trumpet," Tilo proclaimed.

Udela nodded and gazed at the assembled multitude. Thousands of Saxon warriors and their families waited in anticipation. For several long moments, the only sound was the wind and the soft pelting of the rain on hundreds of muddy puddles.

The queen spoke with a commanding voice, "If we are to march to the ends of the earth, it must be as one people. These curs ignored my trumpet, which means they ignored my command. What should I do with such pigs?"

A cacophony of replies rippled across the gray field.

"Kill them!"

"Torture them!"

"No! Spare them!"

Thousands moaned or shouted encouragement. They sounded like braying cattle approaching a stream on a warm summer day.

"My Queen, these men are from a powerful clan of the Nordalbiginians. Their chief is a distant kinsman to Widukind. To treat them harshly might divide loyalty when we most need it," Eberger advised.

Udela raised her hand. "I have taken that into account, Eberger." She turned to the crowd and raised both hands into the sky and chanted in a language they could not understand, "O gods of old, O Wotan!"

Immediately the throng began to chant, "Wotan! Wotan! Wotan!"

She silenced them with a wave of her arm. Many ducked or covered their heads in response. They feared she might throw her thunderbolts at them, as she had at her first appearance.

"I have heard from Wotan." Udela's voice was measured. "He is displeased by these lazy dogs who would challenge my rule. It is at Wotan's pleasure we march as one to the ends of the earth. This spawn of dogs must pay Wotan's price."

"*Wergild*! *Wergild*!" The chant reverberated across the sodden plain.

Udela raised her hands once more. "The *Wergild* is the recompense for honorable killing. Their insolence dishonors Wotan... and me. They shall be taken to the tree of life!"

Chaos began to erupt but then a strange silence followed.

Eberger gave Udela a look. "Are you certain?"

She rolled her eyes towards the distance.

Tilo's men dragged the victims, leather boots sloshing through the deep mud, to a large oak tree standing ominously at the edge of the field. Over sixty-feet high, it had no other trees or shrubs around it for over a furlong. The Saxons considered such a singular tree as the *Irminsul*. The sacred pillar of life.

Suddenly, one victim, an older chief, reached for the *Seaxe* in his captor's belt. "Wotan!" he cried. Before anyone could stop him, slashed open his captor's side, spilling gore into the mud.

The warrior, a sub-chief, staggered back in pain. Four powerful Euci warriors seized the assailant and carried him on their shoulders, writhing like a serpent, to the tree.

There, the Saxon host formed a large square over three furlongs on each side. Udela watched as four massive black oxen were led forward.

"Begin with the leader of this scurrilous pack," Udela commanded.

The Euci warriors bound each of the gray-haired chief's limbs to an ox. He remained impassive the entire time.

With the last knot tied, Udela spoke, "You weak spawn of the Nordalbiginians die because of your arrogance, disobedience, and indiscipline. I demand absolute obedience and discipline!"

The horn trumpeted a mournful sound. Each ox was led forward by two powerful Euci. The oxen moved ponderously, with slow but powerful steps. Very slowly, the ropes stretched and grew stiff. The limbs and muscles of the chief also stretched tautly. His face grew white as his limbs snapped. But he made no sound.

The crowd resounded with gasps and cries with each crunch of the chief's limbs.

"See, My Queen, how a brave Saxon dies," Eberger said. "Show some mercy."

The crowd took up the cry," Mercy! Mercy! Spare a brave chief!"

Udela simply waved her hand. As one, the warriors slapped the haunches of the oxen. The powerful beasts lurched forward. The snap and pop of sinew, tendon, and bone crackled across the field. The throng stood mesmerized as the oxen continued, dragging the chief's arms and legs with them. His head and torso lay at the foot of the great tree.

"I have granted him the mercy of a swift dismemberment, o Saxons. Thus, to those who fail me in obedience and discipline. The others are spared to lead the attack in our next battle."

The entire field erupted in a roar of approval.

"Well spoken, My Queen," Eberger said. "You have shown a perfect blend of mercy and discipline."

Udela looked at him with narrow eyes. "Do not question my justice in the future, Eberger."

A short time later, Alager reported to Udela. "My Queen, visitors have arrived." He pointed through the mists across the river where a band of riders could be seen coming at full gallop.

"Those are Avars!" Eberger said. "I'll form up the warbands."

"No!" Udela said. "See the pennant."

Tilo stoked his hoary beard. "A red scythe on a white background? Who is it?"

"I was told to wait for the red scythe. So I must assume it is our ally," Udela said.

"Dgno?" Eberger asked.

"Dgno, Khagan of the Balaton Avars and a descendant of the great Avar Khagan, Bayan I," Udela replied.

Alager looked agitated. Avars were feared by all Germanic peoples. "What are your orders, My Queen?"

Udela placed her hand on his powerful bicep and allowed it to linger. "Tell my chief servant to prepare a feast. Find suitable shelter for the visitors and invite them to supper with me when they have rested."

Alager scurried off. Udela watched him as she spoke to Eberger, "Have Tilo's men stay within proper distance of the visitors. They may be allies, but they are also Avars."

Eberger nodded and smiled. "Spoken like a wise and powerful queen."

***

Dgno and six companions strutted into the grand hall of the large timbered building that served as Udela's palace and court. They walked with the swagger nomadic warriors always display, eager to conquer new lands and enjoy new sources of booty. Dgno was a nomadic chief in search of a new kingdom. He moved like a panther and his eyes had the glint of a predator searching for its next meal.

"Welcome to the court of Queen Udela," an older Saxon greeted. He was burly and white-haired with half his nose cut off. His face was leather brown from years of sun and wind, broken only by ugly white sun-blotches that appeared like great moths across his face and forehead. He wore a fine red tunic with leather armor and a large *Seaxe* hung at his side. "I am Bruno, Chief of the Issepi clan, and chamberlain of our queen's palace."

Dgno grunted. His head moved side to side as he drank in his surroundings and more importantly, assessed the tactical situation. He wore a conical helmet of bronze covered in leopard skin that came to a point. As with most Avar warriors, chain mail hung from his helmet and down his neck to his shoulders. The same mail covered his lower face and nose, revealing dark slits. He wore an embroidered cream brown kaftan to his knees. Under the kaftan, chain mail swathed his legs down to his thick leather riding boots. A well-used curved sword jangled from his belt, almost touching the ground.

"Take me to the queen you call Udela," Dgno said. He spoke a Germanic dialect that was understandable.

"You speak our language," Bruno said. "That is good."

"I have had many Germanic slaves to teach me," Dgno spat. He had little use for foot warriors and wanted to make it clear.

"I must take your arms," Bruno said. He reached for the long-curved sword hanging from Dgno's belt.

A blade flashed. Dgno's nine-inch dagger sliced a pieced of Bruno's fingertip sending blood spurting down the blade.

The old warrior made no sound and withdrew his hand. Dgno wiped the blood from the blade on his tongue. "I have tasted better blood."

His men laughed. But Bruno merely stared phlegmatically

Eberger approached. "The queen says our guests may keep their arms, but they must remove their helmets. Lead them forward, Bruno."

Helmets were removed grudgingly and the Avars followed Bruno slowly down the hall, the hobnails of their high boots scraping the roughhewn stone floor. Warriors of

Tilo's Eucii tribe lined each side. Udela made sure the fighters, as cold-blooded as the Avars, remained at hand. The shutters of the large windows were thrown open. It was nearly dark, so the high wooden beamed ceiling was lit by a hundred lamps.

Dgno saw the queen sitting on a simple bench on a large wooden dais before him. A line of Alager's guard stood below the dais. Another rank stood before the heavy curtains in the back of the dais. Alager stood directly behind his queen. Dgno halted ten paces before the dais. He and his men looked warily about.

"My men have ridden long and hard to reach this place. I hope you make it worth our while," Dgno said coldly. He was impressed with the looks of this strange woman.

The Saxons in the hall were startled at the cold and impertinent tone taken by the eastern prince.

But Udela smiled broadly. "I am pleased with your eagerness, My Lord. It bodes well for all our people."

"I hope so as well. My warriors are as eager as me." Dgno hung his helmet from a hook on his belt. His entourage did the same. The Avar khagan eyed the Saxon queen with as much lust as interest. He had never seen anything or anyone as beautiful.

"Please join me at the dinner table, o khagan. My cooks have prepared a simple but robust feast for your men. Here is Eberger, chief of one of our great tribes. And that one is Alager, the chief of my bodyguard."

Dgno followed her to the long table and took a place next to Udela. Eberger sat on the other side. Alager's eyes did not leave Dgno. The other Avars took seats at the ends of the table, although one, a bodyguard, took a position next to the khagan.

Servants brought food and ale, wine, and mead as well. Several jesters appeared and began a series of acts to entertain the throng. They danced, juggled, and performed all kinds of somersaults. The crowd laughed and clapped as they rolled their eyes and sang and pantomimed. Even the Avars were amused, but not Dgno.

"Where did you find such fools? I should take them with me," Dgno said. He marveled that these people would demean themselves in such a manner. No Avar would play the fool.

"I found them in a Frank town we sacked. But they come from a place they call Eire," Udela said. "Eberger found them. We need fools such as these to forget the grave problems we face."

"They were in the employ of a fat Christian bishop," Eberger said. "We killed him and his priests. But these two were spared when they performed to save the lives of the Christians in the town. I like to think of them as human gold although I would have preferred real gold."

"I agree, Saxon. Gold cannot deceive. It cannot change its nature." Dgno's dark eyes bore into Eberger like a javelin taking a buck. Dgno recognized his gaze and comment discomforted the Saxon savage chief.

Eberger reached for his ale and quaffed it.

"Life is more than gold and jewels, although I cannot have enough of them," Udela said, as she bit daintily into a peacock leg.

Dgno took a joint of pork and devoured it as if it were a trifle. He then took a heady draught of the ale. "Saxons make good pork and good ale. Warrior's food." He grabbed another side of the pork ribs and sank his pointed teeth into them.

"Save your appetite for the main course, o khagan," Udela said.

"You may call me Dgno."

"Very well, Dgno. Call me Queen Udela."

"We Avars have no queens. Women do our bidding and raise young warriors."

"Saxon women do both. But a Saxon woman can plow a field and swing an ax, and not always to hew wood."

"What does your husband say to that?" Dgno motioned to Eberger.

"He? Eberger is the chieftain of the most powerful Saxon tribe. But he is not my husband." Udela stole a glance at Alager. *If I must choose one...*

"So, you are a free woman?" Dgno asked. He marveled at her light cream-colored skin, long golden hair, and curves that seemed perfectly suited to a woman her size. She was as tall as an Avar warrior. That pleased him. *What sons I could breed with her.*

"I am a very costly woman, Dgno."

Dgno smiled for the first time, a smile he knew looked more disarming than his scowl. "I prefer costly women. It makes things... interesting. What is your price?"

"At least 1,000 Avar horsemen willing to die for me and my cause." Udela's blue eyes gazed fiercely into Dgno's dark slits.

"I have almost 2,000 when they are all assembled. But now they are riding over Frankland as we agreed in our letters. When you are ready, I can gather them, to begin our real efforts."

Udela stroked his sleeve. "I knew that the Khagan of the Balaton would prove the greatest warrior chief in the land. A chief that will lead us to victory over the Franks, their allies, and eventually, even their enemies."

The servants brought out a great silver platter with a stuffed and roasted calf that sizzled and dripped fat down its sides.

"The main course has arrived, Dgno. You and your men must eat your fill. Then we can retire to my chambers and discuss our plans."

Hours later Dgno followed Udela through a series of rooms festooned in typical Saxon style: ornate and colorful carvings of the gods and symbols of the ancient Saxon tribes. Alager walked before them with four of his best men right behind. Dgno's companions were allowed to engage in more drinking. Several young slave girls were brought to them for their amusement. The rest of the Saxon throng departed for their homes.

"This is my favorite room," Udela said as they entered her antechamber. The floors were covered in furs and a sofa of deep golden fabric sat before a fireplace. The fire was small but took the chill from the room. A score of candles glowed brightly.

"Truly a queen's room," Dgno remarked. "But My Queen would be content in an ox-hide tent so long as we are on the march."

"I am not your queen, Dgno. Nor are we yet on the march. But when we are, there shall be palaces and grand demesnes for my taking. A tent is for savages."

"And for warriors, My Queen Udela. We Avars never forget that." He sat on the sofa next to her. Her perfume was sweet, yet fresh.

Alager's face flushed with disapproval. He handed her a rolled-up scroll.

"Thank you, Alager. You may leave. Have you men stand guard outside."

Alager stifled a scowl. "As you command, My Queen."

When he left, Udela opened the scroll. "Can you read, Dgno?"

"Avar khagans have scribes for such things."

"Well fortunately then, this is a map. I read some Latin. Saxons do not care much for writing. But I have a scribe as well. A Saxon priest who is in our employ. He went on a special trip for me and was able to find this."

"What is it?" Dgno was growing impatient. He decided he would bed this woman as much for control of her as the pleasure. He tired of her drawn-out manner.

"It shows all the important Frankish forts between the Rheine and the Iberian mountains and as far south as Rome. This map also contains secrets only Karolus and his *missi* know. This will prove invaluable in our conquest of the Franks."

"I prefer to launch my horsemen. They have an instinct for finding the enemy without the enemy finding them."

"A valuable skill, Dgno. But can they find this and..."

Dgno placed a coarse hand on her soft wrist. "Enough games. What is on this scroll that should delay me here?"

"I am not one of your slave girls. Remove your hand."

He gripped her wrist even tighter and pulled her towards him. "I'll have a Saxon queen before I make any plans with her."

Udela slipped a small pouch of silk from under her blouse and tossed it on the candle before them. The pouch flared and then exploded with a bang and a puff of black smoke. Dgno released her and dropped to the floor, hiding his head under the sofa.

"What evil bit of sorcery is this, My Queen?"

"You have heard rumors that I am a witch?"

"Yes."

"Well here is the proof of it. I have powers that can send you to Avar hell in a trice. Cross me again or try to have your way with me and you shall disappear in a cloud of black smoke. Do you understand?"

"Yes, My Queen." Dgno was fearful of the strange power. But his pride made him angry and resentful of this woman.

"Good. Then rise, Dgno, Khagan of the Balaton Avars, and pay heed to my plan. I do not intend to repeat myself."

Dgno stood up. His slit-like eyes scanned the room – determined to kill anyone who witnessed his groveling before the woman.

"No one is watching, Dgno. Now that you know of my powers, I expect you to ensure your savage horsemen are obedient. They may pillage where I allow it… rape only when I allow it."

Dgno bowed his head and glanced sideways. "As you command, Udela. I have sworn never to serve a queen. But I may serve a witch. Especially one so beautiful."

She smiled. "I accept your compliment and your fealty. Leave it at that. Now let me show you the real secrets this map contains. One, in particular, you might find fascinating."

"And what is that?"

"Karolus's son raided the secret treasure of the Avars years ago. They robbed your people of three centuries worth of booty taken from the Byzantine east and Roman south."

Dgno nodded. "Also from the Bulgars, the Huns, and Turkic tribes too obscure to name."

"And from the Mohammedans," Udela said.

"Yes, and from the Mohammedans. What of it?"

"This map marks the locations of the trove. We'll need it back to succeed in our plan."

"You presume to use my people's birthright?"

"Yes. But in the end, they will have riches beyond what the trove contains. We will control everything from the Pyrenees to the Bosporus. From Britain to Sicily. After destroying the Frankland, we turn south. Then east, to destroy the Byzantines. You will rule the east and I the west. The trove will help us bribe rulers along the way. Pay for mercenaries and ships. And to bring the entire Caliphate to our side."

"The Caliphate? Are you mad?" The Avars knew the power of the Mohammedan armies.

"No, I'm a witch. They will harry the Byzantines and the Franks while we devour the heart of Karolus's empire."

"He can summon 25,000 warriors. Between us we will have maybe 5, 000," Dgno said.

"We will seduce them from their religion and destroy them at their core. Many, once they abandon Christianity, will join us. Others will refuse to fight for a God they no longer believe in and a king they no longer trust."

"Go on, My Queen," Dgno said. He was now intrigued by the scheme.

"Almost half the towns and villages between Fulda and the Rhine are ours already. The Franks have apostatized quite nicely and discreetly. Mannix was a great help. The Bishop at Fulda as well. He is, in fact, not a true Christian, nor a real bishop."

"They say a holy man is in charge of the abbey at Fulda – Baugulf. What of him?" Dgno asked. He feared shamans and the like. Baugulf was described in the east as the great shaman.

"I have mysterious powers, as you now know. I sent a special wine as a gift to the bishop. His name is Willehad. The abbot is in a stupor and cannot leave his chambers. When the time is right, Count Lothar will make an offer to the remainder of the monks. I do not believe they will refuse."

Dgno wondered what this woman had done. "Lothar? The Frankish count at Fulda? He's a paladin of Karolus."

"Lothar will stand with us," Udela said.

Dgno was impressed, but still skeptical a woman could scheme so grandly. "Very well, My Queen. How many men can this Lothar raise?"

"He has a few hundred Frankish men-at-arms. Maybe half are mounted. But he will raise another 1,000. He has approached several nobles already." If they join us, we could have as many as 8,000 well-armed Saxons, Avars, and Franks. We will strike hard. Karolus will not know what hit him until it is too late."

"What? Doesn't he have spies? All rulers have spies."

"He uses his *Missi Dominici* instead of spies. Two of the three are dead."

"He must have some spies, still. You, Westerners, are fools."

"Perhaps he does. It matters not, now that you have the girl."

"How did you know that?" Dgno asked. *She really is a witch!*

"I was wondering when you were going to tell me of her. She must remain unharmed. Do you understand, Dgno? If your savages touch her, the black smoke you just witnessed will be greater. Great enough to send you and your savages back to the snake pits that spawned you."

Udela's words stirred Dgno's lust once again. "The girl is well treated. After all, she is my one guarantor that you will deal fairly with the Avars."

Udela tossed back her long golden plait and smiled. "It is good that we have checks and balances on each other. It makes our alliance more... realistic. United, Dgno, we shall conquer a world."

Dgno grinned like a jackal spotting a crippled zebra. "I do believe your scheme is mad and ferocious, Udela. But we Avars are also mad and ferocious. I like it almost as much as I want you."

Udela smiled a surprisingly fetching smile. "When we own the world, you can have anything you want Dgno, Khagan of the Balaton Avars... anything... except me."

***

The sun's rays turned everything bright and fresh, but already storm clouds could be seen gathering along the eastern horizon. The Avars swung their bandy legs into the air and mounted their sturdy eastern horses.

Dgno drew his coarse leather whip. "In one month, my war parties will be assembled in the great valley before Fulda."

"Will the girl be with you?" Udela said. Behind her, five hundred Saxons stood silently in battle array.

Dgno nodded. "So long as it is in the interest of the Avars, she lives."

Udela frowned. "So long as it is in the interest of the Saxons, she lives."

Dgno smiled a crooked smile beneath his mail. "Then we are agreed, my beautiful queen."

He reached for her hand but she withdrew it.

The Avar horsemen sat impassively through it all. They spoke no Germanic. The sky was leaden and low. A stiff wind snapped the pennants each carried. But the largest, Dgno's red scythe, snapped the loudest against the stiff wind.

Udela smiled grimly. "And the *missus*?"

Dgno looked into the dark sky. "If my ancestors are with us, I shall have the head of this *missus* on my spear point for you, My Queen. Perhaps then you will realize that I am the only man who can be worthy of your yearnings."

"Not love?" Udela asked mischievously.

Dgno regarded her a moment. This woman was different. "Avars do not love. We lust. But you are a queen who might break the oldest of Avar traditions."

Udela's eyes widened and her lips tightened. "Go now. In one month, the Saxons and Avars will meet at Fulda. From that moment, Karolus and his empire's days are numbered."

Chapter 11

Aachen

Mallobaudes struggled as he galloped the last few miles to the cathedral. He was late for his meeting. But he knew the archbishop would understand, once he explained. He gazed up at the leaden sky and caught rays of sunlight breaking through to the west. *A good omen.*

Two armed retainers guarded the portcullis up ahead. Mallobaudes reared his horse. "I have business with His Eminence."

"Your name?"

"Mallobaudes. His Eminence expects me."

"The archbishop is preparing to depart at dawn and wants no more visitors."

Mallobaudes's men-at-arms began to fumble at their sword hilts.

"Tell him Lord Mallobaudes is here on urgent business."

"I am sorry, Lord. But we have our orders."

Deacon Udo stood behind the portcullis, hands interlocked under his robe. "Let the lord pass. His retainers may take themselves to the stables and water the horses."

Mallobaudes dismounted and gave his reins to his squire.

"Follow me, Lord," Udo said.

They walked in silence. To Mallobaudes's surprise, Udo did not lead him to the archbishop's chambers but a chapel at the back end of the cathedral gardens. The chapel was not much more than a log hut with a large wooden cross rising above the entrance. The roof was heavy thatch. The windows had heavy shutters with no adornments. Once inside, Udo threw open the shutters and solemnly lit the candles.

"His Eminence shall join you immediately following *vespers*," Udo said. "Until then, pray the *Pater Noster*."

"I have no beads." For Mallobaudes, religion was a ritual, not a spiritual practice.

Udo handed Mallobaudes a small leather string with knots. "Now you may pray, Lord."

Mallobaudes swallowed. "Pray? Pray for what?"

"Pray for Frankland, Lord. Or your soul."

"But *Vespers* is not for four hours, priest."

"Then pray *Nones*. And I am a deacon, not a priest, Lord." Udo turned and left.

The evening twilight turned dark. Mallobaudes, who had dozed while trying to pray, stirred when the door to the chapel opened. Instinctively, he reached for his long sword.

"We'll have no swordplay in God's house," Archbishop Angilram said. His portly frame almost filled the doorway. "I see Udo was once more sparing with the beeswax."

A servant who had accompanied the archbishop rushed to light the rest of the candles. Soon the chapel was bright enough to see the understated design of the stations of the cross hewn out of solid wood, a few simple paintings, and a plain cross upon the altar. No tabernacle.

"Why the meeting in this swineherd's hut?" Mallobaudes sniffed.

"The chancellery has ears, Lord," Angilram replied. "In any event, this is my sanctuary from worldly worries. I communicate with our Lord here."

"I'm flattered." Mallobaudes sneered.

"Your messenger said you had important news. Why couldn't the messenger simply impart the news? I leave tomorrow at the beckoning of our Lord Karolus."

"Then I am glad I reached you in time. My cousin paid a visit to my lands."

Angilram's face darkened. "And why should your familial affairs be affairs of mine?"

"I am here to discuss the affairs of Frankland."

"You mean the Holy Roman Empire?"

"I'm a Frank. I care only for Frankland and Austrasia in particular."

"Such talk is dangerous. Karolus has rebuilt the empire that the Romans lost."

"Then he should know it is in danger, and I think my cousin plays a role."

Angilram eyed him. "You don't like your cousin. You never have."

"He made me lame."

"God's will made you lame. He was merely the instrument. What do you think he has done?"

"He said he was on a journey to visit Count Lothar."

"He told you that? What more did he say?"

"Nothing. But I believe Melchior might be plotting treason, or worse!"

Angilram grunted. "Indeed. Treason with whom?"

"I saw him meet with a priest." Mallobaudes lied.

"He has two priests, Abbot Jurchen and Father Thomas."

"Not them, with a priest named Mannix." Mallobaudes hoped the planned lie would gain a response.

"Mannix? That name is often repeated," Angilram mused.

"He's Saxon, isn't he? That's reason enough."

"Perhaps. But he is a Christian. I have had Saxon priests here at the cathedral. Lord Karolus believes those who convert should be accepted into the realm."

"But the Saxons are the ancient enemy!"

"Karolus would say pagans are. Now tell me, what did they say? Where did they meet?"

"I followed my cousin when he left my lands. He headed east but then turned north, towards the land of the Saxons. They met at a river."

"What river?"

"A stream. It had no name." Mallobaudes's lies were transparent. But he was convinced Angilram believed them. He once recalled this same archbishop saying that one never knew when a conspiracy, even a false one, might come in handy. But would he take the bait?

Angilram thrust his thick fingers together nervously. "I see. What do you expect me to do with this information?"

"Tell our Lord Karolus that he needs a new *missus*. One he can trust." Mallobaudes almost exhaled the words in fear. Wrongly taken, or rightly, they could mean his doom.

"I have never liked your cousin, but I have always trusted him. Your words give me pause. But I would need to know much more to bring this to My Lord Karolus's attention. I sent the *missus* to Fulda at Karolus's orders. That is all I can say. But if you bring me proof of some perfidy or subterfuge by Melchior, I will reconsider."

"If I do find proof, I want permission to take action at once."

Angilram shook his head. "A *missus* can only be judged by his lord. But he may be the last *missus*. I am trying to convince My Lord Karolus that, in the long term, he should turn to the church for such things. Why send a Frankish warrior when a man of God can do the imperial business?"

"I see. And if some misfortune should occur to Melchior?"

Angilram grinned. "You do hate him. Perhaps I should hear your confession now."

"I would wait until another time. When I have done something worthy of confession to you."

Angilram nodded knowingly.

"But now tell me, Your Eminence, why do *you* dislike my cousin?"

Angilram's jowls turned red and shook like jelly. "Enough talk. You have permission to follow your cousin. Send reports back of any perfidy or treason. But if you are forced to act, you must have ample proof."

Mallobaudes bowed. "I will, your eminence."

"Melchior must fulfill the mission... this journey. After that... go."

***

When Mallobaudes left, Angilram stayed on to reflect. He was not certain why he disliked Melchior, other than he disliked the secular knights who strutted about the palaces and cathedrals, fornicating and fighting like bulls. He knew he could never change that. But when the last *missus* was gone, Angilram hoped his priests and deacons would be the means of managing an empire, a mighty Christian empire, free of pagans and heretics alike. Until then, he needed Melchior to do his work.

Udo arrived. "Everything is ready for the visit, Your Grace. Do you have any words for the coadjutor?"

"Arnulf has my guidance. Serve him as you would me."

"And when will you return?"

"When our lord-and-emperor returns, of course. He has deemed it essential I accompany him, now that Alcuin is gone. Such is his need for spiritual guidance."

Udo bowed his head. "Our king-and-emperor is great. But why do you take so many of the *milites* from the fort?"

"Karolus commanded it. These are dangerous times, as you know."

"Should you not wait until the *missus* returns? From his journey?"

"It is not for us to question Karolus's commands, Udo." Angilram did question this command. He did not want to leave the comforts of Aachen for a meeting with Karolus at some forsaken hunting camp.

"May I say one thing in all candor, Your Grace?"

Angilram nodded his assent.

"I do not trust this, Lord Mallobaudes."

Angilram's eyes widened, and his face flushed. "He is a blooded Frank of no inconsiderable means. And a low-born cleric such as you deign to draw suspicion on him?"

Udo grew white. "Why… why yes, Eminence. There's something about him."

"What is that something?" Angilram eyed the young cleric. Udo was clever.

"Treachery… but more. I get no sense of communion with the church."

Angilram pondered Udo's comment. *Yes, this can be used against Mallobaudes if he does not deliver on his promise. With no heir, his demesnes and Melchior's could easily pass to the church. Or to a suitable lord of my choosing.*

He smiled. "Well taken and noted, Udo. But he has his uses right now. Yet I am sure your point and your candor can be helpful under certain circumstances."

***

Bishop Willehad's Residence, Fulda

Jurchen slid from the saddle and gazed at the large structure before him. It lacked the palatial look usual to such residences. At the opposite end of the town, he could see the abbey. Unlike other bishops, Willehad had no cathedral or basilica. Instead, his residence served as his chancery, and a small church next to it afforded him a place to carry out his ecclesiastical duties. Fulda's large church was at the abbey itself.

To Jurchen's surprise, instead of a cleric, a band of Count Lothar's foot soldiers met him. Their leader spoke gruffly, "What is your business?"

"I'm Abbot Jurchen. Tell his eminence I have news for him."

A short time later, Jurchen was ushered into the courtyard. When Jurchen was last in Fulda, it was still under construction. Now it was finished, and although not large, it boasted granite pillars and a fountain with a large balustrade overlooking it. A servant led him into the building and then to the bishop's dining hall.

"Abbot Jurchen! A pleasant surprise. Come join me for our midday repast, fresh venison, and whiting."

Several other priests sat with the bishop. They were all Saxons. But he only recognized two. *He's bringing fresh fish into his net.*

Jurchen bowed. "Thank you, Your Grace."

Jurchen was given a seat next to the bishop. The Saxon priests ate heartily. There was little small talk during the meal, in the Saxon way. At the meal's end, Willehad sent the priests off on various tasks. But he motioned Jurchen to stay at his side. More ale was brought.

"I am glad you made it back here, Jurchen. It has been a long time. I was beginning to worry. My spies followed you from Aachen, but then somehow Melchior took a devious route, and his spoor was lost."

Jurchen nodded gravely. It was he who intended to throw the spies off their trail. "Melchior is a devious devil. He always plans for the worst. He has taken precautions. He has already lost two companion men-at-arms."

Willehad frowned. "I would have hoped to have killed them all by now, especially Melchior. Killing Karolus's last *missus* would send a signal that times are changing and the time of the Christian Frank will soon come to an end."

Jurchen sipped the ale. "He is seeking Abbot Baugulf. He has some sort of epistle from Karolus to the abbot."

Willehad wiggled in his seat, his rolls of fat nearly splitting the side arms. "An epistle? He sends a *missus* to merely deliver a letter that any courier can bring?"

"It is a special epistle."

"How do you know?"

"The *missus* keeps it on his person at all times." Jurchen skillfully spun the tale Melchior had instructed him to reveal.

"Does Karolus suspect our plot?"

"I don't think so, Your Eminence. If he did, you'd now have 5,000 mounted Franks with full *brunia* riding here, instead of one *missus* and a handful of men. Yet..."

"Yet what?" Willehad took a slug of his ale.

"News of that sort would be best reported to the count."

"Are you being less than truthful to your bishop?"

Jurchen grew evasive, just as Melchior instructed. "No, Your Grace, but the *missus* uncovered indicators of a plot along the journey. All eastern Austrasia feels it. Surely you know that, Your Eminence."

"Yes. And well I intended it so."

"The Avars and Saxon bands should have gone to ground until I brought the *missus* to you."

Willehad rocked his head back and forth and twirled his chain. "Yes, so how do we lure him here if he suspects trickery?"

Jurchen took a deep gulp of his ale and wiped his mouth with his heavy wool sleeve. "I should think a letter from Abbot Baugulf would do it. He is the holiest man in most Franks' eyes."

Willehad leaned back. "The abbot is not in a position to write or even sign a letter. We have given him certain elixirs to control him. Do you think Melchior would consider a letter from me?"

"I don't think so, your eminence."

"How about Count Lothar? He is, after all, a paladin and one of the most powerful lords in Frankland."

Jurchen smiled. "It might work. The letter would have to be crafty. It should admit to certain mischief in the land and malaise of the people. Since Melchior suspects such things, it may disarm him."

"You will go see Lothar tonight. I will prepare a letter of introduction."

"Very wise of you, eminence." Jurchen sighed in relief. This was easier than he had hoped.

***

Jurchen arrived at Lothar's palace as the sun dipped below the western mountains. It was more of a fortress, situated on a knoll, a league from the abbey. Built of stone and oak timber, it rose forty feet in the air with round turrets of granite rising another ten. The walls were irregular to conform to the steep terrain, but each side of the fort measured over a half-furlong. The portcullis was a miniature fort itself, built as a bridge over a wide dry moat. Torches lit the portcullis and the towers, yet the walls of the fortress itself were dark. A sudden break in the clouds and a three-quarter moon shed enough pale light to silhouette the entire structure. *A march count's dream.*

A voice from the portcullis challenged, "Who comes here?"

"Abbot Jurchen, on the orders of Bishop Willehad. I must meet with Count Lothar."

"'Tis late. Come at dawn like the others."

"No, I must come now."

After a few minutes, the rattle of chain on wood signaled the lowering of the drawbridge.

Two armed *warda*, locally raised garrison soldiers, crossed the bridge and led Jurchen's horse into the portcullis. Another five stood on either side, armed with long spears with wicked blades below the spear tips. Jurchen could see that the courtyard was a large open field with stone paths to each tower. One tower loomed larger, with its keep rising high above the others.

One of the escorts pointed at the keep. "Count Lothar lives in the grand tower."

Another pair of guards, this time in fine woolen livery with Lothar's colors of red and black, took over. They each wore a *brunia* of chain mail to their knees and had iron helmets. They carried long swords and the *Seaxe*. Jurchen followed the soldiers through stone corridors and then up a stone staircase that coiled along the tower's outer wall. It was dark and damp. Dim torches barely lit the way. Mice scampered as their feet trudged up the stone.

"Lord Lothar sees visitors in his chambers after dark," a soldier said. He opened a large plank-banded door that revealed Lothar entwined with a pair of young farm girls. Reflexively, Jurchen turned his eyes away and made the sign of the cross.

The guards closed the door and waited outside. Lothar was finishing with one of the girls, whose lithe figure put her at fifteen or so. Barely old enough to marry under Frankish law but prime age in the Saxon lands. Jurchen could see the girls were probably sisters with the same russet hair and country pallor.

Jurchen drew his robe sleeve before his eyes to avoid witnessing the final act. Lothar was panting like a mad bull. The girl squealed as Lothar finished. He could not tell if the squeal was from joy or pain.

"Are you quite done, My Lord?" Jurchen's bravado surprised even him. He lowered his sleeve and clutched at the *Seaxe* that hugged his thigh. He resisted the urge to use it. "I bear tidings from Bishop Willehad."

Lothar had already thrown the girl on top of her sister and tossed a linen cloth over them. He then slipped into a black-on-red woolen tunic and strapped on his own *Seaxe*, a long one, measuring twenty-four inches. "What kind of shit for a monk did Willehad send to me at this hour?"

Jurchen bowed his head courteously. "I am Abbot Jurchen. For the past five years, I served at the cathedral in Aachen under Archbishop Angilram. But I was ordained by Bishop Willehad and am thus under his guidance."

Giggling came from under the linen.

"The girls miss me," Lothar said with a grin. "Go on, priest."

"I was directed to lead the *missus dominicus*, Lord Melchior, to Fulda."

"What? Why didn't you say so? You are Willehad's spy among the *missus's* entourage?"

"Here is my letter of introduction from the bishop."

Lothar read with difficulty and only glanced at the letter. "But you led him to sanctuary."

"No, he is wise to the dangers about. Two of his men were killed by Avars, and he fought a large band of Saxons. He decided to take precautions. He has orders to see Abbot Baugulf."

"Well, then, he should come and visit me first. I am the March Count here, after all."

"I believe he intends to, Lord."

More giggling and squealing came from under the sheets.

Lothar grinned. "They want for something, I fear. Something longer than my *Seaxe*, I'm afraid. Do you have a *Seaxe*, priest?"

Jurchen startled a moment and reflexively stroked the *Seaxe* strapped to his thigh. "I have a prayer book. Nothing more."

"Bah! I know you priests. And I can tell from your way of speaking you're a Saxon. Why should I trust you?"

"That's between you and the bishop, Lord. I am now a priest in Frankland and a subject of Karolus, as you are."

Lothar grinned. "Well put. We need to make accommodation with the Saxons, eh? That's what this is all about. And I've done my part. Why, those two slave girls are Saxon. Don't worry. I'll explain it all to my confessor."

"I am not here to judge you, Lord."

"Well, on that, let's have some ale. Tossing these two has brought out a terrific thirst."

Lothar called for ale, bread, and sausage. He sent the girls off and had a table set.

As they ate, he questioned Jurchen. "So, tell me about our great lord, king-and-emperor. How are things in Aachen?"

"Quiet right now, Lord. Lord Karolus is on a hunting expedition. Alcuin has returned to York, and his family has been relatively quiet. We spend our days in prayer and scripture."

"Alcuin, eh? I never liked him. Bad influence on Karolus. Better he slithered back to Britain. Hunting, you say? Where?"

"I don't know, Lord."

"Hunting's better here. Even better in Thuringia to the east."

"Have you been there, Lord? In the Saxon lands?"

Lothar grew defensive. "Why, yes. As the Count of the March, a margrave, I have a duty to explore lands beyond the march. Why not hunt while doing it, eh?"

"I've lived in Thuringia. The hunting is not so good. Thuringians feed off the wildlife."

"Well, I found it to my liking. Killed a bear there. Ran it through with my spear and finished him with my *Seaxe*. Wish I had brought my *Francisca* along. I swear the Franks have lost their feel for the *Francisca*. It will be our downfall as a race."

Lothar quaffed another slug of ale and burped.

"Lord, I must tell you that the *missus* Melchior is merely the vanguard of a great force that even now marches this way."

"What the devil? You bring foul news! He's a *missus*. Not a paladin. Not even a warlord."

"Lord, they say the *missus* Melchior has killed more men in mortal combat than a pagan gladiator of Rome."

"I say it's all exaggeration. He's an errand boy for Karolus with a fancy title. That's what I think."

"That's not what our lord-and-emperor Karolus thinks. He has ordered Lord Melchior to ride against the evil Saxon queen."

"What? What evil Saxon queen?" Lothar's voice trembled. "Why, if there is a Saxon queen who threatens Karolus, I, as margrave, will destroy her."

"That is what our lord-and-emperor wants. He expects you to aid Lord Melchior. The *missus* requests and expects your assistance as well."

"Such intimate talk of the wishes of kings and nobles from the mouth of a Saxon priest? Why would Melchior send a Saxon to us? Especially a Saxon who serves the bishop? Does he know you serve the bishop?"

Jurchen fought to stay relaxed as he lied, "No, Count Lothar. That secret is safe. The *missus* trusts me as a priest, and the abbot sent me to accompany him on his journey."

Lothar took another swig of the ale and gnawed nervously on a piece of sausage. "I believe you tell the truth. What do you recommend we do?"

"Allow me to visit the Abbot Baugulf."

"That is Willehad's domain."

"He's jealous of his prerogative and, truth told, I believe he feels great guilt at what he has done with the holy man." Jurchen lied. It was a gamble he needed to take.

Lothar rubbed his chin. "So, you know… You are a very capable man, Jurchen. Swear fealty to me. Renounce your bishop, and I'll give the order that you be allowed access to Baugulf. But first, tell me, what good will it do?"

"It will please Karolus and the *missus*. How many men can you muster?"

"A thousand men-at-arms," Lothar said from behind his cup.

Jurchen knew that was an exaggeration. "The bishop said you have maybe fifty mounted warriors and double the number on foot."

"What do clergy know of war? That is all I have allowed him to see. One hundred armed footmen of the *sacra* guard this castle. Two hundred more are ready to march. Of those, one-half are mounted with full mail armor. I can also call up one thousand of the levies."

"The *missus* will bring more than ten times the number. Yet, he would rather move sooner with your men than wait."

"But the Saxon queen has many thousands."

"How do you know, lord?" He caught Lothar in his deception.

The count's face darkened. "I do not like being played a fool. I am the Count of the March. I have spies. I have informants. That is all you need to know, priest!"

Jurchen bowed his head. "Of course, lord. So, may I see the Abbot Baugulf soon?"

"Tomorrow. Meanwhile, I will provide you a room." Lothar tossed back his head and laughed. "If you want, I can send the twins to pray with you."

"No, Lord. If you have a chapel here, I will go there and pray through the night. For if I'm right, Christendom's future needs prayers."

Lothar sneered. "Prayers from a priest, who's no real priest?"

Jurchen shrugged. "I may be no real priest. But I am a real Christian. I will visit Baugulf tomorrow. I also want a letter from you inviting Melchior's assistance here as soon as possible."

***

When Jurchen went to find the chapel, Lothar summoned a powerful young Frank named Hincmar. He needed to get a message to Udela.

"Lord Stilicho said you summoned me. What are your orders at this late hour?"

"You must ride to the camp of the Saxons. Tell the queen Karolus is sending an army to crush her."

"Why would we warn a Saxon of such things?"

"Because things are changing in Frankland and Christendom. There are plots against the king and the church."

"I see."

"You hesitate? You are sworn to me before you are sworn to anyone. You must have faith in my judgment and my orders. I did not raise you from a footman for anything less than complete obedience to me."

"But I am sworn to Lord Stilicho."

"And he is sworn to me."

"Yes, Lord."

"Very good. Here is a message for the queen. Give it to no one else on pain of death."

***

The monks were still at matins when Jurchen appeared at the abbey. Armed retainers guarded the entrance. *This is strange.*

He made his way past the retainers through dark corridors towards the place where Baugulf had his residence. He could hear chanting echoing faintly.

Another guard stopped him. "What brings you here?"

"I am Abbot Jurchen, here to see Abbot Baugulf."

"No one is allowed upstairs unless ordered by Count Lothar or the bishop." The guard thumbed towards a narrow stone staircase lit by primitive torches.

"But Count Lothar himself sent me here."

The guard shrugged and let Jurchen pass. He ascended the stairs slowly. At the top, he was met by a young priest.

"Who let you up here?" the priest demanded.

"The guards, by order of Count Lothar," Jurchen replied.

"This area is under the protection of Bishop Willehad."

Jurchen smiled. "What luck! His Eminence ordained me. I am Father Jurchen."

"I have heard that name. But I shouldn't let you in without ..."

"Here is a note from Lord Lothar."

The priest strained to read it in the dim torchlight. "Very well. But don't be too long."

He motioned at the door with a move of his head. Jurchen pushed hard, and the heavy brass-banded door opened. He stepped into a large antechamber that served as Baugulf's study. Two more priests sat at the table. He recognized them as Willehad's men. *Strange, no monks are with their abbot.*

"I have orders to see Abbot Baugulf. Where is he?"

The priests looked startled.

"He's in his bed, of course. Not to be disturbed," one of the priests said. "What..."

"Ask no questions. It's better that way," Jurchen said boldly.

Baugulf's sleeping chambers had a stygian stench and feel. A musty sheet covered Baugulf to his neck. Jurchen placed his head on his chest and could faintly feel a heartbeat. His skin had a gray pallor. Baugulf's breathing was almost too shallow to detect. He glanced around the room and saw a stone flagon on a table. He went to it and removed the cork. Jurchen recognized the smell, a sleeping potion of the worst sort – one that would slowly kill.

He took the jug and stomped into the study. The two priests stood up.

"Is there a problem?" one asked.

"I'll tell you what the matter is! This is the wrong potion! What fools does Willehad have to do his dirty work?"

"We are no fools. This was provided specifically for Baugulf."

"Provided by whom?"

"Why, Bishop Willehad himself."

"And where did he get it?"

"From…"

"Tell me!" Jurchen demanded.

"Willehad ordained you, correct?"

Jurchen nodded.

"So, you are but one of his agents."

"Yes," Jurchen replied impatiently.

"We can trust him then," the priest said to his mate.

"You never answered my question. Who provided the potion?"

"Vulmar. But they say he received it from the Saxon queen Udela."

"So we are secreting evil potions from witches now?"

"As Willehad's man, you surely know things are changing. We just wish the potion worked quicker. But Willehad wants Baugulf alive a little longer. In case he needs a hostage."

"Very well. I need you to go find a certain lord and ask him to see me at the chapel after matins."

"Who?"

"Lord Stilicho. Now, both of you, go find him. I'll watch over the abbot."

Alone, Jurchen rummaged around the chambers. Under the table where the priests sat, he found wine jugs. *I thought I smelled wine on those sods.*

Jurchen poured the potion meant for Baugulf into a bowl and replaced it with the wine. He then poured the potion into the wine jugs and swirled it around to mix it. *Those two looked weary. This should relieve them of their troubles.*

***

Jurchen found Stilicho waiting in the chapel. With matins over, the place was empty until the next hour of prayer. Stilicho looked like a warrior of old — gray and rugged.

"Lord Stilicho?"

"Yes. Are you the priest they call Jurchen? I am not accustomed to the beck and call of priests. Especially ones ordained by Willehad."

"Yet you serve Willehad," Jurchen said.

"I serve Count Lothar, but not by desire."

"And I served Bishop Willehad, but not by desire."

"Served?"

Jurchen put his fingers on his lips. "I now serve Lord Melchior, *Missus Dominicus* of our emperor Karolus. He sent me here to speak with you."

"Melchior? Where the devil is he?"

"Not far. He must deliver a letter to Abbot Baugulf. But Baugulf has been made listless by potions provided by the Saxon witch, Udela. Both Willehad and Lothar are in league with the Saxons."

Stilicho looked uncomfortable. "I suspected something sinister brewing here. As did my men. We are simple Frankish warriors, but we aren't fools. They have sent couriers east, but none of my lads were ever chosen. Although I serve Lothar, it is with great reluctance. And he has kept me far from his schemes. And I must say, I have preferred it so."

"Things are stirring in Austrasia, Lord. The time for looking the other way has passed. Lord Melchior needs you to commit to him."

"I owe him my life. But I am sworn to Lothar."

"Sworn to a devil?"

"You say that, priest. But I can tell from your speech you're a Saxon."

"Taken as a boy and raised a Frank and a Christian. I am now sworn to Melchior."

"Did he save your life as well?"

Jurchen smiled. "In a way, yes. But he may also have saved my soul by separating me from the evil companions I served. You must do the same. God will understand. Loyalty… fealty to evil is greater than the evil itself."

Turning to the altar, Stilicho dropped to his knees, clenched his hands, and began to weep. "Saxon! You say what I dared not think. What spell from Satan possessed me to follow this pig, Lothar? What madness turned my allegiance from the noblest warrior in Christendom to a dissolute renegade who sleeps with pagans? Where are the Franks of old? I have sinned in my allegiance, priest. Pray with me."

Jurchen fell to his knees, and the two men prayed silently together. After some time in reflection, Jurchen said a final prayer in Latin and made the sign of the cross. They both rose.

"What does Lord Melchior need of me?" Stilicho asked.

"Allegiance, when the time comes, Lord. He is riding here with a small band. We need to succor the abbot and then march on the Saxons."

"March on the Saxons? There are thousands of the bastards, not more than a day or so ride from here. Of the few hundred Lothar commands, my band numbers only fifty."

"Do they all wear the *brunia*?"

"Yes. And all are mounted."

"Well, fifty good men can make all the difference with the right leaders and the right cause. Christ built our holy mother church with just twelve."

Stilicho straightened his back. "And what cause do we serve?"

"The cause of Karolus… and Christendom."

Stilicho made the sign of the cross and bowed his head. "What else does My Lord Melchior need of me?"

"He wants you to act as if you are completely loyal to Lothar and Willehad. When he arrives, keep your men well-armed and ready. He shall attempt to win Lothar over by persuasion and the authority of Karolus. If it fails, who knows? But he'll send one of his men to rally you."

"And if such a messenger can't get to me?"

"Wait for the war cry."

"What war cry?"

"A simple one – *Missus Dominicus*."

Chapter 12

Saxonland

Udela stirred before the morning twilight was an hour away. The lamps in her chambers had long darkened. She raised her head and saw the silhouette of Alager. *A strong youth but in a few years, you'll be bloated by too much ale and meat.*

She held her blankets to her neck. "What are you doing here, Alager?'

"Have I offended you, My Queen?"

His eyes seemed to bore through the sheets, absorbing every curve. This both pleased her and disturbed her. "Yes. You know I like to feel my skin blush before my morning ablutions. Where are my slaves?"

A rattling at the door ended their talk. Udela sat up, her breast heaving in a mix of passion and anger. "What brings you here, Varna? You Bulgars have less sense than Patzinaks."

"I am sorry, My Queen. You wanted to be informed if any strangers arrived. One has just ridden in."

"Who is it?"

"A Frank. He says he was sent by Count Lothar."

Udela turned to Alager. "Go receive him while I change. Give him ale and bread. I will meet with him in the great hall in one hour."

"Yes, My Queen," Alager bowed and left, his long sword scraping the carpets.

Varna stood in awe as he stepped past her. Trained to avert her eyes, she could not do so this time.

Udela saw her look and smiled. "When you are queen, you may command such a stallion, Varna. But for now, prepare my bath." The servants found it strange that this queen insisted on bathing daily. All knew such practices were foreign and dangerous.

"At once, My Queen." Varna went about the task.

When Udela stepped from the bath to be dried and dressed, Varna and the other girl servants marveled at her figure. She was the height of the average soldier with long and muscular limbs that remained graceful and feminine. Her fair skin had a healthy sheen.

"Shall I dry your hair, My Queen?" one of the girls asked.

"Yes. But quickly."

They loved to comb out their queen's long, golden hair. It was far healthier than any seen by them.

"You have the fairest skin and hair in Saxonland, My Queen," the slave girl remarked.

"What makes you think I'm Saxon? Do you think these beasts would make one of their women their queen? Now finish your work and be gone."

They dried her hair and body and then applied oil to both. Then, they dressed her in a shift of rich cloth from the east. It exposed her neck, and the wide silver belt around her waist accentuated her lithe but ample figure. Udela slid into a pair of satin slippers adorned with jewels that the Avar chief had given her.

"These are beautiful, My Queen," Varna said.

"They were taken from a Byzantine princess by the Avars. I could buy one hundred slaves or ten horses with their worth."

Varna ignored the barb. "They are most beautiful. And real rubies and diamonds..."

"How would you know of such baubles?" Udela asked.

"O, queen. I was stolen from my people by the Avars just as they stole these slippers. My father is a Bulgar hetman – almost a khan. I was raised with such baubles."

Udela threw back her head and regarded the girl. "This is true?"

"Yes, My Queen."

"Then, from today, you are no longer a slave. You will serve me as a bondswoman. Would you like that?"

Varna looked at the two other slave girls. "Maya and Radka are also women of means."

Udela looked at them. *Yes, these are the daughters of considerable men.*

"Very well. You will not sleep with the other slaves. You will sleep at the foot of my bed. Except when I have other company."

The girls laughed and beamed knowingly at their queen. Udela stifled a smile.

***

Udela entered the hall, followed by Alager and four of his men. The courier sat drinking a second cup of ale.

"Rise for the queen," Alager commanded.

The courier rose and then bowed before Udela. As a Frank, showing such deference to a woman, especially a Saxon, did not sit well. He made it look obvious.

"You have been here before," Udela said as she took her seat.

"Once, My Queen," he replied.

"Then you should bow to a queen with more ease. What is your name, Frank?"

"Hincmar, My Queen. I am a warrior serving Count Lothar, who dispatched me here with a message."

"A warrior? Where is your chain mail, the Frankish warriors wear with such arrogance?"

"As a courier, a leather *brunia* is better. I can ride faster and longer. Besides, my sword and shield give me more than ample protection."

"Or maybe it lets you flee all the faster," Alager said.

Udela startled. She turned to look at the young warrior standing behind her. *Is he jealous?*

Hincmar reached for his broadsword, and Alager sprang on him with his own. The two locked swords the way a pair of rutting stags lock horns. Alager's companions edged forward with their spears. Ready to strike if he were in danger from the hated Frank.

Udela watched with her hands on her hips. The idea of two young men fighting over her attention warmed her veins. Metal struck metal, and then the blades moved to the hilts, which locked. The two men staggered back and forth, knocking over tables and chairs and grunting like boar hogs.

"I'll gut you, Frank!" Alager's face was red with bloodlust. But Hincmar, the experienced warrior, appeared cool as he positioned his opponent. Finally, Hincmar twisted his sword free and ran the blade across the handsome Saxon's face.

"Arrrgh! Arrrgh!" Alager spat blood.

Hincmar's blade sliced off most of the young Saxon's nose, sending blood gushing across his face. Alager dropped his sword and grabbed madly at the nose. Hincmar moved in for the kill, but the four Saxon guards came at him with spears leveled.

The Frank parried them easily and backed himself to the wall. "Try taking me head-on, Saxon pigs!"

With a roar, the four rushed him. Hincmar's broadsword slashed aside one spear blade. He grabbed another spear by the shaft. With a thrust of his powerful arm, his sword tore open the throat of its owner.

Suddenly, a clap of thunder exploded among them, deafening their ears and stinging their eyes with a ball of fire. Smoke choked their lungs. The blast's power threw them to the floor.

"Enough!" Udela called out.

The men tried to stand, but blasted eardrums and singed eyelids dulled their senses.

After a few moments, Hincmar rose on all fours. But the Saxons still rolled on the floor, moaning. Hincmar's eyes gazed in awe at the tall and stunning woman standing above them. He pointed a shaky finger at her. "You… you *are* a witch!"

Udela smiled in triumph. "Whether I am a witch or not, who can say? But I do possess the power to control the thunder and lightning known only to Thor. That is why I am queen of this tribe of savages. And that is why you will obey me, Frank. Rise! And tell me what Lothar wants."

The doors opened, and twenty more of Alager's men clambered into the hall and rushed at Hincmar, who now stood, brandishing only a short *Seaxe*.

"Stop!" Udela commanded. "Alager is no longer your chief. Select one from among you and get him and his oafs out of my sight. I have business with Count Lothar's messenger."

Udela clapped her hands, and from seemingly nowhere, her newly freed servants appeared with mead, ale, and bread.

"I prefer the mead, but the Saxon ale is quite good," Udela said as they sat at a small table. "I am sad to lose Alager. But his anger in my defense was not intended by me."

"I expect little else from pagan barbarians, My Queen."

Her eyes scanned the young Frank. His blond beard was cut short and his limbs clean. "Well, we are allies now. Count Lothar assured me in his last letter that he would have all Frankland submitting to our rule."

"I don't understand." Hincmar tore a chunk of bread with his teeth.

"I believe you do understand."

"I marvel that a woman could remain so composed after seeing her guardians taken down before her eyes."

"Never mind that. Tell me what message you carry from Lothar."

He reached into his tunic and handed her a small lambskin scroll.

Udela handed it back to him. "This is in Latin. I don't read Latin."

"Then I will read it for you, My Queen."

"You read Latin?"

"Yes, My Queen. It is why I am a messenger. However, most *milites* leave that to clerics," Hincmar said with no small amount of pride. He opened the scroll and read each line carefully.

"What does it say?"

Hincmar hesitated and then lifted his head. "Karolus is sending an army of five thousand."

"He is leading an army against us? Lothar swore to me the Franks were bending."

"Perhaps they are," Hincmar said circumspectly. "But, regardless, a large *scara* is coming to Fulda."

"*Scara*?" The word was unfamiliar to Udela.

"An army."

She rubbed her hands together and paused in thought for a moment. "And Karolus is at the head of this army? Why that may prove an advantage. With my Saxons, the Avars, and Lothar's men, we can crush Karolus and blast his empire to dust."

Hincmar gave a puzzled look. "Blast? What does that mean?"

Udela returned his look with eyes narrowed. "I am not quite sure how to explain. It's a word I use to describe what my thunderbolts do." She regarded him for a moment. "Why, Hincmar, you still have black from the magic powder on your face. Your beautiful golden beard is singed by it. Come here and let me cleanse it for you."

Hincmar's face turned red.

"You blush!" Udela clapped her hands, and Varna appeared with her two friends.

"Get some water and wash the dust from our guest. And try to cleanse those bloodstains too." Udela shook her head. "Our poor Alager."

Varna pushed her friends and grabbed the pitcher and linen. She tenderly applied the water to Hincmar's face, forehead, and beard. She carefully applied gentle strokes and used the moist cloth to wipe away the black powder, road dust, and blood.

Udela could tell Varna was immediately smitten with the strange warrior. She had never seen a man so lean and handsome. With his golden beard, he appeared like a god. Hincmar was equally smitten. He kept his eyes locked on hers the whole time. Udela saw the mutual attraction.

"You favor the young woman? Her name is Varna. She and her companions are Bulgars snatched from their people."

Hincmar shook his head. "She is your slave and…"

"Do not lie to a witch!" Udela laughed. "You favor her. I know it! Well, she is now a free woman and no longer a slave. Perhaps you will see more of her."

"I don't understand," Hincmar said.

"I need to replace Alager as chief of my guard. You can read and you can fight. Are you a Christian?"

Hincmar made the sign of the cross. "Of course!"

Udela smiled mischievously. "Well, no matter. It will all be as one soon enough."

"What do you mean?"

"After we have destroyed Karolus and his army, we shall establish a new empire with a new type of Christianity. One that all can accept."

"Why, that is heresy," Hincmar said.

"No. With our victory, Karolus and the pope's Christianity will be heresy."

Varna finished her ablutions and fetched Hincmar more ale.

"Thank you, Varna," Hincmar said softly.

Udela noticed the pleasantry.

Varna bowed her head and smiled. "You are quite welcome, Lord."

Their eyes met for a second, and spoke more than a thousand shared words.

"You may go now, Varna," Udela said.

When they were alone, Udela placed her soft hand on his. "Read me the letter once more, Hincmar."

He unfolded the vellum and read aloud. When he was done, Udela's mouth twisted in a frown.

"I sense some fear in Lothar in this letter. But I say better we get Karolus here than deep in Frankland. Why, if he gathers forces in western Austrasia and Neustrasia, it could take years to defeat him while we await the rising of the Franks."

Hincmar's face darkened. "My Queen, Karolus will not lead this *scara*."

Udela knew she spoke treason against everything he loved, temporal and spiritual. "Then who will?"

"Lord Melchior, the last *missus dominicus*. He is Frankland's greatest warrior."

Udela's eyes grew wide, and her lips tightened. "Are you sure of this?"

"Yes. He sent a messenger to Fulda and will arrive there in advance of the *scara*."

"Then My Lord Lothar should kill him. Kill him at once, and this *scara* must await the arrival of Karolus. That will give us time to join with the Avars and trap the Frankish leader."

"I am a Frank," Hincmar said defiantly.

Udela's eyes narrowed. "But your fealty is to Count Lothar, is it not?"

Hincmar took a breath. "Yes, My Queen. But through My Lord Stilicho. As he goes, so must I."

"And this Stilicho serves Lothar?"

"Yes, My Queen."

"Then you will follow me. Tell Lothar that when we join together, you shall be my bodyguard. After all, it is only fitting."

"I don't understand, My Queen."

"You ended Alager's role as my guard. You will make a suitable replacement. Lothar will be riding long and hard to raise the Franks against Karolus. I need a strong man. One I can trust."

"You should trust your Saxons before a Frank, My Queen."

"Why should I trust these Saxons? I shall need a strong Frank by my side if I am to rule the world of the Franks. And you can read. That is an advantage."

"But Count Lothar would never..."

"Lothar will do my bidding. He is a weak and pliant man, despite all his Frankish bravado. Now go back and tell him these things."

Hincmar rose and bowed. "As you command, My Queen."

***

As he slid a boot into a stirrup, Hincmar was thinking of a way to avoid the witch-queen's service, as well as his service to Lothar. He resolved to speak with Stilicho and resolve the matter. He rode through the Saxon camp, casting his eyes about for signs of treachery or ambush. The mid-day sun was invisible, turning the high clouds a creamy gray. Surly bands of Saxons stared at the Frank, and more than once, he sensed the point of a spear aimed at his back. But he paid no heed.

At the main gate of the palisade surrounding the camp, Hincmar looked back one last time at Udela's city. *What in Christ's name?*

Hincmar saw a figure coming at him in full stride. He instinctively reached for his sword and swung his shield from his back to his forearm.

"Wait, Lord. Wait!" a girl's voice called. *A girl?* He knew at once it was Varna.

Before Varna reached him, she nearly stumbled. But Hincmar extended a powerful arm and lifted her astride the front of his saddle.

She grasped him tightly. "Take me with you, Lord."

"I can't take you. I must ride hard. Besides, you're the queen's servant. She would have us both killed."

"She freed us today. But freedom among such as these is not true freedom. Besides, when I saw you, I knew if I was to serve anyone, it must be you, O Lord. I can ride hard, too. I'm a Bulgar."

Their eyes locked with intensity. He was drawn to her as he had never been drawn to a woman. He could tell she felt the same. "You are no mere bondswoman, Varna."

She beamed at him with pride. "My father was a hetman of the Bulgars."

"I have heard of these Bulgars. Pagan savages."

Varna dropped her head.

He lifted her chin and smiled. "But pagan savages who breed the most beautiful of women."

Varna's frown turned into a smile, and she stroked his beard. "I see I did not get all the black off your fine beard."

"It will be a remembrance of Udela's black magic. You must stay and serve her. I may return and appear under her control. Know that I am not."

"And in whose control are you?"

"I'm not so sure. Perhaps in yours."

They kissed chastely. Then he took her about the waist and lifted her gently from the horse.

Their fingers interlocked.

"I shall return," he said.

"And I will be waiting."

Hincmar turned his horse south and galloped towards Fulda. He leaned forward in the saddle and looked ahead intently. He did not see the pair of eyes glaring at them from afar, or hear the hissing sound more reptilian than human. Had he looked back, he would have seen a dark figure following at a distance.

***

A light rain fell. The evening had grown dark. In the wooded rocks overlooking the river, Spad and Wala struggled to keep a fire going while they roasted a small doe. Melchior sat, feet crossed, under a small shelter of pine boughs, wiping his blades dry and sharpening them. Audeon entered the shelter and sat next to Melchior.

"Are the horses cared for?" Melchior asked without looking up.

"Yes, Lord," Audeon said. "Werinbert is with them. As it turns out, he was raised on a river but loves horses."

"Aren't we all?"

"My Lord?"

"Aren't we all raised to one thing but drawn to another?"

"I do not understand?"

"A boy is raised by a mother, but leaves her for a strange woman. He is raised by a father, but leaves him to follow a liege. A warrior is raised to serve his chief and king, but is wooed by his enemies. A boy raised a Christian is wooed by paganism."

Audeon regarded Melchior. "Why are you saying all this, Lord?"

"Because, Audeon, we are in a time of great danger."

"Harms? We live in the greatest empire in the world. Not since my great-grandfather, the Martell, defeated the Mohammedans at Poitiers have the Franks stood as tall. My Lord king-and-emperor... my father... rules the Roman empire."

Melchior stopped oiling his weapons and looked at Audeon. *He has much to learn.*

"What do you know of the Romans, Audeon?"

"Not much. They killed our Lord and savior, but then adopted Christianity, and the Church ruled the world as a result."

"The world? This is but a small piece of the world."

Audeon stared dumbfounded.

"You seem puzzled, Audeon. But hear this: the forests to the east become plains vaster than Frankland. Mountains rise, two, maybe three times as high as the Vogues, Pyrenees, or Alps. To the west, where Frankland meets the seas, the waters would swallow Frankland."

"I know. The west is endless water and sea monsters."

"Vast, yes, but not endless. And weeks of sailing bring those who live through it to lands so vast and great, they are almost indescribable." Melchior wondered if this glimpse of things yet unknown was wise.

Audeon said, "Your tales are quite impressive, Lord."

"I am no minstrel here to entertain you, boy."

"I am sorry, *Dominus*."

Melchior placed each of his weapons in its scabbard and looked up. "These are not poets' tales, Audeon. Our world is full of ignorance. It is focused on itself. That will never change. Audeon, no matter what we do, much harm will come this way. Your father is a great ruler. Better than the greatest Romans. But evil forces are lurking in the hope of stopping him before he achieves his destiny."

"And what is my father's destiny?"

Melchior sat thinking. He had begun to piece together his origins. His memories were returning, as was the knowledge he took from years of education. No one in Charlemagne's world would comprehend. Instinctively, he knew it was wrong to reveal too much of the future. For those in the present could only draw false conclusions from prognostications.

"That, I will not say. But his dream is at grave risk from heresy, apostasy, paganism, treason, and sheer evil."

Audeon's face whitened, and his eyes widened. "What should we do, Lord?"

"We are doing it. When empires are at their greatest, come the greatest dangers. I believe your father sensed this, and for that reason, I am on this journey. The Saxons and Avars are uniting with treasonous and heretical Franks to undo your father's work and destroy his dream. He sent me to stop it."

"Why, we need to raise an army. A *scara* of several thousand mounted Franks and the levee will drive them all out."

Melchior smiled grimly. "All he has allowed me is our small band. But if we are true to him and to God, that should be enough."

"But Lord, how can that be?"

"There is an ancient Persian game called chess. Do you play it?"

"No, Lord. I never heard of it."

"I came across it on the Spanish March. Mohammedan prisoners played it. It is a game that appears to be a military campaign or battle. But it is much more. To master it, a player must think two or three steps ahead of his opponent."

Audeon smiled. "Ah, yes, to know one's moves in advance is a great stratagem. But not one I think possible."

"No, Audeon. Not to know one's moves in advance. But to know of one's enemy's moves in advance. To know them, because your moves were calculated to force them. To achieve true victory, one must know an enemy's moves before he does."

"I see," Audeon said.

Melchior smiled. "I don't believe you see, yet. But you shall."

Detleff poked his head into the shelter. "The meat is roasted, Lord. Father Thomas wants you to come for the blessing of the food."

Melchior stood and threw his cloak over his shoulders. "Come, let's eat our fill, Audeon. But mark this, I have confidence in you. No matter what happens to me or us, we are fulfilling your father's command."

They ate in the rain.

"I wish we had some ale. And this wine tastes little better than piss," Fromm said.

"Why, I heard you Norsemen prefer to drink piss," Gaetano said.

"Only the piss of our enemies' wives and daughters," Fromm said. "And damn this deer meat. I need ox meat or pig meat."

"Spad and Walla risked a journey down this mountain to find the deer for us. Do you prefer more hare?" Bavo said.

"Old man, a Norseman fights on a full stomach."

"You'll get your full soon enough," Bavo said. "Isn't that right, Lord?"

Melchior smiled grimly.

Suddenly, they heard a rustling in the bushes.

"Someone's out there," Melchior said.

Fromm leaped to his feet and grabbed his ax. But Cassyon beat him to the brush. He drew his broad sword and cut his way blindly into the foliage. Fromm stood behind him with his blade held high. A robed figure appeared at their side as if from nowhere.

"Is this how you greet a man of God and one sent by Lord Melchior?"

"Abbot! We almost killed you," Cassyon said.

Jurchen smiled. "You were nowhere near killing me. Were I Avar or Saxon, you would both be dead. Now, take me to Lord Melchior."

Alone in Melchior's shelter, Jurchen explained all that happened in Fulda.

"I'm concerned that if we wait here too long, Abbot Baugulf will perish," Melchior said.

"My thought as well, Lord," Jurchen said.

"You have done well, Jurchen," Melchior said.

"If we leave tonight, we can surprise them at dawn."

"No. I will ride into Fulda as *Missus Dominicus* in full daylight. As far as Lothar is concerned, you are leading me into a trap."

"But it is a trap. He'll kill you."

"He will try to kill me. But not right away. Lothar is stupid but sly. He will try to poison us or, more likely, have our throats slit as we sleep."

"What will you do?"

"I won't eat or sleep, to start," Melchior said under his breath.

"Lord?"

"I have a scheme."

"Yes, Lord?"

"If I knew what it was, I'd tell no one. But we'll need a diversion to reach Baugulf. So here is what we shall do…"

***

Alager's rapid descent from the queen's guardian did not sit well with his men. They had watched helplessly as he choked to death, clutching the pulp that once was his nose.

Their chief swallowed and screamed, cursing the Franks, his queen, and his men. In a final death rattle, Alager gripped his sword by the hilt and raised it. "Odin! Odin! Avenge me on them…"

The blade dropped, and he trembled in a paroxysm that filled the hardened warriors with dread. He tried one last time to rise, but fell back, emitting his last breath.

"You are our leader now, Hrodger," one of them said. "You should report to the queen. Maybe she'll take you to her bed."

They all laughed.

"I think not," Hrodger said. "This queen prefers certain types of men. I am missing an eye and two fingers. And I'm too old to be any woman's plaything."

"Make her your plaything, Hrodger."

More laughs and grunts came from the band.

Suddenly, a band of Euduces entered the barracks-room with shields and spears ready.

"What are you doing here?" Hrodger challenged. "This is the barracks of Queen Udela's guard."

The leader of the Euduces band, a small but tough-looking warrior named Loefsige, brandished a long *Seaxe*. "You are correct, Hrodger. But the queen summoned us to take your place as her guard. You will leave immediately."

Incensed as much as by Alager's death, they reached for their weapons, but the leveled spear points and shield wall showed resistance was useless.

"Enough," Hrodger said. "We submit to our queen's will."

With that, the band gathered their belongings and assembled near a small stand of oaks.

"Where will we go, Hrodger?"

Hrodger lifted his face to the low-hanging clouds and let the light rain wash his face. He thought about their lot. None could go back to their tribal units. They had cut those ties when the queen selected them.

"We are our own tribe now. Bound not by blood ties but ties of honor. We are renegades, like those ghostly ancient warriors in service to the god Odin – the mysterious Harii." Hrodger gazed again into the clouds. "Odin, I pledge this band of warriors as yours. We serve our queen, no man… only you!"

The men grunted as one and pounded their spears against their shields. "Odin! Odin! Odin! Odin!"

Hrodger raised his arm, and they grew silent as lambs. "We will take vengeance on the man who killed Alager. That is our sacred duty now."

"But what then?"

"Only the gods know. We must await their bidding. But I know this. Great bloodshed must follow if the queen leads the people against the Franks. I would love to kill Franks. But I do not favor these Avars our queen has allied with."

"Perhaps we'll march north and join Widukind. He is a true Saxon warrior chief," one of them said.

Hrodger nodded. "Perhaps. We are Harii now. We'll let the gods decide. But first, we draw lots to see who has the honor of tracking and killing the Frank named Hincmar,"

Then, in the method of the tribes, they drew stones. Fittingly, the lot was won by Osgar.

"Odin is powerful," Hrodger said when Osgar drew the stone. "He has chosen the warrior, Osgar, whose name means 'spear of the gods.' And as we well know, he is the best of any Saxon with the spear."

"I threw my first spear while still sucking my mother's milk. I can hit the center of a shield at over forty paces in the dark," Osgar said.

They all murmured agreement.

"The Haari wore black, so it is told," Hrodger said. "We'll scour the huts and find clothing appropriate to a Haari." He then drew his long *Seaxe* and waved it at the sky. "Odin...."

The rest of his band drew their long *Seaxes* and thrust them upward in unison, chanting, "Odin, Odin Odin..."

***

The horse kicked up mud and clumps of earth. Hincmar rode fast. But not fast enough. He did not see the lone rider just out of sight. Osgar followed Hincmar's spore, waiting for the right moment to hurl his spear and wield his *Seaxe*. His face and arms were painted black and matched his clothing - the colors of the ancient Germanic Haari. But unlike the Haari, he would not put himself into a frenzy. He would remain calm and deliberate, at least until his spear reached its mark.

Osgar saw a long ridgeline to the east with a narrow trail heading to the crest. *If that trail turns south along that ridge, I might find an overlook from which to take the Frank.* He spurred his horse up the trail and disappeared into the thick pine trees. The trail rose quickly and soon he reached a road long unused but wide enough to put his horse into a gallop. He bounced along under the dark canopy of trees with his head low and clutching the horse's reins and flowing black mane. Boughs scraped his head. The horse blew rhythmically as its hooves thudded on the soft pine needles covering the roadbed.

At last, he reached a small clearing that led to a cliff. Osgar noticed stones piled in what must have been a ritual for one of the ancient Germanic tribes. *Perhaps the Haari worshiped here.* He slowed the horse and dismounted. He clutched two spears, both *angons*, throwing spears with medium-length shafts of ash and a long and narrow iron tip. He also thrust his long *Seaxe* into his belt and crept forward.

Odin's beard! Osgar found the perfect ambush point. Halfway down the ridge was a rocky overhang just above the road to Fulda. The road below was smooth, loamy turf. He did not have to wait long before he heard horse hooves thudding. *Frank blood!*

Osgar saw that Frank had ridden at a steady but not speedy pace. Now he turned the long bend in the road that wended from southeast to Fulda. *He hopes to reach Fulda by dark. Not if Odin has anything to do about it.*

Now, by Odin's blood! Osgar launched the first *angon*. Suddenly, the rider's horse turned its back, and it broke its stride. The spear meant to pierce Hincmar's neck whipped by, missing him by inches. Hincmar spurred the horse, and it bolted into a gallop.

Odin's blood! Osgar gripped his second spear, leading the horse by five paces, and launched it with all his might. His aim was true, too true. The blade squarely caught the iron boss at the center of the shield on Hincmar's back. The heavy metal deflected the point, breaking its impact and turning the tip of the blade into Hincmar's leather *brunia*.

He thought he heard the Frank cry out as the iron tip cut through his *brunia*. The horse slowed to a walk as his victim pulled back on the reins. He saw the shaft angling along his victim's left shoulder blade. Suddenly, the Frank's horse bolted up the road.

"Thor's hammer!" Osgar watched the hated Frank escape. He knew he had wounded Alager's killer, but whether he would live was uncertain. He decided to pursue his stricken prey. Osgar preferred a clean kill. But a slow one would prove enjoyable as well. He returned to his horse to seek a trail to the road and retrieve his spear.

***

Hincmar rode steadily for hours. His back burned and ached. He knew he had lost blood. Just how much, he could not tell. He ached for a drink but dared not slow his pace. Finally, he reached a small stream whose water looked too tempting both for him and the horse. He halted his horse and tumbled from the saddle. The exhausted animal went right to the water.

Weary of the pain and the unwanted appendage, Hincmar decided to remove the spear. He grabbed awkwardly at the shaft until he had the right grip. He grunted and gritted his teeth as he slowly wrenched the spear from his back. He stared at the blood-stained iron tip before he tossed the hated weapon onto the side of the road.

Blood flowed for a moment and then stopped. *Good…. Good… I dare not remove the brunia here to cleanse the wound.* Hincmar staggered to the stream, got down on all fours, and stuck his head into the water, drinking as he dunked once, twice, and then a third time. He staggered to the horse and though now quaking, mounted. He lowered his head and spurred the horse forward.

Chapter 13

Fulda

Melchior rose from a fitful sleep. He stood, stretched his muscles, and took a deep breath. The morning mist had a familiar aroma - the mix of sulfur and burnt metal that came from gunpowder. A glance at the sky revealed nothing. *What was I expecting to see?* He paused a moment. He felt queasy and unnerved. What were thoughts and notions, even dreams, had suddenly turned into reality. *I was looking for aircraft!* His mind flooded with thoughts and images.

He now fully remembered his life as Matthaeus Melchior: medical student, Wehrmacht soldier, and Canadian spy. But he also knew that he was Lord Melchior, *Missus Dominicus*, of Karolus, most serene Augustus, crowned by God, great and pacific emperor, governing the Roman Empire. These realities clashed in his mind and converged in an uneasy alliance.

He bowed his head. A sense of unease mixed with elation coursed through him. "Be not afraid," said a voice within him. *But whose voice?* He thought he knew. But he...

Audeon broke the morning reflection. "Are you all right, *Dominus*?"

"Yes. Where are the others?" Melchior felt peeved at the interruption, but also somehow relieved.

"The men are preparing, Lord," Audeon said. "Detleff will be here in a moment to help with your *brunia*."

"Tell Father Thomas I should like a Mass before we leave."

"But there will be Mass in a proper chapel at Fulda, Lord."

"We may not arrive in time. I want the men's spiritual needs to be attended to. Who knows what physical harm may befall them before the journey's next phase? Perhaps prayer and meditation will help."

Audeon smiled knowingly. "Of course, *Dominus*."

He knew his journey would become a violent one. He sensed it. He felt it. He had no fear. For now, he had accepted his Christianity, a Christianity that had once been merely a form of identity for Matthaeus Melchior. Now, living among these savage yet pious men, had changed his perspective on religion. *Be not afraid.*

Melchior's memory had almost fully returned. He now remembered too many battles to be afraid. Yet, he *was* afraid, not of death, but of fighting for the wrong cause. In all his vicious fighting for an evil cause, he saw many men, both horrified and afraid. But men shattered because they had lost hope — those were the worst.

Now, as he, at last, accepted his need of God, he knew he would never lose hope. Yet Melchior was terrified. Because he knew his failure could cause a great kingdom, a good kingdom, to be toppled by evil. As a man who once defended evil, this terrified him. *Be not afraid...*

"Father is ready, Lord," Detleff said. "Let me help you with your *brunia*."

Melchior stood and spread his arms. Detleff took the coat of leather, covered in iron links, and wrapped it around his master's torso. He then fastened it tightly, leaving enough room for his master to breathe and wield weapons with ease. The *brunia* reached to the knees and three-quarters of the way to the elbow. Under it, Melchior wore his rich blue woolen tunic and woolen breeches trimmed with silver and lined with leather.

"Do you want to wear your leg mail, Lord?" Detleff asked.

Melchior looked at the leather with iron-link leg coverings and shook his head. "Save those for battle, Detleff. These leather boots can deflect all but a battle ax. I don't want to send the wrong message at this point in the journey. I come as *missus*, not a warrior."

Detleff smiled. "Of course, Lord. So, what weaponry shall you bear?"

"You carry my spear and shield. But I'll wear the broadsword and *Francisca*, as well as my *Seaxe*."

Detleff wrapped the thick leather belt around Melchior's waist and fastened it. Detleff marveled at how powerfully built his master was compared to all but the largest of men. His physique seemed unnatural: tall, broad-shouldered, and narrow-waisted.

"Your helmet?"

"I'll carry it on the saddle. Affix the chain mail to the back and sides, in the event I must wear it."

"Very wise, Lord."

"Now, let's go to Mass."

Melchior recalled the time not long ago when he would smile at such a suggestion. Now he craved it. The men had gathered under an oak tree. Father Thomas had his stole around his neck and his linens spread on a felled tree trunk that served as an altar. A few remaining crumbs of bread and the last of the wine served as Communion.

The morning wind whispered through the trees. Melchior's men stood patiently as Father Thomas carefully unfolded his chasuble and reverently put it on. Thomas made the sign of the cross and began to pray. *"In Nomine Patris, et Filii, et Spiritus Sancti... Introibo ad Altare Dei...*

As one, the men dropped to their knees and bowed their heads. *"Ad Deum qui laetificat juventutem meam."*

Thomas went through the prayers with reverence and spirituality that proved uplifting to the band. When the time came for the sermon, though, he truly surprised them. Instead of some discussion of the gospel of the commandments, he turned their hearts and minds to other matters.

"I want to thank Abbot Jurchen for allowing me to pray this Mass... our last as a band of acolytes, followers of our King-and-Emperor, Karolus, and our Lord God. Karolus is the man of the millennium, providing the bridge between the spiritual world of God and God's physical world on earth. For God is indeed in both worlds as the creator and lord.

"Karolus well understands the precepts of Saint Augustine in his great work – *City of God*. Through this, he understands the importance of intersecting the temporal and heavenly. Christians, rather than seeking escape from a fallen society, rather than seeking holiness on earth that is of its essence unattainable, need to practice their faith in and of this world. A world that is not and never will be perfect, because the sacred and profane are ever at war.

"The forces of Satan are arrayed against us. But those forces take many forms. We as Christian Franks face unending conflict against those forces of evil. To triumph as God intends us to triumph, we remain strong and courageous in our physical, moral, and intellectual beings. We will at times sin. But even sinners will kneel before God at times' end. Of course, we have our sanctuaries in our churches, chapels, convents, and monasteries.

"But these offer only respite, not an end. A respite for us as we continue to face Satan's challenge and combat the forces of evil that walk the earth seeking the destruction of men's bodies and the enslavement of their souls. The role of our kings and bishops is challenging. They and their appointed acolytes must bravely face both physical and spiritual evil. In this, the Romans failed. In this, the Franks cannot fail… must not fail… shall not fail."

Melchior looked about him. The men were agape. None had ever heard the humble young priest speak so eloquently on such matters. His words electrified even the lowest and grandest among them. Now they realized that this journey was special and that the fate of Frankland and the new empire might well be in the balance.

Melchior trembled, and his eyes met Thomas's for a moment. *This is no ordinary priest. He knows things. He senses things.*

At the Communion under the canopy of the ancient German forest, each man shook as his tongue received a crumb of host and the barest spot of wine, now transformed into sacred body and blood. Each felt both a moral and physical transformation.

Melchior gazed at the faces of his men. His modern mind finally comprehended he was now in a time when religion was as important and "real" as anything else. An image of Nazis and Bolsheviks flashed. He knew then that no matter how earnestly they tried or Karolus tried, this battle between good and evil, sacred and profane, would continue. *Per omnia saecula saeculorum.*

The Mass ended just as a light rain began to drip down through the trees. Without a word, they finished packing their belongings and headed down the trail, with Jurchen leading the advance. It occurred to Melchior that despite his pledge of loyalty, he could be leading them into a trap.

He motioned to Gaetano, who rode up next to him.

"Yes, Lord?"

"How well can you shoot from the saddle?" Melchior asked.

"I learned from the Arabs, Lord. I shoot better from the saddle."

Melchior pointed at Jurchen, now just one hundred paces ahead as they rode down the dark, narrow trail. "There's your mark."

"I don't understand, Lord."

"If the Franks or Lord Lothar's men ambush us, it will be because of his treachery."

"I understand, Lord."

How little I have learned from the Mass. Melchior felt guilty issuing the order, but he also felt he owed it to his men to see that their deaths would not go unavenged. When they, at last, reached the foot of the mountain, they turned onto the main road. Melchior ordered a halt and signaled for the band to gather.

"How far to Fulda?" he asked Jurchen.

"No more than an hour's hard riding, *Dominus*."

Melchior turned to the men. "I can tell you now, there are evil things taking place at the holy town of Fulda. You should know that Satan's forces are gathering. It may well be Count Lothar has fallen to those forces and is in league with the Saxons and Avars. But we are messengers of our Lord Karolus."

The men all stared at each other. They had never heard a lord refer to his hinds, his followers, in the same context as himself.

"Be prepared to go to arms at a moment's notice. But do not appear ready to go to arms."

A look of confusion spread among them.

"We must give Count Lothar no warning of our suspicions. As far as he is concerned, this is just a journey from a *missus*. We are greatly outnumbered and will likely be killed if it comes to fighting. Anyone wishing to depart can do so with no recrimination from me…" He glanced at Thomas. "Or from God."

They maintained faces of stone.

"Very well. Walla and Spad will be out of place riding into Fulda. Take up a place in the woods near the town. We might need help from without."

"As you wish, Lord," Spad said.

***

They rode east through heavy rain and fierce winds. The sky above was thick and dark. It hardly looked like day. The small column passed by villages, hamlets, and farmsteads. He wanted no one to know they were there. Secrecy and speed were essential. Mallobaudes led a group of twenty mounted Frankish warriors, called milites. Although they had fought under Melchior in two campaigns, since their lands now belonged to Mallobaudes, they were commanded by him. The most experienced was a rugged old milites with one eye, named Guntramn.

"You look discomforted, Guntramn," Mallobaudes said as the two rode at the head of the band.

"I served the king-and-emperor in a half dozen campaigns and Lord Melchior in the last two. It's given me a sense of things. And I don't favor what I sense."

"What do you sense?" Mallobaudes noted the lack of loyalty in Guntramn's tone. He would deal with that when convenient.

"Evil! It's in the air, I tell you. It's all around us." Guntramn looked intensely at Mallobaudes, his blind eye seeming to regard him more closely than the good eye.

"Why look at me, Guntramn? I'm here to rid the land of evil. The bishop himself sanctions this mission."

Guntramn spat a piece of dried pork caught in his gapped teeth. "The companions have been asking why."

"Nor should they know. The bishop wants this journey kept discreet."

"Journey, you say? Did Karolus make you a *missus*? Only a *missus* may undertake a journey. Everyone in Frankland knows Lord Melchior is the last *missus*."

"Well, perhaps not for long. I am to gather proof of his treason to Karolus. After he is punished, I shall be appointed *missus*."

Guntramn laughed and slapped his thigh. "You? *Missus*? You are more crippled than I and have only once gone to war."

"The times are changing. Perhaps Karolus wants a new kind of *missus*."

"Karolus may like a new kind of mistress from time to time. What warrior doesn't? But there is only one kind of *missus*."

"Are you calling me a liar?"

"No, Lord. Only mistaken. But tell me of this suspicion of treason."

"It is more than suspicion."

"I have one other question, Lord Mallobaudes."

"What is that?"

"Why are we taking this long way around Fulda if you have orders against Lord Melchior? We are almost into the Thuringian March. Who knows what savagery we'll find there?"

"I must meet someone first. There is a ford over the river that leads to a large plain, the Huns once claimed as grazing grounds for their ponies. Those we will meet are camped on the hills above us."

"Are we meeting the ghosts of Hunnish invaders?"

Mallobaudes laughed. "In a way, yes. Look ahead."

Guntramn looked across the small river onto a green and gray field a league away. "I see mounted figures in the mist."

"Indeed."

"Avars!" Guntramn shifted his spear and went for his shield.

Mallobaudes reached over and stopped him. "Relax, old man. These are friends."

"Friends? A Frank has no Avar friends. What mischief is this, Lord?"

"Karolus wants me to deliver a message to them. He defeated them in battle. They are now quite submissive to his rule."

Guntramn grunted. "I suppose the emperor must communicate with his supplicants."

"Exactly, Guntramn. As I said, I am being groomed as the next *Missus Dominicus*."

The men behind began to growl when they saw the Avar banners in the distance.

Guntramn called out over his shoulder. "Easy now! Lord Mallobaudes is carrying a message from the emperor to the pagans. But they are Avars. Keep your weapons handy."

"So distrustful," murmured Mallobaudes.

The old warrior spat. "I curse the fate that placed me under your liege."

They rode in silence, crossing a rotted wooden bridge over the river. Before them, some fifty Avars on ponies spread in an arch, sat waiting silently. When Mallobaudes's band was a spear-throw distant, he signaled a halt. An Avar with two retainers slowly rode towards them. When they were a quarter-furlong before the Franks, they halted.

Without warning, one of the *milites* galloped from the pack, heading straight at the lead Avar, who calmly watched the armed horseman bearing down on him.

"Stop!" Mallobaudes's voice choked out the words. "What are you doing?"

Guntramn calmly observed. "The Avars killed Richomeres's father. He has sworn eternal revenge."

Two arrows darted across the sky like lightning bolts, and each pinned the rider's thighs to the saddle. Thick bubbles of blood oozed from the wounds, but Richomeres's frenzy blocked the pain.

Bent on vengeance, Richomeres rode on. Screaming at the hated enemy, he pulled his shield forward and lowered his head. His spear was poised for an overhead thrust at the Avar, who remained motionless. He was a lance thrust away when the lead Avar hurled a javelin just over the shield and fixed its point squarely in Richomeres's throat.

A low murmur of approval that sounded like a swarm of wasps, rolled along the line of patiently waiting Avars. Richomeres's body stiffened but remained pinned to his horse, which galloped off with his torso rocking back and forth.

The Franks began to bellow war cries. In horror, Guntramn braced himself for the attack he was sure would now come.

"No! Sheath your weapons. I will ride to them. If they kill me, you may do as you wish. But for now, hold your men in check."

"Hold fast, *milites*," Guntramn grunted.

Raising one arm, Mallobaudes slowly rode forward. The Avar leader did the same. They met out of earshot of either party.

"Greetings, Dgno," Mallobaudes said. "Accept my apologies. Frank *milites* are headstrong."

"I know it all too well. And we welcome any chance to kill them." Dgno smiled cruelly. "They make it so easy…"

A chill went through Mallobaudes. "My name is Mallobaudes. I come with tidings from Fulda. Have you met with the queen? Is all ready?"

"I have met with my future queen. For I have sworn she will be mine once the Christian Franks are destroyed," Dgno announced haughtily.

"She will make you a willing bride, I am sure."

"It is not a willing bride that I covet. I can have any number of them."

"Of course. Do you have the girl?"

Dgno drew himself tall in the saddle.

"I asked, Do you have the girl?"

"Yes."

"Is… is she safe?"

"Safe… yes."

Mallobaudes could not hide his concern. Karolus's bastard daughter might prove an invaluable pawn to play. "I have orders to bring her safely to Fulda. Where is she?"

"She is safe. With the women."

"Have any of..."

"No! None of my men has taken her. Not that she wasn't eager to have an Avar stallion mount her," Dgno boasted.

"Of course. What young virgin would not want to give her maidenhood to an Avar warrior?"

Dgno nodded. His command of the Frankish tongue was not good enough to catch the sarcasm.

"When can you have her to me?"

"Camp on the far side of the river. I'll send her across at dawn. Alone. On a pony. When shall I be paid?"

"Paid? You will have your stolen treasure back when Karolus is dead. Isn't that enough?"

"No. When Karolus is dead, I want to select one of his surviving sons and the highest nobles for ritual death. Avar vengeance must be reckoned with."

Mallobaudes shuddered. "That... That sounds reasonable."

Dgno laughed. "You Franks are all squeamish when it comes to your own blood. Christian blood. Tell Lothar that Melchior is at the head of the list."

"Melchior?" Mallobaudes was stunned.

"You do know who he is?" Dgno asked.

"Why yes. He's my cousin."

"Your cousin is a great enemy to the Avars. He must be ours to punish."

"I assure you, Lord Melchior will be dead by then if I have anything to do with it."

"Well then, you will make a suitable substitute."

A shiver went through Mallobaudes.

"Are you afraid, Frank? Avars can show humor, too. I like that ring you are wearing."

"It's a solid gold ring, said to have once belonged to one of the Caesars. It was bequeathed to me when I was a boy. It is priceless."

"Then enjoy wearing it for now. But if I am cheated of Melchior's blood, you will choose between the ring and your finger. All Frankish blood is the same to me."

The next morning, the Franks were up before dawn. They ate bread and cheese and sipped at their skins of wine. As the twilight turned to daylight, they donned *brunias* and helmets and mounted.

"I will ride out and greet the girl," Mallobaudes said. "Have the men prepared to charge if these snakes try something."

Guntramn spat. "I thought these Avars were your friends?"

"Allies perhaps, but I don't believe one can be friends with an Avar."

Guntramn nodded grimly. "Now you understand how we feel, Lord." He gazed at the sky. It was covered with dove-gray clouds that looked like loaves of unbaked dough. "No rain and the ground is drying. The ride back should be good."

"Assuming our allies don't follow us," Mallobaudes said.

"Oh, they'll have a party follow us. It's their way. Never be in sight but always be in sight."

"I don't understand."

"That is why you will never be a warlord like your cousin, Lord."

Mallobaudes bit his lip. *This insolence will be repaid.*

"They are coming, Lord," one of the *milites* announced.

Three figures suddenly appeared out of the gray mist before them. Mounted on the small ponies, they appeared like deer to the Franks. They rode to within eighty paces and halted. Then one pony moved forward, very slowly. The other two riders sat passively.

"No quick movement. Those two have their bows at the ready," Guntramn said in a low voice.

Mallobaudes slowly edged his horse forward and halted before a figure shrouded in a colorful robe favored by the Avars.

"I'm Lord Mallobaudes."

"I am… Genofeva," a girl's voice said softly from under the hood. Then she pushed back the hood and looked at him with fear in her eyes. "Why are you taking me from my people?"

"Your people? You are a Frank." Mallobaudes was impressed with her looks. Her eastern blood mixed with Frankish blood made for a rare beauty.

I have Karolus's daughter in my possession. Mallobaudes's scheming mind ran through the possibilities should he manage to keep her in his possession. *I should demand her as my bride in payment for my role in this scheme.*

"I am now an Avar. I went through the ceremony. Dgno himself was my… my patron." She buried her head in her hands and began to weep.

"Patron?" Mallobaudes glanced at the Avars watching them. He sensed they were secretly laughing. He was not entirely sure they would not kill him and keep the girl. But she was too valuable a tool for him to lose now. He grabbed her bridle and rode away.

***

Fulda

Melchior led his band slowly up the road. Walla and Spad ran up ahead. With their hunters' skills and instincts, they combed each bend in the trail for signs of ambush. Melchior reached into his tunic and felt the leather case enclosing the letter for Abbot Baugulf. He wondered about the contents. *Did they really warrant all of this?*

Audeon rode beside him, along with Detleff, his squire. Jurchen and Thomas rode behind him, followed by Bavo and Werinbert. Gaetano and Fromm followed in the rear. The band cautiously descended the high ground and followed a narrow road through the lowland forest that girted the valley of the Fulda River.

"I tell you, I don't like this," Fromm said to Gaetano.

Melchior grimaced at the loud voices that carried from the rear, but then decided their band should seem unconcerned with stealth.

"Lord Melchior knows well that by placing ourselves at the mercy of the foe, he also has them at his mercy," Gaetano replied.

"I don't understand. A Norseman charges his enemy, bludgeons down his defenses, kills him, and takes his women and wealth, although not always in that order."

Gaetano laughed. "In the east, it is different. Eastern princes, the sheiks especially, operate from guile and nuance. Moustafa of Tangiers once took a Byzantine city by riding into it alone. He struck down the general commanding the garrison with his scimitar even as he was pledging peace. The garrison surrendered to his boldness and all submitted."

"Submitted to what?"

"Islam, of course. Its best warriors are infidels who submit. Why, I have seen some of your kinsmen in battle. They are quite impressive."

Bavo whispered to Werinbert, "Nervous, boy?"

"No, Lord Bavo."

"I'm not a lord. I am a free Frank, although I suppose a *milites* is the next best thing to a lord."

"I hope to be taken on permanently as Lord Audeon's squire," Werinbert said.

"Squire to a bastard is no life, boy. Even our king's bastard."

Werinbert twisted his mouth in dismay.

"I am just playing with you, boy. The best offspring of our lords are often their bastards. In truth, I'd say the realm is run by bastards. Many become clergy, you know."

"I didn't know," Werinbert said.

"I envy your youthful innocence. But once you're bloodied, you'll begin to understand."

They emerged from the flat woodlands. The large alluvial plain shrouded in a light mist lay before them. The town of Fulda came into view five miles distant. The mist masked their view. But Melchior could make out the tower and walls of the abbey at one end and the walls of a mighty fort of classic Carolingian style at the other.

"There it is. Two leagues off," Melchior said.

"Fulda is larger than I had envisioned," Audeon said. "Looks to be over eight score buildings!"

"A city at the edge of civilization," Detleff remarked.

"Is this your first time here?" Audeon asked.

Melchior paused a moment. His mind raced with images of the town, now a city, in a more modern era. "Just once. And briefly. I hardly recall it."

"That must be the abbey sitting along the river, Lord," Detleff said. "A big place for a pack of monks to pray all day."

Fulda Abbey is a great center of learning. My father calls it the heart of Christendom north of Rome," Audeon said. "The monks are recording history and ancient writings. Pious and learned men come from all over Christendom to share in the experience of preserving knowledge."

Melchior eyed Audeon. *This lad is more than a lanky warrior in the making.*

"That must be Count Lothar's fort," the youth said.

At the other end of the town, which sprawled along the water, they could see the stone and wooden fort meant to secure the Eastern March. They rode silently for another league.

Melchior gave the signal to halt. "Announce our arrival, Detleff."

Detleff grabbed his horn and blew twice, paused, and then blew a third time. A horn blew once from the fort, recognizing the signal that an imperial *missus* had arrived.

"Raise the banner," Melchior said.

Detleff unslung the long pole with a silver cross at the top and a blue, silver-trimmed banner of light linen cloth. The inscription in silver read simply, "*Missus Dominicus.*"

Melchior spurred his horse forward. The dual tails of the banner fluttered gently in the breeze. As they approached the town, the mist slowly lifted, and afternoon sunshine burst from the clouds to the west, casting a light on the valley.

"Our Lord favors this mission," Thomas said.

The men began to murmur approval.

Melchior raised his leather-gloved hand to silence them. "The Lord favors the pious and the holy. We may be pious, but we are not holy men. We are warriors of Karolus, sent on a holy mission. You may pray for God's help. But make sure your sword blades are sharp, and your wits are sharper."

A pair of *milites* approached on horseback. When they reached Melchior and his men, they pulled up and saluted, "*Ave, Dominus.*"

"*Salve,*" Melchior replied, raising his gloved fist in return.

"I am Arbogast, commander of the watch. Count Lothar has been expecting you. A visit from our king's *missus* is always a blessing. He sent me as your escort, Lord Melchior."

"My Lord Lothar is gracious and generous, Arbogast," Melchior said. "Please lead the way."

The two horsemen turned around and slowly led Melchior's band toward the town.

***

Hincmar reached the Fulda Valley at noon. Weak from his wound and exhausted, thirsty from the ride, he could barely stay in the saddle. Along the way, he dozed while riding. During one of those naps, his horse crossed the river at a ford. When he realized his mistake, he steered along the left bank of the river, hoping to reach the bridge and cross back to the town.

The horse led him to a small orchard, where he fell from the saddle into the arms of a pair of monks picking fruit. Before he could thank them, he passed out. When he woke up, he saw that they had cleaned and bandaged his wound. Once they realized he was awake, the monks offered him some wine.

"Drink this, Lord," one of the monks said. "If you can swallow it, I have some figs and a piece of bread as well."

Hincmar sipped the wine gratefully. He then opened his mouth and took the piece of bread and sipped more wine. When he finished, the monk gave him a fig.

"Thank you, but... how long... have I been here?" Hincmar asked. His voice was weak and halting.

"When we took you from your horse, you fell asleep. Maybe two hours, lord."

"Then it is past noon. Please help me mount. I must see Count Lothar."

The monks looked at each other. "You need more rest, Lord. And the wound may bleed if you ride again."

"No matter. Please help me mount."

One monk lifted Hincmar to his feet while the other prepared the horse. When they got Hincmar into the saddle, one of them spoke, "Ride very slowly, Lord. Think of the wound."

"Thank you," Hincmar said. He turned the horse and spurred it up the road towards the fort. He wended his way through farm fields and meadows along the river, but slowed when he reached a small but thick wood. Just as he entered the wood, the assassin struck once more.

"I have you now, Frank!" Osgar hissed from behind a rock. He stepped out onto the trail and cocked his arm back to throw his spear with the same deadly accuracy as he had done scores of times in the past. Weak from the ride, Hincmar merely sat staring at the Saxon. He barely noticed the wicked missile poised to kill. Yet even in his fevered mind, he sensed he was a dead man. He tried to mumble a prayer.

With a rustle of branches, Spad leapt from the thicket. Moving like a wolf after a doe, he charged the assassin with his hunting spear. But Osgar reacted to the movement. The Saxon quickly pivoted and raised his spear at the old hunter. His eyes widened as Walla's hunting dagger pierced his armpit, sending a torrent of blood down his side. The young hunter twisted the dagger into Osgar's vitals.

The assassin pulled free from Walla's grasp. He staggered, dropped the spear, and collapsed onto the soft earth. His body convulsed. "Odin! Odin!" Osgar gasped. "Don't let me die among the hated Franks!"

With his last measure of strength, Osgar reached for his spear, fingers scratching madly at the black soil. But Spad's *Francisca* sliced through the dying Saxon's wrist, sending a pool of blood that stained the dark earth.

"You'll not use that hand to kill again, Saxon," Spad said grimly.

Osgar's dark visage faced his killer. "A curse on you, Frank..."

Hincmar barely realized what had happened. Spad took the reins and guided his mount to the edge of the wood. There, he slapped the horse's haunches and sent it galloping down the road towards the bridge.

***

Hincmar awoke with two young girls attending him.

"He is awake," one of them said.

Hincmar blinked in confusion while one of the girls wiped his brow. He was on a couch in Lothar's chambers.

Lothar smiled a wicked smile. "I thought you dead, Hincmar. I almost called Willehad to give you unction. For what good it might do. But your lust for life is a good omen."

"I… I thirst," Hincmar said weakly.

One of the girls put a goblet of wine to his lips. He drank a few swallows and stopped. "Water," he gasped.

The other girl brought a skin of water, and he eagerly drank from it as if it were his mother's breast. When he drank his fill, he fell back.

"Now that you are refreshed, tell me what happened," Lothar said. "Who did this?"

"I was ambushed by an assassin."

"An assassin? What kind of assassin?"

"A Saxon. I wounded the commander of Udela's guard."

Lothar flushed with anger. "Why would you do that? She's our ally."

"She is no ally of mine. Her guard has unabated hatred for Franks."

"She allowed this?"

"No, Lord. It happened so quickly. I dispatched him, but the other guards… his men, rushed me.

"Did you even speak with the queen?"

"Yes, Lord," Hincmar said softly.

"Did you deliver the message?"

"Yes, Lord."

"What was her reaction?"

"She was happy."

"Happy? That Karolus is sending his army here for her to destroy?" Lothar smiled mischievously. "She is indeed a warrior queen."

"She's a witch. I saw with my own eyes, an act of sorcery I once only imagined."

Lothar's face grew concerned. "What kind of sorcery? Of course, there are rumors, but…"

"They are more than rumors, Lord. I told you her guard suddenly attacked me. Their hatred of Franks is beyond reason."

"Maybe not beyond reason," Lothar said. "Karolus has chased them from most of their ancestral lands. Forced them from the gods of their ancestors. Who wouldn't hate a people for that?"

"You speak like a Saxon, Lord."

"Do I? Well, soon there may be no difference. Udela will join with me, and we shall rid ourselves of this over-pious king and his onerous version of Christianity. And after him, the pope and the Greek emperor."

Hincmar's eyes burned in anger. He realized his master, Stilicho, served a disloyal noble. "Is My Lord Stilicho in accord with this?"

"He is."

Hincmar could tell he lied. He grew limp with exasperation, pledged to Stilicho and bound by Frankish tradition and honor to follow him over all except Karolus.

"When will Udela arrive?"

"By the moon. She awaits the arrival of Avars. Lord, these are ancient enemies of Lord Karolus. What mischief is this?"

"Your lord Stilicho should have told you. He is pledged to me. I am pledged to Udela, and she is pledged to me."

"Are you pledged to Avars?" Hincmar's voice grew scratchy.

Lothar smiled. "No. They are merely a tool. We need their horses. The *scara* Melchior leads must be destroyed. Avars will give us the advantage."

"Lord Melchior..." Hincmar's voice weakened.

"What of him?"

"Udela wants him murdered when he arrives. I told her he was a messenger of our king-and-emperor." He immediately regretted passing on the evil queen's message. But the wound wore him and had drained his concentration.

"What matter now? Udela is right. I just need to arrange the right time, in case others are as hesitant as you, Hincmar. But you are a good warrior, and I will need good men. My girls will bring you soup and then see if they can arouse your warrior's strength, eh?"

With that, Lothar girded his belt and left. Giggling, one of the girls spooned soup into Hincmar's mouth. Almost imperceptibly, the other began to gently wipe his body with a soft, wet cloth.

***

The blare of a brace of trumpets announced the arrival of Lord Melchior, *Missus Dominicus* of Karolus, King of the Franks, and Emperor of the Romans. Arbogast led Melchior's band over the stone bridge that spanned the Fulda and halted.

"Why do we stop?" Melchior asked.

"Count Lothar wanted to greet you here himself, lord," Arbogast said.

Melchior glanced at the abbey to his right and the fort to his left. The abbey looked run-down. Not like the crown of Christendom Karolus had hoped it would become. Lothar's fort looked no better. The ramparts seemed less than formidable.

"He has done little to improve the place," Melchior said at last. "Karolus will not be pleased to learn of this."

"Lord, the Saxons have kept Count Lothar busy enough. Besides, the fort is secure."

"I don't care about his fort. Lord Karolus wants his people protected. And the abbey."

They waited for twenty minutes, but Lothar did not arrive.

***

Willehad was in heated consultation with Lothar as to when and how to eliminate Melchior. "It must appear a natural act," Willehad said. "Perhaps Vulmar's potion can be ingested. Once he has sickened and dies, you can find a pretext to disarm and execute his band."

Lothar scoffed. "It sounds easy. But after all these weeks, the potion has failed to send Baugulf to his maker."

"I have investigated the matter. The oafs charged with caring for him are to blame. They mixed up the potion and consumed it, giving Baugulf their wine."

"How long have you known this?"

"A few days." Lothar's questions irritated Willehad.

"Why didn't you tell me?"

"What happens with the clergy is my domain, not yours, Count Lothar."

"It is when our plans are in jeopardy, Your Grace." Lothar paused a moment and then spread his hands. "Very well. Perhaps we can arrange it so both our pastoral and temporal victims are stricken by the same malady."

Willehad twisted the cross on his chest. "Now you are speaking like the king-and-emperor you shall be!"

The blast of trumpets turned their attention.

"That's Melchior," Willehad said.

A scowl crossed Lothar's face. "I must greet this interloper sent by Karolus. I will have a great dinner arranged for the *missus*. I suggest you get the potion prepared."

"I have but little left. Somehow, the fools who ingested it also managed to spill the remainder. I must await Vulmar's return."

"And when is that?"

"Soon, Count Lothar. Very soon."

***

From the fortress gate, a small party rode out to meet them with trumpets blaring. Lothar's banner fluttered in the hands of his squire. Beside him rode Willehad, his squat figure nearly crushing the pony he rode.

"A likely pair your lord and his bishop make," Melchior said.

Arbogast bristled. "The count and bishop of Fulda are two of the noblest men in Frankland."

"Indeed? And this is now Frankland?"

Lothar pulled up on his horse as Melchior finished speaking.

"*Salve, Missus Dominicus*," Lothar said with a gloved hand raised in salute.

"*Salve*, Count Lothar… Your Grace." Melchior nodded at the pair but did not raise his hand.

"Is this your *scara*?" Lothar sniffed as he looked at Melchior's small band of *milites*. "There are rumors of an army led by you."

"Don't be quick to dismiss rumors. I am a general as well as a *missus*. I have ridden ahead to prepare the way and to deliver official messages from our King-and-Emperor, Karolus."

Willehad flashed a broad but somehow menacing grin. "Excellent! I was hoping to hear from our king and our good Bishop Angilram."

"I bring secular tidings for Count Lothar and ecclesial tidings for Abbot Baugulf, but unfortunately, none for Your Grace." Melchior disliked the faux bishop.

Willehad's eyes widened. He pursed his lips and fumbled for his gold cross. But he made no reply. Melchior could tell he was up to no good.

"How far off is the rest of your *scara*, Lord?" Lothar asked. "The rumor is you have five thousand *milites* advancing this way."

"I would rather discuss all of this after my men are properly refreshed." Melchior did not want to answer too many questions too soon.

Willehad smiled pleasantly. "Of course! Count Lothar is ever about business. It is I who must remind him of pleasantries and pleasures. He works hard to preserve our lord Karolus's interests here on the march."

"I'm sure he does," Melchior said. "Here on the march."

"Count Lothar, let us lead these bold Franks to the barracks where they and their mounts can rest," Willehad said.

Lothar nodded. His eyes bored into Melchior's, trying to measure his mettle. Melchior's eyes glared in return.

"Of course, Your Grace. Arbogast, lead us in."

Arbogast and his escort led them through the narrow street leading to the fort. Lothar and Willehad fell in with them, and Melchior and his men followed. From the high ramparts, more trumpets sounded.

Melchior's men rode silently. Each felt that death surrounded them. Fulda, the most Christian and pious town, looked ominous. None of the inhabitants were to be seen, and most of the mud and timber buildings were shuttered tight. The horses' hooves made sucking noises as they plodded through the sea of mud that covered the winding streets. Then, they saw the fort up close.

Embrasures incomplete... towers unmanned... many stones have fallen to the dry moat – half-filled with mud and the stench of sewage and garbage. Melchior noted the decrepit state of the defenses. The smell permeated even the coarsened nostrils of these hardened warriors.

"Look at the garbage they filled the moat with," Cassyon observed.

"Saxons like to bathe in that shit." Fromm's deep voice could be heard at the head of the band.

"Smells worse than five hundred dead Saxons," Cassyon replied.

Laughter erupted.

"I do not believe Lord Melchior wants us to make light of our friends here," Audeon said. "In such circumstances, it is better we observe but not comment."

They all looked at him in surprise. The easy-going Audeon seldom offered his opinion, and when he did, it was usually in support of another's opinion.

"I believe Lord Audeon is right," Jurchen said.

Melchior was anxious that his men could give something away, but neither Lothar nor Willehad heard the banter.

"Interesting tactic, filling your moat with offal and detritus, Count Lothar," Melchior said. He pointed upward as they drew closer. "Why isn't there a full complement on the towers?"

"I'll give a complete accounting of our defenses in good time, *missus*," Lothar said. The anger in his voice was obvious.

"Count Lothar is being modest," Willehad said. "Truth is, his forays across the march into pagan lands have kept the local Saxons in hiding. Just as our Lord-and-King Karolus wishes."

"Our lord, king, and emperor wishes the Saxons Christianized into his dominion or…" Melchior hesitated. He did not like the second part of his mandate.

"Or what, Lord?" Willehad asked.

"Or nothing. He wishes them all to follow Christ," Melchior said. His mind had trouble accepting Karolus's ultimatum until he recalled serving a regime that did not even offer the option of conversion.

"I have personally converted many Saxons, lord. Why, your priest there, Jurchen, was once a pagan lad from yonder. I brought him into the light of the church and ordained him."

"*Ad majorem gloriam dei*, I suppose," Melchior said.

"Indeed, Lord," Willehad said with a grin. "We do everything for God's greater glory."

"And Karolus's I hope," Melchior said.

Neither Lothar nor Willehad responded. They rode through the trellis gate, and a half score of servants scrambled to help with the horses. Once their horses were stabled, Melchior's men were led to barracks. Melchior started to join them.

"No, no, *Missus*," Lothar said. "I have a room for you near my chambers."

"The priests will stay at my residence," Willehad said.

"I prefer to stay with my *milites*, Count Lothar," Melchior retorted. He realized they were dividing his men. But he also realized he had little choice.

"Nonsense, you are a lord. I insist."

"Very well. But I insist that my squire accompany me. And Lord Audeon."

"Lord Audeon? Since when does a *missus dominicus* travel with a lord?"

"Since our lord, king-and-emperor ordered it," Melchior said.

"Audeon is a son of the great Karolus," Jurchen interjected.

Lothar and Willehad looked genuinely surprised.

"As for the priests, they too must stay with me," Melchior said.

Lothar signaled agreement with a wave of his hand.

"Mass is in two hours," Willehad said. "Then we shall have a welcoming feast."

"At the abbey?" Melchior asked. He glanced back across the town at the half-finished steeple of the Fulda abbey.

"No," Lothar said. "In the chapel right here in the fort."

"But shouldn't the abbot be part of this?"

"I am a bishop," Willehad said. "Once out of the environs of the abbey, I rule." He glanced at Lothar. "When it comes to things ecclesiastic, that is."

***

Although a dozen voices chanted a haunting hymn, the Mass was understated by Frankish standards. Willehad officiated, and along with his secretaries and deacons, he ordered Jurchen and Father Thomas to assist. Melchior's entire band attended, except the pagan Fromm, who found the canteen suited his needs better. They had ample ale, and the barmaids had ample curves.

Over a score of candles cast a dim glow, but the dark, damp chapel remained mostly in shadows.

"This is the sparest chapel I have ever seen," Audeon said to Melchior as they knelt.

Melchior nodded. "Willehad is the sparest of clerics. He calls himself bishop but was never officially approved by the pope."

"But our king-and-emperor approved him?"

"As a last resort to placate his clan. An accommodation to solidify his status as the sole king of the Franks. Normally, the pope is in concord, and these things are a mere formality. But the pope objected strongly to the appointment and never sanctified him."

"Why not?"

"That remains a mystery."

"Yet our lord Karolus retained him."

"Yes," said Melchior. "Even the greatest among us can err. And can have flaws. Karolus decided that he did not want to risk losing the support of such a powerful family."

Although Melchior defended Karolus to the king's son, he was vexed by the idea of this false bishop. But he trusted Karolus had his reasons to look the other way. he just hoped that the decision would not prove too costly.

"I suppose at the proper time, he will be defrocked," Audeon said.

"Pray that it is not too late." He did not tell Audeon that he feared it might already be too late.

***

Heavy boots echoed down the stone corridor as the worshipers entered the hall of Lothar's fort. Several rows of long tables were arrayed before them. Although unadorned with cloth, the oak was scrubbed clean. Soon, plates clattered, and eager hands grabbed for loaves of bread and hunks of steaming hot meat. The warriors ate with zeal, and soon the hall reverberated with the hubbub of hungry soldiers at mess. Melchior sat at the high table with Willehad and Lothar. Audeon sat beside him, as did Jurchen and Thomas.

"Lord, they separated us from your men-at-arms," Audeon whispered.

"That's normal," Melchior replied. "At your home, among your people, things are more intimate. But great lords and kings sit in a hierarchy of church and nobility, warriors and freedmen, then peasants and slaves."

"So much for me to observe and learn, Lord," Audeon said.

"That's why our lord Karolus sent you with me," Melchior said.

"What's all the snickering about?" Lothar guffawed. "Franks eat first and talk later!" He dug into a large haunch of venison set before him. He gripped a small *Seaxe* and carved a chunk and chewed it off the point of the blade. He speared a second chunk and brandished it high.

"Lord Melchior, you are feasting on game taken from the Saxons," Lothar said proudly.

At one of the back tables, Cassyon mumbled to Gaetano, "I prefer to feast on Saxon women."

Gaetano laughed, "Or any women. I don't favor wild game such as this. I find it tolerable in the forest. But here in a *demesne,* a civilized meal should present itself."

"I think your wish has been granted," Cassyon said.

"Here comes the ox meat!" Bavo exclaimed. He sat at a table between them and Melchior, aligned with other senior *milites.*

Jurchen took it all in as he sat next to the bishop, who gave him knowing glances. It occurred to him that Lothar had separated Melchior's men. Although this was normal for such feasts, he suspected foul play. He decided to try to pry the secret from the bishop. "When will you act, Your Grace?"

Willehad smirked. "I don't know what you mean, Abbot."

Jurchen took a sip of his ale. "I mean what I said, Your Grace."

Willehad leaned over, his wine-sotted lips almost touching Jurchen's ear. "When Melchior's band is beyond their senses, Count Lothar will strike."

A dark figure appeared in the shadows near the alcove that led to the kitchens.

"And from the looks of things, that should be none too soon," Willehad said.

"Who is that?" Jurchen asked.

"Vulmar... I hope he brought spices for the drink. We wouldn't want our guests to drink flat ale and wine."

Jurchen looked a second time, but the figure was gone. He glanced at the men-at-arms. Cassyon, Bavo, and Gaetano were drinking heavily. Detleff seemed more controlled. As did Werinbert.

"Those two are not drinking with much gusto. I should go and encourage them," Jurchen suggested.

"By all means." Willehad turned to Thomas. "Father, you must try more of this excellent wine."

Jurchen hovered over Detleff and Werinbert. He made a sign of the cross as if to bless their food. "Warn the others that Willehad and Lothar aim to dull your senses with drink and then seize you."

Detleff's eyes widened. He pushed his way through a table of Lothar's warriors, who shoved him and jeered as he went by.

"Drink more!" one said.

"Men from east of the Rheine can't down their ale like we men of the marches. You West Franks have grown soft," said another, a big man with a fat belly and a mustache dripping with foam and animal fat.

"But we can down pigs who can't mind their own business," Cassyon said. The ale was getting to him, but unlike Lothar's men, Melchior's men were far from sotted.

The large Frank rose and slid the table aside. "I'll gut you like a..."

Jurchen jumped between the two men and held them apart. "Peace of God! Peace of God! We can't have drunken brawls in the hall of Count Lothar and in the presence of the bishop."

The soldiers were all up on their feet. They formed a ring around Jurchen, Cassyon, and the Frankish warrior. "Show him, Maiuel! Show him!"

Maiuel blinked and slurred his words. "Fa, fa…you are no priest to me." He pulled a *Francisca* dangling from his wide belt and raised it over his head. "I'll cut through you, priest, just to kill this puppy who lets men in robes protect him."

"Out of my way, Abbot Jurchen. I can handle pigs like him." Cassyon reached for his *Francisca*. But he had brought a short *Seaxe*. He reached for it, but Cassyon, slowed by drink, fumbled the *Seaxe*, dropping it to the floor.

An evil glint came from Maiuel's bloodshot eyes. The large Frank roughly pushed Jurchen aside and raised his *Francisca* to split Cassyon's skull. But his arm suddenly fell limp as Jurchen's *Seaxe*, hidden under his cassock, cut deep into the exposed side of the Frank. Maiuel made a sucking sound. He stiffened and fell to the oak floor with a resounding thud before the *Francisca* tumbled harmlessly to the floor. The fall of this imposing physique silenced the few warriors cheering him on.

One of Lothar's men pointed at Cassyon. "You killed Maiuel!"

The Franks drew closer.

"He's killed Maiuel!" several of them murmured.

They were all now looking at Cassyon. Jurchen had moved his blade so quickly that no one realized the man in robes had made the mortal cut. True to their Christian upbringing, none expected it either.

"Retrieve your weapon, Cassyon. You killed him fairly and in self-defense," Jurchen said, slipping his *Seaxe* under his robes.

Cassyon's eyes widened. "What have I done?"

"I want no more fighting from you, Cassyon," Jurchen commanded.

"Yes, abbot."

"Give me your weapon for safekeeping."

"Of course, abbot." Cassyon retrieved his Seaxe from the floor. He passed it, handle-first, to Jurchen. Maiuel's compatriots failed to notice it was clean of blood.

The Jurchen knelt, said a prayer over the body, then stood up. As he did, he made sure Cassyon's blade was dipped in the dead man's blood and vitals. "Take this man away. No one should disturb the peace."

With that, he walked through the throng towards the dais bearing the weapons of both fighters.

"What happened?" asked Willehad when he returned to his seat.

"I heard the sounds of fighting," Lothar said.

"Indeed, Count Lothar. One of your men attacked one of Lord Melchior's men. It was *Francisca* against *Seaxe*. Seems the *Seaxe* triumphed over the old Frankish weapon."

Jurchen tossed the *Seaxe* and the *Francisca* on the table in front of Lothar.

Melchior looked at Jurchen and gave a faint nod.

"Who was killed?" Lothar asked.

"Some bear of a man they called Maiuel. I said the prayers for the dead over him. He can receive a Christian burial in the morning."

Lothar's face hardened. "What? Impossible! Maiuel is one of our best fighters."

"Perhaps he had too much ale, Count Lothar," Willehad said smugly.

"Perhaps," Lothar replied.

"Have more ale, Lord," Willehad said.

"Yes, drink the ale. It is quite good," Melchior said.

Jurchen gave a knowing glance at Melchior before taking up his tankard. It occurred to him that killing men had become a little too easy — even for him.

Chapter 14

Fromm liked the canteen. He had already had two of the better whores. Both were Saxon women and slaves of the old Frankish warrior who ran the canteen. The warrior, named Boso, had taken over the canteen when he put down his arms. It was a fitting sinecure for a landless warrior who had served his masters well. Hook-nosed, creased of face, and bald of pate, the wily old Frank was a deal-maker with a strong sense of garrison politics, gossip, and rumor. Fromm knew the type. The deals he kept to himself. The gossip and rumor he passed on to Lothar.

"You look like you're ready for your third wench, Norseman," Boso said with a wink and a nod.

Squeals and grunts came from behind the dirty blankets that lined the back wall, behind which several ale-soaked soldiers thumped away.

"I'm ready. But first, let's have another draught of that ale and a joint of something to gnaw on," Fromm said.

"Anfelisia!" Boso made a sign, and one of the slaves, a slender dark-eyed girl, ran quickly to fetch the food and drink.

"That's a right pretty lass." Fromm belched.

Bozo glared. "She's no whore, Dane. If she were, I'd be a rich man."

"I find that hard to believe. She's the comeliest wench I have seen here."

"Do you think you are the first sod to drool over her?"

Fromm's mouth broke into a wide smile as the girl placed a large mug of ale and a leg of mutton before him. Her doe-like eyes and long dark hair on caramel skin were unlike anything he had seen in the north.

"You Norsemen like dark-eyed girls. That much I have learned in my forty years," Boso said.

"Who wouldn't? Although I do prefer a bit more meat on them. She can't be more than thirteen. Slip of a girl, she is."

"She's eighteen. And a virgin, if you'd like to know."

Fromm put his ale down. "I find that hard to believe."

"She is under the protection of Willehad."

"His mistress?"

"I told you, she is pure, as they say. The rumor is the fat old cleric fathered her on a journey to Italy. She says she's a Lombard, but clearly, Roman blood runs through her veins."

Fromm laughed. "Why didn't the bishop marry her off? Or put her in a convent? You Christians seem to like to do that to your women when it conveniences you."

S.W. O'Connell

"That's because we are civilized. Unlike you pagan Norse. They say someday the entire race of Norsemen will sail from their homelands to raid, leaving their women behind."

"An interesting idea." Fromm took another gulp of his ale.

Boso leaned forward and spoke softly. "Some say Willehad plans on making her his wife. Others say he looks to sell her to the Avar chief, Dgno."

"I don't know which would be worse for a poor lass like that."

Boso shrugged. "You came in with the *missus*, didn't you?"

"You're an observant man, Frank," Fromm said.

"I rode with him once. Yes, it's hard to believe, but I once wore the *brunia*. Melchior was but a lad. But even then, a great leader. Would that he were the count, instead of that sod Lothar."

Fromm sensed something wrong and concocted a tale. "I rode in with them. But I only joined the pack of Franks a day earlier. I am on my way to offer my services to the empress in Miklagard. I saw signs of Avars about and figured I'd join them for security."

"You want to serve the Byzantine empress, Irene? She's a greater witch than the Saxon queen Udela. Why, she blinded and killed her own son to attain sole rule of the Greeks who call themselves Roman."

Fromm grinned, letting some of the mutton fat mixed with ale dribble through his beard. "I hear she likes Norse manhood. Figure if I can't fight my way to riches, I could try shagging my way."

Boso eyed the big, muscular Dane. "Yes. I suppose she'd add one like you to her Varangian Guard. But women like Irene are most dangerous. Besides, if you sign on with Lothar, you might make that wealth without the trouble of crossing to the far side of the world. If you had taken the head of the *missus* while you were with him, Lothar might have granted you a vast estate and the pick of the Saxon women."

Fromm's face remained passive. "Tell me more. Perhaps I can still do it."

"No need. They are filling the *missus* and his men with ale. My ale. I know they laced it with something to send them to their dreams. Then, the dungeon, followed by a painful death."

"How do you know they laced it?"

"I saw that other sod Vulmar about. The exorcist. He probably taps Satan on the shoulder and says go home to mother."

Fromm smiled, but he feared devils like any true Norseman. "You served this *missus*. How could you be part of killing an old comrade in arms?"

"You Norsemen are so romantic... and so stupid. That was then. This is now. The rumor is... Lothar plans on supplanting Karolus. There's a stirring in the land. A big lad like you could do well."

Fromm realized he was on to something. "Tell the count that my services are for sale."

"What should I tell him you want?"

"I want five bags of silver." He would have taken three.

Boso bowed his head in agreement. "A bargain price, Norseman."

"And the girl." Fromm realized the outrageous demand would make them take him more seriously.

Boso's face reddened. "The girl? Anfelisia?"

"Anfelisia. As you said, we Norsemen like the dark-eyed ones. Why else did you think I was heading east? You just saved me the travel."

"I am afraid that Willehad would not give her over to a..."

"To a pagan?" Fromm laughed.

"No, to a Norseman. They say the day is coming when pagans will be treated as Christians."

"Besides, he is saving her to bait a certain Frankish lord."

"Which one?" Fromm asked.

"Mallobaudes. Curiously, he is Melchior's cousin. When Melchior dies, they say Mallobaudes gets his land. His influence will be useful when they..." Boso hesitated. "I will talk to Count Lothar. Be satisfied with your silver."

***

The meal was grinding into its third hour. Outside, the marchland had long grown dark, both from the setting sun and the gathering of storm clouds that soon drenched everything in a cold rain. Melchior's head began to nod. Jurchen noticed the men at the table had already passed out, as had Father Thomas.

"Not feeling well, Lord Melchior?" Lothar asked with a devious grin.

"Just tired. We will depart for our chambers... "

"Your men have passed out. Can't take ale well, can they?" Lothar taunted.

Jurchen watched it unfold with a growing feeling of horror. He suddenly realized the ale was spiked. *They used some of the same potion reserved for Baugulf.*

"My men..." Melchior's eyes grew heavy.

"You will be escorted to your chambers, Lord," Lothar said.

Melchior opened and closed his eyes, looking dazed.

"Are you all right, *Dominus*?" Jurchen whispered. He did not want to arouse suspicion. Willehad and Lothar believed he was still with them.

"That ale... it..." Melchior slumped forward, and his head hit the table, spilling ale and sending fruit and nuts spilling in all directions.

"This proved easier than I had thought," Lothar said. "I should cut all their throats right now."

"Selling them as slaves to the Avars might prove profitable," Willehad said.

Jurchen was disgusted and fearful. He thought the plans were to get them drunk. He realized now that Willehad had used the potion on the *missus* and his band.

"What of his *scara*? With five thousand men-at-arms, it can wreak havoc on this place and ruin all of your plans, Your Grace," Jurchen said. *I need to stall until I have a plan.*

"Perhaps Jurchen is right. Count Lothar, I suggest you hold them ransom. The *scara* might hold off on an assault if they know we'll kill their commander."

Lothar scratched his beard and nodded. "Perhaps... Chamberlain! Have what men are still sober drag the *missus* and his retainers to their quarters. Secure them there with a sturdy lock and chain. And post two guards."

The chamberlain bowed. "As you command, Lord."

"Keeping them alive is a wise decision," Jurchen said.

Lothar scoffed. "It's no decision, priest—just a tactic until I decide on how to dispose of them. I think my fair Saxon queen would not mind a slave such as Melchior. Of course, we'll maim and blind him first."

"Yes, every queen wants a blind and maimed slave about."

Lothar did not react to Jurchen's barb.

"I suspect our Saxon friends would like some Christians to sacrifice at the next offering to their gods," Willehad said. "I don't favor such heathen practices, but a *missus* of Karolus as a sacrifice might send a bold message to the other nobles of Frankland."

Jurchen shuddered. He knew he had to act quickly to save them from death or something even worse. He needed to find Stilicho... and Fromm.

***

Melchior's head pounded like a heavy *Francisca* against a war shield. His dry mouth burned from a coating of his intestinal juices. He lay immobile in the darkness. *Am I dead? Did they poison me? No, I can move my limbs, and I smell something putrid. My innards...I threw up most of Lothar's poison.*

Melchior heard low groans. "Detleff, Audeon... is anyone awake?"

A slow moaning was the reply. He finally managed to get to his feet. But he felt wobbly like a newborn fawn.

Detleff's hoarse voice brayed, "I'm awake, Lord. But I wish I were dead."

"I think Lothar tried to poison us." Melchior saw a faint light from what looked like the door. He stumbled toward it and tugged at the latch. "We're barricaded in here."

"I think these are our chambers, Lord. I feel our saddlebags here against the wall where I left them," Detleff said. "Oh God, my head hurts, and my throat burns."

"We need to find a candle and get some light," Melchior said.

Detleff rummaged through the bags. "Let me see if I can find your amulet."

"My amulet?"

"Yes, Lord, you told me to hold it for you... that it came from the Avar trove and held the power of the world."

Melchior recalled no amulet. "Very well. See if you can find it then."

Detleff rummaged in the dark for some minutes. "I found it. Lord, I found it."

Melchior made his way over to his squire. The others began to stir, but their sounds were those of the living dead.

"Here it is, Lord." Detleff's powerful hand opened, and he placed a leather pouch attached to a thin rope into Melchior's palm.

Fingers fumbling in the dark, Melchior opened the pouch and extracted something metallic and square. He rubbed the smooth edges with his fingers. Muscle memory caused him to flip the metal box open, as if by magic. The smell of alcohol permeated his nostrils. *Lighter fluid!*

"My Ronson!" Melchior said in surprise. Despite the headache, his mind cleared its thoughts.

"What, Lord?" Detleff asked.

"My Ronson! This... this is the amulet?"

"Yes, Lord. You wanted it secreted until the right time. I thought this was the right time."

He remembered the Ronson he carried through the war. The one the Canadians... A thousand memories flooded Melchior as he ran his fingers on the smooth sides... steel. He remembered smoking untold cigarettes and the quick flame that lit them. He remembered smoking in university... in the army... in Canada...he held the first physical proof that... *I am not mad! I really did come here from the future...*

Any doubt about his time in the twentieth century was gone. He had traveled here through time. Ever since he awoke at Aachen devoid of memory, he had tried to ignore the glimpses into the future as some madness he carried. But now they were clear. The Canadians had succeeded. *What can this journey gain for people more than a thousand leagues and a thousand years distant?*

A small flame erupted, and Detleff covered his eyes in fear.

The damned thing still works! The Ronson's fuel traveled with me!

Melchior admired the flame and took in the smell. He raised it, and as his eyes adjusted, he scanned the shadows of the room. "There!"

Melchior made his way to a lantern and lit it. The dull rays flooded the chamber.

"That's better." He found a second lantern and lit that. "Even better."

"What happened?" Audeon said as he struggled to his feet. "I feel like a battle-ax has hit me."

Melchior closed the Ronson, put the stainless steel "amulet" back into the pouch, and secured it around his neck. "The ale had something in it. We were... drugged."

Audeon held his temples. "What do you mean... drugged, Lord?"

It occurred to Melchior that he used a word unknown to this time. "They put a potion in the ale to force us to sleep. We are locked in our chambers."

Cassyon and Gaetano began to stir, along with Bavo and Werinbert. Groans and moans filled the room.

"Our water skins are here. Give them something to drink, Detleff," Melchior said.

"The bastards didn't kill us," Bavo said.

"They are going to use us for something," Audeon replied.

"For what?" Cassyon asked. "Oh, my head. Say, where's Jurchen?"

"That false priest betrayed us," Bavo said. "Bugger a bunch of priests."

"But he saved me in that fight with that big Frank, Maiuel," Cassyon said.

"Bulls' balls, lad! I saw you kill him," Bavo said

"I saw the blood on your blade," Gaetano said.

"I too," Werinbert said.

"No. The *Francisca* was coming down on me. I was going to die. Then the one they called Maiuel fell to the ground with a blade in his armpit. Jurchen killed him — with what, I didn't see. But he did it. He saved me. And he tried to warn us of the ale. He may be a rogue priest, but he is no traitor."

"Then why isn't he in here with us?" Bavo asked.

"Maybe they discovered his actions and killed him," Werinbert said.

"No. Because I told him to pretend he remained in league with his master, Willehad," Melchior said. "Enough babble about Jurchen."

"They took my *Seaxe*. I had it with me at the feast," Audeon said.

"Mine too," Cassyon said. "And my broadsword."

"Lord, my weapon is where I left it," Detleff said. "And yours, Lord."

"They left mine," Werinbert said.

"Mine too," Bavo said.

Gaetano reached under his sleeping cloth. "Bow and full quiver. Long *Seaxe*."

"Well, they make mistakes then. That's good. We need them to make mistakes if we are to succeed."

Thomas had recovered. "God has given us this gift, *Dominus*."

Melchior girded himself and secured his *Seaxe* and broadsword. "*Wehrt euch.*"

"Lord?" Detleff asked.

Melchior had slipped into 20th century German. "I said, arm yourselves."

Melchior handed his *Francisca* to Audeon. "Make sure you take the sword and shield from the first of Lothar's men you kill."

Audeon hefted the blade in his hand. "Yes, Lord."

"I suppose we'll have to do without some of our weapons for now," Melchior said. "But we'll use what God has given us. As for you, Cassyon, I think we'll find another long blade somewhere in the fort. Meanwhile, take Detleff's *Seaxe*."

"What shall we do now, Lord?" Audeon asked.

"Pray," Melchior said, dropping to his knees.

The men all got to their knees and bowed their heads.

"Pray for what, Lord?" Bavo asked.

"Pray Jurchen can get us help from an old friend. Now, Father Thomas will lead us in prayer. Pray!"

Thomas began to pray in Latin. They followed along. Even the lowest peasants of Frankland knew their Latin prayers. Melchior was amazed to find that he was once again following along fluently.

"*Pater noster qui es en caelis sanctificetur nomen tuum adveniat regnum tuum fiat voluntas tua sicut in caelo et in terra panem nostrun quotidianem da nobis hodie et dimmitte nobis debita nostra sicut et nos dimmitimus debitoribus nostris et ne nos inducas in tentationem sed libera nos a malo, Amen.*"

The men prayed fervently. Raised in pre-Nazi Germany with a weak form of Christianity, Melchior felt devotion he had never seen in the 20th century. Devotion freely emanated from these simple men. *The twentieth century could learn something of true piety.*

For a moment, Melchior forgot that these pious men who evoked such spiritual power were also warriors of unimaginable courage, physical power... and savagery.

***

Hincmar pushed the young girl away. She had turned her medical ministrations and ablutions into something less modest.

"Find my clothes... my *brunia*.... my sword," he commanded in a soft but firm voice.

"But Count Lothar said we should satisfy you in every way."

He regarded the young girl with a mix of desire and disgust. "And well you have. Now, do as I command."

"But your wound, Lord?"

Hincmar felt a burning stiffness where the blade struck. "Bleeding has stopped. Lying about will not make me better."

"But Count Lothar..."

His burning eyes showed that further hesitation was futile. The girl scampered off to find his things. A half-hour later, with her help, he was properly fitted with his *brunia*, sword, *Seaxe*, and *Francisca*. He put on his heavy leather gloves.

The girl looked at him demurely.

He regarded her. *She is not un-pretty.*

Hincmar stroked her cheek. "I will tell Count Lothar you served me well and followed his instructions flawlessly."

The girl blushed and lowered her head. "You are more than kind, Lord."

After months of serving Lothar's every demand, she finally had an encounter that stirred her heart as well as her body. She caressed his beard and kissed him fully on the lips. "You are the finest warrior I have ever known, Lord."

"I must go."

"What should I tell Count Lothar when he asks about your whereabouts, Lord?"

"Tell him I am doing My Lord's will."

She smiled. "He will be pleased."

Good... she thinks I meant Lothar.

Hincmar nodded and left through a back door. He had to find Stilicho. Hincmar avoided Lothar's guards and made his way to the barracks of the mounted warriors under Stilicho's command. The girl had told him of a great feast. That meant most of Lothar's warriors would be eating and drinking.

He arrived at the barracks, where one of the warriors greeted him.

"Hincmar, you are back!"

"I am back, Chlodwig. Didn't Count Lothar inform Lord Stilicho of my return?"

"No, Hincmar. And he did not say where you went."

"I carried a message to the Saxons for Count Lothar."

"The Saxons? And they let you return?"

"Yes, and if things go wrong, they may well return here."

"What do you mean?"

"I can't say just yet. I must talk to Lord Stilicho."

Chlodwig led Hincmar to Stilicho's chambers.

"You are back!" Stilicho jumped to his feet.

"Some hours ago. Count Lothar insisted I stay in his quarters to be tended to."

"Tended to?"

"A Saxon assassin tried to kill me. He almost succeeded."

"But Lothar has made peace with them. And you were an emissary. They broke the peace, then?"

Hincmar shook his head. "I, I do not think so. I think it was a rogue who wanted me dead."

"And why?"

"I killed a few of the queen's guards at the queen's palace."

"You what?"

"In self-defense, Lord. The queen admitted as much. "She... she likes me."

"The Saxon witch likes you? Are you mad? Has she used her foul magic on you?"

"I think she tried, Lord. But I resisted - most of her charms."

Stilicho eyed the long-limbed and strong-muscled warrior. "But not all of them, eh?"

"There are evil things about. The queen and her Saxons are coming. Frankland is threatened. And I'm afraid Count Lothar is part of the plot."

"I know. And the sod of a bishop as well."

"You know already?"

"I just learned. From Father Jurchen. One of Willehad's false priests."

"Why would he tell you?" Hincmar asked.

"Why would the queen tell you?"

Hincmar flushed. "She trusts me."

"Well, Jurchen sought me. He warned me of the plot. Melchior is in danger."

"Lord Melchior?"

"Yes, and..."

Chlodwig returned. "Lord, a priest is here. He wants to speak to you. He says it's urgent."

"What priest? They are all with their bishop getting sotted."

"He is the priest they call Jurchen... the Saxon." Chlodwig spat the last word out like a curse.

"Jurchen? This bodes ill. Bring him in."

***

Stilicho and Hincmar listened attentively while Jurchen related what had happened to Melchior.

"Evil doings have descended on us," Stilicho said.

Hincmar said nothing.

Jurchen nodded. "If we don't act, Lord Melchior, his men, and possibly Baugulf will all be dead or enslaved by this time tomorrow."

Stilicho poured a cup of wine and drank as he pondered. "Things are moving quickly. I hoped this plot would evaporate into the Fulda mists. But I was wrong. Yet I am pledged to the count. I hesitate to break an oath like that."

"Lothar has not hesitated to break his oath to Karolus. And that is the greater oath," Jurchen said.

Hincmar lifted his chin. "Is it? The Queen of the Saxons wanted my allegiance, but I told her my first bond is to Lord Stilicho. That I would do only as he orders. Whether it is right, or even lawful."

Stilicho said nothing and took another draught of wine. He had much to ponder.

"And if it is immoral and sacrilege? Would you serve up your soul for fealty to a lord?" Jurchen retorted.

"You are a sacrilege, are you not? A priest by the hand of a false bishop is sacrilege itself," Hincmar said.

Jurchen's face reddened. "I suppose I *am* a sacrilege, as you say. But now, I'm not speaking as a priest, but as a warrior pledged to Lord Melchior and our king-and-emperor. So, Lord Stilicho, what say you?"

Stilicho hesitated, staring into his cup. At last, he spoke, "To break my oath to a count of the realm is a grave crime."

Jurchen's anger burst like a bolt of lightning. "In the chapel, we prayed together. I thought you stood with Melchior. Now you say you stand with Lothar, a man who is conspiring against his rightful ruler and the true Church. What kind of Frank are you? I'm a Saxon, yet I can see the evil that has descended on us."

Hincmar reached for his sword. "I'll strike you down for those words, Saxon pig!"

Jurchen's *Seaxe* flashed from under his robe, and its blade caught Hincmar's broadsword squarely. The strike was so quick that Hincmar let his iron grip go and his blade scampered across the floor.

Hincmar reached for his own *Seaxe*. "I am weak from my wound, Saxon, or you..."

"Enough! Put down your weapons." Stilicho's voice stopped both men.

"The Saxon must pay for this," Hincmar said.

"Your temper with Saxons has already unleashed killers against you, Hincmar. I think it's time to make friends, not enemies." Stilicho knew Hincmar was a hothead, but was sworn to him. Yet he realized something had changed ever so slightly in the young warrior. *The witch's magic?*

The Frank bowed his head and sheathed his *Seaxe*. "As you say, Lord."

Stilicho eyed Jurchen. "You too."

Jurchen shrugged and carefully slipped his blade under his robes.

"What have they done with Melchior and his hinds?" Stilicho asked.

"They are locked in their rooms under guard. Willehad convinced Lothar to sell them to the Avars or make them a gift to the Saxon queen."

"Melchior would not last long as a slave," Stilicho said with a grin. "I have my men ready for action. But the garrison outnumbers us four to one at least."

"Lord Melchior says your men are the best."

Stilicho nodded. "They are. How far is Melchior's army? These thousands of men? Maybe we can wait."

"There is no time for that."

"If I were Lothar, I'd hold Lord Melchior as barter when his army arrives," Stilicho said.

"Willehad advised as much. But who knows what Lothar will do?" Jurchen said. "We should act quickly."

Stilicho rubbed his chin and tugged at his beard. "We should. But if I strike now and lose, Melchior is lost. But if his army is nearby…"

Jurchen gave him a strange look. A very troubled look, but said nothing.

Stilicho nodded. Jurchen was telling him the truth. No army was coming. Stilicho knew Melchior well. The plan was nothing but a bluff.

"What are you going to do, Lord?" Hincmar looked at this master, then at the Saxon in priest's robes. "Do you believe this?"

Stilicho paused a moment and then said softly. "I do believe this. And though I am now pledged to Lothar, I once swore fealty to Melchior. No legal or moral authority ever released me from that pledge."

"I have studied some law at court. The earlier pledge takes precedence," Jurchen said.

"Lord Stilicho, this has implications for our entire band," Hincmar said. "Is it wise?"

Stilicho realized Hincmar's loyalty had switched, although the young man might not realize it himself. "No. It is not wise, Hincmar. But it is just. Therefore, I release you from your oath to me. You may pledge directly to Lothar. Go tell the others as much. If I have to face him and Willehad alone, with just my broadsword – I shall."

"You'll have my *Seaxe* as well, Lord," Jurchen said.

Hincmar glared at the Saxon. "I'll speak to the men. What should I say?"

"Say Lord Stilicho has decided that under both Church and Frankish law an earlier oath makes his current allegiance to Count Lothar null and void," Jurchen said.

Hincmar reddened. "What? This can't be true?"

Stilicho nodded. "Yes, Hincmar. Tell them that. They may all swear to Lothar directly, as may you."

Stilicho could tell Hincmar was confused. *This witch-queen has had her influence in some way. The hot-headed young Frank had followed me since he was a teen. I was more than a father to him in many ways. Yet he holds no allegiance to Melchior. And, even if Hincmar disliked and distrusted both Lothar and Willehad, in his mind, they are the rulers of the march.*

"You are truly noble, Lord," Hincmar said. "What do you propose we do?"

"I propose we pray with the priest." Stilicho dropped to his knees. So did Jurchen, who fumbled for his prayer book. Hincmar did the same, and together they prayed.

"Ave Maria gracia plena Dominus tecum benedicta tu in mulieribus et benedictus fructus ventris tui ihesu. Amen."

When they finished, Stilicho stood erect. The old warrior exuded a spiritual vitality that gave him a commanding presence. "Hincmar, go and do as we spoke. Father Jurchen and I will continue in prayer."

Chapter 15

Bishop Willehad's Chambers

When they finished the prayers, Jurchen trudged through the rain-soaked streets to see Willehad and learn his plans for Melchior or even influence him in some way. A priest Jurchen once knew stood at the door to the bishop's chambers.

"Father Anfeald?"

"The bishop is not to be disturbed, Jurchen," Anfeald said.

"Are you now his guard?"

"No. I'm his secretary."

"Then let me see him."

"He's busy."

"Busy? At what? We both know he rarely prays, even when he says Mass."

"That is not your affair, Jurchen."

"I want to know why I can't see my bishop."

Anfeald shifted his weight. He was a mid-sized man in his early thirties, but already suffered from rheumatism and was nearly bald. He squinted in the faint light. "Bishop Willehad is preparing correspondence."

"To whom? About what?"

"We both know that is not your affair."

Jurchen grabbed the front of Anfeald's robe. Twisting the cloth tight, he pulled the priest to him and lifted him, so he stood on the tips of his toes. "There is the matter of the copper coins, Anfeald."

"What.... What copper coins?"

"How we forget our little sins but dwell on the big ones. Yet the little sins can add up. Especially when the sins are committed against the laws of the church and the realm."

"I... I have no idea what you speak."

"Oh, but you do. Our little visit to the towns south of here. Was it, three years ago? Time flees us when we don't respect it."

Anfeald's eyes widened. "What do you want?"

"So... you remember now? A few coins from this chapel... a few from that chapel. I think we visited almost twenty in that one visit. The first time I watched you, I thought my eyes deceived me. But I watched you a second time, and my worst fears were confirmed. Those poor *villeins* trusted you, a representative of the church and the emperor. I suspect you have been doing it for years. You should have quite a little stash by now."

"So this is about money? I have none. It's all gone." Anfeald's face flushed crimson. *The fool just admitted to the accusation.*

"I accept your confession, Anfeald. At least your temporal one. As we both know, neither of us is a real priest. Now, what did you do with the coins? Is there a mistress? A wife? Come now, Anfeald." Jurchen twisted the cord tighter.

"I...I can't breathe Jurchen."

Jurchen loosened his grip and eyed him. "I don't care what your scheme was, Anfeald. Just let me in."

"You won't tell anyone?"

"No."

"The money was paid to the father of a girl I once knew...." Anfeald lowered his eyes. "I once killed a girl."

"Killed a girl? How... why?"

"A girl who resisted my advances."

"So, it's worse than I thought," Jurchen hissed.

"I committed a grave crime and needed *wergild* to pay for it. To do otherwise would have cost me my robe and maybe my life. It happened before I was ordained. Yet I'm still paying."

"No difference to the girl whether you were a priest or not. And we both know you are not. Stand aside."

Anfeald let Jurchen pass. Jurchen pulled the heavy bronze doorknob and stepped over the threshold. The bishop was indeed at his desk with a stack of vellum and a pot of ink.

"Your Grace, I have come to speak with you of Melchior."

"Who let you in?" Willehad had a look of guilt.

"Anfeald, of course," Jurchen said.

"He had strict orders to bar all from my chambers. What did you do to get by him?"

Jurchen smiled. "You ordained me, Your Grace. I heard his confession. You might want to check the accounts on any collection he has done for you lately."

Willehad shook his head slowly as if to will Jurchen away. "I can't have you in here."

"Who are you writing to at this hour, eminence? You should be leading services."

"My administrative duties take precedence. You know that. I am writing a letter to..."

"To whom, Your Grace?"

A smile slowly widened across the bishop's jowls. "Well, since you shall be the messenger, I suppose I should tell you."

"Messenger? Messenger of what?"

"I had intended to send Hincmar on the mission. But he is Lothar's man. I prefer my own. You are my own, aren't you, Jurchen?"

"You are allied with Count Lothar," Jurchen said.

"Indeed. But in certain matters, it is better the clergy be in charge. Don't you agree?"

"In charge of what?"

"The world, of course."

Jurchen knew Willehad as a dishonest and craven man driven by his desires, but he realized now he was a mad schemer of vast proportions.

Willehad dipped his nib into the inkpot and continued writing. His fat hand moved slowly, marking the vellum with the precise letters prescribed for ecclesiastic correspondence.

At last, Willehad finished the letter and held up the sheet to admire his work. "There, it shall be dry in a few minutes. A work of art, I must say. I could surpass any of Baugulf's wretches when it comes to official writing."

Jurchen grimaced. "Those wretches are preserving sacred scripture and capturing what little we know of the ancients. They do God's work. That is not something we should make light of, Your Grace." His pique at Willehad's comment surprised even him.

"I simply state the fact." Willehad's face brightened as he glanced at the stiff parchment. "Maybe I should have become a monk. Perhaps I am on the wrong side of this town."

Jurchen resisted the urge to respond. He needed to play along.

"There's a flagon of wine over there, Jurchen. Fetch it and two cups. Pour us each some refreshment, and I will tell you what you are going to do."

Jurchen silently poured the heavy red liquid into a pair of pewter cups. He glanced over at the drying parchment in the hope of reading it, but could not make out the words.

Willehad sipped the wine and smiled smugly. "I am so glad you took the trouble to disturb me, Jurchen. It must have been divine intervention."

"Your Grace, an idea suddenly crossed my mind. Who among the Saxons can read Latin? Shouldn't I read your missive to them?"

Willehad put down his cup. "No, that won't be necessary?"

"But Your Grace, how else are the pagans to know its contents? Wasn't Hincmar to do as much?"

Willehad grinned smugly and then touched his wine-soaked lips with a fat finger. "Oh, the beauty of things! But no. There is someone among the Saxons who can read the letter."

"A Saxon read Latin? Is there a priest among them I don't know about?"

"Father Jurchen, you have heard rumors that their Queen Udela is a witch, have you not?"

"Why yes, but…"

"No but about it. For a woman, and a Saxon woman to read Latin, a language taught only by the church and for the church, is that not a form of witchcraft?"

"I'd say so…. You mean?" The fact that the witch-queen could read the language of the church did strike Jurchen as a form of sorcery. *What evil walks the earth?*

"That is a form of sorcery I can vouchsafe." Willehad laughed, a sound like a pig's squeal.

***

Lothar's heavy hand struck the young girl's buttocks with a fierce smack.

"Oh… oh Lord please…"

He struck again. "I should turn you over to the men. Then send you to be a scullery maid. You'll die of knobby knees and hands worn to the nub!"

His voice was only half angry. He did not care enough for his playthings ever to be jealous of them.

"But you told me to care for him. I did my duty."

Another blow landed with a crack on her plump rear end.

"Ohhh..."

"Your duty was to keep track of the boy. Where did he go?"

"To you... I thought to you, Lord."

"You are lying. He never came to me. Where did he go?"

"I... don't know. He said he was going to see his lord. I suppose that was you, Lord."

Lothar raised his arm to strike the girl again. But a firm hand gripped his wrist and pulled it down gently, but assuredly.

"No need to strike the girl, Lord. I'm here," Hincmar said.

Lothar stepped back. His face flushed with anger. "You dare interfere with me? You touch your liege lord in the act of disciplining one of his servants?"

"I am sorry, Lord. As a Christian warrior, it is my duty to protect women and children, the weak and the poor. Lord Karolus so commanded it in the name of our Lord Jesus Christ. In this case, I fulfilled my duty in all areas."

Lothar regarded him. "You are serious. Yes, I can see that you are. Very well, Hincmar. I won't have you blinded—although I should. Now, tell me where you went. The wench said to see me. To see your lord. Those are one and the same. So please explain."

Hincmar bowed his head in deference and spread his hands. "I attended my Christian duty."

"What duty?"

"To be thankful. I went to the chapel and prayed. Prayed to our Lord Jesus Christ, whose grace delivered me from a Saxon assassin."

Lothar nodded. "Of course you did, Hincmar. I should have known. But I'm glad you returned. I have need of your services."

"I'm at your command, Lord."

Lothar smiled. "Good. Well, there was blood spilled at the feast. I ordered Lord Melchior and his hinds held prisoner until I can decide what to do with them."

Hincmar nodded back. "As it should be, Lord. What do you plan to do?"

"Sell them. Or, more properly, give them to Queen Udela."

"Give them to a pagan witch? I'm confused."

"Why yes. Udela is now our ally. The rest of the Saxon race reviles her Saxon followers. She, in desperation, has turned to me for succor. We have an understanding. Hincmar, mark my words. As one of my key warriors, you are destined for greatness."

Hincmar smiled. "Greatness, Lord? What kind of greatness, Lord? Serving Count Lothar is as great an honor as anyone could hope for."

Lothar rubbed his chin thoughtfully. "Of course, it is. Yet I'm thinking you could serve as a duke or even king of a realm someday."

"A realm? What realm, Lord?"

"Why, any realm you might fancy. Hincmar. Big plans are unfolding. Your part in this could make you a king." He hoped to tantalize the young blood. Greed and lust for power were universal traits, but decidedly so among blooded Franks.

"A king, lord? King of what?"

Lothar saw the look flash in his eyes for a moment. *I have him.*

"Let's say of Neustrasia, or maybe Austrasia. What do you think of that, boy?"

Hincmar stiffened. "Why... I am flattered, Lord.... flattered."

Lothar smiled. "Excellent. You are in this all the way now."

"In what, all the way, Lord?"

"High treason for one. Sacrilege and heresy for another. Murder. Regicide. These will give you every reason not to fail me, Hincmar."

Hincmar put his hands to his head. "This can't be true. How can you... We do such things?"

"First, we must dispatch of the *missus* and his band. They must be escorted east to join our good queen. You will lead the escort. They will serve as slaves. But first, we must blind and maim them. I'll leave that to you."

Hincmar blanched. "But Lord, it is a grave crime to maim a free-born Frank. And to maim a noble Frank, well.... such is the work of the Mohammedans.... Or Saxons... Or the Greeks... Or Avars. But not Franks. Not Roman Christians."

Lothar shook his head. "We shall have new laws, Hincmar. Not Roman laws. Laws of my making. And I say a threat to the new kingdom must be dealt with harshly."

"Very well, Lord. But if I might, I suggest we wait and give your queen the option of deciding the particulars."

"Particulars?"

"Yes, Lord... which hand to sever... which eye to pluck."

Lothar smiled wickedly. "You speak well. My new bride's gift."

Shouts came from the anteroom. A knock on the door brought a breathless servant.

"What is it?" Lothar asked.

"The guards have a pagan warrior, Lord."

"Have him? A prisoner?"

"No, Lord! He has them. And he demands to see you."

"Me?"

"Yes, Lord."

Lothar grabbed his belt and buckled his broadsword to his waist. Hincmar unsheathed his sword, and the two stormed into the anteroom, where they saw the towering frame of Fromm. He had two stout Frankish guards pinned against the stone wall with the shaft of his broad ax.

"Lord, be... beware!" one stammered. "This pagan seeks you... he is most... dangerous – ooof!"

Fromm snapped the staff sharply against the guard's chin, sending bright red blood dripping down his face. Fromm twisted his wrists and snapped the neck of the second guard, cracking his skull against the stone. With surprising agility, Fromm spun about and raised the battle-ax.

Hincmar lunged with his broadsword, but his injury slowed him. His weapon smacked the head of the battle-ax. The power of Fromm's blow sent the weapon tumbling harmlessly to the stone floor. Fromm took a quick diagonal step and rammed the shaft's point into Hincmar's midriff, collapsing him breathless.

More guards arrived with battle swords and shields. Fromm laughed as they made the mistake of rushing him individually. He sliced off the head of the first assailant as effortlessly as swatting a fly.

"Enough!" Lothar called out. "What is it you want? And who are you?"

Looking relieved at the reprieve, the guards halted. Each squinted at their comrade's head, which had rolled into the dark recesses of the room.

"My name is Fromm. I'm from the Dane Mark."

"A Norseman? What brings you here?"

"I'm on my way to Miklagard, the great city. The empress pays her warriors well. The land is warm — the women warmer and the food and drink abundant."

"Yet you want to see me? Why in Christ's name?" Lothar asked. His tone was authoritative but respectful. He knew this savage could easily take a score of his warriors.

"Your canteen-keeper, Boso, was supposed to speak with you of my services."

"I don't deal with canteen-keepers," Lothar scoffed. "And why would he say that?"

"He thinks you need my services. I understand there are things afoot, and I like action. The right consideration might save me a long journey to the east."

"You are indeed a powerful warrior. But I need my warriors disciplined."

Fromm laughed. "Well, I have disciplined three of them for you. Send me the rest, and I'll gladly discipline them all."

Lothar looked at his men. There was terror in their eyes. Hincmar, one of the ablest Franks, was getting to his knees. "Very well. What is your price?"

"Well, it was five bags of silver. But now it's twenty bags. And the girl."

"I'll give you fifteen bags. If your services prove worthwhile, perhaps a county on the Danish March."

"Agreed," Fromm said. "And the girl."

"What girl?" Lothar looked startled.

"Anfelisia."

"The serving wench?" Lothar laughed along with his men.

Fromm shook his battle-ax. "What is the joke?"

Lothar shook his head. "Willehad fancies her somehow. She is of no consequence to me. You'll have to get him to agree. Meanwhile, we have plenty of slave girls for you."

Fromm shrugged. "The offer suits me. I'll deal with the bishop in my own time."

Distant trumpets blared. Lothar's guards stirred back to their posts. None looked the great Norseman in the eye.

"Your warriors are quick to scurry off," Fromm said.

"They are trained to follow the summons of the trumpet. It announces a visitor of importance," Lothar said. "Hincmar, retrieve your weapon and find out who has come."

"As you say, Lord," Hincmar said. He picked up the broadsword but glared at Fromm with an obvious look of hate as he left.

Fromm laughed. "I don't think your Frank lieutenant likes me. I'll have some ale now, Lord. Killing Franks is thirsty work."

Lothar motioned to a servant who rushed to find a pot of ale. "I suppose it is, for a Norseman. We'll partake of the ale in my chambers."

As they sat drinking, Lothar regarded the Norseman with a mix of hope and suspicion. He was impressed by the sheer brutality and lethality of this immense warrior. He needed just such a man as a check to the ambitions of the Avars, the Saxon queen, and even his men.

Hincmar returned with news of the visitor. "Lord, it is Lord Mallobaudes, himself. He…"

Before Hincmar could finish, Mallobaudes stormed through the door.

His face looked thinner and his skin paler. Lothar noted his hair and beard were also beginning to fleck white. "I hope you have good cause for storming into the chamber of a Count of the Realm."

Mallobaudes waved his leather glove dismissively. "I have undertaken to meet with the savage Avars, Lothar. And I have brought back the girl."

"I believe those were your orders, Mallobaudes. I am pleased you have accomplished them."

"I have accomplished them. Now I want you to live up to your part of the bargain."

"My part? And what is that?"

"I want my cousin out of the way. I want his lands. And I want them now."

"All in good time. Your cousin is to be given over to the Saxons along with his men. He will be blinded and enslaved."

"I don't want him blinded. Damn you, I want him dead!"

Lothar stroked his beard. "I am sure you do, Lord Mallobaudes. And I wanted them blinded. However, my mind has changed. They would make little use as slaves if they were all blinded… or dead. But the Saxon yoke is harsh. They will all likely be dead in a year. Meanwhile, take comfort in their suffering. And in the significant lands you will soon possess."

"He must die for me to have his lands," Mallobaudes said.

"Yes. But by joining with me, you stand to win much more than Melchior's demesne."

Mallobaudes's eyes widened. "What do you mean?"

"I mean, Lord Mallobaudes, how would you like to be Count of Fulda?"

"But that is your title."

"Soon enough, I shall be king-and-emperor. I'll have little need of the title or the lands."

Mallobaudes bowed his head. "I'm overwhelmed, Count Lothar."

"You are most welcome, Count Mallobaudes."

Fromm watched the two Franks while sipping his ale.

"What are you glaring at, you oaf?" Mallobaudes sputtered.

"I was musing that if I took this girl from you, Frank, I could trade her for the one I want." Fromm poured ale down his mouth and spilled it down his chest. He slammed the cup on the table and laughed.

"My Lord Lothar! How can you allow a Norseman affront a Frank lord?"

Lothar looked at the ale-sodden Fromm and then at Mallobaudes. "Fromm is my man, now. Part of my plan. A more important part than you, Mallobaudes. So be respectful."

***

The rattle and scrape of a deadbolt woke Melchior and his men. Audeon, always quick to action, drew his weapon and made a panther-like move toward the heavy door. Slowly, it began to swing open.

"Hide your weapons," Melchior said. "You forget I am *missus* on an official journey for the emperor. We must see where this leads." Melchior had little doubt where it would lead. He just needed time to adjust his plans.

Audeon's mouth curled in a frown, but he slipped his sword beneath his cloak.

Four large men-at-arms marched through the threshold. The iron links on their *brunias* made a grating sound that somehow disturbed Melchior. He stood and confronted them.

"Why are we locked up? Where is Count Lothar?" Melchior took their measure. *We can easily take these men. But then what?*

The leader grasped the hilt of his broadsword and shifted his shield. "You are to be transported from this place, Lord."

"Now?"

"No, Lord. At dawn tomorrow. You ask where Count Lothar is. That I don't know. But I do know you are to be transported by his authority."

"Where are we going?" Audeon demanded. Melchior saw him grasping the hilt of his weapon under the cloak.

"I am speaking to Lord Melchior, boy. Who are you to interrupt me?"

"I am Audeon."

"Audeon? Ah, yes, Karolus's bastard," one of the men-at-arms said.

The men-at-arms laughed.

Audeon stared stone-faced.

"Well, from what we have heard, any one of a score of swine herds might be your father," another said.

They guffawed in amusement.

Melchior tried to hold Audeon's sword arm, but he was not quick enough. The young Frank stepped forward and, with his sword blade swirling, rushed the four. A swift blow brought the blade down, cutting through the leader's *brunia* and slicing his arm open at the shoulder.

"They have weapons!" the leader exclaimed. His sword fell, and his arm dangled limply. His ashen face stared blankly before he toppled, landing at Audeon's feet.

"Murder! Murder!"

"Sound the alarm!"

"Kill the bastard!"

With angry screams, the three men-at-arms drew long *Seaxes* and charged Audeon, with blades flickering like fiery tongues in the dim lamplight.

"Pay for your treachery, bastard!" The lead man caught Audeon's blade with his shield and lunged sideward to slice his ribs with his *Seaxe*. Before the short sword struck, the attacker lurched, dropping his *Seaxe* to the floor. Blood now pouring from his lips, he staggered back, clutching frantically at the arrow in his throat. Gaetano sprang forward and, with a twist, tore the arrow from the dying man's throat and placed it in his quiver.

The last two men-at-arms turned towards the archer but then hesitated. Melchior's men did not. With blood lust up, they drew blades as one and sprang into action. The men-at-arms backed to the door with panic in their eyes.

"Alarm! Alarm! The prisoners are armed!" one of them shouted in desperation. Sentinels throughout the fortress picked up the cry. Sounds of excited voices and hoarse commands began to fill the stone walls.

In the room, blade met blade. Melchior's men grunted and strained to take down the two now fighting desperately for survival. Despite their skill and strength, the two went down quickly, and the chamber grew quiet.

But the growing echo of voices and the tramp of boots on stone reverberated from the depths of the castle.

"More men are coming, *Dominus*," Audeon said.

Melchior looked at the fallen men-at-arms. "Take their shields and what blades you fancy. We'll need them now."

Audeon looked at Melchior with a face ripe with shame. "I'm sorry, Lord. I lost my temper. It is not like me to do so."

Melchior regarded the young man. *He is indeed Karolus's son. Calm to the breaking point. Quick to act when it's crossed. And remorseful at killing.*

"Your lack of control lost us the element of surprise, Audeon. What do you propose we do to rectify that?"

"The lad did the right thing," Bavo said. "Franks kill for much less than this."

The others murmured in agreement.

These are truly men of a distant time, Melchior thought of *a different world.* Suddenly, he recalled the butchery of his own century. Villages on the steppes of the Ukraine burning... Simple soldiers, reduced to murdering civilians. *Maybe not so...*

"That will be the last time anyone disobeys my orders. I'll personally kill the violator," Melchior said. *Maybe not so...*

"Aye, *Dominus*," they replied in unison.

"Well, Audeon? What do you propose we do? Lothar will have fifty armed men, seasoned Frank warriors, upon us soon." Melchior eyed the young man intensely. Already, the cries and footsteps made that abundantly clear.

"They no longer serve my father, so they might as well be Saxons. I say we pay them for their treachery."

Audeon clambered over the dead men and into the hallway. Melchior and his men followed. Audeon pointed toward the stone staircase. "Lord, we can defend the stairs and slay half their numbers before they take us."

"Yes," said Bavo. "The boy is right."

"Only half right, Bavo," Melchior replied. He needed to take control and act quickly. *"Dominus?"*

"I came here to fulfill my mission to Karolus. We can't do that by dying in a useless fight."

"What do you propose, *Dominus?*" Audeon asked.

Melchior glanced up. "The ceiling above our chambers has large wooden beams holding up the roof. Find a rope and climb up… try to pry open the window. If you escape, make your way to the abbey. But first, find Jurchen. He can lead you there or to Stilicho. He is pledged to Karolus and me."

"Jurchen? He's a Saxon and a half-priest. Can we trust him?" Audeon asked.

"We have no choice. And he is pledged to me as well. Here is the scroll I am to deliver to Baugulf. It contains your father's command, Audeon. Guard it with your life."

Audeon was about to protest, but the piercing glare of Melchior held his impulse in check. The sound of the approaching Franks ended the talk.

"All of you go. Bolt the door behind you," Melchior said.

"Dominus, I will stay with you," Bavo said with a conviction that surprised Melchior. "I am too old to climb. I prefer to fight or face my end in your service."

Melchior fingered his talisman while he assessed the old warrior. Then he nodded and tucked it under his *brunia.*

***

A distraught-looking man-at-arms rushed into Lothar's chambers. His face told Lothar all he needed to know. "Count Lothar, the prisoners have escaped!"

Lothar remained calm. Somehow, he had felt Melchior would not succumb without a struggle. Perhaps this offered the opportunity to rid Frankland of him more quickly. "Escaped? How?"

"I, I'm not sure. The guards cried the alarm. There are cries of murder."

Lothar drew his *Seaxe* and stuck the blade deep into the oak plank table. "What of the prisoners? Are any killed or wounded?"

"There were screams, Lord. I believe the prisoners killed the escort guard. That's all I know. The first banner is assembled and awaits your orders."

"Fifty men sitting on their asses waiting for orders? Where is Hincmar?"

"I'm here, Lord," Hincmar said, stepping into the chamber in full *brunia.*

"Never mind!" Lothar snapped. He buckled on his broad sword while a servant placed his conical hat on his head and handed him his shield. "No one is to be harmed if possible. Do you all understand?"

"Yes, Lord."

"Any delay may cost us our prisoner. Take the banner forward, but try not to kill them, especially Melchior. He still has some worth to me. I want to please my new bride."

"I should go with him," Fromm said. "Melchior knows me and my prowess. Perhaps he'll submit sooner."

Lothar grinned. "I like the way your pagan mind thinks, Fromm. Go! Both of you."

"As you command." Hincmar turned and left.

Chapter 16

The heavy boots tramped through the halls, signaling the arrival of a cruel horde. The Frankish banner, so-called because fifty men marched under a flag, marched in column four abreast and twelve-deep.

Hincmar approached the officer in charge. "Count Lothar placed me in direct command until he arrives."

"The banner is at your command." But the officer cast a suspicious eye at Fromm. "What of this one?"

"Sworn to Count Lothar." Hincmar glared at Fromm. "He will follow in the rear. Form four ranks."

Hincmar marched at the head of the banner, with Fromm behind the fourth rank. Even as he led the warriors, his thoughts were of the slave girl, Varna. He took a deep breath, hoping his service to Lothar and Udela might win him the girl. He could not shake her from his mind. He was glad he had thrown his lot in with Lothar after all.

The dark corridors swallowed the column, which moved like a snake slithering through a burrow beneath the soil. In the dim lamplight, their shadows cast eerie wraiths on the walls. At length, they halted at the bottom of a long, narrow staircase. Hincmar glanced up into the darkness.

The ranks parted as Lothar made his way through the banner. He gazed up the dark staircase and grasped Hincmar's shoulder. "Take the first rank with you. Find out what has happened."

"Yes, Lord." Hincmar grabbed a torch from his servant and slowly made his way up the stairs. His own shadow bounced before him. Somehow, it made him feel more secure. Then he saw what he thought was a dark form at the top of the stairs.

"Who's there?" Hincmar asked.

Stillness accompanied the darkness.

"I'm Hincmar. I speak in the name of Count Lothar… who is there?"

After a moment, a powerful voice came from above. "I speak in the name of Karolus, King of the Franks and Emperor of the Romans. Advance…but slowly."

Hincmar slowly climbed the dark steps. The staircase suddenly narrowed at the top, leaving room for only one man at a time. Hincmar knew the design was intended to restrict the number of attackers. It had the desired effect. The young warrior, normally beyond courageous, felt a slight unease. *What fiendish trick awaits?*

"Stop right there. Sheath your sword and step to the top. Your hinds can remain where they are."

"How can I trust you?" Hincmar asked.

"I am Lord Melchior, *Missus Dominicus.* I speak for the king-and-emperor on all matters, secular and ecclesiastic. You represent a traitor and a heretic. Which of us can be trusted? Step forward, slowly."

Hincmar strained to see if there were more men behind the form. He thought he heard a blade drawn from its scabbard. When he reached the top, he saw a powerful figure standing with arms crossed. *Melchior!*

Another figure stood just behind Melchior. This one held a broad sword menacingly. *I was right!* "Who's in your shadow, Melchior?"

"Bavo. A brave veteran of Karolus's wars. A brave Frank *milites.*"

Hincmar thought he saw lifeless forms strewn behind Bavo. "I am sent to demand your surrender. I have a banner thirty steps below. Fifty *milites* anxious to climb these stairs and avenge their comrades."

"I'm sorry my men killed your guards. But they are charged to defend me and serve Karolus."

"And now you would kill me. I was a fool climbing here with my blade covered in leather. A good Frank dies armed," Hincmar said.

"A wise Frank dies in bed," Melchior said. "Which do you want to be, Hincmar: good… or wise?"

Hincmar gripped the hilt of his sword. Lothar offered him a chance for new glory and lands he could never have dreamed of possessing. Varna's face passed before him. He imagined her as his consort in his new demesne, and he took a breath. "My duty is to Count Lothar, now. Karolus's days are numbered."

"All our days are numbered, Hincmar," Melchior said. "The question is whether this is your day… or mine."

Hincmar's long sword sang from the scabbard. "Draw your blade, *Missus!*"

Melchior drew his sword but then threw the blade at Hincmar's feet. "I did not call you up here to kill you, Frank. But to yield my sword…"

But before Melchior could finish, Bavo sprang forward with a speed that denied his age. He raised his blade high and bounded toward Hincmar. "Karolus forever!"

"No!" Melchior said, but too late.

Bavo's heavy iron blade crashed against Hincmar's shield like a thunderclap, splitting it down the middle. Hincmar's left forearm was cut, bludgeoned, and cracked like kindling. Grimacing in pain, Hincmar staggered and then twisted aside as Bavo lunged at him. The old warrior tumbled down the staircase.

Cries and shouts from the first ranks of the banner were heard. "Treachery!"

In a frenzy of rage, the Franks slashed at the figure sprawled before them and, with repeated blows, cut Bavo's body to pieces.

Lothar made his way to the front of the banner with Fromm beside him. "Is that the *missus?*

Fromm turned the head over with his broad ax and grunted. "No. This is Bavo – a brave warrior of Karolus's campaigns."

As Bavo tumbled headlong into the darkness, Melchior snatched Hincmar's sword from his hand and, in one motion, tossed it down the dark staircase. He then held Hincmar to keep him from tumbling.

"Are you all right? I have yielded to you," Melchior said.

"Your man attacked me," Hincmar sputtered.

"I had no idea he would. Tell your count I am his."

"What of your band?" Hincmar asked, panting in pain.

"I cannot account for their goodness or wisdom. They are Franks, after all."

A half dozen *milites* raced up the stairs. Melchior could easily have cut them down one by one. Instead, he stood holding Hincmar.

"Unleash Hincmar or we'll carve you up like your bastard friend," one of the Franks threatened.

"He is my prisoner. Do not harm him," Hincmar said.

"We should kill him where he stands," another said.

The dark figure of Lothar suddenly appeared at the head of the stairs. "Do as Hincmar says."

"As you command, Lord," the lead warrior replied.

***

Count Lothar's Chambers

Melchior sat before Lothar. A servant set a goblet of wine before him, but he remained indifferent.

"We found no sign of your men, *missus*." Lothar sipped at his wine.

Melchior cast a sideways glance at Fromm, who sat in the corner slugging ale.

Lothar scratched his beard. "You haven't touched your wine, *missus*. You suspect another potion, I suppose. But the time for tricks is passed. I want to know why you're here."

"To bring Karolus's laws back to the marchland. It seems his chosen count is not up to the task."

"Hardly the case, Melchior. Soon, the only laws will be my laws."

"Not when Karolus arrives with his *scara*."

A weak smile crossed Lothar's face. "Dgno's Avars would have warned us of that. I suspect there is no scara coming here, or anywhere else. I suspect Karolus is prancing about with his concubines or off on another quest for boar and bear. He is a boy at heart. Well, now it is time the Franks were ruled by serious men, not by a boy and his monks."

"Karolus will have something to say of that... as will the Pope."

"The pope? He's Karolus's puppet. Or is it the other way around? It matters not. Soon there will be a new pope and a new emperor."

"Emperor of Avars and Saxons?" Melchior's face twisted in contempt.

Lothar ignored Melchior's tone. "And of Franks, and of more."

From the corner, Fromm let out a burp. "Count Lothar plans to march on Miklagard, *Dominus*. Seems I'll get there yet."

Melchior cast an angry look at the Dane. "Is this meant as a joke? How will he do it?"

"Once I have destroyed Karolus's followers, I shall turn my new Frankish-Saxon army east. We will reach out to the Mohammedans and divide the empire of the Byzantines."

"What makes you believe the Mohammedans can be trusted? They'll cross the Spanish March while you are in the east and march up your ass," Melchior said.

"They wouldn't dare. This won't be Franks alone. Frankish heavy cavalry, Saxon footmen, and the Avar light horse will make an unstoppable force. Besides, I plan to pay off the Caliph in Cordoba with treasures from Karolus's churches. In our new realm, the church will belong to me, and I will decide what wealth it may have."

Melchior held his tongue. He racked his memory and recalled none of these events from his study of history. *No point in arguing against something that will never happen. Or could it, if I fail?* "What does any of this have to do with me? You have already butchered the valiant Frank Bavo for naught."

"For naught? He wounded my best warrior and would have killed him. At least our blades struck quickly and true. Be thankful for that."

"I was surrendering on my own. Hincmar can attest. Bavo was headstrong."

Lothar rose and walked over to Melchior. He jabbed with his finger like a dagger. "Where are your men?"

"I have no idea. The cowards deserted me. That's why I surrendered."

Lothar balled his fists. "Very well, Melchior. You will be happy to know that I am not killing you. You will have the honor of serving the queen of my new realm, Udela of the Saxons."

"Serving? My sword will not serve a pagan queen!"

"I said nothing about swords, Melchior. You shall be my lady's slave. Like a lap dog but without actually sitting on her lap." Lothar laughed, and Fromm joined in.

Two armed retainers moved on Melchior. Each was hand-picked for strength and size. The larger of the two had a short blonde beard, wore a polished conical helmet, and had glistening scales on his brunia. He pulled Melchior to his feet, grabbed his wrists, and squeezed them together with vise-like power. Melchior grimaced but stood firm. The second, with a long brown mustache and a scalloped helmet, wore blackened scales over his brunia. He slapped a set of chains on Melchior's wrists and locked them shut.

"I was going to blind you, Melchior. But I decided to leave that decision to Udela. Saxons are peculiar about such things." Lothar gave a sly laugh and raised his wine cup in a mock toast. "To my future bride and queen! May she ever keep her slaves in lowly submission to her will."

Melchior struck when Lothar's cup touched his lips. He lowered a shoulder and rammed the retainer with the blonde beard, sending him staggering. Melchior then spun, swinging the chains into the face of the retainer in the scalloped helmet, hitting him with a savage smack.

"Aaargh!" The retainer threw his hands to his face, but they could not staunch the blood flowing from his nose and mouth. Melchior twisted left just in time to catch the first retainer squarely in the throat. The heavy links cracked his windpipe, sending him to his knees, choking for air through a windpipe flooded with blood.

Lothar threw his wine cup to the ground and drew his *Seaxe*. "Guards! Stop the prisoner!"

Melchior whipped his chains from side to side and moved toward Lothar, who stepped back from his attacker, holding his Seaxe defensively before him. A dozen broadswords descended on Melchior, who now whipped the chains to ward off their blades.

"A bag of silver to the man who takes him," Lothar screeched.

Melchior grunted from anger and exhaustion, continuing to parry sword thrusts and blows. The result of his strenuous training in Ottawa, though, was only a blur in his memory as he traveled through time.

The heavy chain clanked against the long blades and thudded against the heavy wooden shields. He was holding his own when a low sword thrust caught his boot, slicing it open and sending him stumbling. Now, enraged by Frankish bloodlust and greed for silver, the guards began jostling each other in a frenzy to be the one to strike the blow.

Then a voice roared above the din, "Odin!" The bellow of a stuck bull could not have been more frightening. "Odin!"

The Frank *milites* turned back to view the enraged face of Fromm, now purple with *berserker* frenzy.

A devious smile crossed Lothar's face. "Yes, Fromm, yes. Show him what brute strength can do!"

Melchior turned to face Fromm, but realized Lothar had misjudged the scene unfolding before him. The count's eyes tightened in anger and dismay when he realized Fromm's anger was not directed at Melchior.

"Beware the Norseman!" Lothar shouted. "Guards! Call out the watch!"

Fromm's eyes bulged with excitement, and he moved with the fury of an enraged bear suddenly awakened from hibernation.

"Odin!" Fromm stepped forward, twirling his two-handed battle ax over his head as easily as a feather.

Two of the Franks moved to face the new threat with long swords swirling.

"You Franks make killing too easy!" Fromm struck swiftly. His ax cut a diagonal arc, slicing through both attackers like soft cheese, entering one man's shoulder and exiting the other's hip. Both died without a sound.

"Send me more Franks to butcher," Fromm spat as he moved towards the others.

They now ignored Melchior and formed a small phalanx three ranks deep.

"Stay shoulder to shoulder," their leader ordered. He did not join the phalanx but stood over Melchior, his blade ready to kill the prisoner. "Lock shields. Present your sword points."

As one, the block of fighting men advanced on Fromm. But the Dane moved surprisingly quickly for his size. He stepped back, and when the block clambered over its slain comrades, he struck with a low swipe that cut the first rank at the knees. Franks toppled like ninepins. Fromm reversed his grip and twisted upward, sending another Frank's head spinning from his body, eyes staring and tongue moving in surprise.

Hesitating a moment, the second and third ranks edged toward Fromm, their fury in tow. Men whose forbears had fought Romans, Goths, Huns, Mohammedans, and Saxons had little to fear from a solitary Dane.

***

Lothar rushed into the main hall and summoned his lieutenants. "Where is Stilicho?"

"He's nowhere to be found," an officer replied.

"There's much treachery afoot," Lothar muttered.

Then, the chanting of the ancient Germanic war cry, once borrowed by the Romans, began to echo through the dark corridors and into the halls of the fort. Demonic chanting from scores of voices slowly grew in power, sounding like a powerful bull bellowing in its death throes.

"The *Barritus*!" Lothar exclaimed. "The ancient war-cry. Good... more soldiers are coming!"

A runner staggered into the chambers. "Count Lothar, Lord Stilicho's men are armed and marching!"

"Excellent. I wondered where he was."

"No, Lord, he is marching on us!"

Lothar turned to his lieutenants. "Stilicho is the son of a whore! He has sworn fealty to me personally. Now he has broken his sacred oath. I'll see him flayed alive."

The lieutenants nodded.

Lothar's attention was on his new threat. "Thanks to Stilicho's treachery, our forces are divided and will appear weaker to the Saxons and the Avars. Appearing weak is something I cannot afford. Nithard, summon the horsemen. Wandregisel, muster the infantry. This treason must be ruthlessly crushed and quickly."

"But Lord Stilicho has considerable warriors. And Frank fighting against Frank is not..."

Lothar grabbed the officer's throat. "No one can claim the title Frank if he marches against me. Now gather your men!"

"As you command, Count Lothar." Both lieutenants saluted with *Seaxes* extended.

Lothar glanced into his chambers and saw what looked more like a pack of wolves – the growls and snarling were vicious.

"None of you will admit that Lothar, and therefore all of you, are breaking a sacred oath to Karolus," Melchior shouted.

The officer guarding Melchior struck at him with his sword, but Melchior slapped the chains around his wrists and pulled them tight as bones cracked and the officer swooned in pain. "Aaaagh..."

On his side of the room, Fromm felled man after man until the remaining six locked their shields one last time and pressed the powerful Dane. Thrusting the points of their

Seaxe's over their shields, as their Roman predecessors had, they backed him against an oak pillar.

At the arch of the doorway, Lothar stood with arms akimbo. "That's it, Franks! Kill the traitor Norseman. Kill him... then kill the missus."

"Odin!" Fromm bellowed. He had felled half a dozen men and wanted more. But the expertly placed blade thrusts had cut him in as many places. His arms and face were soaked in blood and sweat. He staggered.

"Now's your chance, Franks!" Lothar shouted.

Lothar now considered joining them for what seemed an easy kill. But he saw one of the *milites* drop his weapon. The Frank's eyes suddenly widened and bulged from their sockets, while his tongue hung distended like a lifeless slug. Melchior's iron chains tightened around his neck. He gave a quick *snap*, and the *milites'* neck bones cracked. His body hung lifeless.

One of the Franks tried to help his mate, but Melchior's chains smashed his face into a bloody pulp. His hands went to his face, and he slumped to his knees. "I'm blind."

A second blow cracked against his *brunia,* and he fell sprawling to the ground.

"Odin!" Fromm regained his footing and his strength and raised his long ax, bringing it crashing into the helmet of the Frank before him in an ear-splitting geyser of brains and blood.

"Odin!" The sound chilled the bones of the last three warriors, who began stabbing frantically in all directions. Melchior's chains pummeled another to oblivion while Fromm's ax cut through the last men standing.

Lothar stood aghast. *I must get help.* He stepped quietly back through the archway.

***

Fromm stood over the blinded swordsman and raised his battle-ax for a final, killing blow. But Melchior's chains snapped around the Dane's powerful arms, holding them back.

"Hold, Fromm," Melchior gasped between breaths. "He's no longer a danger."

"I thirst for more Frank blood," Fromm said.

"You'll be swimming in a river of it soon enough. Cut these chains."

Fromm smiled. "Cut them? You'd have me destroy your new toy?" His ax head smashed the iron links in a powerful blow. The chains broke open, and Melchior shook them off.

Lothar was gone before they looked up. The fortress was now a din of commands, tramping boots, and war cries. The demonic braying sent a chill through even the pagan Fromm.

"Thor's hammer! It sounds like Loki has set the hounds of hell upon this place," Fromm exclaimed.

Melchior nodded grimly. "Something like that, Fromm. The *Barritus* is a Germanic war cry borrowed by the ancient Romans. The Franks have reclaimed it for their own."

"Those are Franks?"

Melchior picked up one of the Franks' broadswords and a *Seaxe*. "Yes." He saw shields scattered about—no time for a shield.

"If I am correct, those are Stilicho's men. That means he has turned from Lothar's cause to ours. A battle for the soul of Frankland is taking place."

Fromm grinned. "Then we should waste no time joining in. Where are the rest of the lads? Don't tell me they're dead?"

"No Fromm. I sent them to find Jurchen with a message to rouse Stilicho. It seems they have."

"I think we should find Lothar and kill him."

"No."

"Then what will we do?"

"Find the fat bastard of a bishop, Willehad. He's the brain behind Lothar. Besides, he may have some church silver he'd be willing to part with if you ask him nicely."

Fromm grinned. "Lead on, *Missus Dominicus*."

***

The Saxon Village

Udela lingered longer in her bath than usual. She liked the feel of the soapy water on her skin. *It may be some time before I feel this clean again.*

"Rub the cloth on my back one more time, Varna. Make sure you use lots of soap," she said in a soft voice.

Varna began rubbing her mistress. She noticed the strange mark on her arm. The mark she used to prove she was both a witch and a queen.

Varna whispered to herself, "So strong and harsh in public is My Queen, yet so gentle in private. In my heart, I believe the private queen is the real queen."

Udela closed her eyes and fell into a deep sleep, dreaming great dreams. There were large castles adorned with decorations never seen in Frankland. She dreamed of wonderful bridges and roads—better than those left by the Romans. She dreamed of a powerful, content people—all under her power. At no time did she dream of Lothar at her side, nor of the wretched Avar, Dgno, who would have her if he could. Instead, she dreamed of a man by her side whose face evaporated before her gaze. Then she dreamed of terrible sounds—thunderclaps and lightning as she had never imagined. And destruction greater than her entire stash of black powder could ever wreak on a helpless people. Udela was startled and woke from the dream.

"Are you all right, My Queen?" Varna asked. "You seemed troubled in your sleep. You spoke of a great many things."

"What did I say?" Udela asked.

Varna shook her head. "I am sorry, My Queen. But I could not understand the words. They were so very strange to me."

"But you speak perfect Saxon now."

"It was not Saxon you spoke, but something else."

"Frankish? Norse? I speak those languages."

Varna shook her head. "I don't think it was those languages. I can't say what it was."

Udela pondered this as Varna finished bathing her and washing her hair, then oiled and perfumed her entire body. She selected a shimmering gown of fine material encrusted with jewels.

"Not that, Varna. We are on the march beginning this morning. I need something more suitable."

Varna selected a black woolen dress trimmed with blackened leather, giving it the appearance of a warrior's *brunia*. Soft leather boots and a silver diadem completed the look.

"Hand me my gloves, Varna. And my dagger."

Udela carefully slid the dagger into a special sleeve woven inside the dress. She then took her sack of powder and filled half a dozen silk pouches. "Keep the lamp lit at all times, Varna."

"Yes, My Queen."

Udela stood in her majestic splendor. The chambermaids all marveled, and a sense of pride flushed through them as each identified closely with their queen.

"Summon the captain of my guard and the chamberlain!" Udela commanded.

A maid scurried from the chamber, and a few minutes later, Hrodger entered. Udela did not quite trust the ruthless Saxon as she had Alager. But he served her purpose.

"Form your men for a long march, Hrodger."

Hrodger nodded. "As you command, My Queen. Can you say where we go?"

"We march on Fulda!"

Hrodger bowed and departed. She sensed a certain reserve in his demeanor. She was not sure whether she liked that. It often meant conflicting loyalties. And Udela needed full allegiance from all her tribes.

Another chief pushed past the chamberlain and stepped into the room.

"You called, My Queen?"

"Of course I called you, Bruno. We march on Fulda. I want your Issepi in the rear guard of the march."

"Who will lead the van?" Bruno asked.

"Eberger."

Bruno's eyes narrowed. "Always the Nabo in the van."

"You question my command?"

His face reddened. "No, My Queen."

Udela's voice softened. "Hear me. The Nabo are the most powerful tribe in our force. But I trust your Issepi more. That's why they will take up the rear. When all the tribes have departed, I want the camp burned."

Bruno's eyes widened. "Burned?"

Her eyes bored into him. "All the supplies and possessions are too heavy to carry on the march."

"But it's the wealth of the people."

"*Was* the wealth of the people. We shall take Fulda and from there march west to conquer new lands... acquire new wealth. I want no one to look back. Only looking forward. Do you understand?"

He bowed his head. "Yes, My Queen. "

"Then go and make ready."

***

Udela's horse plodded along the cow path that served as the road to Fulda. The Haari guards surrounded her like a ring of black iron. Her people marched, organized by clan and tribe, with the families following each group. At the large field beside the road, she raised her gloved hand, and they halted.

"Halt here, beside the *Irminsul*." She planned once more to use the ancient Saxon oak tree of life to encourage her people.

She turned and scanned from left to right, the morning sun at her back, straining to break through the gray clouds. Udela beheld her people. They had cast their lot with her because she refused to wage a war of resistance like the great Saxon leader Widukind, and because she was a witch with special powers.

She nodded to the head trumpeter. At the sound of the horns, the entire column faced the queen, who sat high on her horse. Her black clothing and long blonde hair cut an impressive figure among the superstitious pagans. She raised her hands to the sky.

"My people, the time has come for you to take what is yours! The Franks and their priests have ruled the world for too long and oppressed the Saxons: stealing their lands, insulting their gods, and bathing our children in their water... their priests are using the water's powers to turn Saxons into Christians. Well, I tell you — my powers are all the greater!"

Varna handed her one of her small silk bags and a taper from the lamp. Udela took one in each hand and joined them as she pitched them onto the pyre prepared before her. A flash of fire and a boom exploded. The throng of men and women ducked, cowered, or covered themselves to shield themselves from the magic.

The Haari began to howl like wolves, while long *Seaxes* beat upon their shields. "Udela! Udela!"

Next, the Nabo took up the cry, "Udela! Udela!"

Then each clan and tribe in succession down the line, until they reached the Issepi.

Udela extended her gloved hand at the pyre. "Thus, shall I destroy every Frankish fort, church, village, and town!"

Roars of approval erupted from all along the line. "Udela! Udela! Udela!"

She turned and pointed back at the Saxon camp. "Regard your Saxon homes for the final time!!"

At that moment, the village camp burst into flames, sending smoke and sparks hundreds of feet skyward so that everyone in the long column could see it. Udela smiled and nodded in knowing satisfaction. "The gods have proclaimed that we shall depart these lands and seize the land of the Franks, and more. This is proof of their will."

The sun suddenly broke through the clouds, bathing Udela and her entourage in its light. Then just as quickly, the clouds smothered it, and the dim gray of the day returned. She nodded in approval as great warriors and lowly slaves alike cowered in fear and awe before the mysterious and beautiful queen, who was, indeed, a witch. But a Saxon witch!

The cry was taken up once more, "Udela! Udela! Udela!"

"How did you do such a thing, My Queen?" Bruno asked.

Udela eyed him suspiciously. "You question my powers, Bruno?"

"Of course not, I just… "

"Never question my powers, Bruno." Udela feigned anger but was pleased that the elements cooperated. For she well knew that the key to her powers was not overestimating them, as the Saxons had. The horns sounded. As one, the assembled masses turned and began trudging toward Fulda and a glorious future.

S.W. O'Connell

Chapter 17

Fulda

The fort erupted into the chaos of close combat as Frank fought Frank with the demonic fury only factional strife and civil war bring. Melchior recalled close-in fighting of a different kind, with acrid smoke and flames as bullets tore men apart at close range and grenades burst, sending hot shards into the bodies of desperate men. Somehow, this seemed worse. Suddenly, his mind returned to the reality of his situation as he gazed down at the courtyard.

"It does me good to see Christians killing each other, Lord," Fromm said. "So long as you are not among them."

Melchior looked for Fromm's usual smirk but found none. "For now, their fighting serves a purpose. Let's keep going."

They moved quickly along the stone catwalk that ringed the fort's walls. There were no guards to avoid. All had joined the fray, taking one side or the other – some for Lothar, others for Stilicho. Melchior grimaced at the cries for quarter that went unheeded. When they reached the end of the catwalk, Melchior looked down.

His eyes narrowed at the sight. Over a hundred Franks lay bleeding or dead. *Not too many more, and the Saxon witch will walk through here with none left to resist.*

Stilicho's powerful band seemed to have the advantage. Swords slammed against shields. Blades scraped against blades. The *thud, clang,* and grunts of close combat among hundreds of hardened warriors were deafening and sickening.

"Lock shields and push," Stilicho's voice could be heard over the din. "Kill all who would betray their king! Kill all who would betray Jesus Christ to the pagans!"

"Reform ranks and prepare to charge," Lothar called to his men. "A bag of silver goes to the one who brings me the head of Stilicho, the traitor to his liege lord."

Once more, the masses slammed into each other with a dreadful crash. Iron swords thudded against wood and leather shields or scraped against the iron and brass bosses. Sword blades shrieked as metal struck metal. Men grunted as they strained, their arms growing weary after only minutes of combat. The tired fell first. Fatigue was the grim reaper in such combat.

Melchior could see that Stilicho's men, although more skilled and experienced, were slowly reduced by the greater numbers employed by Lothar.

"We need to move quickly, Lord," Fromm said. "When the Franks cease fighting, they will come for us."

"Not if Lothar is defeated, Fromm. That is part of my mission." Melchior scanned the yard. "No horsemen have entered this battle. Good."

"Good?"

"We will need all the mounted *milites* we can muster to fight the Avars and Saxons."

"Fight the Avars? What ale did they give you, Lord?"

"Do Norsemen fear Avars? What do you think the Greek emperor will have you do if you get to Miklagard?"

Fromm grunted.

"Heed," Melchior ordered.

They watched as Melchior's mind raced for a solution. Lothar sent a small band of hand-picked warriors who methodically cut a path toward Stilicho. Time was running out. "If Stilicho falls, all is over here."

"What will you do?"

"I will join the fight— on Lothar's side."

"Lord, has Loki seized your senses? What mad joke is playing with you?"

Melchior checked his broadsword and *Seaxe*. He tucked a *Francisca* in his belt. He pulled a shield hanging from the wall and checked its weight. "This will do."

Fromm lifted his battle-ax and grinned. "I thank you for the chance to enter Valhalla. I can think of no better way to do so than by killing Christians and Franks."

"No. Valhalla will have to wait. You go find the others and save the abbot from Willehad."

"My place is with you, Lord. And killing Franks."

"It is my wish and Karolus's command. Besides, you need the bishop's silver for your trip to Miklagard."

"And to marry a fine young servant girl," Fromm said.

Melchior did not hear his reply. He had already made his way toward the staircase. No guards barred his path. The entire place was deserted, as the great fight in the courtyard and the great hall had sucked every Frankish man-at-arms into its vortex. At the bottom of the steps, Melchior peered through a high-arched doorway into the courtyard. The combat was a swirl of steel now. We need such ferocity against the pagans. Both sides were locked in mortal combat, each knowing that giving in meant certain death. Melchior knew his intervention needed to break that notion.

At the bottom of the stairs, Melchior saw a plain iron helmet discarded by one of Lothar's men. He donned it, fastening the leather strap tightly. With the shield emblazoned with Lothar's colors, he now looked like part of the count's scara. Melchior drew the Seaxe, preferring its twenty-two-inch blade for close-in fighting. He made his way into the great courtyard and found a band of Lothar's men loitering behind the lines. *These men will do.*

He made the sign of the cross and advanced towards them. "What is this? Shirking your duty to Count Lothar? Take up your arms and follow me!"

"The men are tired," one of the warriors replied. "Besides, we do not favor fighting Franks."

"There'll be time enough to rest. And I agree. So follow me, and we'll put an end to this madness."

"And who are you?" another warrior asked.

Melchior raised his *Seaxe*. "I am Lord Melchior, *Missus Dominicus*. Sent by Karolus, whose authority supersedes your liege, Count Lothar. If you are true Franks, follow me!"

The men murmured. Finally, one of them spoke, "Aye, *Dominus*. Lead, and we will follow!"

"Form two ranks and stay with me. Strike down only those who would strike at you. Follow my commands as if they were Karolus's and the Lord God's."

The warriors seemed to rejuvenate. Their moral compass had just found its true north after months of Lothar's questionable leadership.

Melchior stepped in front of the group and began to beat his Seaxe against his shield. "*Deus adiuta Romanis! Deus nobiscum!* God help the Romans! God be with us!"

"*Deus adjuta Romanis!*" the band responded as one. The traditional war cries of the Romans and now Karolus's armies were the links to the Roman Empire, they believed was now Karolus's empire—their empire.

The wall of men stepped forward, Melchior in the lead. Their blades beat against their shields to the chant, "*Deus adjuta Romanis…Deus nobiscum! Deus adjuta Romanis… Deus nobiscum!*"

***

The deep-throated battle cry grew in strength and timber with each step they took. Its stirring sound and deep meaning began to stir their warrior blood, and soon it began to drown out the din of combat.

When Lothar and his retainers heard the battle cries, they halted.

"What is that?" Lothar snapped.

"The battle cry of the Romans, Lord… Karolus's battle-cry!" Hincmar exclaimed.

"What does it mean? It comes from the rear of our forces. Who's responsible for this?"

"I'm not sure, Count Lothar. But I think some of our men have rallied to Stilicho."

"Melchior! It's his treachery again at work."

"Perhaps, Lord," Hincmar said. He knew Lothar was right, and he knew what was coming.

"Hincmar, I shall take fifty good men and stop him and his pack of traitors. You must lead the final assault on Stilicho."

Hincmar startled. Stilicho was his one-time liege and mentor. Now he was boxed into the worst kind of treason.

"But Count Lothar…"

"You're already a dead man, Hincmar. If our great effort fails, Karolus will have us all executed, or worse, blind us and sell us as slaves to the Muhammadans. Assure me of your loyalty by killing Stilicho yourself."

Hincmar felt a surge of anger mixed with guilt. But he had thrown his lot in with the devils and now had no other recourse but to see it through. He thought of possible riches and of Varna. "As you command, Count Lothar."

Lothar smiled grimly. "Wandregisel, Master of the Foot, pull back your infantry. Nithard, Master of the Horse, form the cavalry for a final charge. We'll break the back of this bastard, Stilicho."

"Yes, Lord," they replied in unison but with obvious hesitancy.

"And I warn you. I want every traitor of a Frank killed. Take no prisoners."

Wandregisel and Nithard looked at each other and then at Hincmar.

Hincmar shook his head in submission. "We are sworn directly to Count Lothar. We must do as the count commands."

Hincmar watched as Wandregisel drew his long sword and stepped into the ranks of his infantry. "Captains, close up your ranks and draw back. Pull back your ranks, I say!"

It took a few minutes, but soon the infantry stood twenty paces from Stilicho's band. Hincmar gazed at his former lord. He looked weary but proud. Hincmar's mind raced with a mix of anger, fear, and guilt. His wounds ached, and he was tired beyond measure. But he despaired of prayer and forgiveness for what he was about to do. *I must kill my former liege.*

Stilicho wasted no time in reforming his men. He ordered the dead and wounded pulled back and their shields locked. Then they began the *Barritus*. The mournful chant again filled the fort with the sound of howling wolves.

"It's the *Barritus*, Hincmar," Wandregisel said.

"No matter, Wandregisel. We have our orders." He pulled himself onto his horse. "I have obeyed mine. Now you must fulfill yours."

"The horses are ready, Hincmar," Nithard said. "They will charge at your command."

"How many have we?"

"We have the two *cunei* at my command."

Hincmar looked at Stilicho's force. "They're depleted from fighting and dismounted. Better than two to one odds in our favor. Yet they are still too many for my liking. And Stilicho's *milites* are seasoned warriors."

"But they're on foot. A charge will break them," Nithard said

Hincmar glanced up at the walls that bounded them all in. "I'm not so sure. In such tight quarters, a footman's disadvantage is negated."

The sound of the *Barritus* grew louder.

"The horses grow skittish, Hincmar. We should charge now."

Hincmar drew his broadsword. He grabbed the reins firmly and turned his horse toward Stilicho's massed ranks. "Not much room to charge. We'll advance at a walk."

Nithard grabbed Hincmar's arm. "Look, Hincmar! Stilicho's men are advancing on us! We must charge now!"

With a mournful tone, Stilicho's *milites* stepped in unison, banging their shields, which were locked and held at eye level. "*Karolus...Karolus... Dominus et imperator...*"

Nithard spurred his warhorse forward, his broadsword raised high. Half the horsemen followed him in a pell-mell rush. The snorting horses struck shields with a series of thumps and groans. Stilicho's footmen had fought barbarian horsemen before, but never their brother-in-arms, who were heavily armed and mounted on powerful horses. Yet they resisted with a zeal that demoralized the mounted warriors. Scores of broadswords flicked from behind the shield wall like sparks from a flint. The long blades pierced the horses, sending more than a dozen to their knees or squealing in retreat.

Riders toppled from their saddles, some never to rise. But many leaped to their feet and rushed the wall of shields, *Seaxe* or *Francisca* in hand. The dismounted warriors hacked at the shields, but few lived long enough to harm, for the longer swords of Stilicho's wall cut and stabbed with cold accuracy. Nithard rode back and forth to encourage his men onward. At last, frustrated, he galloped forward in a frenzy and leaped his horse over the shields. There, the second rank gutted his horse with their broadswords and then hacked him apart with their *Francisca*.

A mounted Frankish nobleman rode up. "Hincmar, Count Lothar orders you to carry out his command at once!"

Hincmar regarded the man before him with anger. "Mallobaudes! I don't recognize your authority."

Mallobaudes smirked. He raised a small gilt staff, the symbol of a Frankish commander's authority carried by their aides. "Lothar just appointed me his lieutenant. Now go!"

"Why don't you join the attack yourself, mighty warrior, you claim to be?"

"I am charged to ensure you carry out the order."

Hincmar raised his sword in desperate fury. *Now, I have no choice but to lead these men against their kin.* "Form on me and charge!"

The remaining horsemen drew their swords and spurred their excited horses over the wounded men and horses before them. Men screamed, and creatures snorted. The sound of bones breaking was drowned out by the din. The mounted Franks slammed into the shield wall with a thundering crash. Horses reared. Hooves flailed, knocking men to the ground. Blades plunged into animal and man alike. Screams and shouts from both sides added to the din. Hincmar lowered his broadsword and drove through a pair of Franks. Despite the desperate efforts of the footmen, the charge broke the shield wall, albeit only at one point. Hincmar and a handful of the riders fought their way through the footmen.

We may yet disperse them. Hincmar bellowed, "Finish this madness!"

The horsemen around Hincmar were hacking left and right, felling many of Stilicho's second rank. But Stilicho himself led a dozen mounted milites in response. With savage blows, they cut down the attackers one by one.

Suddenly, Hincmar found himself alone. He whirled his horse from side to side, flailing madly at the swarm of footmen. Then he saw Stilicho. The old Frank stepped up to Hincmar's horse and struck a powerful blow, knocking Hincmar from the horse and tumbling him to the ground. Hincmar felt one stab and then another as a swarm of dismounted Franks descended on him.

Hincmar's mind swirled with pain, terror, and anger. A glimpse of Varna's face crossed his mind and then vanished with the flash of blades. *I'll not die without a fight.* He drew his *Seaxe* and fought off blows from *Francisca* and broadsword. Finally, he saw a Francisca blade descend on him, sending all into darkness.

***

When Hincmar launched his attack, Melchior acted. His band of Franks struck Lothar's remaining infantry from the flank. The surprise caused the ranks to buckle in confusion. With no leader at the point of attack, they fought recklessly and without purpose. It was Frank against Frank in a confused brawl.

Melchior shifted his shield and struck, plunging his blade into the chest of the warrior facing him. The snarling and cursing of men in close combat filled the air. He looked for Lothar and spotted him with his retainers. He thought he saw a familiar figure, but he turned his attention back to the Frank before him, a tall, broad-shouldered warrior named Enurchus.

"Treason must be paid!" Enurchus struck his broadsword against Melchior's shield, striking the boss squarely but glancing off the polished bronze.

Melchior plunged his *Seaxe* deep into Enurchus's shield, missing the metal boss and piercing the wood and leather. Melchior's blade cut through the leather glove and split Enurchus's forearm in a rush of blood.

"Aaargh!" Enurchus tried to drop his shield, but the *Seaxe* pinned it fast to his arm. While he struggled in pain, Melchior struck like a python. He pulled his *Francisca* and brought it down on Enurchus's shoulder. Enurchus slumped to his knees.

A Frank aligned with Melchior tried to kill Enurchus with his broadsword, but Melchior grabbed his arm. "We don't kill helpless Franks, even when they serve a traitor."

"Yes, Lord." The Frank then addressed Lothar's men, "Enurchus is down. Lord Melchior has defeated Enurchus. Enurchus is with Melchior. Join us now. Count Lothar is a traitor to Karolus. Death to Lothar! The Franks, still fighting, lowered their weapons. And one by one, then by twos and more, they began to chant, "Melchior! Melchior! Melchior!"

Finally, a voice called out, "We yield to Lord Melchior. We yield to Lord Melchior, *missus dominicus!*" A warrior in full, resplendent *brunia*, stepped through the disheveled, sullen ranks and bowed.

"Who are you?" Melchior asked, his body quaking from the frenzy and shock of close combat that affects even the victor.

"I am Wandregisel, Count Lothar's remaining lieutenant. I surrender the fort to you, *Dominus.*"

***

Lothar surveyed the scene before him. He watched Hincmar and Nithard fall to Stilicho's men. He called Wandregisel, "I have seen enough. Gather our remaining forces and rush their shields."

A confusing mix of sounds filled the air. A shiver went through Lothar. "What's that?"

"Some of the *milites* are turning against us in favor of Lord Stilicho," Wandregisel said.

"Under whose command? Who is the traitor?" Lothar demanded.

It was then they heard the cries, "*Deus adjjuta Romanis...Deus nobiscum!*"

Mallobaudes arrived, his chest heaving and beads of sweat forming on his brow. "My cousin is leading them. You must send soldiers to seize him."

Lothar turned to Wandregisel. "Take our rearguard and break this attack. Bring me, Melchior, dead or alive."

"I think his cousin, Lord Mallobaudes, should have the honor," Wandregisel responded.

"Do your lieutenants routinely countermand your orders, Count Lothar?" Mallobaudes asked with a sneer. "Is this how to raise a new empire? With insubordinates at your side?"

Wandregisel's face darkened, and his eyes narrowed. He began to draw his *Seaxe*.

"Hold, Wandregisel. I am your liege. Do as I command," Lothar said.

Wandregisel slipped the blade back into hits sheath and glared. "As you command!" Without another word, he turned to gather his men.

"He is an insubordinate, Count Lothar. If you make me your lieutenant, I will never question your authority," Mallobaudes said.

Lothar watched and listened as the fighting grew to a crescendo and then quieted. "What is happening?"

"Count Lothar, I believe Wandregisel has given his sword to Melchior," Mallobaudes said. He has betrayed us!"

"We should leave. Gather who we can and go. But go where?" Lothar's mind raced with fear and confusion. His arrogance and bravado now drained from him.

"To join your allies."

"The Avars? They'll laugh at us and sell us to Melchior."

"No, to the Saxons. The queen, Udela, will welcome you. With your great knowledge of things military and her savage tribesmen, we can retake this place and still march west. Besides, I still have the girl."

Lothar regarded the man before him. *Could he be trusted? No!* But he needed him now. "Yes. The girl could be useful. We must get a message to Willehad. I have my silver packed on mules and ready to go west. But we can use it to pay the Saxons. How many men do you command?"

"I have half a dozen retainers."

Lothar looked around. He still had twenty stout Franks standing beside their mounts, waiting for his orders. "This band, my bodyguard, is all I have left."

"Then let us ride," Mallobaudes said.

Lothar gave a last look at the devastation before him. "Yes, we must depart this place. Udela will help us."

Chapter 18

A udeon and the others scrambled across the rooftop and down a narrow ladder to the outer wall. The blaring trumpets had all but emptied the battlements.

But two sentries spied the band. "Who goes there?"

Audeon tried to bluff. "In the name of the Risen Lord and Count Lothar, we have been sent to summon the bishop."

The sentry eyed Auden's band. "So many of you to summon one bishop?"

"The count believes he is in some danger. The prisoners are proof of it."

"We must verify this with one of the lieutenants."

"We have little time to waste." Audeon fumbled at the hilt of his broadsword.

"I must follow orders." The guard turned to his mate. "Be quick about it, Ouus. We don't want to put the good bishop at risk."

Ouus nodded and turned back. Before he took a step, an arrow pierced the back of his neck, the serrated point slicing open his Adam's apple like an apple. Ouus grabbed at the point protruding from the front of his neck. He choked on blood and took a step, then collapsed into a convulsion and died.

Audeon stepped forward and ran his broadsword through the other guard's armpit. He wiped the blood from the blade and sheathed it. "A worthy shot, Gaetano. Grab their *Seaxes*. We must move quickly before any others arrive."

They scurried in the darkness to the next tower.

Cassyon hefted the *Seaxe* he took from the guard.

"That's some *Seaxe* you have now, Cassyon," Detleff said.

Cassyon smiled. "Just long enough to reply to the stroke of a broadsword."

They now heard the stirring of the Frank-on-Frank fray.

Audeon peered carefully over the battlement. "There's some sort of action below."

"We might be able to save the *Dominus* in the confusion," Detleff said.

"First, we must fulfill our mission," Audeon said. "But of course, that requires a way out of here."

"I see something, Audeon," Father Thomas said.

"What is it, Father?"

"This door."

"A closet of some sort. Do you think it contains weapons?" Audeon asked.

Father Thomas said, beaming. "No, something better. A *Pater Noster*,"

"A what?" Cassyon asked.

"A rope and pulley contraption to move goods up to the battlements. In the cathedral, we had one to move our casks of food."

"And ale, I wager," Cassyon quipped.

"Well, it was also used to get a tardy priest to Mass on time," Father Thomas said.

"Let's have a look." Audeon cracked open the door to reveal a wooden box just large enough to fit a man.

"Usually, it is worked from a wheel at the bottom," Father Thomas said. "We'll have to work it from here until two of us are below. I'll go first."

Audeon glanced down the dark shaft, and a shiver went through him. "It looks like the way to hell."

Father Thomas nodded. "All the more reason for a priest to go first… so I can wrestle the devil and clear the way."

The priest slipped into the box and made the sign of the cross as they began to lower him. He was shrouded in darkness until the box struck the bottom with a thud. He yanked the rope to signal the next man down. Audeon made sure he was the last to depart. When he stepped out of the *Pater Noster*, Father Thomas handed him a loaf of dark bread. He saw the others hungrily chomping on the same.

"Is this some sort of new Communion, Father?" Audeon asked.

"No. It seems this contraption led to the canteen pantry. The men had not eaten in a while, and who knows when we'll next eat."

Audeon nodded and took a large bite. "We must be off."

A girl's soft voice came from behind the pantry door. "What is going on here?"

Cassyon grabbed her. "What do you think, lass?"

"I think you are robbing the larder."

"We're hungry. I think you know who we are," Audeon said.

"Followers of the *missus*? I heard the prisoners had escaped. But now with the terrible fighting, I don't know what to think."

"What's your name?" Audeon asked.

"Anfelisia. I am a slave to Boso, the master of the canteen."

"This Boso has good taste in women." Cassyon squeezed her more tightly.

Anfelisia twisted and struck him across the face. "I am no whore to be mangled by the likes of you. I'm a Christian woman."

"Leave her go," Audeon said. "We're not here to fondle women of any kind. Can you direct us out of here?"

"Where are you going?"

"To the abbey," Father Thomas said.

"Then I will lead you," Anfelisia said.

Anfelisia led the band through a passage known only to those responsible for delivering victuals, wood, and other goods. Soon they were in the town itself. The buildings were shuttered tight. Strangely, many barn doors swung open in the breeze. Cows, chickens, and pigs roamed loose.

"It's awfully quiet here," Werinbert said.

"Most are at services. It's a holy day," Father Thomas said.

The faint pealing of bells could be heard.

"All the better," Cassyon replied.

"Perhaps, Father. But most of the villagers have fled. They know that Fulda is in danger from within and without," Anfelisia whispered.

She led them past the half-timbered buildings along muddy streets piled with dung until they reached the road leading to the abbey.

"You should leave us now, Anfelisia," Audeon said.

She lowered her head. "No, Lord. I would come with you."

"For what reason?"

"To escape bondage, of course. I was not always a slave. I was brought here from the south as a little girl. But I was told my father was a great Frankish warrior."

"And who is he?" Audeon asked.

Moisture welled in her eyes. "I... I am not sure."

"And yet, you hope to find him?" Audeon had found someone with a greater problem than he. He, at least, knew who his father was.

"No. But I would take the veil and pray. I desire to serve God, not Frankish brutes in the canteen."

Audeon looked at Father Thomas.

The priest folded his hands. "It is frowned upon for the church to offer a refuge to slaves. But perhaps we can buy her freedom. The monks of the abbey would be fortunate to have your services until you can take the veil."

"Very well. We owe Anfelisia our freedom. Now let's be off," Audeon said.

***

The Abbey

Jurchen stood next to the bishop. Willehad was intent on presiding over a Mass to celebrate the holy day. The bishop could not even recall the feast. "This is my last service under Karolus's edict. Who are we even celebrating? Some Roman martyrs no doubt. Karolus had made all things Roman and Christian his priority. I'll change that soon."

Normally, the chapel would be full of monks under the offices of Baugulf. But with the abbot secured and drugged and the monks mostly confined, the Mass was attended by a score of Willehad's retainers – priests and deacons he had ordained into his special branch of the church. Jurchen knew they were armed and devoted to their master even more fervently than Lothar's *milites* were to him.

Jurchen tried to stall for time. "This is most unusual, Your Grace."

"What?"

"You are a bishop. To serve a Mass with less than a score in attendance is an insult to your office and you."

"What do you suggest?"

"Send for some townsmen. Fill the place with devoted Franks. Devoted to their bishop... to you."

Willehad smiled. "Yes, you are right, Jurchen. As bishop, I deserve no less."

He waved to one of his Saxon priests. "Father Derian, the services will wait until you can gather some townsfolk to join us. Be quick. I have real work to attend to after the Mass. Meanwhile, let us all pray in silence and remind God of our unworthiness."

Indeed, Jurchen thought.

The retainers dropped to their knees and prayed silently.

Willehad nudged Jurchen. "After the service, I want you to fetch Baugulf."

Jurchen grew alarmed. "To what purpose, Your Grace?"

"I will try one last time to win him to my cause. He could still rule over a great center of Christian learning. But it shall be the learning I dictate. Not Karolus's. And not Rome's."

"But your potion has him near death." Jurchen was worried that Willehad would discover that the abbot, although weak, had not suffered the worst.

"Do what you can. If he dies, at least I tried to reason with the man. But I have reconsidered my earlier plan. Having him as an ally, however unwilling, is to my benefit."

"And how can you be sure of his allegiance, should he agree?" Jurchen asked.

"Why, I'll leave you to be his assistant. You'd like that, wouldn't you? To serve at the center of learning for all Christendom? That is, my Christendom."

"I suppose I have no choice?"

"You always have a choice, Jurchen. Isn't all Christianity based on free will? It's just the outcome we have no choice over, eh?"

"Of course, Eminence." Jurchen's mind raced for a way to connect with either Stilicho or Melchior. He changed the subject. "What will Lothar do with Melchior and his men?"

Willehad smirked. "It won't be pleasant, whatever he does."

Since Melchior and his men had been drugged, Jurchen struggled with how to save them. Although he managed to win over Stilicho, he could not be sure if he would act.

A servant came into the chapel and whispered in Willehad's ear.

Jurchen saw his eyes widen. "Is something the matter, Your Grace?"

"I don't know. Trumpets have been heard from the fort. Lothar is rallying his men to action."

"Perhaps he has decided to act now. To march and meet the Avars and his new queen?" Jurchen suspected otherwise. *Stilicho must have acted.*

A commotion erupted in the narthex opposite the altar.

"Ah, I hear some of the faithful come to join us," Willehad said.

A handful of reluctant-looking men entered at the prodding of Father Derian.

Willehad put on a smile. "Welcome, my children. We celebrate a feast day Mass and welcome the faithful of Fulda..."

"We have not come here to pray, Your Grace," Father Thomas said. "But to secure the safety of the Abbot Baugulf and deliver unto him a letter from our king and emperor, Karolus."

"Father Derian! You dare bring these prisoners here?"

Father Derian stammered, "But, but Your Grace? These were the first folk I encountered. They seemed very eager to attend services under you."

"Father Derian could not have recognized these as escaped prisoners, Your Grace," Jurchen said. His eyes met Audeon's, motioning toward the side door along the chapel's ambulatory.

From behind a pillar emerged a slender form.

"I see you have the lovely Anfelisia with you. Now that is fortunate. Lothar has always delayed giving me her charms. Now, I'll claim what is mine."

"No! I want to take the veil and serve in the abbey…"

"Seize the girl!" Willehad ordered.

Two of Willehad's men grasped Anfelisia.

Anfelisia! Jurchen had heard of the girl before. She was indeed beautiful. But Willehad could have any number of peasant girls who would be compliant, if not willing. Jurchen could see in the girl's face that she would die a martyr rather than submit to such sin. *Why fix on this girl now?*

Audeon edged toward the door, but the retainers left their pews to block the way. The sound of short seaxes slipping from sheaths beneath robes broke the chapel's silence. Willehad hurried from the altar to join his men.

Audeon and his men flashed their blades.

"No!" Father Thomas called out. "No violence is permitted in God's house."

Willehad smiled. "Of course. Father Thomas is correct. You have violated God's laws by bringing weapons into a Christian place of worship. Drop them now or be condemned!"

"What crap is this?" Cassyon asked.

"He's right," Detleff said. "No Christian warrior may draw his sword in a place of God. It's sacrilege."

"Then why do the bishop's priests carry weapons?" Werinbert asked.

"A bishop or an abbot may negate the rule," Father Thomas said glumly.

Willehad threw back his head and laughed. "The only other who can break the rule besides me is Baugulf, Abbot of Fulda. And he is, shall I say, indisposed."

"Was indisposed, Your Grace." A lean figure in a dark cape and hood stood at the opposite side of the ambulatory, the side that connected to the abbey. The figure dropped the hood, exposing his face, which no one expected to behold.

***

"Baugulf!" Willehad exclaimed.

"I have been revived by the good offices of one of your priests, whom it seems was not as vile as you supposed."

Willehad looked at Jurchen with eyes burning. "Traitor! You were not sent there to revive him."

"Traitor to whom, Your Grace?" Jurchen replied.

"Seize them all!" Willehad screeched.

The armed priests and deacons moved quickly to surround Audeon and his band. A ring of blades encircled them.

Cassyon, Werinbert, and Detleff brandished their weapons.

Audeon raised a gloved fist. "We'll not sin against God in this sacred place. No blade shall draw blood in a chapel."

"But God made no law against arrows," Gaetano said with a grin.

Everyone looked up. Above the flickering chandeliers, they saw the hawk-like outline of the bowman, arrow drawn and aimed straight at Willehad.

"This archer has lived among the heathens and developed some bad habits, Your Grace," Jurchen said. "He's an expert shot, and the missile is aimed at your heart."

"No! Wait!" Willehad fumbled nervously at his gold chain and cross. "We can make an arrangement yet."

"If you are thinking that Lothar will come to your aid, think again," Audeon said. "He is much beleaguered."

Willehad looked again at Jurchen. "More treachery, Jurchen?"

"As you said, Your Grace, we all have free will. I have made my choice. Lord Stilicho has decided to remain faithful to Karolus and the true Christian faith. Without him, Lothar's power is diminished, as is yours. I think you should take up the pen and prepare your confession to Karolus and the pope."

"Never! The Avars are near... as are the Saxons. Both armies march here as we speak and should arrive by dusk tomorrow."

"That's something you'll not see," Audeon said. "One false move and Gaetano will extinguish your capacity for evil in this world. We'll see if your pact with the devil carries with you to the next."

"My men outnumber yours," Willehad said.

"These are Frankish warriors who have each killed more men than your faux-priests can dream of," Audeon replied. "Are your men prepared to die, in violation of church decree, for the likes of you?"

Willehad looked at his men. "I have something that Melchior will want."

"Lord Melchior can't be bought," Audeon replied. "He is the *Missus Dominicus*."

"There is." Willehad pulled Anfelisia in front of him and stepped behind a pillar, blocking Gaetano's shot. His men closed around him. "We are leaving. Follow, and I'll cut the slut's throat."

"What do we care if a servant girl is the last person you kill?" Cassyon said. "Let's spring on this band of pigs. I care not if I meet them in hell. I'll just kill them again!"

Werinbert and Detleff stepped forward as well.

"No," Father Thomas exclaimed. "Desecration and the death of an innocent is no way to uphold the church."

"Father Thomas is correct," Baugulf said. "They tried to kill me and destroy the abbey's work. But I'll not commit sacrilege to correct that."

Face flushed with anger, Audeon drew his weapon. "Tell me why we should care whether this girl dies or not."

"Because her father will skin you all alive," Willehad said. "That's why!"

"Her father?" Audeon asked.

"Yes, the very *Missus Dominicus* you all revere," Willehad exhaled. "Melchior is her father!"

Anfelisia swooned. One of the monks grabbed her tightly.

"Yes... The idiot canteen keeper let on as much. That's why I wanted her so badly. But I could not let Lothar know, or he would have used her for his purposes."

"How... How is she his daughter?" Audeon was confused but also stalling for time.

Willehad laughed. "I should have been more precise, bastard daughter. There's a difference, as you must surely know, Audeon."

Audeon's eyes narrowed. *I'll kill this false priest.*

But Father Thomas held his sword arm. "Easy, Audeon. He is desperate, making him more of a danger to the girl."

"How do you know this, Willehad?" Baugulf asked.

"Mallobaudes's revenge on his cousin. He rode with Melchior in Lombardy some sixteen years ago. Boso was his squire. It seems Melchior had too much to drink, or not enough, and impregnated a farmer's daughter named Aniela."

"That can't be," Detleff said. "I would have known."

"Does a lord confide his trysts to a hind?" Willehad mocked.

Detleff turned red. "Why..."

Willehad continued. "As a lord, he could not do the honorable thing. Fortunately, Boso was enthralled with Aniela and later returned to Lombardy, where he married her. He despised Melchior, as did Mallobaudes, so taking his wife and daughter was a double pleasure. But one he dared not reveal. When he left Mallobaudes's service, for the weakling cousin never went on campaign again, Boso enlisted under Lothar. He finally retired at Fulda to run the canteen."

"And how do you know all of this?" Baugulf asked.

"Because it is true," Boso's voice came from the narthex. "I'm a sworn enemy of Melchior."

Willehad smiled grimly. "Boso... You arrived just in time."

"Count Lothar sent me to warn you. He's fleeing to the Saxon lands. What is Anfelisia doing here?"

"She is serving her bishop. Tell these men the truth about your servant... the bastard daughter of your dead wife."

Boso gazed blankly.

"You see, Boso could not bring himself to raise her as his own. After all, she was a bastard of the *missus*. But he recognized she could be valuable someday. And she is — to me."

"What do you want, Willehad?" Baugulf asked.

"You will allow us to leave. When we have arrived safely, I will release the girl."

"How can you be trusted?" Audeon asked.

"I am a bishop of the church."

Audeon looked at the figure in the dark cloak. "Abbot Baugulf, I have a message from my father, the emperor and king, Karolus. Perhaps you should read it before you decide."

Willehad's face contorted at the news of the letter. "What mischief is this?"

As they talked, Jurchen worked his way closer to the girl. He drew his *Seaxe*, aiming to thrust it at Willehad.

But Boso went from silence to anger, then to action. "You'll not take her without a price, Willehad." He charged into the band of faux-clerics, *Seaxe* held high. A powerfully built deacon pushed Jurchen aside and thrust a *Seaxe* into Boso's ribs.

Boso dropped his blade and clutched his side. "You've slain me!" he fell to his knees and sprawled face-first onto the marble floor.

Anfelisia screamed. Gaetano unleashed a shaft, striking one of the clerics in the heart.

Audeon's men looked to him for orders.

"What do we do, Lord?" Cassyon asked.

Willehad and his men quickly dragged Anfelisia through a back door. She kicked and grabbed at the men holding her. One of them drew his cloak over her head, muffling her cries.

Audeon raised his broadsword. "They have left the sanctuary. But they'll not get far. Follow me."

"Father Thomas and Jurchen will stay with you. We must save the girl."

"Perhaps not, Lord," Werinbert said.

They all looked at the young man.

"What do you mean?" Audeon asked. Werinbert was not one for much comment.

"We could offer an exchange," Werinbert said.

"Exchange for what? Willehad can't be swayed by silver or even gold. It is power and control that he craves," Baugulf said.

Werinbert shrugged. "I don't know, it's just..."

"Perhaps another girl," Jurchen said.

"What do you mean?" Audeon asked.

"Willehad said Lothar sent Mallobaudes to ransom back a girl who could prove very valuable. A very beautiful and young girl, coincidentally also fathered by a powerful lord but raised by one of his *milites*."

"Genofeva," Werinbert said.

Audeon reddened. Hearing her name made his heart skip a beat and his stomach churn. "I wish that were true, but she's lost to the Avars."

Jurchen stroked his beard. "That could be the name, " I heard someone mumble. That might be the name. How do you know this girl?"

"She is... my sister... of a sort. My father raised her as my sister. An Avar pack stole her from under our very noses. I am ashamed of it," Werinbert said.

Audeon lowered his head in shame. *I loved a girl and yet failed to boldly ride in her defense or to pursue her captors. What kind of milites am I?*

"And I heard something else," Jurchen said.

"What's that?" Audeon asked.

Jurchen gave Audeon a strange look. "From the way, they were speaking... I suspect she is Karolus's daughter."

Audeon's lips tightened, and his face turned pale. *Genofeva... my sister? It can't be!*

"I am sorry, Audeon," Jurchen said. "I know you favored the girl. You mentioned her so often during the ride east. I had hoped to spare you the shame of falling in love with your half-sister, but I had to say it."

Audeon stared. A hundred thoughts and feelings flashed through him. *What sin have I committed...?*

"Are you all right, Lord?" Werinbert asked.

Audeon nodded. "Never... never mind who she might be. Anything that would return Genofeva from these evildoers is worth doing. An exchange... or a fight."

"Where is this girl?" Cassyon asked.

"Mallobaudes has her secreted away. So we must get to him," Jurchen said.

"And where might he be? Perhaps fallen in the fight within the fort," Audeon said.

Baugulf spoke, "Lord Mallobaudes, the *Missus Dominicus's* cousin, is a coward who will not expose himself if he can avoid it. If the girl is indeed Karolus's daughter, he must have her under guard somewhere. Find Mallobaudes, and you'll find the girl. But why would we trade the illegitimate daughter of an emperor for the illegitimate daughter of his servant, Melchior?"

"We'll use the trade to trap Willehad. We must save both maidens," Audeon said. "It is as my father would wish. It is our Christian duty."

"Very well. Make haste then," Baugulf said.

"We are wasting time here," Cassyon said. "Let's ride."

"You'll need horses and better equipment if you venture into a land infested with Avars that soon will be infested with pagan Saxons," Baugulf said.

Suddenly, a party of twenty heavily armed Franks burst through the narthex with broadswords drawn for action. Audeon and the others held their weapons at the ready.

"Who breaks the Lord's sanctuary?" Baugulf asked calmly.

An officer stepped forward. "Who challenges me?"

"I am Baugulf, Abbot of Fulda and representative of Karolus, the Holy Father, and God."

The officer and his men bowed their heads and made a quick sign of the cross.

"I apologize, Abbot," the officer said. "My name is Imninon, Commander of Lord Stilicho's first banner. I was sent here to secure the abbey and you."

"As you can see, Lord Imninon, I am in good hands," Baugulf said. "You say Lord Stilicho sent you?"

"No, Abbot. I didn't say that. Lord Melchior, *Missus Dominicus*, sent us. Lothar is defeated. Lord Melchior wanted to ensure your safety. He and Lord Stilicho are organizing forces to defend against the expected attack of Lothar's allies — the Saxons and Avars."

"God be praised," Father Thomas said.

"God's word!" Audeon exclaimed. His thoughts were on the girl he loved — whether she was his sister or not.

"Yes, praise be to God," Baugulf repeated. He made the sign of the cross, as they all did.

***

"Bread and wine never tasted so good." Melchior downed the wine quickly and munched on the black bread. He was exhausted beyond belief.

When Lothar and his band fled and the remaining Franks pledged their loyalty, he turned the defense over to Stilicho and begged for time to rest. Even the ever-strong Fromm seemed whipped. But after just a few hours' rest, they rose and ate while Stilicho gave his account.

"How are your wounds, Fromm?" Melchior asked.

"Mere scratches inflicted by Frankish puppies."

"I thank you for your efforts on my behalf. But tell me, did you go over to Lothar?"

Fromm gulped more ale and scratched his ear. "In the name of Loki, I don't know."

Melchior had a feeling he knew. "Well, I'm glad you intervened when you did."

"I have a feeling I may never get to Miklagard." Fromm quaffed his ale.

"Are you disappointed?" Melchior asked.

"I'm not sure. I favor the girl, Anfelisia, here. But I favor the pleasures and the loot of the east more."

Melchior nodded thoughtfully. "I feel better. A Norseman in love is no pleasant sight."

"Loki toys with such men," Fromm said.

They both laughed.

Stilicho entered the room. A servant poured him ale. The gruff old warrior seemed to have a new lease on life since the formal break with Lothar.

"What does the new Count of Fulda say of our situation?" Melchior asked.

"I'm no count," Stilicho intoned.

"I am *Missus Dominicus*. That gives me Karolus's authority in his absence. I just exercised that authority."

Melchior felt he had a more complete knowledge and understanding of the world he now lived in, as though it were always his world. Yet, he was still in all ways a man of a later century, a soldier, vagabond, and spy.

Stilicho grunted.

Fromm laughed. "Stilicho knows full well this makes his fate worse. How many men do you have?"

"Maybe fifty mounted milites and one hundred footmen, worth counting. But all wear the metal *brunia* and are proven veterans. If I reduce the area we defend, I believe it can be held. Certainly, against Avars and Saxons, who have little skill with siege warfare."

"They'll just move on and ravage the lands between the Rhine and us," Fromm said.

Melchior realized the brutish warrior had a keen mind. "Well said, Fromm. No, that is what they will expect. And they will march to the Rheine. Who knows how many local lords have secretly pledged to Lothar and his evil queen?"

"What do we do?" Stilicho asked.

"We attack them," Melchior said.

Fromm smiled with excitement. "Exactly! Always attack!"

"But we'll be outnumbered by twenty to one," Stilicho lamented.

"True, but we will choose the place and time of the attack. I am not convinced the Avars can be trusted. And we know Lothar is a coward. He may flinch if we strike boldly. But the key is to sow discord among them all. What do we know of this Saxon queen? The one they call Udela... the one they say is a witch?"

Stilicho frowned. "Hincmar was witness to her witchcraft. Summoning thunder and fire at will..."

"I should like to fill her with Thor's thunder," Fromm said, making an obscene gesture.

"Perhaps you will," Melchior said.

Fromm half grinned. "Meaning what?"

"Meaning... you may go among these Saxons and offer your services," Melchior said.

"Lothar will never allow it," Stilicho said. "Fromm betrayed him once."

"But Fromm is a Norseman. They expect as much. Anything for silver, drink, or women. His tale is that he seeks all three. Tell them I did not reward you sufficiently and forbade your travel to Miklagard. Say you seek the girl Lothar promised. Say you realize the Franks will never willingly part with their silver. Say you are tired of Christians and seek the company of good pagans. Say you yearn to serve a beautiful queen."

"Lord Melchior is right. It might just work," Stilicho said.

Fromm nodded but then considered the idea and frowned. "How can this be?"

Melchior looked at him intently. "I can only say what can be. You must determine how it can be. If you are willing."

There was a long pause. Finally, Fromm nodded his head. "I'm willing."

"You leave tonight. Stilicho, have a horse made ready for him."

"How do I get there?" Fromm asked.

"Hincmar was at their camp. He knows the way," Stilicho said.

"So he lives?" Melchior asked.

"Yes. I did not execute him with the other leaders. But his wounds are serious."

Melchior smiled. "You are a wise man, Stilicho. Tell him I guarantee Karolus's mercy and full restoration of his position if he agrees to guide Fromm.

S.W. O'Connell

Chapter 19

Campus Unofelt

Fromm and Hincmar left when Fulda lay in darkness. The village was deathly quiet. A moon shrouded in clouds made reaching the village and the minor abbey northeast of Fulda a ponderous journey.

"Thor's breath! I can barely see the end of this horse," Fromm quipped.

Hincmar rode in silence. His pain worsened with each movement of his horse. His body ached from the bruising of blows and a half-dozen blade cuts. He wished he had died in the struggle. Guilt, shame, and resentment overwhelmed him. Still, the *Dominus* had given him redemption of sorts, and no matter what, he remained a milites of Frankland.

"What do they call this place?" Fromm asked.

"Campus Unofelt."

"What does that mean?"

"It's Latin. Karolus established it some years ago for the Benedictines. Another religious center. Not ten years old and it already has two churches."

"We Norse don't need so many holy places."

A vague shadow appeared before them, then vanished into the darkness. Hincmar drew his broadsword and spurred his horse in pursuit, gritting his teeth against the pain. The horse neighed, and suddenly the figure stood before him. "Whoa." Hincmar pulled back on the reins.

The figure fell into the muddy lane. Before Hincmar could strike, it knelt, folded its hands, and bowed its head.

Hincmar noticed the bald pate against the faint moonlight. "Who in the name of the holy saints are you?"

"Kill me quickly, as I have made my peace with God." The figure groveled and hugged the ground like a worm.

Hincmar's horse snorted and moved its feet nervously.

"Stand and answer my question, or you'll feel the flat of my sword and be quick about it."

The figure stood. "I am Brother Paul, a Benedictine... but you are... a Frank?"

"Of course, I'm a Frank. We are maybe six leagues from Fulda. Why did you flee from us in the dark?"

"I... I thought you were a Saxon... or an Avar," he said nervously.

"But the Saxon camp is leagues from here. I rode there once myself just days ago."

"No! The Saxon vanguard was just two leagues from this very place at dusk. They ambushed some of the brothers while they were gathering mushrooms. They killed all but two. I assumed the rest of the Saxons had arrived, and you were they."

Hincmar felt woozy and wobbled in the saddle as he said, "Saxons don't like to fight in the dark."

Fromm's horse halted beside Hincmar. "Who does?"

"This monk says the Saxons are just outside the village. Where are the villagers and the rest of the clerics?"

"Some are hiding behind their shutters. Most ran off. Several monks are in the church praying for deliverance."

"And why were you about, Bother Paul?" Hincmar asked weakly. The pain from his wounds bit him with a burning sting.

The cleric tried to hide his robes.

"What have you there?" Fromm asked.

"Nothing."

Fromm's long ax reached out and smashed the jug of ale hidden beneath the robes, sending the dark liquid oozing through the cloth.

Brother Paul jumped back like a frightened puppy. "You could have killed me with that."

"Wrong, monk. I should have killed you... making me waste perfectly good ale."

Brother Paul pointed at a small mud-and-thatch building. "There's more in the cellar."

Fromm grinned. "Well, what do you know? A monk gives up his ale cellar to a pagan."

"No time for this." Hincmar felt guilty about what he was about to propose, "Fromm, if you are going to desert to the Saxons, a cleric would make a good trophy. Then lead them to this town for plunder. It will gain their trust for a short time at least."

Brother Paul shook with fear. "You can't be serious! You are a Frank *milites*, sworn by Karolus to uphold the church."

Hincmar nodded grimly. "In my own way, that's exactly what I'm doing."

"Say it not if you are truly a Christian *milites*." Brother Paul shook his folded hands.

Hincmar swayed weakly in the saddle. "It... must be... so, Brother Paul. I must return..."

A thick rope was wrapped around Brother Paul, and he was tied to Fromm's horse. "You can't do this!"

"I am doing it. Act like a man, in the name of Odin," Fromm said. "If you're lucky, you'll soon die a martyr for your god. I know Christian priests like that."

Brother Paul stood quaking. Fromm mounted and spurred his horse along the dusky road. The monk's legs pumped as Fromm's horse swayed down the wooded trail.

When they disappeared into the dark, Hincmar turned his horse around. *I have betrayed my king twice, two of my liege lord's and now my God by turning this monk over to the pagans.* He tried to pray for forgiveness as his horse moved along, but a fever soon gripped him. A half league later, he tumbled from his saddle into the brush.

***

As another gloomy dawn broke, Fromm entered the thickly wooded forest. He saw no sign of the Saxon advance guard. The trail wound through the heavily wooded high ground. Nothing stirred, but Fromm kept his ax ready. Brother Paul stumbled along the trail behind him, whimpering and mumbling desperate prayers. *One powerful shout to Odin is worth a hundred of these mumbling Christian prayers.*

The dull twilight began to cast a gray light through the heavy branches above them. This made Fromm uneasy. Dusk and dawn were the favored times for Saxons to attack. Finally, they reached a draw.

"Here is where they attacked us." Brother Paul cast his eyes nervously.

The ground sloped upward on three sides. Fromm scanned the dark tree line.

"Yes, this is where I'd come for an ambush. They likely ran off for leagues after the raid," From said as he surveyed the land.

"So... can you let me go?" Brother Paul asked.

"I need a hostage."

Brother Paul lowered his head and folded his hands in prayer as tears welled in his eyes. "I'm prepared to meet Our Lord as a martyr to the faith. I only ask that you kill me quickly yourself if they decide to submit me to Saxon torture."

"A fair bargain. But I don't fancy hearing you squeal like a pig. And I don't kill for Saxons. Now take off your robes,"

"What?"

"Strip now, before I change my mind, Thor's breath."

Brother Paul dropped his robes to his ankles but firmly held his crucifix.

"I'll have that too, priest. The Saxons will want proof I killed you in this forest."

"I'm a Benedictine brother. I'd die before I'd give up my crucifix to pagans."

"Is your crucifix worth your churches? And your people? For if the Saxons have their way, all your holy places and holy people will die as surely as Odin rules Valhalla."

Brother Paul kissed his beads and looked to heaven.

"Answer me, by Thor's breath!"

Trembling, the monk nodded and handed him the silver cross bearing the broken body of Christ.

"Now run back and stay in the shadows. I don't want a Saxon scouting party to spot you and turn me in for a liar."

Brother Paul ran through the forest, panting and huffing.

Fromm turned his horse up the trail. He rode another half-hour and then stopped to get his bearings. He hoped the Saxons had not moved in a different direction. He knew that under their war leader, Widukind, they moved quickly and struck even more quickly. *Will this evil witch, their queen, fight as well?*

The answer came not a moment later. A pack of Saxons clad in black dashed from the trees with horrific screams that would frighten most men, but not Fromm. He turned his horse left while drawing his broad-ax with his powerful right hand. A Saxon leaped at him and met the ax blade with his open mouth. The blade sliced through flesh and bone, sending the upper half of the attacker's skull spinning into the earth.

The second Saxon grabbed the neck of Fromm's horse and plunged his Seaxe into Fromm's side. The blade caught on his heavy belt stud and plunged into his wineskin full of ale.

"Thor's piss!" Fromm grabbed the Saxon's wrist, snapping it with a crack.

"Aaargh!"

Fromm twisted the horse about, dropping the Saxon into the pine needles and facing the other two. They stood with their short spears poised, ready over their round shields. Fromm slipped off his horse and raised his broad ax over his head. "Come and taste Thor's little brother, my Saxon piglets."

They rushed him, shoulder to shoulder, with spear tips darkened and pointed at his chest. But Fromm easily stepped to the side and swung his broad-ax, cleaving their spears in two. The Saxons stood with mouths agape, then drew their long *Seaxes* and charged forward as one.

"Hold! By Thor's hammer. I came here to treat with Saxons, not kill them. Spare me this."

He spoke in their tongue. They looked at one another. "Who are you, Norseman, who rides with Franks and speaks our tongue?"

"I am a worshiper of Odin and Thor and all the great gods. They call me Fromm. And who are you? You look and speak like Saxons but are far beyond the Saxon lands."

"These are our lands now, as they were before the accursed Karolus took them. What brings you here, Norseman?"

Fromm's mouth broke into a wide grin. "Silver. And now that your dead friend sliced open my skin, I need more ale."

"What makes you think the Saxons have silver for the likes of you?"

"I'll let your queen Udela decide that. I heard she is very beautiful and favors powerful men, especially those who bring news of the Franks and their defenses."

"What makes you think our queen will receive a Norseman?"

"What makes you think she won't?"

An hour later, they reached the edge of the forest, and Fromm saw a vast open plain fed by a gentle river. It occurred to him that such fine land was rare in his homeland – another reason to travel. Thousands of Saxons were camped along the river, but he saw not a single campfire. They are staying on the move.

"Do you know where your queen is among such a large host?" Fromm asked.

"Of course. We are Haari. We follow Hrodger. He serves the queen directly."

"Then lead on, Haari."

Fromm rode through the Saxon camp behind the two Haari warriors. Women and children scurried after him to take the measure of this stranger. They had never seen anyone so big.

"Is he a Frank?" many asked.

"No. A Norseman!" someone said.

"A curse on all Norsemen!" murmured another.

"Until Widukind came to lead us, those beasts of the north raided Saxon lands along the coast with impunity. Lately, they have been quiet. Is he the beginning of a new invasion?"

Fromm nodded grimly. He knew the Saxons feared the Norse as much as they hated the Franks. The crowds parted before them and then closed behind them. Finally, they reached a large leather tent, almost as big as a house. Two warriors in black stood at the entrance.

"Impressive guardians of your queen," Fromm said.

One of his escorts nodded. "They are Haari as well. We were banned by the queen after a Frank bested some of them. But we have since proven ourselves by bringing her plunder and trophies from the Franks. We are raised above the Nabo and Euduces."

Fromm nodded. "I have heard of the Haari. Our forefathers fought them. Savage *bezerker* fighters beyond even our own."

The Saxon pounded his chest in pride and grinned for the first time.

Thanks be to Odin – they are as stupid as they are brave. "I hear your queen is allied with certain Franks. How can that be? No follower of Odin can trust a Christian, especially a Frank."

The two Haari shot knowing looks at each other.

"You agree with me?" Fromm asked.

They nodded. "We think the queen is herself bewitched by the idea of working with them. But we are sure she will turn them over once we have our victory and take the place they call Fulda."

A powerfully built Saxon in polished black leather and fur emerged from the tent. He was followed by six others. Even by Fromm's standards, they looked brutal.

"Who is this? Where are the others?" the Saxon demanded.

"Hrodger, this is Fromm the Norseman. He sent Brunger and Frumirih to Valhalla. But it turns out he abandoned the Franks to join us. He asks to meet with the queen."

Hrodger's face contorted in fury. "Kill my warriors? Meet with the queen? I'll kill you myself, Norseman!" His powerful hand grasped the long *Seaxe* hanging at his belt.

The others began to bellow and bang their javelins on their shields.

Fromm slid from the saddle and drew the broad-ax. "I come in peace, Hrodger, to meet the queen, Udela. But I will gladly go to Valhalla and take her Haari lap dogs with me!"

Hrodger's eyes took in Fromm's mettle. He slammed his *Seaxe* into its scabbard. "Very well, Norseman. A Haari who dies so easily is best gone. Come, let us drink ale while they inform the queen. But we must be quick, for the people will soon move."

***

Fromm's broad girth balanced on a crude stool as a plump Saxon girl poured ale into his greedy mouth. Between gulps, Fromm spun his tale of betrayal by Melchior and the Franks, who deprived him of his silver and the girl Anfelisia.

Hrodger swigged his ale. "I have seen the girl, Anfelisia. She is most beautiful. But the fat Christian priest has her. I'm not so sure he could mount her with that belly of his."

Fromm blanched. "She is no mere trifle for him to mount."

"What do you mean?"

"Didn't the priest... they call him a bishop... tell your queen?"

"Tell her what?"

"She is the daughter of Karolus's favorite warrior. The one they call the *Missus Dominicus*, Melchior."

"I know nothing of that," Hrodger said. "But the queen has many secrets."

"You sound as if you don't like that she has secrets."

"Haari warriors do not favor following a woman."

"Not even a witch?" Fromm laughed. "I've heard stories."

"They are true! The only reason we follow her. Her magic..."

"Nothing else?"

Hrodger took another draught of ale. His eyes narrowed. "We wait for Widukind. He has allowed the witch to serve as our queen. He had hoped she would distract the Franks. But now she has allied with the Avars. This puts the Saxons in danger."

"Avars?" Fromm feigned ignorance.

"Dgno, that walking serpent... leads thousands of mounted warriors. Avars are not to be trusted. But Widukind is shrewd. Avars and Saxons, combined with rogue Franks, are not a force Karolus can ignore. He must march to Fulda to counter it."

Fromm peered over his cup. "I've heard he has. Melchior is the vanguard."

"That is what Lothar told Udela. He quivered as he spoke of it."

"Lothar should shake in his boots. Melchior smashed his army and sent him running from Fulda."

"You were there?"

"Almost a score of dead Franks can attest to that," Fromm spoke the truth. *How easy it is to fit the truth into this narrative.* "But Lothar... where is he now?"

"With Udela. Pressing for early nuptials. The fat priest called Willehad is here too."

"Willehad claims he is a bishop. To Christians, there is a difference. Do they know of my arrival?"

"No, Norseman. I have decided to keep your presence secret among the Haari. There are those among the folk who do not favor us. We have usurped the traditional guardians of the queen and others. But I will send your words to Widukind and await his orders. Until then, we must march on Fulda."

"Under Melchior, Fulda will not easily fall. And when Karolus arrives, your forces will be blown away like dust."

"No matter. As I said, this is a diversion, although our queen does not know of it. Widukind has ten thousand warriors, some fifty leagues north of here. While Karolus wastes his energy here, Widukind will retake all the lost Saxon lands from the Elbe to the Rhine. While Karolus plays at Fulda, Widukind will pillage Aachen and move into Frankland to the west."

Fromm sat stone-faced, but his mind raced with excitement. *So Widukind was using the renegade queen Udela to invade Frankland. These Saxons are craftier than I thought.* "He thinks like a Norseman – your Widukind. I hope for your sake he fights like one."

Hrodger nodded. "He learned much from the Norsemen. Speed and surprise raise as much fear as savagery. And in combination, a nation trembles and falls with little resistance. And I need my surprise. So, you will remain here until I decide it benefits us both."

"There is the matter of the girl, Saxon. The crowds saw me. Word of my arrival surely reached the queen."

"In good time, Fromm. I'll tell the queen you are resting. Finish the ale. Eat some cold meat and bread."

"What will you tell her?"

"That you are about to join the Haari. True, you are not Saxon blood. But any warrior who can fell his enemies as you did belongs with us. We are a small band, but we're *berserkers* who can defeat five times our number, or more."

"But I want assurances the girl is safe."

Hrodger smiled. "Are Saxon women not good enough for you?"

Fromm raised his cup and grinned. "I plan to find out."

***

Udela's gaze moved from Lothar to Willehad and back. She knew each had his own agenda. Lothar, now a Frankish outlaw, was desperate to bind himself to the Saxons. Willehad, too, had gone from schemer to outcast, hoping to use the girl to make a deal. These were the men Udela relied on to gain a victory over the world they called Christendom. But she also longed to replace Widukind as the revered leader of the Saxons. She cast her eyes over the Saxon leaders. Hrodger and Eberger stood beside her, arms crossed and faces intent. Tilo alone sat in a corner, quietly watching. She was not so sure of him.

Lothar pumped a fist into the air. "We will move out at dusk. Tilo, you will take the Euduces out first and secure the way. In the mountains near Fulda, fell a dozen large oaks and prepare them as battering rams."

"We will charge the gates in the dark," Tilo said proudly.

"No. Wait until the main body arrives," Udela said.

"Eberger will take five hundred of his warriors and attack the abbey. It is weakly defended," Lothar said. "A mere diversion, but if they take it, so much the better."

"I agree," Udela said. "Eberger, sound a trumpet as the signal when you are engaged. The Franks will send help to the abbey. That's when Tilo assaults the gates."

"The fort has an outer wall," Lothar said. "It will be lightly defended. But the inner wall and towers are more compact. An experienced Frank can hold it for a long time,"

"Can an experienced Frank take it?" Tilo asked.

Udela realized she held a fragile alliance. Each of her leaders would gladly kill the other, and none of them liked the alliance with Lothar or the Avars. *And where were the Avars?* She needed Dgno's savage horsemen to make the victory complete.

"Count Lothar knows the fort. He built it," Udela said.

"There's an underground passage with a stream that carries water to the well. We can dam the source so a body of men can take the passage and climb up. With a hundred warriors in the middle of the defenses and Saxons storming the walls, the fort will succumb," Lothar said.

The room filled with grunts and nods. Udela was not convinced of the plan.

Willehad's jowls began to wiggle. "I want Baugulf alive. I can convince him to accept our new arrangement. We need him to influence the Frankish clergy. They need new leadership, and I'm just the one to give it to them. But when we take Aachen, I want the entire inner circle, including the bishop Angilram, killed."

"Fulda is the key to Aachen," Udela said. "But Aachen is the key to Frankland and beyond. Once we take Aachen, even Widukind will bow to our leadership."

"The queen and I will marry at the chapel in Aachen. A fitting end to the first phase of the campaign and the beginning of the second," Lothar said.

Udela nodded politely. *There will be no marriage!* She had no intention of loving a man. And something deep inside her, something she did not understand, told her she could never marry without love.

Tilo's voice came from the corner shadows. "So, Count Lothar, what part of this plan was your loss of Fulda? The Euduces don't favor alliances with cowards who flee their fort."

"Are you all not fleeing Saxonland?" Lothar reached for his broadsword.

But Udela placed a gentle hand on his wrist. "That was no insult, Lord. Saxons speak truthfully. The Euduces are our oldest tribe. Speaking thus is their way... their right."

Tilo folded his knotted arms across his chest and glared.

"I forsake my honor only out of my love for you, Udela," Lothar said.

"Spoken like a man of noble blood – like a future king," Udela said.

Lothar bowed his head. She noticed his eyes shifting, scanning the room to check on the others. In her heart, Udela knew she could never marry such a man.

"I will gather my warriors at once, My Queen," Tilo said. "The Euduces are not quibbling cowards. We shall lead the way to your victory, should Odin so deem it."

Udela raised her right hand. It occurred to her she had never done that... as a queen. "I praise the bold Euduces in advance. I am sure your brave deeds will follow."

Tilo stood and strode out.

"I expect every warrior to fight like there is no tomorrow. For if we lose, there will surely be no tomorrow," Udela said.

"We shall not lose. Our cause is just," Lothar said. "And our queen is a powerful ruler of men."

Udela knew he spoke with ignorance that exceeded his confidence.

"I have a spy still at Fulda," Willehad said. "He will warn us if the Franks make a move."

"And who is this... spy?" Udela did not like the bishop's deviousness.

One of my priests," Willehad said. "He is there to keep watch."

"You have a spy at Fulda in anticipation of our attack?" Lothar asked. "Why didn't you tell the queen of this sooner?"

"Such things are best kept secret, Count Lothar. I can say that you are wrong. Melchior does not think like other Franks. Why, I am not so certain he is a Frank."

"Are you saying he is an outlander?" Lothar asked.

Melchior? Udela's turned toward the fat cleric. This comment was more interesting than the revelation of a spy. She had always wondered about such things.

"Perhaps. Perhaps something else." Willehad's pig-like eyes glared at Udela. "Best we burn him at the stake when he falls into our hands. After all, we can only stand one sorcerer at a time."

Udela's skin tingled with alarm. *This priest is a danger. More so than the others.*

She smiled a false smile. "You have your angels and saints… we have our sorcerers, Willehad. Is there any difference?"

Willehad did not answer.

"Who is this Melchior? Why do you fear him?" Udela asked.

"He is nothing. A simple messenger from the simple Karolus," Willehad said.

Lothar pulled at his beard. "Why do you speak thus of Melchior, Eminence? He has long been *Missus Dominicus*. I have known his family for years."

"Have you known this man? Are you sure? Truly sure?" Willehad asked.

"What exactly do you suggest, eminence?" Lothar stroked Udela's arm.

Udela's lips tightened. *I'll allow this now, Frank. I must learn what this all means.*

"That he is not of us at all. Perhaps he is a heretic… or a sorcerer," Willehad said.

Udela was startled at the comment, and a shiver went through her. The idea that there could be a Frank sorcerer never occurred to her.

"Our queen has powers… we have seen that. But she is our queen."

Udela thought she caught a subtle hint of sarcasm in Lothar. She realized that these Franks were using her just as she was using them. Suddenly, her way forward seemed more precarious, but surer.

***

The fire in Lothar's chambers sizzled and spat embers. On the nearby oak table, a half-gnawed joint of ox meat and a loaf of bread sat unfinished. The flagon of wine stood half empty.

"Secure the door until I say otherwise, Detleff," Melchior commanded. "

"As you wish, Lord." Detleff nodded and ran the bolt across the latch. He then stood patiently at attention.

Melchior broke the seal and slowly slid the heavy vellum parchment from the hard leather pouch. He glanced at the page. It was a *diploma*, a very formal document framed with religious symbols in Latin and written in highly stylized black ink calligraphy. The seal of Karolus at the bottom ensured its authenticity. He stared at it a moment.

"Perhaps I should read it. It was intended for me," Baugulf said.

"Not just for you, Abbot," Melchior said. "There is a message in it for me as well."

"*Epistola de litteris colendis*," Melchior read aloud.

"A letter... that concerns... the cultivation... of letters?" Baugulf rubbed his beard pensively.

Melchior's eyes scanned the elegant script. "Of knowledge... Karolus writes of the importance of knowledge and conduct, stating that because knowledge precedes conduct, people must learn the norms, both ecclesial and secular. He wishes the people the knowledge necessary in this world and the next, as they are to be one. Errors should be shunned by men and avoided at all cost, so that these chosen people can become the servants of truth."

The abbot's eyes widened, and he tilted his head. "So true. We hoped this monastery would be a beacon for such truth. I suspect Alcuin influenced this."

"I think he was also warning you of the heresy around you, Abbot."

"And warning you to seek knowledge before you take action," Baugulf replied.

"I suppose that was the real purpose of my journey. To bring knowledge to the knowledge-seekers."

"And to destroy the Saxons and their evil queen?"

"To convert them, Abbot. Karolus knows we cannot fight them forever. As true Christians, we must all unite. Karolus seeks a united Christendom. You shall provide the wisdom and knowledge that Christendom needs to be a wise and righteous realm worthy of the next."

"And you, *Missus*?"

"As it is written. Knowledge begets action." Melchior handed the bull to Baugulf and poured himself wine from the flagon. He drank a deep draught and tore a piece of the bread.

Baugulf looked up. "What next, Lord Melchior?"

"We have much to do. A better question is, where to start?"

"Start with your basic task," Baugulf said. "I will start by weeding out the false priests and monks. Those who truly wish to follow the cloth will be educated correctly. The others offered work rebuilding the place. God knows the monastery needs it. Fulda needs it."

"My basic mission..." Melchior again read the code contained in the *Epistola*. His mind flashed to scenes the abbot could not know... of times and places he could not imagine... he remembered the great battles... he remembered gunshots and a train... his mission... He placed his head in his hands as if in prayer.

"Are you all right, *Missus*?"

"Yes." But he was not all right. A million more memories rushed through his mind. Memories spanning time and space. Memories of people living and dead... his parents... Kristel... von und zu Zelinsky, Weber, Captain Doolan... Doctor MacKay... Brooke... Patricia... *Where will this end? How will this end?* "Perhaps just too much wine, Abbot."

"Maybe. But I have seen Franks drink more and suffer less. It is not the wine."

Melchior shook his head slowly and placed it in his hands. "No. It is not the wine." A knock on the door snapped Melchior from his dark thoughts.

Detleff removed the bolt, and Audeon walked in, wearing full *brunia*. "Count Stilicho says the men are ready, *Dominus*."

"Detleff, fetch my *brunia* and arms." Melchior rose to his feet.

"Is it wise to leave Fulda completely unprotected, *Dominus*?" Audeon asked.

Melchior looked at Baugulf. "How many monks do you have?"

"Perhaps fifty. Why?"

"Secure the arms of Lothar's dead. Equip the monks and place them on the battlements while we're gone."

"Men of God are not permitted to fight," Baugulf said.

Melchior's thoughts turned to the Teutonic Order — religious knights a few centuries removed. "Not true, Abbot. They just can't kill. But they can make a show for the Saxons or Avars."

"I don't know the first thing about such matters."

"No. But Stilicho does. He is, by my order, the new Count of Fulda. I'll leave him here with a handful of *milites* to back him. If you put up a good enough show, no one will attack."

"And if they do?"

"Stilicho will drill your monks in the rudiments. Remember, knowledge begets action."

Baugulf stared at the bull in his hands. He gently rubbed the seal and regarded the religious symbols around it. "*Deus vult.*"

Melchior thought of his journey across time and space. Perhaps what they do here and now can lessen the harm he knew would come. "I certainly hope God wills it. With his blessing, we'll use Fulda as the anvil while the *milites* forge the hammer that will once more crush the enemies of the Franks... and of Christendom."

***

Some forty mounted soldiers and twice as many foot soldiers marched in the dark under a misty rain. No one noticed. The few inhabitants remaining in Fulda huddled around fires to keep out the night chill and to pray for the town's deliverance.

Stilicho stared down at the column, winding serpent-like along the road that hugged the Fulda River. "I should be with them, abbot. I long to sink my broadsword into a Saxon's belly."

"My monks should be preparing for compline, not battle. But God wills it otherwise," Baugulf said.

Stilicho shrugged. "I shall check the sentinels. If a Frank fails to remain alert, we usually flog them. I'll be more forgiving to your monks and merely box their ears a time or two."

"You are most kind, Count Stilicho. I will return to the chapel and pray."

"We all must pray," Stilicho said. "I will instruct your monks to pray as they stand watch."

"You are a pious and good Christian warrior, Count Stilicho. Not like your predecessor."

"Are you afraid, Abbot?" Stilicho asked.

"No. Willehad tried to poison me and failed. I believe God has other plans for me and for the abbey." He pointed towards the dark outline of the town below. "It's them I fear for. Those loyal souls who did not flee are at the mercy of Saxon or Avar."

Stilicho nodded. "Pray for them. And pray the *missus* finds the Saxons first."

***

A figure cloaked in black lurked in the woods across the bridge. When the column of *milites* snaked its way east, he counted the torches along the parapet. Left behind by Willehad to spy on the Franks, Mannix had observed the comings and goings at the fort from the village. None of the villagers questioned him as he wore the habit of a priest. *They have a sparse garrison. I must report to Willehad.*

Mannix led the mare out of the woods. Anyone who saw him would take him for one of the column's stragglers. Mannix knew a shortcut through the mountains that led to where the Saxons were assembling. If he could get there in time, a trap could be set for the Franks. He had escaped the fighting. Instinct told him to flee to the east. But Mannix had sworn an oath to Willehad's cause and to Vulmar. He had had enough of Christian piety. The time to destroy it forever was still within their grasp.

Suddenly, his mare convulsed. Snorting in pain, it sank to its knees, sending Mannix tumbling into the wet grass. Powerful arms roughly yanked his woolen cloak. A stout pole slammed into his stomach, driving the air from his lungs. As he struggled to breathe, another pair of arms trussed him to the pole like a hunter's game.

"What is this? No!" Mannix kicked and struggled.

"Silence him, lad," Spad grunted as he twisted the leather strands around Mannix, binding him tighter to the pole.

"He is a priest, Uncle," Walla replied.

"You saw what evil he brought to our village, boy. He's no priest, but the pagan spawn of the devil."

Spad drew his dagger from his belt and raised it over Mannix's head.

Mannix's eyes widened. "You can't kill me!"

"And why not? I've killed better men than you, pagan priest," Spad said.

"Because I know things Melchior will want to know." Mannix looked into the big hunter's eyes for a sign of belief. He saw it.

"Tell me," Spad said.

"Can we trust such a man?" Walla asked.

"No. But let him talk."

"I know where the Saxon camp is." Mannix knew they had left their camp. He would give these buffoons just enough to stay alive.

"That's not enough, pagan priest. Tell me something useful."

"The Avars…"

A spear flew past Spad, its shaft gliding over his shoulder. Mannix's eyes widened in desperation as the spearhead pierced his breastbone, pinning him to the shaft like a cloth doll. His mouth exploded in a spray of blood.

-250-

***

Before Spad or Walla could react, the killer escaped into the thick woods on horseback.

They drew their daggers and crouched, blending seamlessly into the foliage, spears at the ready. Spad signaled to Walla with his eyes. The boy dropped to his belly and moved quickly as a fox under the low boughs, making his way up a rise. He returned to Spad.

"Any sign?" Spad signaled.

He shook his head.

"To move on us without our knowledge in woods such as these takes a special kind of being."

Walla gave a puzzled look. "Avar?"

"No. Not Avar."

"Saxon?"

"Perhaps. But whoever did this can do it once more. Next time, it could be one of us. Or worse."

"Worse?"

"It may be the abbot he wants. Or the *Missus*."

"Who could do this, uncle?"

Spad's eyes narrowed as he scanned into the depths of the wood. He dared not say the name he thought.

"You know!"

Spad slowly nodded. "It must be the real devil's spawn himself: Vulmar!"

"Vulmar!"

Spad made the sign of the cross, as did his nephew.

"The assassin sent by the devil. He murdered half the priests in the valley," Spad said. "It seems he has traveled back east."

"That is bad."

"At least he has not spread death any further into Frankland. His presence means the *missus* has drawn him back."

"He's hunting the *Missus*?"

Spad shrugged. He was not sure what to tell the boy. A mere lad, yet he had witnessed so much evil and mayhem. *Thank God he's solid in his faith.* Spad knew that only their faith protected them from the evil that walked Frankland.

"We should warn him," Walla said enthusiastically.

Spad shook his head. "No, boy. We'll stay in these woods near Fulda. Melchior is first among the *milites*. He can handle things." Spad glanced at the town and the abbey. "The abbot is still at Fulda. He is Karolus's spiritual leader in the Marchland. We'll stay close to him."

"What do we do?"

Spad glanced at Mannix's body. "Bury the vermin. Then move to better ground."

S.W. O'Connell

Chapter 20

The Avar Camp

Dgno grunted and thrashed like an animal. The young woman beneath him showed no sign of pleasure, but she yielded to his every move and demand. Everyone knew what happened to girls who denied the khagan of the Avar tribe. In his mind, she was a substitute for the object of his real desire, merely practice for what Dgno planned for his future queen and slave. He regarded her for the fifth time. The fear and pain in her wide eyes only stirred him more.

"Please Lord, no more. Let me rest. I can make you happier that way." She tried to caress him, hoping to calm him.

He pushed her back and drew closer. "Well, I'm not so tired."

She stiffened in fear. "No, Lord, no…"

Her whimpering brought an evil grin to Dgno's reptilian face. "Good. I like to break steppe ponies. You will be one I…"

The tent flap suddenly flew open and a large and hideous-looking Avar stepped in. "Lord, the ponies are ready."

"Good, Otmak. We can ride… now…."

The girl squealed in pain and shame. Dgno shoved her head forward smashing against the leather hides that served as his bed.

"Please, Lord, no," she moaned again, painfully.

"You should cry for joy that a khagan would take you to bed," Dgno muttered.

"That was… joy… Lord," she whimpered and began to sob.

Dgno yanked her thick dark hair and roughly pinched her chin. "There now, little pony. Dry those tears. He handed her a dirty rag and she wiped them. Dgno regarded her fleshy figure with regret. "Were you the queen I desire, this would be all the better. But you pleased your khagan."

A forced smile crossed her lips. "That… pleases me as well, Lord."

Dgno grunted. "Good. A pretty Christian should die happy." He plunged a long, curved dagger into her belly and twisted upwards. She stiffened and went limp. Dgno pushed her body onto the dirt floor.

"Do we leave, now, Lord?" Otmak seemed almost oblivious to what his master had just done.

Dgno stood, drew up his leather breeches, and slipped on his riding boots. "We leave everything behind but our ponies and weapons. What we need, we shall take from the Saxons and the Franks: food, gold, weapons, horses…women."

"Your spy is here with news," Otmak said.

Dgno flashed his dark-stained teeth. "Why didn't you say so? Bring him in."

Vulmar entered the tent. He glanced slyly at the lifeless form sprawled before him but remained fixed on Dgno.

"So what do you have?" Dgno asked.

"Good news. Queen Udela and her Saxons are marching on Fulda."

"That's good news? They break their pledge to me?" Dgno asked.

Vulmar's eyes narrowed. "Isn't that what you wanted?"

Dgno's eyes narrowed, and his mouth twisted mischievously. It was exactly what he wanted. He never intended to keep his bargain with the Saxons. He was using them for his own wicked purposes. They would bleed the Franks, so he could sweep in and take everything. The surviving Saxons would then be forced to become his vassals. He would take their queen as his bride and rule them not as equals but as a true khagan should rule.

"Who guards Fulda?" Dgno asked.

"A handful of monks. You should strike it quickly. My spy Mannix was captured by a pair of Frank peasants. They questioned him."

"How do you know?"

"Because I stopped it. But I can't be sure what he disclosed before my spear ended his miserable life."

Dgno grunted. "Fulda will yield when the time comes. And not to the Saxons... to me. Where are the rest of the Franks?"

"They rode out to meet the Saxons. Will you join them? The Saxons?"

"In good time. I want Saxon and Frank to spill each other's blood. Then we'll sweep in. Udela will beg me to marry her because she'll not have enough warriors for her plot."

Vulmar nodded. "And what of me?"

"You get to rut with the Frankish girls of your choice and rule the place they call Neustrasia."

Vulmar smiled. "What of Lothar? He's still with Udela. As is the fat bishop. "

"You'll join them in the great battle. When no one is looking, kill them both."

Vulmar grew nervous. "You see me. I'm no warrior."

Dgno grabbed the Vulmar by the neck and lifted him off his feet. Vulmar was taller and bigger than Dgno, but the Avar was mostly muscle and sinew and more powerful than most men. "I don't need you to be a warrior, Vulmar. I need you to be an assassin."

Dgno stepped through the tent flap and looked east. Sunlight caressed the horizon, its rays caressing the gathering clouds. The plain before him was bursting with men, fierce men mounted on equally fierce steppe ponies. The Avars had their own breed – mixed with the larger European stock, they were larger than their ancestors and carried more weight, yet were equally hardy. He sniffed the morning air and caught the aroma of smoke mixed with horse dung. *A good omen.*

Dgno mounted his pony and raised his whip over his head. "Our gods give us a morning sun to put at our backs. Who rides with me?"

A thousand voices rang out in reply, "We ride!"

Dgno twirled the lash over his head. "And who are we?"

"Avaaaars!" Their reply became a roar that reached a thunderous pitch.

Dgno cracked the whip, and his pony bolted across the wet, grassy plain. His warriors followed as one. Though it looked like a horde to the casual eye, with one flick of his whip, Dgno could order his warriors into tactical formations or send subgroups to attack villages, towns, or whatever the khagan marked for destruction.

Ears back, the ponies rumbled across the plain for an hour. Then Dgno rose in his stirrups and slashed his whip in a dance of signals. His sure-eyed captains each responded with their own. As one, the Avar host split into ten units, each heading eastward in a different direction. But in just a few hours, they would all arrive at the same place, ready to plunge into the one thing they loved more than their mounts - war.

***

Thundering hooves pounded the muddy strip that served as a road in the far-flung marches of Karolus's realm. Melchior's *milites* rode through a draw that led to the mountain passes. Most passes from the east to Fulda were narrow and winding, but Melchior selected one that was wide and ran straight. The one he knew the Saxons would use as they advanced on a city ripe for the taking.

The midday sun is a good omen, *Dominus*," Audeon said.

"I don't believe in omens, only the work of God." Melchior felt uneasy saying it, but he had to admit it was the truth. How else could he traverse time and space without the help, no, the act, of God? Raised Catholic but always a casual believer, Melchior had changed. Transformed by what he did not know – into a devout... That too he did not know, or would not admit.

"*Dominus*, I have a question," Audeon said.

"Does it involve the girl?"

"Yes, *Dominus*."

Melchior shifted his weight in the saddle and glanced back at the column of men bouncing behind them. "I'm listening, Audeon."

"I think I am in love with Genofeva, *Missus*."

Melchior thought he heard the gulp in the young man's throat, a sign he meant it.

"Your father will be a judge of who you love, Audeon. Some loves are never meant to be." The thought of Kristel flashed across his mind, and for a fleeting moment, electrified his senses.

"And how will he judge me, *Dominus*?"

"That depends on how successful we are." Melchior looked over at Audeon and smiled. "We must defeat these Saxons. I believe the girl you love is among them. But it may be a love forbidden to men."

Audeon nodded, lowered his head, and spurred his horse forward.

He loves like a Frank, Melchior thought.

They rode on. Less than an hour later, Melchior raised his hand.

The column stopped. Warriors dismounted. Each checked the fittings on their tack, belts, and bridles, and for those who had them, stirrups. Horses nibbled oats from open palms. Others took gulps of water from cupped hands.

"Where is Jurchen?" Melchior asked.

"Right behind us, *Dominus*," Detleff said.

"Pass me my lance and shield, Detleff. Then fetch him."

Minutes later, Jurchen trotted up. Instead of priestly garb, he wore the *brunia* of a Frank warrior. Father Thomas arrived with him.

"I am glad to see you brought Father Thomas. I want a prayer."

Jurchen looked puzzled. "A prayer, *Dominus*? What sort of prayer?"

"Why, a prayer for victory. Constantine had his sign, the cross. I have no such sign."

"But you do, *Dominus*," Detleff said. "Your talisman."

Melchior stiffened. *The Ronson!* He reached under his *brunia* and drew out the leather pouch containing the polished metal. His mind flashed with images and sounds of a rubble-strewn city smothered in smoke and scorched by flames. The blasts of explosions pounded his head. He trembled in the saddle. *Remain calm. Be not afraid.*

"Are you all right, *Dominus*?" Detleff asked.

"He looks ill," Father Thomas said.

"Let me help you, *Dominus*," Jurchen offered.

"I am fine." Melchior was. The voice had put him at ease.

"Take this as your Christian talisman, *Dominus*." Jurchen handed him a simple crucifix on a plain-metal chain. "I won't need it any longer."

Melchior placed the chain around his neck and tucked the crucifix under his *brunia*. The feel of the cross against his flesh gave him a sense of comfort.

"Lead us in prayer," Melchior commanded.

Father Thomas began to make the sign of the cross.

"No! Instead, Abbot Jurchen should lead us."

"But I am no longer playing at priest," Jurchen implored.

"I don't care. I want you to lead us. Is that all right with you, Father Thomas?"

"Of course, *Dominus*."

The column of warriors dropped to their knees in a jangle of chain mail, armor, and scabbards. As one, they made the sign of the cross. Jurchen began, *"Pater noster, qui es in caelis: sanctificetur Nomen Tuum; adveniat Regnum Tuum; fiat voluntas Tua, sicut in caelo, et in terra…"*

As they prayed, Melchior raised his head and looked down the line. He was moved by the sight. More than 100 hardened warriors in full battle dress, praying reverently like children, heads bowed in adoration of a God they had never seen but served and adored. And they did so with a devotion to a God the Nazis and the Bolsheviks once fought but could never understand. He recalled a time when he could not understand God either. But now he was beginning.

Their chant went on, *"…Panem nostrum cotidianum da nobis hodie; et dimitte nobis debita nostra, sicut et nos dimittimus debitoribus nostris; et ne nos inducas in tentationem; sed libera nos a Malo. Amen."*

The *Amen* erupted with the fervor of a war cry. The line of warriors rose as one. He nodded at Audeon, who signaled mount. As the horse's hooves beat the damp earth and the bridles jangled once more, Melchior reflected. *What was he? The spurned fiancée of a beautiful woman? The defeated and broken Wehrmacht officer? The agent of a desperate experiment in science and spirituality? Was he Matthaeus Melchior any longer? Had he ever been?*

Everything is the sum of the past... Be not afraid...

***

The column of armed men strode quickly and with purpose. The Saxon warriors were now arrayed by clans and sub-tribal units. The Euduces, led by Tilo, marched at the front, followed by the Nabo under Eberger, then by the lesser tribal units. Nothing distracted a Saxon from the one thing he liked more than hunting, pillaging, or the rituals of their pagan worship – killing Franks.

Lothar rode with Udela at his side. A ring of Haari on foot, led by Hrodger, raced beside her. They moved in silence. The Haari's dark clothing and hunched backs gave them the appearance of wolves, Lothar thought. *My wolves.*

He had come to an understanding with Hrodger. When he fled Fulda for the Saxon camp, Lothar quickly learned that the Haari were feared by many and hated by all. He realized their allegiance to Udela was opportunistic. The Saxons feared her powers, and the Haari leader, Hrodger, was bent on wresting them from her. Lothar knew he had gotten himself into a dire situation that offered an opportunity if he made the right move.

"Where is the fat priest?" Udela asked.

"The bishop? Willehad stayed back with the women and children," Lothar said.

"Is it safe to let such a man out of our sight? To trust him?"

Lothar realized her question was aimed at Hrodger, not him.

"He has the girl Anfelisia with him. He can't do much harm with her in tow."

"I don't trust him," Udela said.

"What do you want me to do, My Queen?" Hrodger asked.

"Send some men to keep watch on him," Udela said.

"Better yet, I will send Mallobaudes," Lothar said. Mallobaudes had the girl Genofeva in his possession. Lothar did not like her being so far forward. She was worth too much to bargain with Karolus if they failed.

"I have left my most powerful warrior back at the camp. He will watch the fat priest," Hrodger said.

"What warrior?" Udela asked.

"A powerful Dane recently accepted into the ranks of the Haari."

"A Dane? And what's his name?" Lothar was suddenly suspicious.

Hrodger grinned. "Why, did I not tell you? He's called Fromm."

Lothar blanched. "By Christ! He's a follower of Melchior!"

"No longer," Hrodger said.

"Who is this Norseman?" Udela asked.

"A bold warrior, on his way to Miklagard. Joined Melchior to make passage through Frankland. Deserted Melchior and is now Haari," Hrodger said.

"How is a Norseman among the Haari? Why doesn't he continue to Miklagard?" Udela asked.

Hrodger smiled. "I convinced him killing Franks is a more worthy endeavor."

"You should have told this to the queen... to me." Lothar held his temper. He still needed the help of the Saxon. "Very well."

Udela said nothing. He saw her looking at a Saxon youth running toward them. A pair of powerful Haari spears barred his way.

"Let him through," she commanded.

The Haari opened their ranks, and a young warrior of maybe fifteen armed only with a short *Seaxe* halted in front of Udela, panting."

"What news do you bring?" Udela asked.

"The van has arrived at the pass, My Queen."

Lothar realized his time had come. "My Queen, place me in command now, and I will lead your warriors to victory."

"No. I must wait for Dgno. He's a reptile. But we need his warriors."

"My Queen, I have learned striking swiftly is more important than striking with great numbers."

"I have learned great numbers defeat small numbers," she replied.

Another figure galloped up on horseback, swaddled in a hooded cloak that hid his face. The ring of Haari opened for him. They halted before the queen, and the figure dropped his hood.

"Vulmar! You arrive at just the right time," Udela's eyes strained toward the horizon. "But where is Dgno?"

"He'll be here soon. With his full army."

"How soon?"

"He said you must strike the Franks as soon as possible. He is timing his approach to strike their flank just as you engage. But you must be quick."

Lothar grew suspicious. He knew Vulmar, one of Willehad's false priests and a killer. But then, the thought of crushing Melchior and exacting revenge overcame his caution. "As I said, I will gladly lead the attack."

"Very well, Count Lothar. Follow this boy to the vanguard, where the Euduces and Nabo lead. But take Bruno and the Issepi forward with you." Udela said. "Your Mallobaudes can accompany you."

Lothar glanced back. He could see the Issepi warriors a half league behind them. He wanted to send Mallobaudes back, but events were moving too swiftly. "Very well, My Queen," he said.

Lothar formed the Issepi and Nabo into two attack columns. Behind them, he arranged the rest of the warriors. Tilo and his Euduces slithered forward in small packs to screen the advance. Lothar regarded the Saxons as brutes, not much better than the horse he rode. But he could see their killer instincts were finely honed. More importantly, they were eager for battle. *Yes, you filthy dogs. Yap and yelp for Frankish blood.*

Lothar drew his broadsword and raised it into the air. "Let no man sleep with his wife or another man's wife without drenching his blade in Frank blood... Christian blood!"

Some 2,000 voices rumbled in a slow, steady crescendo that quickly grew into a ferocious roar, "Odin! Odin! Odin!"

A shiver went through Lothar. He still retained just enough of his Christianity to fear the pagan war-cries. He shook his shield and replied in a voice he scarcely recognized as his own, "Odin! Odin! Odin!"

Then he turned to Bruno and Eberger. "Are your men ready to fight to the death?"

"They welcome Valhalla, Frank," Eberger said with a look of derision.

"Not so with your Christians – who fear death," Bruno said.

Lothar grunted. He was not so sure. "Tilo's wolves will gather logs to ram the gates. I expect the Frank archers will kill most of them. No matter, though. If your men do their work properly."

"I have five hundred of the best Nabo whom I will lead forward," Eberger said.

"That will give Tilo a chance to run his rams at the gates. Bruno, I want your Issepi ready to move with me."

"With you?" Bruno grew agitated.

"There is a tunnel that runs under the walls. I will lead you to it. While the Franks are engaged with Tilo and Eberger, the Issepi will slip in and claim the city."

"Very well," Bruno said.

"What of me?" Mallobaudes rode at the head of the handful of Frankish warriors who escaped Fulda with them. Genofeva sat astride a pony, hands bound to the saddle.

Lothar regarded the girl. He found her beautiful. The thought of her falling into the hands of the Avars or being taken by a renegade Saxon disturbed him. *She is valuable.* "Stay just behind the main body of Saxons. We'll use the girl only if we must. But I don't think we'll need her to bargain, at least yet."

"So long as Melchior is killed," Mallobaudes said.

Lothar knew Mallobaudes's hatred of his cousin was fierce – even greater than his own hatred of the *missus*. He glanced at the leaden sky. "Darkness comes soon. We must move. Once the Saxon fury was unleashed on Fulda, there would be no controlling it."

A young Saxon warrior, grasping for breath, grabbed Lothar's stirrup.

Lothar pulled on his reins, backing his horse and forcing the youth to let go.

"What news have you?" Bruno asked. "Be quick, boy."

The young Saxon stood erect. "Tilo's scouts are in sight of Fulda. They have felled a dozen trees and are even now binding them. He plans to take the main gate at once."

Lothar's face flushed red with fury. "No! He was to wait!"

The youth smiled matter-of-factly. "He said to tell you the Euduces always lead and are always first to battle. Bring the rest up at your leisure."

"No one countermands my orders!" Lothar drew his broadsword, swung it in an arc, turned his horse, and brought the heavy blade across the youth's neck, sending his head toppling into the soft earth.

"Send the columns forward then. Right behind the Euduces," Lothar ordered.

A cry went up the line. Saxon *Seaxes* and spears began a steady beating against their shields.

Lothar pushed through the low brush until the wide plain and the bending river came into view. He could see the outline of the town he had lost to the *missus*. He saw figures moving in the distance — the Euduces approaching the main gate. Along the parapets, he saw the outlines of armed men. Something did not look right.

Lothar grabbed Bruno's arm. "What do you see?"

Bruno shook it loose. "I see Tilo's dogs leading where I should be leading. I see the other columns moving across the river."

"Then what *don't* you see?" Lothar asked.

"The Franks have no archers. They are not throwing spears or rocks on the Euduces."

"The castle is not fully garrisoned," Lothar said.

"What does that mean?" Mallobaudes asked.

Lothar turned in his saddle. "A trap by the *missus*. Bruno – we must take the castle quickly. Form up the main body, and I will lead them myself. A curse on the Avars. If they were here as planned, they would cover our flanks."

"We shall destroy them," Bruno said flatly.

Lothar was impressed with the swagger of the Saxons. He now knew why Karolus had such difficulty subduing the savage tribesmen.

Lothar turned to Mallobaudes. "Ride with the girl to Udela. She must be taken to a safe place. We might yet need to barter Karolus's flesh to preserve our own."

Before Mallobaudes could reply, the count galloped forward with four of his staunch Frankish retainers in tow.

***

The last drop of ale slid down Fromm's gullet. His hairy arm wiped the foam from his lips. He belched and pushed the young girl off his knee. "I've had enough of this ale and your charms, Radka. It's time I checked on the puppies."

Fromm enjoyed frolicking with the queen's handmaid. Yet he was unhappy to be left behind with the women and children. He needed to be closer to the action so he could steer Lothar and the Saxons into the trap Melchior had set. But the Haari chief was wise to leave him behind. Rather than protest too much, he decided to take advantage of the situation while he figured out another way to help Melchior.

The Saxon baggage was light. Most of their possessions went up in the great holocaust ordered by the queen. Small wagons were pulled by old men and boys, donkeys, and the occasional pair of oxen. It stretched for a furlong along the muddy rut they used as a road. He found a group of boys armed with primitive spears. He looked at their pale, smooth faces. *Saxons guard their wealth with twelve-year-old boys.* He counted over 100.

"Who's the leader?" Fromm bellowed.

An old Saxon warrior approached. His hair was white and tied behind his head. His face was crinkled brown from years of sun and wind. But his eyes were clear, and he did not stoop. *A proud old warrior.*

The old man stood before Fromm, a hand resting on the hilt of a long Seaxe. It looked as if it had seen decades of use.

"Are you the one they call Fromm?" the old man asked.

"I am. And you?"

"My name is Bomani. We were told to await your orders."

"Told? By whom?"

"The chief of the Haari."

Fromm grunted. "I would form those carts into a circle for better defense. Strung out along this rut you call a road makes you all a target."

"But we are to follow the attacking columns. It's the Saxon way."

Fromm rubbed his beard. "You were told to await my orders. My orders are to form a circle. There might be Avars about. You wouldn't want your fat young girls… or your tender boys to fall prey to those demons?"

"The Avars have made a pact with the queen."

Fromm laughed. "Avars are devils. Their word means nothing. Do as I say, or you'll have more to worry over than Avars."

The old man's eyes narrowed to slits. His lips tightened. But he shouted out some words in Saxon, and the boys began scurrying to the wagons. Soon, the women and girls joined them, and they began dragging carts and baggage over the muddy ruts. Fromm watched in amusement, but then his eyes narrowed. He saw something that both disturbed and delighted him. *The fat priest and Anfelisia!*

But Willehad saw Fromm first. He shoved Anfelisia onto a small horse and mounted his own. A pair of robed men rode with him. Fromm mounted his horse. He sought out the old man. "I have business elsewhere. Make sure there's no gap between your carts. Avar ponies are small."

"The Avars are our allies," the old man replied once more with a shrug. He suddenly seemed feeble.

Fromm grimaced. "Where I come from, men with white hair and beards are considered wise. I know now that among Saxons they're just old. Trust no one until I return."

Fromm urged his horse toward Willehad. The bishop had ridden east. Fromm did not like that. There was but one thing to the east — Avars. He soon spotted the party bouncing along on their mounts. Fromm closed on them, but slowly. His size and girth strained his horse's muscles and lungs with every step of its hooves. But Willehad's fat body did the same. A half-hour later, he closed to within earshot.

Willehad said something to his robed retainers. They turned towards Fromm while Willehad led the girl into a heavily wooded area.

Fromm smiled. *They are fools for not attacking me in the woods.*

But the robed men threw back their hoods, revealing iron helmets with nose guards. They slipped from their mounts while pulling short bows from under their robes.

Before Fromm knew what happened, a pair of arrows snapped past his body, so close he saw the flechettes. *Archers — not monks!* He turned his horse to approach them from a different angle. But the archers drew a second arrow, firing it before he could turn again. One arrow pierced the horse's neck, sending it tumbling to the wet grass. Fromm fell far from the horse, avoiding its hooves. The animal squealed in pain and thrashed its legs in agony. He scrambled to the dying animal and retrieved his battle-ax from the saddle. Two more arrows whisked past his ear. *Can I outrun arrows?*

Crazed with anger, Fromm lowered his head and charged the two archers, now just twenty paces away. "Odin!" He was almost on them.

Steely eyes let loose another round of arrows. One struck his shoulder with a sickening squish and crack. He ignored the pain and barreled forward, his ax poised to strike. The archers dropped their bows, reached for their belts, and drew weapons, one a long *Seaxe*, the other a *Francisca*.

Fromm grimaced. *They should have launched more arrows.* He brought the ax head down on the archer with the *Seaxe*, crushing his helmet like an egg and smashing his skull into red and gray pulp. Fromm struggled to free his ax from the body.

The second archer brought his *Francisca* down to strike Fromm's neck. But the Norseman pivoted and caught the blade with his own. The two heads struck with a sharp clang, sending hot sparks from the metal. Both men took deep breaths and stared intently.

"Prepare to meet your God." Fromm's eyes were blurred from sweat and blood. The archer looked like a shadow.

Suddenly, the archer drew a dagger from his belt and plunged it into Fromm's side. Fromm felt the familiar burn of iron slicing into his ribs. He smiled and grabbed the archer's wrist. "Now you are unarmed!"

With two quick moves, he yanked the blade from his side, bent the archer's wrist around, and twisted the man's dagger into his belly. A whooshing sound ensued as the man's entrails spilled onto the grass. Fromm pushed him off, and he fell in a heap into his own offal.

Fromm staggered back. The arrow wound had stopped bleeding, but his ribs still oozed blood. He felt weak, a feeling he had had many times before. He knew he needed water and rest to recover. Yet the thought of Anfelisia drove off any hope of rest. He staggered to the two horses and found a skin. He pulled out the stopper and took a deep drink. It was wine. He took two more and put the stopper back.

Fromm picked up his ax and mounted the stronger-looking horse. It skittered under his weight but then regained its footing. "I'll be gentle. Now, let's go for a ride."

Fromm plunged into the dark woods, muttering to himself as the horse pushed through the thick pines. "Odin, give me strength. Thor, give me courage. Loki, bring me luck."

Chapter 21

Fulda

Hordes of Saxons swarmed the fields and woods. Stilicho stood impassive as they felled trees and bound the trunks together to fashion primitive rams. The walls and gates were strong, but he knew they could not hold the Saxons for long. He paced the ramparts to bolster the courage of the monks disguised as warriors. A humming sound pierced his ears. *They are praying in unison! We'll need all the prayers Our Lord will receive. For if Melchior does not strike soon, we are surely doomed.*

A roar of excitement erupted from the Saxons.

Stilicho looked down at the gathering enemy. *Soon they will attack.* He stopped, and dropping to his knees, said a *Pater Noster* himself.

Baugulf placed a hand on his shoulder and smiled weakly. "So, we make monks into warriors and warriors into monks."

Stilicho made the sign of the cross and rose to his feet. "I was praying that Melchior be quick about his work, Abbot."

Baugulf shrugged. "It's in God's hands now. Lord Melchior is under his guidance. If he can strike a blow to the Saxons, so be it."

"They're coming!" a sentinel announced in a voice shrill with fear.

"We have time. They'll likely sack the town first," Stilicho said.

Baugulf gasped. "The people… we should get them inside these walls."

"Too late now, abbot. Most have fled anyway."

"And those who couldn't?"

Stilicho's jaw stiffened, but he did not reply. He knew what would become of them.

"We must pray they make their way safely west," the abbot said.

Stilicho would not tell him that those who escaped the Saxons would fall prey to the Avars. The humming grew louder.

"Who among your monks can fight as well as pray?" For the first time, Stilicho was worried. Not for his safety; he had faced death countless times while serving Karolus. But he did not want to let down Melchior or his king-and-emperor. Nor did he want to die in defeat.

Baugulf smiled. "No matter whether they can fight, so long as they can pray. For of the two, prayer is the more potent weapon. This abbey is to be the seat of all Christian learning in the realm, that is, in Christendom. God will not let it fall to pagans or heretics. Have faith in that, Count Stilicho."

"Saxons approaching the gates!" a sentinel screamed.

Stilicho shouted to the monks on the walls above the gate. "When they reach the gate, drop the baskets. If God wills it, the stones will drive off the pagans."

He looked at the abbot. "It's no sin to cast stones over a wall, is it, abbot?"

Baugulf slowly shook his head. "So long as they don't single out any of them for death."

"My *milites* are standing ready at a barricade behind the gate. Should the gate fail us, they'll resist as long as they can."

"My monks will die as well. If God wills it."

Saxon war cries now drowned out the sounds of prayer. Tilo's warriors scampered over the bridge and charged the gate. Stilicho cursed himself. If he only had archers.

"Thor!" they bellowed, invoking the god of thunder.

"Thor!" The ram plunged into the wooden gate, and an ear-splitting crash resounded.

"Thor!" Another boom erupted as the ram slammed the heavy oak again. Like a bellows pumping, the Saxons' cries grew more intense with each blow.

"Thor!" Boom. The ram slammed the gate once more.

Stilicho watched as the next Saxon party advanced with its ram. *The next blow will be the last. The next boom will signal our end.*

"Thor! Thor!" Muscular arms, glistening with sweat, strained as the Saxons drove the heavy ram for a final blow.

"Drop them now!" Stilicho ordered.

But the expected boom did not come. Instead, the air filled with the rattle and crashing of dozens of stones. They scattered across the bridge, a mix of cracking and thumping as they struck the Saxons like a deluge. Disrupted by the stones, the Saxons fled the bridge. Stilicho counted a dozen dead, plus two left for dead, before the gate. He had no way of knowing that among the stricken was Tilo, chief of the Euduces.

Nervous monks and determined *milites* watched as the pack of Saxons gathered once more in a swarm. Stilicho felt something was different.

Soon, vengeful cries from Saxon voices signaled a renewed attack. Angry men, grunting and cursing, shouldered four long oaken trunks lashed together with leather ropes. Bearing an even larger ram, made from four stout oak trunks, they shuffled quickly toward the bridge. This time, they had a mounted warrior in the lead.

"Lothar! The spawn of a snake. My arm for a score of archers," Stilicho murmured. "I would have them place a shaft in his traitorous eye."

The monks along the battlements began praying more loudly.

"Prepare the baskets!" Stilicho commanded. "This is the main attack. They'll not stop until they are among us."

"Thor! Thor! Thor! Thor!"

The cries came fast and furious in a babble that sent chills through the monks and even some of the *milites* waiting below.

Stilicho raised his sword and brought it down. "Loose the baskets, now!"

Three heavy baskets were hoisted and tipped over the stone battlements. The backs of more than a dozen Saxons cracked as rocks the size of a man's head and pavings the size of a fist rained down. Skulls were crushed. Men collapsed as stones smashed into exposed shoulders, backs, and arms. The Saxons gasped in pain and cursed in fury, but none cried for mercy. Instead, they renewed their efforts.

Boom, boom, boom — the heavy ram crashed against the door. A distinct crack meant the heavy oak planking began to buckle.

"It's giving way, Count Stilicho!" a *milites* called out from below.

Stilicho gripped his shield tightly and rushed toward the courtyard barricade. His broadsword flew from its scabbard just as the gate's bindings broke and the stout planks collapsed like chaff. The Euduces rushed in, hell-bent on vengeance. Spears and seaxes filled the gate with menace. Yet they carried no shields. Still, the proud Euduces leveled their spears and charged the barricade.

"Step back and lock shields." Stilicho had only eight men, but they snapped into a shield wall with a precision that made the old warrior feel good. *I can die with men such as these.*

The Euduces crawled onto the pile of carts, logs, and furnishings. Scrambling down, they threw themselves against the shield wall like rabid dogs, poking and prying with their blades. But Stilicho and his eight men cut into them in a businesslike manner, stabbing and slashing at the human wave pressing against their shields. Blood-curdling ancestral war cries filled the yard, but the Franks held firm. Saxons went down, one by one, then two at a time. The *milites* then began to push forward until the remaining Euduces had their backs to the barricade.

More fell. Finally, the remaining few tossed their weapons and scrambled frantically back over the barricade. The Franks butchered them mercilessly. Bloodied sword blades stabbed into backs, slashed open legs, and gashed necks and heads. In minutes, all the Saxons entered Valhalla.

As his men cut the throats of any suspected of living, Stilicho ran to shut the gate again. Alone, he lifted and reset the brass hinges, once more securing the heavy planks. *This should hold a while longer.* As he was finishing, the clopping hooves of war horses caused him to turn. He saw four mounted Frank *milites* in full *brunia* — led by Lothar.

"Finish bolting the gate!" Stilicho ordered.

His men ignored the command and rushed to his defense.

Stilicho brandished his longsword. "In the name of Christ's blood, close the gate! Secure the fort!"

This time, his men obeyed and slowly pulled the heavy gate closed. A rattle and snap meant the heavy bar was set, locking the planks tight.

Pounding hooves grew closer. Lothar was leaning forward in the saddle. The horse galloped across the bridge in a flash, barely giving Stilicho time to set his feet.

Smack! Lothar's sword struck Stilicho's shield with the full weight of the horse's impact. The blow sent Stilicho reeling but saved him from a second, fatal strike. Stilicho's left arm was numb from the blow, and his shield was cut through.

Lothar turned and spurred his horse. "Die like the dog you are, Stilicho!"

But suddenly, a single paving stone tumbled from the walls above, striking Lothar's horse and causing it to twist aside and limp. Lothar's retainers now galloped to their master's aid but several more pavings dropped like manna from heaven, forcing them back.

Lothar dismounted and let his horse hobble away. But he grinned as he hefted his shield before him and pointed his longsword. "You betrayed me, Stilicho. By God's justice I have you in my grasp."

The shattered remnants of the shield fell from Stilicho's now useless arm. He clutched his broadsword tightly in his good hand. "You betrayed Karolus and our God. You're the work of Satan. I'll gladly die fighting you."

Lothar's feet clattered across the wooden planks, and he threw himself at Stilicho. Sword met sword in a *clang, clang, clang* punctuated by grunts and deep gulps for air. Fatigue began embracing Stilicho. The numbness in his arm was replaced by a throbbing pain from shoulder to wrist. He felt a gooey liquid seep through this mail. *Blood.* He had little time. His *brunia* felt like lead but his powerful legs stepped firmly toward the menace before him.

At the last moment, driven by a ferocity mixed with desperation, he sprang. Lothar tried to block him with his shield. Stilicho anticipated the move and dropped to one knee and swept his sword under it, slashing Lothar's left leg just below the knee. The blade sliced right through the leather and chain links, tearing flesh, cartilage, and bone.

"Aaargh!" Lothar staggered before he fell tumbling from the bridge and plunging into the rancid water of the moat.

Stilicho gazed at the frantic eyes of Lothar who tried to speak but the weight of the metal *brunia* pulled him down. The gray water closed on his face, filling his mouth with a putrid liquid that choked him before he could utter his last earthly curse.

Stilicho braced himself for the onslaught of Lothar's men but when he looked across the bridge, he saw the backs of men and haunches of horses as Lothar's lackeys quickly rode to safety. Then his eyes locked on something that turned his stomach. Not a quarter-league away, rank upon rank of Saxon tribesmen formed for battle with spears leveled. *They must number over a thousand!* He began to tremble and staggered.

The gates flew open and the steady arms of two of his *milites* ran to Stilicho to help him under the portcullis.

"Are you all right, Lord?"

"Yes. Lower the portcullis. Help me re-set the bolts on this door. Pile what debris we can behind it."

"Then time for more fighting, eh?"

Stilicho shook his head slowly. Beads of sweat dribbled slowly down his neck and under his *brunia*. "No lads, I believe it's the time for praying."

The valiant Frank slumped to the ground—his face drained of blood.

***

Melchior watched the scene unfold from a wooded hillside just under a league away. He had arrayed his mounted *milites* in a column of four abreast. He had spent the past few hours training them for this moment, a massive charge with lances low. Franks typically held their spears high and stabbed them like elongated swords. But he taught them to hold the lance under the arm instead and to charge home using the power of the charging horse to do the work.

"The effect will shock the Saxons and then the Avars," he told Audeon and the others.

"But Lord, I don't understand. Franks have always fought so," Audeon said, raising his lance over his head.

"We must shock an enemy that outnumbers us, understand?" Melchior said. "Lean forward in the saddle and mark your spearpoint low. The swaying of the horse and your nerves will naturally raise it."

They nodded, but he realized they did not fully understand. But they would soon. Or so he hoped... and prayed. Melchior grabbed two items from under his *brunia* – the Ronson that somehow made the journey with him and his cross. *Is this truly a Christian world? Is this a world I should help Karolus build?* He thought about what the future held for Christendom: doubt, heresy, war, strife, and worse.

"You seem in reflection, *Dominus*." Father Thomas sat next to him, his Psalter in hand.

"The Lord Melchior is preparing his mind for battle," Jurchen said.

Melchior looked at the pair. *Saxon and Frank, priest and pseudo-priest.* "My mind is already prepared for battle. It's my soul I am preparing."

"Your soul?" Father Thomas asked. "I have given absolution to all the men."

"Does Christ really want warriors to fight for him?" Melchior asked.

After some hesitation, Jurchen spoke, "I think he wants us to die for him if need be. If that includes fighting, so be it."

"Devils do walk the earth, *Dominus*. We should fight them spiritually always and physically, when necessary," Father Thomas said.

This young priest is right. I have fought against the devil and for him. For whom do I fight now? Melchior gazed out across the open fields and toward Fulda in the distance. Despite the light gray sky, he could make out the fort's battlements, where Stilicho held the Saxons at bay. He knew it would not be for long.

"Does Christ favor only Christians?" Melchior asked out loud, but was speaking to himself. "If so, why is half the world... un-Christian?"

"That is why we are so fortunate in our king-and-emperor. He will bring God to them all again," Father Thomas replied.

Melchior realized the simple and open faith that filled this young man was genuine. "But if we lose... as we did lose in the Pyrenees?"

"Then we will die as the martyrs once did," Father Thomas said. "Better to die for one's faith than live without it."

Melchior thought of Baugulf and the letter.

"But we will not die... or at least we will die in victory, " Jurchen said.

Melchior closed his eyes. The simple faith of these two men, so different yet so alike, gave him confidence. He opened his eyes and looked up at the tin-colored clouds. He sensed the sun was trying to break through and give him a sign, but it did not.

"You are correct, Jurchen," Melchior said.

Audeon rode up breathlessly. His horse snorted and pranced with anticipation. "*Dominus*... the ranks are formed. Two battles, as you ordered."

Melchior looked toward Fulda again. This time, a small break in the clouds let the sun's rays beam on the town like a beacon. He thought he saw Stilicho. Then he saw the Saxons swarm across the bridge. He put his helmet on. Jurchen did the same.

"I'll lead the first battle. Jurchen rides with me. Audeon, you'll lead the second battle. Hold them back, no matter what. If the Avars arrive, you will charge them as I ordered. Then make your way back to Fulda. I will try to do the same. But get to Fulda and wait."

"Await what, *Dominus*?" Audeon asked.

"You will learn soon enough."

"But the girl, Genofeva?" Audeon asked.

"You love her, don't you?" Melchior asked.

Audeon's eyes widened. "I, well, I… "

"And well you should. But she is gone."

"Not if I charge the Saxons and rescue her," Audeon said.

Melchior's eyes narrowed. "My command is to strike the Avars when they come. Then take your battle back to Fulda, where Stilicho commands. Do you understand?"

"But how do you know the Avars will come?" Audeon asked.

"They'll come." Melchior signaled for his men to gather. Cassyon, Detleff, and Gaetano drew near. "You are all good men. If I don't emerge from this battle, I order you to follow Count Stilicho to Fulda. Karolus, our king-and-emperor, has great plans for Fulda."

"We will die with you, *Dominus*," Detleff said.

"I don't plan to die. But you will follow Stilicho until Audeon is of age. Then you will follow him. Now, mount your horses. And remember, your spear is neither a projectile nor a sword for slashing. Let your horse do the work. Drive the tip through a Saxon and ride the next."

Melchior slipped his boot into the stirrup. His horse snorted. "Easy, Timbo." He patted it and swung into the saddle. He realized for the first time that Timbo was a Frisian, somewhat larger than the modern breed but still a warmblood. Melchior's mind conjured an image of riding with Brooke, then suddenly lost it.

He patted Timbo's neck. "Let the horses do the work."

"Beware, *Dominus*," Father Thomas said. "Beware the evil witch-queen, Udela." He made the sign of the cross.

"Fear not, Father Thomas. I have the cross under my *brunia*." He looked at Detleff. "I have my talisman as well. The combination should preserve me from an evil Saxon queen… even if she is a witch."

Melchior's men broke into the laughter of men who knew it might be their last. None of them noticed that Melchior did not.

***

After struggling through the dense pines, the horse staggered and slowly sank to its knees, exhausted. Fromm swung his heavy leg out of the saddle. He stroked the horse's muzzle. "It's all right. You did your best. Now I must do mine." He took a swig from the wineskin and wiped his mouth. The pain in his ribs had grown intense. His left arm was stiff, but the pain was manageable.

A ray of dim gray light broke through the dark canopy overhead. Fromm listened. The forest was silent. That meant one thing: man. He put on his helmet and retrieved his battle-ax. After a moment of hesitation, he took the shield as well. It was a crude Saxon shield of wood and leather. But it bore runic markings. Two lines converged at an angle, pointing left: <

"*Kaunan*," he muttered. All Norsemen knew the meaning— mortality, and pain. He grunted and took another swig of wine. *If I am to go to Valhalla I will bring as much wine with me as I can.*

Fromm made his way slowly. The pine needles under his feet felt good, and the smell refreshed him. He pushed through pine boughs as thick as the fur on a northern bear. He came to a glade and paused. When his eyes adjusted to the light, he saw a dark form in the center. Fromm stayed in the trees and worked his way in a circle until he had cleared the wood of any possible observer. Then, slowly, he approached the form in the glade. It moved. Fromm tightened his grip on his ax.

"Stay away! Let me die in peace," whispered a shallow voice.

If it talks, it can be killed. Fromm drew closer. He recognized the robes of the fat bishop, but the face was not recognizable, covered in blood that had oozed from the sides of his head and dried nearly black. *He has no ears!*

Fromm looked around once more and then knelt beside Willehad. "Where's the girl?"

"Gone. They took her."

"Who took her?"

"The devils… the Avars…"

Fromm now saw he had several darts stuck in his torso. "How many?"

"I… I don't know…"

Fromm grew angry. "How many, in the name of Odin?"

"Maybe six… Maybe ten…You'll not catch them on foot. And if you do, they'll cut your ears off as well."

Fromm sensed some glee in Willehad's voice. *Christian pig.*

A sound stirred from the underbrush deep in the trees.

"They're back! They'll cut you too now, pagan. I thank Christ I'll live to see you go down by their hands. Pagan killing pagan."

Fromm listened attentively. The sound stirred again. "That's not the sound of the Avars. I must go. You can greet your new friends when I leave."

Fromm went back into the trees and again headed east. The sounds grew louder. At first, a faint rustling. Then a louder rustling. Then snorting.

Willehad's voice cried out. "Stay away, you devil… stay away…"

Fromm heard a ukh, ukh sound, followed by a high-pitched, ear-piercing cry. He glanced back and saw a large black boar—over 300 pounds. The animal's dull eyes blinked. Then, suddenly, it charged Willehad. In one swift move of its powerful head, it ripped open Willehad's belly. Willehad screamed shrilly. The boar snorted, grunted, and snapped as it ground its tusks into Willehad's fat belly. With each grinding move, Willehad screamed more shrilly.

Fromm turned away from the sight just as a last, blood-chilling wail left Willehad's body, along with whatever had served as his soul. *The work of Loki...*

***

Udela listened to her army from afar. The sound of the Saxon warriors thrilled and horrified her. She knew how little control she had over the passions of these wild men who served her and her cause. But what was her cause? She had only a vague notion of conquering the west, then turning south and east. She had an even vaguer notion of why. She moved on impulse, passion, and hope. Hope that she would understand the forces that made her the witch-queen to these wild men.

A messenger struggled up the road. She could see he was another youth, perhaps fifteen. His shock of yellow hair and fuzz-like beard gave him away. But he struggled like a man, she thought. He arrived at her side, gasping. Two of the Haari warriors held him before Udela.

"Have you news from Count Lothar?" she asked. "The sounds of battle are indistinct from this distance."

The youth took a breath. "The attack is underway."

"Is Count Lothar not inside the fort?"

"Not yet, My Queen."

"Tell me what is happening." Udela's tone was soft and patient.

"Tilo's men took down the gate. But the Franks drove them back and closed it. A second attack also failed."

"How could this be?" Udela asked. "And the attack by the main body?"

"Eberger's Nabo anxiously await their orders."

"Why doesn't Count Lothar give the order?"

"He rode to the fort but fell at the hands of a Frank."

"And Mallobaudes? He has the Frank girl. Some believe she is of value."

"He was seen riding off before the attack."

"In which direction?"

"East, My Queen."

"To the Avars! And where is Dgno? Never mind. We shall not wait for the reptile. The Saxons will do this alone."

"Eberger awaits your command. I'll gladly carry it back," the youth said.

A strange sensation surged through Udela. "No. I will not leave this to the wiles of men. Even good men like Eberger. I am your chosen queen for a reason. I shall lead the attack. "Varna, do you have my belongings?"

"Yes, My Queen," Varna said. Since gaining her freedom, Varna had become Udela's closest confidant. She handed Udela one of the long leather bags strapped to her pony. Udela looked through it carefully.

Udela's lithe legs swung easily into the saddle. "Varna, you and Maya will stay well to the rear. Can you do that?"

"Should we join Radka with the baggage?" Varna asked.

Udela pointed towards the high ground west of the Fulda River. "No. Find a place along those hills."

"What is your name?" Udela asked the Saxon youth.

"Drucfred."

"Can you ride, Ducfred?"

The youth nodded, his hand grabbing his long *Seaxe* firmly at the hilt. "But I would rather fight against the Franks, My Queen."

"All in good time. I have a suspicion there will be more fighting than even a fine young warrior like you will care to see. You have strong legs. Come with me."

Udela rode toward Fulda with Hrodger and his Haari at her side. Ducfred ran alongside her like a pet dog. They made their way through green fields intermingled with woods. The sky was gray and heavy, but suddenly light broke through the clouds. She could see the gray walls, the spires and dome of the abbey, and the towering fort. Fulda. Between her and the city was a mass of powerful warriors, the Nabo. She spurred her horse toward them.

"We await your command."

Her eyes bore into Eberger. "I will ride to the fort with the Haari. When you hear the boom of Thor's hammer — launch your men."

"But My Queen should not..."

"Hold your tongue, lest I have Hrodger slice it from your head. This is my destiny." Udela had no idea what possessed her to act. She recalled what she had been told... what she had learned somewhere in the mists of time and place.

Eberger lowered his head.

"Keep watch for the Avars. The thunder of Thor's hammer will call them."

Bruno arrived, breathless but eager for orders.

"How go the *Issepi*?" Udela asked.

"Many have gone to Valhalla. But those who remain are ready to send the Franks to their hell."

"Good, Bruno."

"But, My Queen, Count Lothar is gone. You must appoint a new commander."

"I know he is gone. I am leading the next attack. Join me with your warriors." Udela felt relieved that Lothar was gone. He was only a tool. Now she would happily accomplish her goals on her own. She realized she needed no man, no prince, to achieve them.

Bruno smiled grimly. "We are not expert at attacking such forts but welcome any chance to kill Franks or find Valhalla."

Udela frowned. She was tired of this Saxon desire for Valhalla. "Valhalla must wait! We shall send the Franks to their hell."

"When Thor's hammer strikes, you and your warriors must rush the fort. I will grant uncommon gifts to the warrior who brings me the abbot alive and his possessions... his writings... undamaged."

The warriors let out a roar and struck shields with spear, *Seaxe,* or *Francisca.* Udela raised her hand, and they grew silent. "O my Saxons... my brave Saxons... You will take this bastion of Karolus and his hated Franks. It will be just the first of many until we tear apart his palace with our hands. Move out now! Move like the lone wolf closing on its prey... until Thor's hammer strikes.... That will be the signal... until Thor's hammer strikes!"

Against a thousand years of instinct, the Saxons marched in silence toward their quarry. Udela had commanded it. Silence until Thor's hammer struck. And so, it was. Thousands of Saxons grimly advanced on the fort... the castle... the symbol of the hated Karolus... the symbol of the hated Frankland.

***

Fromm stumbled on them just as the sun broke over the horizon. After hours of struggling through the dark wooded hills, he had almost given up hope of finding them. *They are likely halfway to their homes in the east.*

After leaving Willehad to the tusks of the boar, he continued moving east in search of the Avars and the girl. He began to move his left arm gingerly, and the ribs wound no longer stabbed him with each heavy step. He crossed two streams, stopping at each to lap up the refreshing water and cool his hot face. He decided to follow the second stream. Shortly after that, he smelled and then spied horse dung in a place where no horse would go on its own.

He looked down at the pair of steppe ponies nibbling on the sweet grass along the stream. He could hear another pair just twenty paces away. The heavy morning mist shrouded the area in a deep gray. He looked up and silently thanked Thor for the weather. He rubbed his hand along his rough leather boot. His dagger was in place, an eighteen-inch blade with two edges. He wiped the dew from his battle-ax's blade and adjusted his helmet.

Fromm's feet took baby steps to avoid disturbing the ponies. He stopped just a few paces away from the sleeping Avars. There were three. Little men, he thought, but so deadly. *But where is the girl?* He heard one of the ponies nickering in the mist, then the subtle jingle of stirrups. *The girl is trying to mount one!*

Suddenly, the three sleeping Avars roused and sprang to their feet like cats.

Fromm bolted from his cover and charged them with his battle-ax already in motion. "Odin!" The powerful arc cut through branches and foliage, slicing the first Avar in two. Fromm thundered past the torso, which sprayed a geyser of blood in all directions.

A second Avar hurled a dart, striking the side of Fromm's helmet. The Avar quickly drew a short, curved sword and charged at Fromm like a leopard taking on a bear. But the bear's heavy paw struck with surprising speed. The battle-ax came down on the Avar's shoulder and cleaved his arm off. Before he fell to the muddy earth, the Avar's blade struck Fromm's thigh, cutting through the heavy leather breeches.

Fromm staggered for a moment but shrugged off the pain. Then he felt a sharp sting at his chest. The third Avar's dart struck him, burying itself in his chain mail tunic.

Fromm grimaced. *Odin's blood.* He heard the sound of whinnying and the hooves of the ponies lurching across the muddy riverbank. *The girl is escaping with their ponies.*

The Avar must have had the same thought. He picked up his short bow, notched an arrow, and in one motion launched it into the gray mist. The squeal of a pony made Fromm's blood curdle. *Odin's beard!*

Before Fromm could act, the Avar launched a second and then a third arrow toward the squealing pony. Fighting through the pain coursing through every quarter of his heavy frame, Fromm slogged across the mud with his battle-ax held high. He was now struggling to breathe and had to strike without his usual battle cry. The Avar turned just as Fromm's breathing turned into grunts. A wolf-like face with dark slits for eyes met Fromm. *A devil!*

The Avar grinned wickedly. Fromm's pain was evident as he staggered forward. The Avar sidestepped his move and drew a curved Asiatic dagger, plunging it into Fromm's side.

"Odin's blood!" Fromm grunted in pain and rage, dropping his beloved battle ax into the alluvial mud.

He pulled away from the Avar, who struggled to tear the weapon from Fromm's side. Fromm shook off the pain and ignored the blood oozing from his side. He crouched and weaved, this time deliberately, causing the Avar to let go of the knife hilt. Fromm reached down and drew his own knife from his boot. He staggered toward the Avar with only one purpose left —to tear the devil apart. The Avar's eyes widened, but with ease he drew his last dart from his belt and fought off Fromm with its pointed blade.

Ignoring the frantic jabs to his chest and torso, Fromm grabbed the Avar by the throat and lifted him off his feet. The warrior wriggled like a game fish, despite the crushing of his windpipe, and stabbed madly at the brute that held him. Fromm plunged the blade of his dagger into the Avar's belly and twisted upward. His boots grew warm from the Avar's entrails, now hanging limp in his grasp. In a rage, he hurled the body like a toy and cried, "Odin!"

Fromm then closed his eyes and collapsed into the Avar's offal.

Chapter 22

Fulda

The morning fog had lifted, and what passed for sunshine lit the Fulda Valley. The clop-clop of hooves struck the soft earth in a strange rhythm. The footmen's heavy leather boots slogged through wet grass that reached almost armpit level. Still, the Franks trod with measured steps.

Melchior hoped to intercept the tribes as they deployed in the open fields around Fulda. He glanced back toward the wooded hills, wondering whether he was right to divide his force into two battle groups. He shrugged off his doubts, but his thoughts turned to his journey. He thought he understood its purpose, yet he did not understand his own. *To deliver a letter? Destroy a witch? What is the meaning?*

As Timbo pressed forward, Melchior's mind raced with images of his life in both worlds: friends and family, wartime *Kameraden* — comrades in a war unthinkable even to these fierce Franks, the brutish Saxons, and the Avars. Images of tanks, machine guns, and bombs flashed. Always bombs. The blast of artillery shells bursts with deadly effect. Sound and fire. The crack of rifles and the rattle of machine guns. Smoke and chaos. He thought of the Canadian researchers and their desperate plans for him. A gunfight at night on a train. Fighting on steppes and in deserts. The strike of a sniper's bullet. He thought of the Bolsheviks, and he realized this very ground was the divide between godless Bolshevism and what remained of Europe... of what these people called... Christendom.

At last, he thought of Kristel. *Why had she never written? Why didn't she join him as promised? Was she ever his true love? Which world was his true world?* He reached under his *brunia* and grasped the Ronson. It was his only proof of the other world. He fumbled for the metal cross. *Was this the only proof of God's other world?* He did not see himself as a man of God, but suddenly realized a truth he had been avoiding. He was a man for God.

In the distance, he could see the throngs of Saxons swarming over Fulda like an army of killer ants. But the Frankish pennant still snapped in the breeze. Stilicho has done well so far. Just a little longer. If God wills it...

***

Udela raised her hand, and her eager warriors broke into a run. The youth Ducfred advanced with them. Her plan was risky. *Can he follow my simple instructions?*

She looked up at the battlements. Random pavers torn from the streets and walls bounced off the column, but only a few of her thousands fell. If we can only take down the gate. She saw a Frankish warrior atop the portcullis. Ducfred carried the sack on his shoulder. The Saxons were silent in their final approach. The walls of Fulda buzzed with a strange sound — prayer. *So it is Thor's hammer against these chanting monks. We shall see...*

Ducfred, surrounded by a ring of Saxons, rushed to the front of the Euduces. Udela grew nervous. Her magic would be difficult for someone unused to it, and she had no time to demonstrate. She hoped her instructions were clear enough. The boy seemed brighter than most and willing to risk all… for his tribe and his queen. Udela suddenly felt a pang of guilt. She was sending this innocent boy to… But realized it must be done… if her plan were to succeed.

The ring of Euduces tightened around Ducfred. Udela lost sight of him. The warriors were now at the gate under the portcullis. It amazed her that the Franks had no archers. And as she scanned the battlements, she realized the Franks were few. *Yet they had managed to defeat Lothar…* Precious minutes went by. Udela considered riding forward to do the deed herself.

"Is something wrong, My Queen?" Hrodger asked.

Udela shook her head. She was glad she had reinstated these beasts as her praetorian guard. They were savage, but they had no clan allegiance. Udela had lived among the Saxons long enough to know that blood ties of clan and tribe trumped allegiance to a chieftain, a god, or even a queen who was a witch. Suddenly, she saw the flash, then the *boom.* The valley reverberated from a thunderous explosion greater than anything that had rained from the heavens. A cloud of black smoke enveloped the ring of warriors. As one, the entire Saxon host, including the Haari, dropped to the ground in fear.

"The hammer of Thor! Acknowledge the hammer of Thor!" Udela exclaimed. She could scarcely conceal her smile. Then her lips turned down in a grim frown. *The boy Ducfred is dead… No matter, it had to be done.*

The portcullis collapsed. A larger brown cloud of dust and debris now enveloped the black smoke from the explosion. The gate that once blocked their way into the fort was now just a heap of rubble. The entire Saxon host rose as one.

With howls of victory and vengeance, the Saxon advance guard filled the breach. But as the first Saxons clambered over the bodies of Ducfred and his ring of escorts, they found the pile of debris almost impossible to climb. A handful of desperate Franks stood atop the pile and hurled stone after stone. Spears cut through the air as the Saxons tried to drive them from their position.

"What is happening, My Queen?" Hrodger asked. The usually confident and imperious Haari seemed subdued to her.

"I should have expected this. Thor's hammer smashed the portcullis, but the rubble is blocking the entrance."

"Eberger must continue to attack."

"The Euduces are in confusion."

"Look there— horsemen!"

In the distance, she could see a swarm of horsemen riding at the Saxon warriors who now had fallen into confusion as their chiefs plotted their next move.

"My Queen, the Avars are coming to our aid," Hrodger said. "The hammer of Thor must have awakened them."

"So the reptile has come, after all," she said.

Udela watched eagerly as Dgno's horde charged across the field. It occurred to her that their archers could cover the walls while her warriors fought their way through the pile of debris.

"Riders approach," one of the Haari said.

Mallobaudes galloped up with a pair of his men-at-arms and the girl, Genofeva, in tow. "Hail to your victory, Queen Udela!"

"Where have you been?" Udela asked. "You were with Count Lothar in the attack, were you not?"

"I was. But before his attack, Count Lothar sent me back to stay by you with this young beauty. I had her in a safe place, but when I heard the dreadful sound, I decided to come right to you."

"And why did Lothar send you back?"

"Because we need her more than ever. He suspects the *missus* has left the fort with a body of men. Monks guard the fort. And Melchior is at large."

Udela again startled at the sound of that name, *Melchior? Melchior!* She regained her composure. "These monks have held off the cream of the Saxon race. I doubt that is possible. But no matter, our allies have at last arrived."

Hrodger smiled. "They too must heed the hammer of Thor."

"I think a force should be sent to find the Melchior," Mallobaudes said.

"Then go find him," Udela said. "I'll watch the Avars and my people take Karolus's shrine and begin the destruction of his realm."

"Count Lothar promised me a prominent place in the new realm."

Udela sneered. "You may keep your lands. That's all I promise."

"And the girl?" Mallobaudes stroked Genofeva's arm, but she recoiled.

"I think she prefers neither to be your bride nor your concubine."

Mallobaudes edged his horse closer to Udela. Two Haari blocked him with crossed spears. Udela signaled to let him pass.

He spoke softly, so only Udela could hear, "She is the daughter of Karolus. Whoever possesses her possesses the link to him. Once he is gone, she will make a useful tool to control the Franks — to make them willing followers of you, Queen Udela."

"My Queen, the Avars attack our warriors!" Hrodger announced.

Udela looked across the valley. "Those aren't Avars!"

Mallobaudes's face twisted into a dismissive frown. "No, My Queen. That is my cousin— he, Karolus's *Missus Dominicus,* Lord Melchior, riding at the head of his band."

A chill coursed through Udela. *Who is this... Melchior? Where is Dgno?* She quickly composed herself. "Saxons will prevail."

As she pronounced this, a column of mounted *milites* followed by footmen crashed into the flank of her Saxons.

***

The Frankish horsemen charged with spears lowered. Melchior struck a Saxon squarely on his shield. The spearhead cut through the leather and transfixed the warrior, sending his dangling body back into the mass of men behind him. Melchior looked to his side. Detleff struck home, as did Cassyon, as did they all. *Good! Let the horses do the work.*

Surprised and confused, the Saxons turned to face the onslaught. But the Franks rode furiously, breaking the Saxon force. Some ran. Others stood their ground with mocking bravado.

"Finish them with blades!" Melchior cried.

The riders drew their broadswords and struck Saxon after Saxon. The Saxons tried to slip under the horses and gut them with *Seaxes*. Lacking armor, they were easily slashed and stabbed. Now the Frank footmen struck in their steady phalanx.

The Saxons fought back savagely. Cries of "Odin!" rang out as Saxon bands, large and small, rushed at the Franks. Years of hatred and conflict reached a boiling point as these ancient Germanic enemies fought a battle to the death.

Melchior pulled back to assess the combat around him. Detleff and Cassyon rallied to him. He pointed at a mounted *milites* savagely slashing all around him. "Who is that?"

"Jurchen, *Dominus*," Detleff said.

"He fights more like a Frank than most Franks," Cassyon quipped. "May I join him, *Dominus*?"

Melchior turned and looked to their rear. "Perhaps, but first…"

"What is it, *Dominus*?"

"I hear something. The rumble of hooves."

"Perhaps young Lord Audeon could not hold his *milites* from such a battle," Cassyon said.

"No, those are not horses' hooves, but ponies."

"Avars!" Cassyon and Detleff exclaimed together.

"Cassyon, rally who you can from the melee. Make sure they have lances."

"Detleff, ride back to Audeon and tell him…." Melchior hesitated.

"Yes, *Dominus*?"

"Tell him to wait for the outcome and to send a message to his father." Melchior knew the outcome was forlorn. He decided he would at least save his squire and the son of Karolus.

"So Karolus is nearby?" Detleff asked.

"Only in spirit. But perhaps that's enough. As long as Audeon is ranging with his forces, they will think Karolus is coming."

"I'm your squire. Send someone else, *Dominus*."

"Obey my command. Deliver my message and serve Audeon as his squire until I return. Now go!"

Detleff shot a doubtful look but then nodded and rode off.

Cassyon had rallied a dozen mounted *milites* and some forty men on foot. The rest had fallen or were too busy finishing off the Saxons. The horsemen spread out in an arc in front of the footmen. The footmen formed a block. With spears lowered, they marched toward the approaching swarm.

"Shields over your heads until we charge," Melchior commanded.

As one, the men hunched forward and swung their shields onto their shoulders. They drew closer to the pounding hooves. Eerily, the Avars had no war cry except the singing of their bowstrings and the plunging of their shafts.

Melchior's men cringed in fear as the first arrowheads plunged into their shields. They looked like porcupines. Like porcupines, they moved forward. The air soon grew heavy with arrows, and the *szhit-szhit* sound drummed against the shields like a hailstorm. The panicked wail of horses chilled them to the bone. The Avars had given up on their human prey and decided to take out their mounts! Melchior knew they had to break out of it now or the Avars would simply pull back and continue the onslaught from the air.

The Avars were now barely forty paces away. He swung his shield in front of him, lowered his lance, and charged.

As one, the *milites* lowered their lances and lurched forward in a desperate charge. The lances struck true. But the Avars began to ride away, peppering the oncoming wall of steel with arrows. Some *milites* fell, but most charged home. Blades skewered archers from their ponies. More horses fell. Undeterred, their riders rushed the Avars on foot, seizing bridles or stirrups and slashing their hated enemies with broadswords or chopping off limbs with the *Francisca*.

The Frankish footmen joined the struggle. Though only half the original number, the stolid footmen struck the mass of Avars, sending ponies into a panic. But the Avars pulled back from the phalanx and replied with a volley of arrows that stung the air with *zhit – zhit – zhit*.

Cassyon appeared beside Melchior, covered in blood, and two arrows jutting from his arm. "We need more horsemen, *Dominus*. The footmen are almost done. Let me ride to get Audeon and the rest of the mounted *milites*."

Melchior saw the phalanx had melted to barely a dozen men. "If they take the Avars in the rear, we might yet best them. But I can't risk it. We must face the Avars with the men we have."

He cursed himself for not anticipating this. He had committed the sin of pride, thinking a few Franks could defeat twenty times their number in Asiatic horsemen. *The Eastern Front should have been my lesson. Now, good men have died. And a kingdom could fall. Am I to lose history in one act of foolery? We have slain at least three hundred, but they have more. One last effort...*

Smoke still hung across the portcullis at Fulda, but now swarms of Avars began shooting at the remaining Saxons. *We did their dirty work. Now we all pay the price.*

Melchior leveled his lance at the Avars. "On me, men of Frankland! *Deus vult!*" He turned his horse toward the Avar line. With a roar of "*Deus vult*," the remaining Franks joined Melchior. Some held shields to cover men who were dragging the wounded with them. The arrows continued to rain down on the field.

Only a half-dozen milites rode behind him—the rest were dead. The surviving Frankish footmen ran behind the horses. Melchior and his band struck home and once more sent the light horsemen scattering. With a *smack*, Melchior's spear tip hit home. He skewered one, then another, and another. His arm ached from the impact on his last target. His lance snapped in two, and his shield was ripped from his hand.

But Timbo kept plunging through the Avar ranks. Melchior slashed and struck with a broadsword and a *Francisca*. As Avars fell, more joined them. They launched darts at close range and slashed with curved swords and daggers.

Only two mounted Franks remained with him. One was Jurchen — the other Cassyon.

"We've done God's will here. Ride and find Audeon," Melchior ordered.

"We stay and die with you, *Dominus*," Jurchen said.

Melchior hardly recognized him. Covered in dust and blood, with sweat dribbling down his cheeks, he looked like a true Frankish warrior of old.

"Do as I command."

"I shall, *Dominus*. But first, I will exact a penalty on the Avars."

Before Melchior could reply, Jurchen lurched forward and pressed into the Avar line, thrusting with his lance and hacking with his *Seaxe*. Cassyon followed him into the swirl of horses, dust, and death. Melchior turned back and saw the remnant of the phalanx of footmen lying where they had fought. Not one cried for mercy as silent bands of Avars rode among them, cutting the ears from the dead and dying.

Melchior shook his head as if to drive the scene away. He never knew there could be such death and destruction without the use of bombs, bullets, and automatic weapons. With one hand, he grasped the Ronson, his talisman, and his silver cross. He quickly uttered a prayer, one he was not sure he wanted answered.

A band of Avars galloped toward him. He dismounted and drew his broadsword. His horse snorted a warning.

"They're my enemies, not yours, Timbo," he whispered. "Run free, my warm blood." He slapped Timbo across the rump with the flat of the blade, sending the horse galloping towards the dark, distant forest.

The clatter of pony hooves drew near. Devil-like faces and the buzzing of bees seemed to engulf him. Melchior raised his broadsword high, both hands tightly wrapped around the hilt. "*Deus vult!*"

He disappeared as the Avars swarmed around him like a tornado of death.

***

Like mounted vipers, the Avars had now sunk their fangs into the unsuspecting Saxons. Arrows darkened the sky with a rain of death. Those with shields managed to take cover, but most fell as the black shafts plunged from above, iron tips plunging into flesh and breaking bone. Desperately, the Saxons sought cover or raised their hands to ward off the onslaught, but to no avail. Some crawled under the bleeding corpses of their comrades. Still, the shafts plunged through them. Soon, more than a thousand warriors lay groaning or motionless, eyes staring wide into the gray sky.

Udela's eyes filled with tears as she watched the destruction of her people. The Nabo and Euduces were nearly gone. So were the Issepi. She saw only a handful make their way up the wooded slopes where the Avars rarely ventured. When she first saw the swarm of Avars, she felt relief, but when the Franks fell on her people, the betrayal shocked her. She thrust her face into her hands in anguish. What the Franks did not do, the betrayal by Dgno did. Of more than 2,000 warriors, perhaps three hundred escaped. Now she had only the Haari and some stragglers to secure the women, children, and baggage.

"Have we heard anything of the camp?" she asked.

"I sent a messenger as you commanded, My Queen. But let's move into the mountains before Dgno turns his men on us." Hrodger replied.

"His mounted serpents, you mean. Yes. I counted several hundred warriors who made their way into those hills. If we join them, we can wait for Dgno to take Fulda and launch a surprise attack."

"My Queen is bold," Hrodger replied with a smile. "The Haari will gladly follow you to hell."

"See how they loot the Saxon bodies. We must exact revenge."

Udela was undaunted. Her ploy with Lothar failed. Her own attack failed. The Avars had betrayed her, yet she remained confident. She would concoct another plan. This one, aimed at Dgno.

"Dgno must pay for this treachery! I want your Haari to swear they will fight to the death to avenge the Saxon blood that has stained the fields before Fulda today."

The Haari pointed their spears into the air. "We swear it!"

Udela saw Mallobaudes fidgeting with his horse's bridle. The girl was already mounted as were his Frankish retainers.

"Where do you think you are going?" Udela demanded.

"The politics of Frankland have changed. I plan to meet with Dgno. He will need me..."

"Do you think a man who would betray his queen would hesitate with a man like you? Dgno will kill you and keep the girl for himself."

Udela's mind raced to find an advantage in this. "But perhaps there is a way we all can benefit."

"I am all ears, My Queen," Mallobaudes replied with a slight bow of his head.

Hrodger had signaled his Haari, who now surrounded Mallobaudes and his handful of *milites*.

"You will go to Dgno as my emissary."

"And then?"

"Tell him I will submit to become his queen. We must set aside today's work and consider the future. The West can still be ours. And I will reconsider your role, Mallobaudes. You should make an excellent king of the Franks. Under the suzerainty of the Saxon—Avar alliance."

"With all respect, My Queen, I think your Saxons are a subdued race this day."

Hrodger's men growled and shifted their spears in their hands in anticipation of the signal to strike.

Udela raised her hand. "Nevertheless, Dgno will treat with me. He needs a powerful consort. I need his warriors. It's that simple."

"What do I tell him?"

"Tell him I will meet him in three days at the Christian church in Fulda. If he has not taken the fort by then, he will need what Saxons remain and my special powers. Thor's hammer will strike once more."

Mallobaudes nodded.

"And the girl remains with me. As a matter of precaution."

"No! She is…"

The *Haari* sprang like wolves. Before they could react, Mallobaudes's men-at-arms were struck down in a flurry of spears, thrusts, and *Seaxe* cuts. Hrodger himself secured Genofeva. She made no resistance.

Udela pointed at Mallobaudes. "The girl is now under my protection. Remember, three days. Now go."

Udela and her bodyguard hurried west. An hour later, they were in the wooded hills where they found Varna and Maya.

Varna ran past the Haari guards to Udela and threw her arms around the queen's legs. She sobbed hysterically.

"We are together, Varna. Soon we'll find the others and…"

"O, My Queen. We have learned of the worst…"

She pulled Varna to her feet and looked into the girl's tear-stained face. "What is it?"

"The Avars raided the camp before they attacked the main body at Fulda. Almost all were put to the sword, including Radka."

Bitter anger coursed through Udela. But she maintained her composure. "They are savages. But we must treat with them. Until…"

"My Queen?" Varna asked.

"Nothing. It is what must be. For now, we must treat with Dgno." Udela glanced at Genofeva. "At least until I can use this girl to a better purpose."

The next day, the *Haari* scouts managed to locate the Saxon survivors, a mix of Nabo and Issepi. Between the Frankish blades and Avar arrows, the Euduces were killed to the man. Udela knew the massacre of the women and children would inspire untold rage in her remaining warriors. She had to act quickly and without hesitation to exploit this.

That evening, she summoned the remaining warriors under a canopy of tall fir trees. A large bonfire cast shadows across the dark woods as Udela mounted a log platform.

"Saxons… Saxons… we are forged by blood and iron as a people…. a people strong and determined. The perfidy of the Avars and the sly tactics of the Franks have dealt us a blow. But it is Odin's will that the blow makes us stronger and more resolute."

More than three hundred angry throats bellowed approval. Spears and blades struck shields in thunderous applause. "Udela! Udela! Udela!"

Udela scanned their faces. The men looked undaunted. *Perhaps even more ferocious in defeat than other men in victory.* She took that as a good omen.

"I welcome your acclaim. But I need your complete trust even more. I swear on a sacred oath to Odin… to Frig… to Thor and Loki. I will not rest until we crush the Avars and the road to the very heart of Frankland is yet ours. Our acolytes have gone forth and sown seeds of doubt and derision among the Franks. Because of this, many doubt their god and their king. But we Saxons have never doubted our gods or our rulers."

Voices erupted in a roar of shouts, and eager spears and blades thundered on shields. "Udela! Udela! Udela!"

Udela's eyes were aflame as she gazed at the people before her. She raised her hands high. "I will go to the serpent Dgno and offer myself as his bride."

"No! Never!" came the response.

Udela raised her hands, and the throng fell silent. "Dgno will welcome me as his willing bride. But I shall bring the hammer of Thor down upon him in a thunderclap that even the Christian king will fear… a hammer that will signal your time for vengeance… vengeance for his betrayal!"

The warriors exclaimed their approval, "Udela! Udela! Udela! Death to Avars! Death to Franks! Long live the Saxons!"

Udela glanced down at Varna. She looked so frail and innocent. An inner shudder ran through Udela, for she knew that before her journey was complete, the young Bulgar would lose that innocence, one way or another.

***

Anfelisia listened to the Avars whisper among themselves as they guided their ponies through the thick woods. She thought they were arguing over her fate. She had escaped from the first band of Avars in the dark woods, but other packs prowled the area. She was soon back in the hands of the beastly men from the east. The narrow trail wended its way below the crest of a series of hills that led to Fulda. She heard that word spat several times among her captors. The trail forked, and the Avars halted. From their gestures, she could see they were in a heated discussion about which trail to take.

Finally, one of the Avars snapped his whip, and his pony lurched up the right fork. For reasons she would never know, the choice gave her comfort. The trail leveled and then began to descend. A break in the thick woodline revealed the winding river and the town of Fulda, about four leagues distant. Home, she thought. But her heart sank when she saw the plume of black smoke rising from the bridge leading to the fort. The plains along the river seemed dotted with something. Men on horseback were riding back and forth. She was witnessing the end of a great battle. Anfelisia averted her eyes and folded her hands in prayer.

They came to a stream that flowed off the hills toward the river valley. The Avars halted and unsaddled their ponies. A dim light filtered through the heavy canopy above, signaling dusk. The Avars lit a small campfire and began preparing a strange mix of horsemeat and porridge. They sat in a circle and drank from what looked like wineskins. Their banter was hushed and sober at first, but after an hour of drinking, they grew more relaxed.

One Avar tried to feed her some of his porridge, but the smell was rancid, and she demurred. He grinned and said something. The laughter from his mates made her suspicious. She toyed with reaching for his curved dagger, which hung loosely from his belt. He mumbled something and gave a rakish grin. Dark eyes glimmered like slits across brown cheekbones marred by pox marks. He bent over and grabbed at her cloak. His hands moved wildly over her. The others seemed to cheer him on.

The Avar straddled her and pulled down his dirty breeches. What must she do as a Christian girl of virtue? Anfelisia instinctively knew. She smiled longingly at the Avar. He nodded knowingly. He thrust his hips forward and downward to mount her.

Anfelisia seized his dagger and plunged it into his side. The Avar's eyes widened in confusion. He glanced to his left and saw the hilt of his blade protruding from his side. Anfelisia twisted the hilt up and down, skewering his innards. He slumped over her without a sound.

His mates cackled and whispered in approval of their leader's conquest. Anfelisia lay quietly as the Avar lay atop her. Her mind raced with what to do next. After some minutes, the calls from the other Avars changed in tone. She realized they each wanted their turn. She slowly drew the dagger from the body of her would-be lover and held it ready for the next. *I can take one more before they have me.*

After what seemed an eternity, one of the Avars scrambled over to her. He mumbled something to his leader. Hearing no response, he pulled him from the Anfelisia, and the lifeless form rolled into the wet grass, eyes staring glassily into the dark canopy.

A cry from hell erupted from the Avar. He drew his dagger and launched it in an arc at Anfelisia's bare breast. But she plunged her dagger into his belly and twisted it wildly in her panic. The Avar gasped a series of strange sounds and collapsed onto her. She struggled to push him off, but he was too heavy. A series of cries and the thud of boots came from the camp circle. Try as she might, she could not move the Avar. *This is the end. So be it.* She closed her eyes in prayer. *Take me quickly, o Lord.*

Then came more grunts and cries. She opened her eyes and, in the dim firelight, saw two of the Avars with spears protruding from their squat bodies. The others reached for their curved swords and darts. Two large figures emerged from the woods and began hacking the other Avars with Franciscas.

A voice called out in Frankish, "Be not afraid, girl. We are friends!"

The *Franciscas*, in the hands of Spad and Walla, made quick work of them in close quarters. All the Avars lay dead.

"Who are you, girl?" Spad asked as he pulled the Avar's body from her.

"My name is Anfelisia. I worked in the canteen at Fulda. Until the pig of a Bishop Willehad took me."

"What happened to him?"

"I don't know. A man named Fromm, a Norseman I met in the canteen, tried to save me from him. But Bishop Willehad's men managed to kill him, I think. Willehad was fleeing with me when the Avars appeared from nowhere. They left the fat bishop for dead. But one of them took his ears as a prize. If you had not arrived, they would have…"

Anfelisia began to cry.

Spad took her in his arms. "You are safe now. No one can get to Spad and Walla in the forest. We will keep you safe until we see what Lord Melchior can do."

"Lord Melchior! I helped him escape Fulda with his men. I hope he can end the misery that has engulfed Fulda and Frankland."

Spad gently placed her down. "Can you walk? Where we go, no pony or horse can follow."

Anfelisia gazed up at her two rescuers. "I have ridden to hell. I believe with God's help I can walk to wherever you lead."

S.W. O'Connell

Chapter 23

Fulda

The sun was not to be found on a day of threatening clouds. The pennant snapped rhythmically in the stiff winds that swirled through the battlements. Stilicho heard no chanting. It was mid-way between Lauds and Prime. The few monks on the walls knelt, holding well-worn psalters in silent prayer. The old warrior stood beside Baugulf looking down from one of the embrasures. The sight below dismayed them. A column of Avars slithered through the narrow winding streets of Fulda like a dark serpent.

"They are remarkably quiet," Baugulf said.

"It's their way. The Avar is like a night hawk in silent search of prey. They have their bellies full of it. In one move, Dgno has destroyed Melchior's forces and the Saxons."

"Not entirely, Count Stilicho. While you were defending the portcullis, I was watching. The *missus* left almost half his force back. For what reason I don't know…"

"Because he is the most skilled warrior in Frankland and Christendom, abbot. Dgno thinks he has won a war. But he has only won a battle."

"Melchior fell to their arrows and swords."

"I suspect he left Audeon in command. Karolus's blood will figure out a way to defeat the devils of the plains, as his father once did."

"My monks are praying with a fervor that you are right. I will pray for Melchior's soul."

Stilicho nodded glumly. He, in fact, had no idea why Melchior struck with just half his force. He was an old warrior whose experience told him to strike with everything at once. Never a time or place for guile. The sound of galloping hooves broke the morning silence.

Then the buzzing sound of the Avar voices filled the air. Stilicho could only make out one word from the babble. "Dgno!"

The Avar khagan wore his mailed helmet with a black kaftan over his chain mail and carried his bow high over his head. Behind him rode a score of retainers holding large banners of various colors. Dgno galloped through the streets. His horsemen turned their mounts and faced inward as their ruler rode between them. He worked his way to the church and monastery.

"The desecration begins," Baugulf said. He made the sign of the cross. "I should have stayed to protect the church… the vestments… the manuscripts…"

Stilicho watched tears form in the monk's eyes. "I thought you had them all moved to the fort."

"Not all… not all… perhaps one quarter."

"But you saved the most important."

"Who knows if I did? Perhaps those I chose were not the most important to mankind... not the most important to God."

"I can take my men and raid the monastery tonight. Perhaps we can retrieve some more of them."

Baugulf wiped his face with the long sleeve of his robe. "You know that will not be possible."

Stilicho did know it was impossible. "Nothing is impossible if God wills it."

Baugulf managed a smile. "You are right. Nothing is impossible to God. If he wills it. I believe he wills me to save the quarter. It would be a sin of pride to attempt more. Let us hope we can save what we have."

"Avars cannot take a walled fortress. That's why Dgno allied with the evil witch, Udela. Then he turned on her. He will have to move his horsemen on once he has his way with Fulda."

Baugulf stared a few moments with his hands clasped in prayer under his sleeves. Then he turned to Stilicho. "Why not assist God in this enterprise?"

"Assist God? How can we assist God, Abbot?"

"We should send a messenger out who can get past the Avars, avoid the remaining Saxon bands, and find Audeon."

***

A column of weary but determined men marched along the rutted road toward Fulda. Bands of Avars on small ponies raced around them but offered no resistance. The dull sound of Saxon war songs mixed with the steady beat of spears, swords, and Seaxes striking shields. A league from Fulda, they halted and formed a shield wall. Udela rode out from behind the ranks. Hrodger and four Haari followed her.

"We need more men. We cannot trust Dgno," Hrodger whispered.

"Are you afraid, my brave *Haari* chief?" Udela glanced at Varna, who rode beside her with two large bags across her saddle. "Besides, more warriors would have been a threat, but would not defeat his Avars."

"My men have made an accounting. The Avars have lost more than half their number—yet they are double ours."

"And still well mounted. I need them to feel superior. That is what he did to us. Struck us when we were at the point of victory and felt victorious. I aim to return the favor."

"By going to his bed?"

Udela's eyes narrowed, and her face darkened. "Whom I choose to bed is my choice. You must learn that quickly if you are to remain chief of my bodyguard. They say I'm a witch. I tell you. No mere witch will ever possess the power I have."

Hrodger hung his head. "I only meant I can kill the serpent for you if you wish."

"I ask only that if things fail... save the girl. Do not let the Avars have her."

A score of Avars galloped across the field and spread out before them.

"Here's our escort," Udela said.

They followed them through the town. The *Haari* stared in amazement. They had never set foot in anything more impressive than a peasant village. They marveled at the stone buildings that rose almost to the height of trees that seemed to block out the sky.

"Your first time in a town, is it not?" Udela asked.

"Yes, My Queen," Hrodger replied. "It must contain great treasures."

"Of a sort. But these hovels are simple Frankish cottages, not palaces. The church and monastery, on the other hand…"

They had come to the monastery gate. The Avar escort grabbed their bridles and led them into the main yard.

"Where is Khagan Dgno?" Udela asked.

"He awaits you in the chambers of the priests."

She nodded at Hrodger and dismounted, making sure she had the sack under her cloak and her dagger in her belt.

***

Melchior opened his eyes to darkness. His head throbbed. His limbs ached. The dank air told him he was in a chamber. He bent his head and saw dim lamplight from under a door. He tried to rise, but he could not. *Is my leg broken?*

After some hesitation, he moved it slightly. *Not broken.*

He could feel the sting and pain from at least a half dozen cuts and blows. *Nothing mortal.* The Avars had slashed and riddled him with darts, but none seriously. His *brunia* had saved him. He grasped at the silver cross. *Deus vult…*

He tried to recall what had happened, but his mind was a jumble of events. Some from the 8th century… some from the 20th… He smiled grimly. I have seen worse… felt worse… He heard the Avar guards chortling in their language.

He was thirsty — terribly thirsty. Thirstier than in the desert of *Afrika*. He noticed a wooden bowl next to him with some sort of liquid. Trembling hands managed to lift it to his mouth. He downed it, spilling some but getting most down. It tasted of blood mixed with sour milk. He recalled from somewhere that Avars lived off such concoctions. *So they want me to live. But for how long?*

"Are you there, *Dominus*?"

Melchior startled. "Who is that?"

The voice came from the next chamber. He realized these were monastic rooms for the monks with small windows between them for sharing things.

"It's Jurchen, *Dominus*."

"Jurchen! With you here, I know it's a sign. God willing, we'll fight our way out of here."

"No, *Dominus*. That's not to be."

"Of course, you are wounded. I saw you charge into a cloud of Avars. Where are your men?"

"All dead, *Dominus*. And I'm afraid I can't help you escape."

"I'm wounded as well. But we'll shrug off our pain just long enough to make our way out. We did as much, once before."

"That was different, *Dominus*."

"Yes, the others are not here."

"They're all dead, *Dominus*."

A shudder went through Melchior. "Cassyon too?"

"I saw an Avar arrow pierce his neck."

"Gaetano?"

Jurchen did not reply.

"Gaetano?"

"The last I saw of him, he was loosing arrows into the Avars. But he was surrounded. He can only be dead. They're all dead, or worse, like me."

"But you survived, and together we can…"

"No, *Dominus*. I… I'm blind." Jurchen whimpered softly. "Rather, I would die in combat. For God."

"I would rather you live for God. Are you sure? It's dark as Hades in here."

"They blinded me by… I won't repeat it. No matter. We'll both die soon. They said so. We are to be sacrificed for the Khagan Dgno's new bride—Udela."

Udela! The witch! Melchior cursed himself. His journey was to save Fulda and convert or kill the witch-queen. He had done none of that. He was the last, and the worst, of the *Missi Dominici*.

***

Udela entered a large room where the monks once took their meals. It held almost a score of long tables of rough oak. These were now filled with Avar chiefs who had come to celebrate the capture of the town, their victory over the Saxons and Franks, and the wedding of their khagan. The raucous laughter, the banging of tambourines, the whining of strange eastern flutes, and the pugnacious revelry of the men proved they had no trouble finding the abbey's ale.

At the far end of the room, Dgno raised his hand in a sign of victory. "Come to me, My Queen."

He, too, has been drinking. That could be exploited.

The room fell strangely silent as Udela walked toward Dgno with her head held high. These barbaric men of the east had never seen a woman like her: taller than any of them, slender, with fine white skin, golden hair braided to her hips, and fierce blue eyes. They all knew she was a sign from the gods.

"With a consort such as this, the Avars will rule the world," many whispered.

Udela sensed the power she held over these dwarf-like creatures. Her high bosom heaved in anticipation as she drew near. She knew her task would be difficult.

Dgno motioned her to sit beside him.

"Welcome, My Queen. Your husband has long awaited this moment."

"Awaited what?" she asked.

"Destroying a Frank army. Taking possession of what is my right, by conquest."

Her eyes glared at him. "You betrayed our pledge and attacked my bold Saxons, killing women and children and worse."

Envoy of the Lord

"I needed my Avars to be first in this alliance. I think we showed your warriors that Avars will rule all in this land."

"They are still a powerful force to reckon with."

"Your Saxons?" Dgno sneered.

"No, the Franks."

"The Franks! Bah! I have taken their capital in the east, Fulda." He waved an arm about.

"Their fort has not fallen," she replied. "There are rumors that their king Karolus comes with another army."

"I have taken you." Dgno licked his lips. "And I don't believe rumors."

"I am only taken by whom I wish."

Dgno smiled. "Before this day is over, you will wish. I have gold and silver from the monkish church. Jewels as well. These will be my gift to you."

"But I have no gift to give you."

Dgno smiled his serpent-like smile. "Your body will be my gift... and the bodies of your remaining Saxons. The men will besiege the fort for me."

"And if they don't?"

"Then they will see their beautiful queen and my beautiful bride torn apart before their eyes. After our wedding night, of course. Unless..."

"Unless what?" Udela did not betray her feelings. But for the first time in a long time, she sensed a loss of control. She felt fear.

"Unless you use your powers to destroy the fort."

Udela did not want to use her powers on a fort that had no value. Her powers had limits. Yet now she had an opportunity to unleash the hammer of Thor.

"I can only do it under certain conditions. My powers remain, so long as I take no husband!"

Dgno's eyes bulged in anger and disappointment. "What trickery is this, Udela? I know you have had men."

"Never a husband. Once a wife, my powers are lost. Think hard, my khagan, as to which you prefer – my powers or my body."

"I would think they are the same, but no, you are right. You, My Queen, are different. I must reflect on this. Meanwhile, let us celebrate. We have food, ale, and wine. A guest will join us."

"Who?"

A man in Frankish garb stepped from the throng with a twisted gait.

"Mallobaudes! I sent you as an emissary to the khagan. Why are you reveling with his warriors?"

"The great khagan has promised me more than you ever could, My Queen. With Lothar gone, it seems I am to rule what is left of Frankland. So, I am celebrating my new domains."

"You are a traitor to all, then!" Udela said.

"Which makes me a traitor to none," Mallobaudes said with a fiendish smile. He moved to the main table and took a seat.

"I believe it is time to revel, for we have much to celebrate," Dgno said. "In a month, we'll be at the gates of Aachen, while Karolus and the Saxon Widukind destroy each other along the Elbe."

Widukind! Udela blanched at the name. He was the one man in the world she feared.

Dgno quaffed a goblet of ale and turned to her. "Mallobaudes tells me he had the girl Genofeva. The one my warriors once took."

"She is held by the Nabo, o khagan," Udela said.

"But she was in Mallobaudes's possession, was she not?"

"Yes."

"Now Mallobaudes has given her to me. There are rumors that she is the bastard of Karolus. Holding her may prove prudent."

"I see."

"She is one of us," Dgno said smugly.

"What do you mean?"

"When we first held her, she had passed through the ceremony of the veil and the snake. That makes her an Avar woman, subject to Avar law and custom."

"I'm to be your wife. I demand to know. What is the custom?" Udela's mind raced for a way to exploit what Dgno was saying.

"It involves certain rituals. You will learn of them, all of them, in good time. You will be My Queen. But she will be first among my concubines."

"But the plan is to use her in some way against Karolus," Udela said.

Dgno took another gulp of the abbey's ale. His eyes moved in their slits like a lizard sizing up its prey. He motioned for more of the brew.

Udela realized he was craftier than she thought. *He means to make the girl the mother of his heirs to solidify his claim on Frankland.* She also realized that she must die as part of his scheme. *I must bring down the hammer of Thor sooner than later.*

Dgno suddenly sprang to his feet and danced across the wooden tables. His chiefs clapped and cheered as his feet thumped and the obnoxious sounds they regarded as music filled the air.

Udela suddenly felt a hand rubbing her thigh. She reached down and slammed Mallobaudes's wrist with a tin cup.

"Argh," he exclaimed and reached for her wrist.

Udela drew her dagger and drove the point into Mallobaudes's thigh.

He gushed with pain. "Argh… argh!

Udela's fierce eyes bored into him, deeper than the blade. "A thumb's length closer, and you would have died in minutes. As it is, I merely pierced your fat to gain your attention."

She sheathed the blade and threw him a cloth from the table. "Bind it tightly. It will mend soon enough."

Mallobaudes gasped. "You are a witch!"

"They call me that. I suffer traitors poorly, Mallobaudes. Now talk."

His eyes widened. "Talk of what?"

"Where is he?"

"Who?"

"Your cousin. The hated *Missus Dominicus,* as they call him. This Melchior."

"He'll kill me!"

"Who?"

"Dgno."

"Of course, he will, you fool. Once he has the girl Genofeva, you'll be in his way."

"Why... why do you want to know where Melchior is?"

"To speak with him before he is executed."

"Why?"

"I'm a witch. How do you think I derive my powers? There is great power in the spirit of the condemned."

She saw Mallobaudes's eyes struggling with what she said. She knew then he believed her tale.

"Give me some ale... or wine..."

She handed him a cup and filled it with ale. He swigged it and motioned for more. She obliged. Mallobaudes finished and wiped his mouth with the back of his hand. This practice disgusted her.

"Talk, now."

"Melchior and another prisoner are in the monks' chambers. Small cells where they pray and read... work on their manuscripts."

"Manuscripts?"

"They spend their days preserving the writings of the ancients... the gospels and the like... It's of no consequence to me if priests waste their days at such useless pursuits."

Udela regarded him. Mallobaudes was the most deceitful, conceited, venal, and treacherous Frank. *Were they all like him? Was his cousin like him?*

"You shall take me there."

"What? No!"

Udela's eyes bore into Mallobaudes like a *Seaxe* in an exposed belly.

He lowered his eyes. "Very well. When?"

Udela waved her elegant hand at the reveling Avars. "When the ale and wine and sour milk send them to whatever dreams such creatures have."

***

One of the Avars in the hall was not drunk. He sat quietly, munching on a chunk of bread with cheese and watching. He wore a tan kaftan and chain mail, heavy boots, and a helmet with cheek guards that covered most of his face. He waved off the slurred attempts to have him remove his helmet and join the feasting. Under the table, he cradled a bow across his knees. His mind raced with one thought. *Who to kill first?*

The night grew long. Most Avars had passed out and lay snoring, their faces in their vomit. A few staggered out to sleep among their ponies or to roam the deserted town for women. The lamps were beginning to dwindle. He saw the queen slip out, followed by the Frank, Mallobaudes. The Avar khagan, Dgno, realizing his bride had departed, stood up to pursue her. He staggered forward and almost fell, but his bodyguards held him.

The only sober Avars in Fulda. The chamber was now mostly in shadow. He rose from the table and, as fast as a hawk's swoop, loosed an arrow and then another into the lead guards. They staggered forward, clutching desperately at the shafts buried in their necks. Dgno hit the floor with a muffled thump. The other two guards drew their swords and came at him. They struggled over the tables and piles of stupefied warrior chiefs. A difficult shot in the darkness against men who were moving shadows. *Zhit... zhit.* Each clutched at the arrow in his throat.

He moved among the chiefs, dagger drawn, cutting throats as he made his way to Dgno. The khagan lay in a dark ring of his own drool. Those who awoke would blame the witch and the rogue Frank, Mallobaudes. He took his dagger and cut the tip of the khagan's right middle finger. He well knew Dgno would be hard-pressed to lead a tribe of warrior-archers if he could no longer draw a bow. Dgno merely grunted as the blade severed the finger, leaving it in his hand, and then passed out.

***

Mallobaudes led Udela through the monastery's labyrinth. Her limp, from a bad hip and a fresh wound, vexed her. They had little time. Her eyes took in their surroundings. The simple but elegant artwork of the abbey impressed but did not amaze her. The dim lamplight revealed array after array of frescoes, mosaics, and tapestries depicting a mix of biblical scenes, angels, saints, and dedications to the Christian God. For some reason, these portrayals of piety, devotion, and the divine sent a shiver down her spine. *What are these to me? I am no Christian?*

Their footsteps echoed as they passed a small chapel at the end of an alcove. A tabernacle sat on a simple marble altar, a red lamp burning brightly. Another shiver went through her. The hallway narrowed, and a steep stone staircase, inlaid with crafted oak planks, led to an upper floor.

"We'll need light. I don't know if his chamber is lighted." Mallobaudes reached for a lamp.

The Avar guards were squatting in front of a door in the Asiatic manner. As Udela and Mallobaudes approached, they rose and stood, blocking the threshold. They were barely visible in the shadows cast by Mallobaudes's lamp.

A guard issued a challenge. But she knew they recognized her as the khagan's future bride. Udela moved in closer and motioned for them to let her pass. She pointed at the keys hanging from the belt of one of the guards. He reached to protect them with his hands. She smiled seductively, plunged her dagger into his side, twisted upward, and watched the life drain from him. The other Avar lunged toward Udela. She gave him a piercing look. As she hoped, the Avar hesitated for a moment, giving Udela time to plunge the dagger into him. The lithe but powerful Udela killed two savage Avar warriors with but a dagger.

"Why look so shocked, Mallobaudes? I'm a warrior-queen, after all. Take the keys and open the door. Set the bodies against the wall. It will look as if they are squatting, as is their way."

Mallobaudes obeyed. She could see that the leg wound hampered his movement. Once the guards were propped up, he worked the key into the lock. After some rattling, the lock sprang open. The hinges creaked.

"Give me the lamp," she ordered.

Like a man mesmerized by something he could not quite comprehend, he lamely handed her the lamp. "As you command, My Queen."

His hands were trembling as she snatched the flickering light. Udela stepped into the room. It was small, and it smelled of what, she could not tell. The figure of a man was lying across a narrow bed. She took careful steps with her knife in one hand and the lamp in the other. Her heart raced with excitement. Her next actions would change the course of Christendom... and thus the world.

She stood over the bed. "Now, Melchior, so-called *missus dominicus*, I, Udela, shall make you the last of the *Missi Dominici*!"

Her dagger rose. In the shadowy light, she could see his eyes had been burned out of his sockets. "Is the mighty Melchior a blind man?"

Mallobaudes sputtered in shock and anger. "What? They blinded my cousin? I wanted him to see his own death coming."

The figure reached up and grabbed Udela's wrist. "You are indeed a witch from hell, sent by Satan to kill a blind man."

Udela was startled. It took all her might to free her wrist from the blind man's iron grasp. "So, Melchior the Frank, you speak the Saxon tongue as well. Shame the Avars blinded you. I too wanted you to look upon the face of the one who killed you."

"I care not if I die. I have prayed to the one true God and am ready. Better a day in heaven with no eyes than an eternity in hell with eyes."

"That's not Melchior's voice," Mallobaudes whispered.

"I don't care. I will send him to his Christian hell!" Udela plunged the dagger downward, but a powerful hand grabbed it from behind and roughly twisted her around, thrusting the tip of the blade so it caressed her breast. She swung the lamp at him, but his other hand grabbed her wrist, holding it as easily as if it were a sparrow's wing.

For a second that seemed an eternity, she stared into the dark stranger's eyes. She stared more deeply. At first, the eyes glinted with dark hatred, but then they softened. Udela's eyes widened as a thousand thoughts ran through her mind, spanning not a moment but a thousand years.

Mallobaudes drew his *Seaxe*. "This is Melchior, who hides in the shadows like a rat! I will gladly kill him for you!"

Mallobaudes lunged forward, the Seaxe pointed at Melchior's exposed back.

"No!" Udela screamed. Melchior released his hold on her. She stepped past him, and as Mallobaudes thrust the *Seaxe*, her dagger flashed. The point pierced his right armpit, deftly avoiding the chain links of his brunia.

Mallobaudes's eyes widened. He slumped to his knees, dark red staining his side. "I would kill the hated *missus* for you, and you do this? You are... a witch..."

"So they say. But you are a double traitor."

"Then I implore... turn your evil powers on Melchior. I die in peace knowing he is next."

Mallobaudes collapsed. His crippled torso lay crumpled in the shadows.

"Then die in peace." She stepped past his lifeless form.

Chapter 24

Incredulous eyes fixed on his face. The dagger, still warm with blood, clattered to the floor. "You are... Melchior?"

He gazed back with a mix of hate, fear, and shock. His pulse raced and his eyes narrowed. "Are you Udela?"

She lowered her eyes. "Yes."

Their forms came together in a rush of disbelief, longing, and passion.

Melchior held Udela's arms in his vice-like grip for what felt like an eternity. Her eyes met his, and they seemed to fuse in a maelstrom of charged emotion. Mesmerized, each felt their eyes read their minds, then their hearts, and finally, their souls.

At length, he released her. "Kristel? Is this really you?" Melchior asked in German. "Or some crazy illusion? Some twisted dream?"

Udela's eyes brightened, and her lips softened into a smile that answered his question. "Yes, it is I. How do you know...? But Matthaeus. Is it really you? How can you possibly be this Melchior, the *Missus Dominicus* who holds the Saxon nation in fear? I recognized the name, but I never thought..."

He was stunned. She had replied in German, not in Saxon or Frankish. He looked closely at her. Such beauty could not be created twice. "I am, indeed, Melchior, missus dominicus, and the last of the *Missi Dominici*. And you are Udela, the witch-queen of the renegade Saxons?"

Tears flooded her eyes.

Unable to stand it any longer, they fell together like a thunderclap. Melchior swept her into his arms and kissed her madly. She returned his ardor with a fervor neither had known before. Melchior had no idea how long they embraced. These were moments he had longed for and would never end if he had the power.

The rasping voice of Jurchen ended their idyll. "*Dominus*? What is happening?"

Melchior loosened his embrace and spoke in Frankish. "All is well, Jurchen."

"How did you get in here, *Dominus*?" Jurchen asked.

"The monks have trap doors between their cubicles. The Avars never checked for them. I did."

He gazed at the woman in his arms. "Kristel, you speak German. So if I'm not mad, it's proof that it really is you and that my thoughts about the future were not the rantings of a crazed man or poisoned dreams sent by Satan."

He caressed her, carefully running his fingers across her face. He recognized each crease and curve. "Yes, it is you," he said.

Her eyes teared again. "I, I was sent back to this desolate time and place for a reason."

"Then you are more fortunate than I. I was sent for no reason I can recall, just to see if I could make the… journey. Those Canadians… somehow would use me against the Bolsheviks in a war of shadows."

"As I was used, Matthaeus, by the Bolsheviks. They learned of the Canadian plot and used me to counter it. They sent me here to kill Melchior. I had no idea it was you. No idea I was sent to kill my only love. I… I have indeed become a witch. I have done evil, Matthaeus… true evil. They told me it was for the cause… which I was convinced was a good cause."

"What cause?"

"World socialism."

Melchior did not understand. "Why didn't you join me in Canada as planned? Why no letter? No explanation?"

"The Bolsheviks… Stasi agents and their KGB masters took me right after you left Germany. I was in a prison where they worked on me day and night. They told me I had special gifts and that they knew the Amis held my brother Klaus prisoner."

"Zet? A prisoner? I told you he died in the rubble at Aachen. The *Amis* didn't hold prisoners long after the war — the Bolsheviks did."

"They convinced me the *Amis* had him. Because of our powers. Our minds… They said he had the same kind of mind as me… That they only needed that power to protect and spread socialism. That they were the only ones who had stood up to Hitler and the fascists. That the West was no better than Hitler."

"And you believed them?" He paused for a second. "Of course, you did. *Ach mein Schatz.* They are masters of deceit and control. Did they harm you?"

"In the beginning, a little. Then they… There was a man they sent to me… to make things… better. They said he was a doctor, but he was too young and… he… he…"

Kristel began to sob.

"Say no more."

Melchior crushed her to his chest. He stared into the damp shadows of the monastery, seething with anger at what he knew they had done.

"They turned me into a witch. I am trained to kill without a second thought. Trained to manipulate. Trained in other things…"

"Your evil powers?"

She shook her head. They had an ancient manuscript that told of men from the east – from China — who brought black powder to Europe, destined as a gift for Karolus.

"Nonsense. Everyone knows Marco Polo brought gunpowder from the East in the 13th century."

"No, Matthaeus, everyone believes Marco Polo brought the first black powder to Europe. He was some centuries late at it. They knew these emissaries had spent some time traveling through the lands of the Saxons and never made it to Frankland. My first task was to find them."

"Did you?"

She nodded and closed her eyes. "I found them, and I killed them. As I was ordered and trained."

"Programmed is more like it."

"That's never an excuse for evil."

"Killing isn't evil in itself."

"It is when you take pleasure in it."

He bristled. "And did you... Take pleasure?"

"I took satisfaction in doing my job well. That I might somehow help my brother free himself from the *Amis*. That I was furthering the cause of socialism."

They programmed her. "This sounds like slogans straight from that club foot Goebbels, Marx, or Stalin. Or worse – that shit SED leader Ulbricht."

"Yes. I met him."

"Met who?"

"Walter Ulbricht. He dined with us the night before they sent me on this...as you say... journey. Ivan Serov was there too."

"The one they call "The Butcher" in the western papers?"

"Yes. He joined us. They made a big deal of this."

"Us?"

"The Stasi and KGB men who trained me and..."

"And..."

She averted her eyes. He knew better than to ask further. He knew enough from experience that people can be made so vulnerable that they respond to a person specially trained to exploit that vulnerability.

Melchior fingered her hair. Despite what she did, he knew she was not fully responsible. And he still loved her so. "That's all right Kristel... that's all right..."

Her body shuddered. "What do we do?"

"We are in an ancient monastery surrounded by savage Avars and your Saxons. And I have Jurchen to worry about. They blinded him."

After the two stood in thought, Kristel spoke. "I can use my... powers..."

"What powers?"

"I told you. I brought black gunpowder from the Orient, from China. It arrived long before Marco Polo, but it disappeared. History has no idea it disappeared into my hands. I use gunpowder to demonstrate my magical powers. I place a small amount in little cloth pouches and ignite them with a candle or lamp. The explosion is mostly noise and smoke, but it suffices to have them cowering. I tried to have my Saxons ignite a larger amount to blast open the gates to the fort, but the amount was not sufficient."

She placed the back of her hand against her forehead. "I've killed many people, Matthaeus. I fear I am truly a witch." She began to sob again.

"You were a tool of the Bolsheviks."

"I see that now. I was a tool in their grand plot. But still, it was I who did those horrible things."

"What plot?"

S.W. O'Connell

"Oh, Matthaeus, an awful plot. The Soviets wanted to change the course of history."

Melchior's eyes narrowed. He would not tell her that he hoped to as well. "History? How so?"

"By destroying Christendom... by destroying Karolus and his empire. So the march of history would not lead to a powerful German state led by..."

"Hitler?"

"Nor a Kaiser. Nor a King. Nor a president. And certainly, no *Führer*. But an eastern ruler. With the West as the outer rim of civilization and the East as the heartland. Somehow, they thought the East would then become the center of gravity. Yes... that is the word they used. Center of gravity... not western Europe."

Melchior laughed. "So they thought they could challenge geography?"

"I don't understand."

"One can challenge many things, Kristel: the mind, the body, ideas, even time —as we both have learned. But it is geography that governs how nations develop, which nations trade, which nations invade, and which nations are invaded. Man can challenge many things— but not geography. Only God can do that."

"God? I had no idea you were an ardent Christian."

He paused to reflect and then pulled out his cross. "I wasn't when I arrived here. But I am now. And as a Christian, I know you are no witch. Just a sinner."

"How do you know?"

He held up his silver cross. "This! A witch would have averted her eyes from the cross. You didn't."

"So what do we do, Matthaeus?"

"First, we pray. Jurchen was a priest. He can lead us. Do you remember your Latin?"

"Some."

Melchior switched to Frankish. "Jurchen. Queen Udela and I wish to pray with you. Can you lead us?"

"*Dominus?*"

"Lead us in prayer... then we can decide how to escape this place."

Jurchen sat up and then dropped to his knees and clasped his hands. Melchior and Udela did the same.

"*Pater Noster...*"

***

Stilicho's heavy boots paced the walls. He looked down toward the monastery. The revelry of the Avars had ended. The night was clear, and a faded moon could be seen. He turned his gaze toward the open plain where, hours earlier, over a thousand had fallen in mortal combat. He said a silent prayer for the dead... the Franks.

A monk standing guard challenged him. "You should be sleeping, Lord Stilicho," he said.

"My fighters are sleeping. Frank warriors can slay a man in mortal combat and sleep like a newborn. Meanwhile, I watch... and pray."

"You can join the others at prayers. Matins is over, but Lauds begins in a few hours."

The monk looked awkward in a *brunia* and with weapons that were no match for his slender, almost frail size. His pale brown beard was straggly, as was his hair.

"What is your name, monk?"

"Brother Giffin. I'm from beyond the Rhine."

"Flanders?"

"Yes."

"How old are you?"

"Twenty-five Easters, Lord. I've been a monk for five."

"You are no priest. Why are you here?"

"To transcribe the sacred word of God, as well as the words of the ancients. I'm skilled with quill, vellum, and parchment. I live to do this."

"Your family all serve the church?"

"My father is a freeman farmer. He served Karolus's father as a warrior. His father served the great Martel in the battles against the Umayyad invasion."

Solid Frankish stock, Stilicho thought. "Well, it's good you're here. Your blood will tell."

"We shall again fight?"

Stilicho looked down into the dark streets of Fulda. He could hear the snorts of the Avar ponies and the occasional scream of a girl or woman unlucky enough to have been taken by the Avars.

"I don't know. But if they come, I need your prayers and your arm. The Avars have seized the town. There are Saxons across the river. Not many, but enough to take this place. The *missus* is likely dead or worse."

"What should I pray for, Lord?"

"Pray that Audeon comes... that the *missus* lives and that the Khagan of the Avars dies. And after that, you may pray for a bountiful harvest for your father in Flanders."

"For my father in Flanders, lord?"

Stilicho grasped the young monk by the shoulder. "Because this is why we fight here and now. So men like him can continue in God's work. So the earth can yield God's bounty and people can live and honor God. So there can be a Christian peace across Karolus's domains."

***

Eager men in leather and mail lay in the deep grass, resting perhaps for the last time. Powerful battle horses grazed along a stream that fed the Fulda in a large glade known to few. Audeon walked pensively among the horses, listening to his men's snores as he pondered his next move. What that should be, he was unsure. The *missus* had fought a battle, but he did not know the outcome. Ordered to hold back, he felt like a coward, not a son worthy of a great father.

A sentry raised a challenge. "Who approaches?"

Audeon drew his broadsword and raced through the darkness towards the sounds.

"A Frank... a Frank..."

Audeon recognized Detleff's voice. "Let him pass!"

The figure who emerged from the dark shadows of the night nearly tumbled from his horse. His face was so covered in mud, blood, and gore that he was hardly recognizable.

"Lord Audeon..." Detleff panted. "I have ridden for hours to find you."

"Have you word from Lord Melchior?"

Detleff was exhausted. His eyes had the vacant look of a man who has given all and lost it.

"Yes and..."

"And? Speak, Detleff."

"There are many dead. The entire battle was destroyed."

"What of the enemy?"

"Hundreds of Saxons... hundreds of Avars fell. I left before the end. The *missus* insisted I ride to you. I did as ordered. But I feel ashamed."

"You followed orders—the orders of your lord. There is no shame in that. Now, what were Lord Melchior's instructions?"

"To warn our king-and-emperor. And to hold back until Karolus sends help or arrives with an army."

"I don't understand the reason to hold back. My battle could turn the tide for the Franks."

"The *missus* was quite clear, lord."

"And what of Lord Stilicho and Abbot Baugulf?"

"They still hold the fortress, but the Avars have taken the town. Now a force of Saxons is outside the town as well."

Audeon rubbed his chin. "This is a curious twist."

"Lord?"

"Avars in the town... Saxons in the field."

"Yes, Lord."

"What do you think, Detleff?"

"What do I think, Lord? I'm but a simple *miles,* a soldier. I don't think, I fight."

Audeon's face lit up. "Of course! You're right!"

"Lord?"

"We'll ride to Fulda at first light. If the *Dominus* is dead, we shall avenge him. If he's alive, we shall save him. We shall kill Saxons and Avars alike. We'll free Stilicho and the abbot."

"Yes, lord Audeon! You are truly the son of Karolus."

Audeon caught the nuance of Detleff's remark. His father would surely ride into danger when Franks and the church were threatened.

"Lord?" Detleff interrupted his thoughts. "What of the second part of the *missus's* command?"

Audeon pondered the question. He was new to making such decisions.

"Lord?"

"I'll send my two best *milites* to seek my father. But I shall lead this battle to Fulda at first light."

***

Dgno woke with a head that felt as if it had been kicked by a horse. He rose, wiping vomit from his face, only to have blood smear his chin. His eyes, blurred by darkness and drink, slowly focused, and he saw that his fingertip was a bloody stump. "Arrrrgh! Arrrgh! A thousand deaths! A thousand deaths!"

The khagan cast his eyes about the darkened hall. His chiefs began to stir, but slowly. He ran among them, kicking and cursing, even cursing in ways pagans dare not utter. Some of his chiefs roused more quickly at the blow. Others just lay there. He managed to rouse thirty cranky chiefs, but as they examined their comrades, Dgno realized almost half that number lay dead, their throats slit.

"What fiend from hell has entered the Avar circle?" He strode from body to body, turning over each slain chief. The throats were expertly cut. His mind burned with such hate that he forgot his finger. When he, at last, regained some composure, he grabbed a rag and tied off the bleeding digit. Then he grabbed a flagon of wine and poured it over the finger and finally over his head.

Otmak and a band of Avar warriors arrived to help.

"Chiefs, summon your warriors!" Dgno bellowed.

"What can I do, o khagan?" Otmak asked.

"Find twenty of our best warriors and follow me. This is the work of the evil witch, Udela. I shall make her my Queen and myself a widower on the same day. Then we'll storm the fort and kill every Saxon and Frank we see."

Otmak smiled. "Yes, my khagan speaks like a great Avar ruler. Blood for blood... flesh for flesh."

When the warriors assembled, Dgno addressed them. "Search every corner of this place until the witch is found. I want her alive, along with her companion. Only I will take my revenge. The warrior who deprives me of my vengeance will die a worse death, as will all his kinsmen."

The Avars raised their swords in approval. "For Dgno, and the death of our enemies!"

With battle cries echoing across centuries of war, the Avars marched off behind their leader. The sound echoed throughout the once-holy monastery like the barking of hell's guard dogs.

***

Melchior held Udela in his arms for what felt like hours but were only fleeting moments. They said little. He was still confused about how it all came together. Until the moment he saw, no, touched Kristel, he had still regarded his journey as some kind of dream. Now he wondered if his entire life had been merely an extended dream. *Could it really be her?* He drew in the sweet fragrance of her skin and hair. He touched her. Regardless of the century or millennium, it was Kristel.

From the darkness, Jurchen's voice broke Melchior's idyll. "Listen. They're coming, *Dominus.*"

With Kristel once more in his arms, he had forgotten poor Jurchen. "What did you say?"

"They're coming, *Dominus*. Take the woman and save yourselves."

"I don't hear anything."

"I have lost my eyes. So now my ears must work all the harder for me. The Avars are rousing. You must flee."

"I can't leave you here, Jurchen. Grab my arm, and I'll guide you."

"If we can make our way out of here, some three hundred of the best Saxons are waiting," Udela said.

Melchior retrieved the sword from one of the dead Avars and thrust it into his belt. Kristel secured her dagger.

"Come, Jurchen." Melchior extended his hand.

As did Kristel. "With two, we can make it with him."

"No, *Dominus*. Is there lamplight?"

"Yes, but why?"

"Douse it and flee with the woman. Just give me a sword. In the dark, I'll be on equal footing with the Avars."

The buzzing of what seemed like a thousand hornets began to echo through the halls.

"Hear it now? The Avars draw near. Go now, *Dominus*."

Melchior nodded grimly and placed his hands on Jurchen's shoulders. "You are a great Christian warrior, Jurchen. Greater than I'll ever be."

He fetched the Avar's weapon and placed the hilt in Jurchen's hand. "Remember that the point kills, whereas the blade merely hurts."

A sound that seemed like a cross between the howling of wolves and terrified bleating sheep rose in crescendo.

"Go now!" Jurchen said. "It is God's will!

Tears welled in Melchior's eyes. "*Vale*, my friend."

Melchior would never have left him. But when he looked at Kristel's pale face in the shadows, he decided to save her. The irony was not lost on him. His mission was to kill her or convert her. Now he could only convert her. But first, he had to save her.

Kristel doused the lamp. They slipped out of the chamber. Melchior turned the key, and the tumbler rattled shut. "It will take them some time to open it."

He and Kristel padded down the dark passage, away from the sounds of hell pursuing them. They moved down an ever-narrowing corridor that seemed to wind along the outer monastery wall. The damp smell filled their nostrils. They heard horrible buzzing-like screams and frantic pounding.

"The Avars found the chamber. When the pounding stops, Jurchen is done for."

Melchior took Kristel's hand, and they hurried down the dark causeway for minutes that felt like hours. Suddenly, they smacked into solid stone.

"We are trapped in the dark." But then he remembered his talisman. "The Ronson!"

"What?" Kristel asked.

"You were one of the few women I knew who didn't smoke. Ronsons were...are...will be... the lighters of choice. Here is mine."

He flicked open the lighter, and the small flame lit the darkness like a Roman candle.

"Matthaeus, look," Kristel said.

Along the wall to their left was the outline of a passage almost as high as a man. Melchior ran his hands along it. Halfway down, he felt a notch. He extinguished the flame and pushed the hilt of the Avar sword into the notch. A click snapped, and the stone doorway moved.

"The stone is a façade. This is a wooden doorway," Kristel said.

"You're right. Help me."

Together, they pressed, and slowly the heavy door eased inward. It opened into a large, vaulted chamber with lanterns still glowing. Before them stood a dozen wooden desks with ink pots still full of dark ink. The room was bright with ambient light from above. The smell that assaulted their nostrils was unbearable.

"What is this?" Kristel asked.

At half the desks sat the decomposing bodies of monks who had refused the order to evacuate, choosing instead to continue with their God-appointed tasks.

"A *Scriptorium*. The monks did their transcribing here. The Avars simply slew them at their desks."

Kristel covered her nose to smother the stench. She gazed upward. "It must be day, look."

Above them, along each wall of the chamber, were stained-glass windows, but every other window was tilted open, letting in subtle rays of daylight. The finely inlaid colors of red, blue, gold, and cream-white splashed the room with a rainbow of light. Unbridled beauty combined with unspeakable horror. Melchior locked the door behind them and, despite the urgency of their situation, examined some of the sheets of vellum that lay on the desks. The letters were large and very artistically drawn.

"Such fine calligraphy," Kristel said, running her fingers over one of the parchments.

"Yes, they were transcribing knowledge for the ages. This must be preserved." He looked at the corpses at their work. "And they must be avenged."

"But not now, Matthaeus. We must make our way from here. If the Saxons can strike the Avars while they are away from their ponies, we can destroy them. Dgno must still pay for his mistake, as well as his treachery."

She is indeed a warrior-queen.

Melchior took one of the lamps and led her from the chamber. They soon came to a stairway that spiraled downward in a tight spiral. They trod carefully down the damp stone steps. The stairs ended in a large room that opened onto the courtyard.

"The gate must be out there," Kristel said, pointing at a doorway.

Melchior carefully opened the door and surveyed the scene. In an expansive courtyard, he saw several score ponies tethered in circles, casually eating from crude leather buckets.

Kristel gently put her hand on his arm. "The Avars have them in circles, just as they do on the plains."

"I don't see any sentries."

"They're all looking for us," Kristel said. "If we can seize just two of the ponies, we might make it through the gate."

"If it is open."

Their eyes met with finality.

"If it is open."

Suddenly, their bodies came together as one in an outburst of long-unrequited love and passion. They kissed and embraced with devotion and longing neither could imagine, each knowing this could be their one chance to blend their souls.

She reached her hand under his *brunia* and tunic. "You have a scar?"

"A sniper at Normandy Beach," he murmured. "Or a Saxon sword point. What matter?"

"My poor Matthaeus," she said.

Kristel found the silver cross hanging from his neck. "Your cross?"

"A gift… from God. A priest gave it to me. If we survive this, it will only be through God's will."

"You are a Christian, then."

"I told you. I hope you will become one too. You were Christian, once."

"That was long ago, as well as in the future."

"Did the Soviets drive God from your heart?"

"The war drove God from my heart. The Soviets only made me realize it and act on it. When I arrived among the pagan Saxons, the transition was simple."

"So, you are a pagan?"

"I am. I mean, I was. But now that I have found you again, I can begin to think differently."

"Take your time, Kristel. I did. God will come to you when the time is right. Although he separated us, I believe now he planned to unite us all along."

"For what purpose?"

"We can never know God's purpose, only his love."

She nodded and held him closer.

Finally, they separated.

"Perhaps I know the purpose, Matthaeus."

"What do you mean?"

"There's something else. Something I overheard. Something I was not supposed to hear."

"What on earth?"

Kristel put her lips to his ear and whispered.

"That can't be… are you sure?"

"Yes. I'm quite sure. I think we should go now."

"Yes, My Queen. We'll talk of this later," Melchior said with a vaguely sardonic smile. But her secret was not lost on him.

They left the building's cover and made their way to the outer ring of ponies. The first few snorted and snapped at him. Melchior had never realized how small yet ornery the beasts were. He missed his warm blood. He found one that seemed compliant.

He took Kristel around her narrow waist and lifted her onto the pony.

"Can you manage this?" he asked.

She smiled. "I am a queen. Besides, you forget how often we rode together."

"But those were Thuringians—real horses."

"I think I can manage this pony."

As if on cue, the pony reared just a bit and snorted.

"Hold tight," Melchior cautioned.

He leaped onto the next pony and turned its head toward the outer gate.

The rings of ponies began to snort and stomp. Suddenly, Avar war cries erupted from the building. Melchior cracked his pony's rump, and it sped towards the gate. Kristel followed behind.

Melchior looked back at her. "Quickly! The gate is open!"

They sped through the gate and reached the town's outer buildings. The whinny sounds from behind told them pursuit was coming. Kristel pulled up next to Melchior. Her riding skill amazed him.

"My Saxons wait just across the river and over the rise."

"If they obeyed your command."

"They always obey my commands."

The tiny hooves thumped over the plank bridge, and the ponies began to scramble up the slope.

"My Saxons are just beyond."

The sudden *zhit – zhit* of arrows began to sting the air. An Avar band pursued them, letting loose shaft after shaft while on the fly. Just ahead, an Avar sat astride a pony. The Avar drew his bow and elevated it to establish his firing arc. Alarm surged through Melchior. He felt sure the arrow was meant for Kristel. *Avars never miss at this range!* He spurred his mount forward to shield her from the deadly missile.

The arrow was released and sailed exactly where the archer aimed, over their heads. It struck the lead Avar in pursuit.

The archer lifted his hood.

"It's Gaetano!" Melchior exclaimed.

"Who?"

"One of my men."

"Follow me, Kristel!"

They reached the summit and pulled back on the reins. Now Gaetano began shooting shaft after shaft at the oncoming horde. The Avars began to tumble from the saddle, but now their arrows began to reply.

"We must rally the Saxons." Kristel turned and looked toward the place where the remnant of her tribes waited. She cried out in disbelief. "Oh, my God... Oh... my God!"

"Don't tell me they are gone," Melchior said.

"No! They're all dead!"

Melchior looked at the circle of bodies. Almost three hundred lay slain behind a wall of shields.

Gaetano turned to Melchior. "The Avars ambushed them, *Dominus*. I watched the entire scene. Dgno left a force of more than three hundred in hiding. He was wary of being trapped in the town."

"Take the queen-witch and ride, *Dominus*. I will hold them off as long as possible."

"You must come too. I command it."

Gaetano shook his head. "I will not last, *Dominus*. No matter. I killed a score or more in the hall. Many of them were chiefs." He smiled grimly. "I deprived Dgno of his shooting finger— a fate worse than death for an Avar. But now it is my turn to die." He raised his arm to reveal an Avar arrow that had penetrated his mail tunic.

Melchior was enraged. He would not let another of his men die so he could live. He drew his broadsword. "Then I will fight here," he said.

Melchior spoke to Kristel in German, "I must save this man, as he tried to save us."

With a panther-like move, he struck Gaetano's pony with the flat of his sword. The creature bolted across the fields toward the wooded hills.

"Follow him, Kristel. I have another battle under Lord Audeon, Karolus's son. He's out there somewhere. Find him…"

An arrow suddenly struck Melchior's pony, sending it to its knees. The terrified creature twisted its neck, sending Melchior tumbling into the tall grass.

"Matthaeus, climb on with me," Kristel pleaded.

"No, it will slow your pony down. Flee now, Kristel!"

Two more arrows struck, this time sending her mount to the ground. Melchior now realized the Avars meant to take them alive. He placed himself between Kristel and the Avars. He drew his broadsword high over his head in a defensive stance. But they were quickly surrounded by more than fifty horsemen. The Avars sat silently. Their ponies snorted and stomped as if to plead for them to finish their work.

A single figure rode from the rear and spoke in halting Saxon. "I am Otmak. You have aroused the ire of the khagan, My Queen. Consort or not, I fear you will pay a price. But if you have this pig of a Frank surrender now, I am sure Dgno will show you some mercy."

Otmak spoke in a proud yet respectful tone. Melchior realized the Avars were still aware of and wary of the witch's powers. Hoping to save Kristel, he thrust his sword point into the soft, black earth.

Chapter 25

Stilicho and Baugulf had looked on helplessly while the Avars slaughtered the ring of Saxons and made off with the few women and children who had survived. Several *milites* joined them on the turret.

"I should lead my remaining warriors and seek God's justice," Stilicho said.

"They are just pagans," a *milites* replied. "What matter is it to us?"

"They are the Lord's children, pagan or not," Baugulf said. "Fulda is established to bring the Saxons and other pagans to God, but not like this."

"Our lord king-and-emperor might disagree, abbot," Stilicho said.

"Perhaps. But he, too, knows that it is better to baptize men than kill them. His *episcola* says as much."

***

The sentries on the tower stood their watch impassively. The early dawn light bathed the entire valley in a silver-and-copper tint. Suddenly, they saw the ponies gallop across the field, followed by a swarm of Avars thundering in pursuit.

"There, it's the *missus*!" one of the *milites* exclaimed. They watched Melchior's escape unfold before them in awe mixed with dread.

"I thought him dead," Baugulf said.

Groans rose along the line as the Avars captured and dragged Melchior and the Saxon queen back into the town. The monks began to pray.

"He will surely die now. We can't hold out much longer," Stilicho said.

"We will hold out as long as God wills it," Baugulf replied.

"I see the glint of steel, Lord," one of the *milites* said. "I fear more Avar bands returning. Our cause is hopeless."

A series of groans went along the line. Several of the monks dropped to their knees, whispering in prayer. Baugulf bent his head and prayed silently. When done, the old monk lifted his weathered face to the sky. "Let God's will be done."

Sensing something, Stilicho climbed to the top of the turret and squinted against the sun. His eyes teared from the piercing light as he tried to peer through the haze. More glints of steel. Then more.

"Lord?" one of the *milites* whispered.

"What?"

"How many Avars do you count?'

"The sun and the haze... my guess, perhaps one hundred men. But they are not Avars!"

"More Saxons?"

"No, Franks! The *missus* divided his force into two battles. I feared both destroyed, but it appears not."

The cry went up along the walls. "Praise be to God! Praise be to God!"

***

Audeon drove his battle hard. The trails through the forest were winding, leading up and down the hills. The footmen struggled to keep up with the mounted *milites*. He led the van, with Detleff at his side. The men who rode and marched with him were hardened veterans of more than a decade of fighting. Audeon realized that the missus had left the better troops with him. Now he had to lead them to relieve their master. He hoped he was up to the task.

At length, they came to an overlook. Before them stretched the valley and the town of Fulda. Father Thomas rode up next to them.

"How long now do you reckon, Detleff?" Audeon asked.

"The town is some four leagues away, Lord. But the distance is deceiving. If the footmen keep up, perhaps four hours."

Audeon looked up at the sky. Remarkably, it was blue, with a haze. "The sun is already in the west. We shall strike as soon as we arrive. It will be light enough. Strange that the sky would be clear everywhere, except for that strange-looking dark cloud before Fulda."

Detleff squinted. "That's no cloud, Lord."

"No cloud? What is it then?"

"Buzzards… vultures. They are feasting on carrion - the remains of the warriors who fell before Fulda," said Lebuin, an experienced veteran and commander of the mounted *milites*.

A shiver went through Audeon.

Father Thomas made the sign of the cross. "God, protect us from such devilishness and grant that if we must die, we receive Christian burials."

"I would rather you pray that we don't die, Father. I would rather you pray for victory." Audeon spurred his horse down the winding trail that led to the valley floor.

"He is truly Karolus's son," Father Thomas whispered to Detleff as they followed him.

After hours of riding, they reached the approaches to Fulda. Audeon deliberately avoided the area where the vultures still circled. It did not matter. Each Frank saw the vile creatures flocking to the east and knew what it meant.

Audeon raised his gloved fist.

"Why do we stop, Lord?" Detleff asked. "We are only a league from Fulda."

"I want the men and horses to rest. At dark, we shall advance and storm the town. I don't want to risk the Avar patrols alerting Dgno." Audeon's real reason was indecision.

"But Lord Audeon, time is of the essence. Any delay could put Lord Melchior at greater risk."

"If he yet lives, Detleff. I'm trying to think of what he would do in the same situation. He would not risk everything merely to save his own life. This is hard for me, but it's what I must do."

"I can say a Mass and grant absolution to the men, Lord," Father Thomas said.

Audeon nodded. "Let them eat what food they have and drink what wine or ale they have. Then an hour of rest. After that, you may attend to their spiritual needs."

Less than two hours later, the battle was assembled in full *brunia*, helmets, and shields. Father Thomas had finished the absolution and the Mass. Now he led the devoted Franks in the *Te Deum*.

Te Deum laudámus: te Dominum confitémur.
Te ætérnum Patrem omnis terra venerátur.
Tibi omnes Angeli; tibi cæli et univérsae potestátes.
Tibi Chérubim et Séraphim incessábili voce proclámant:
Sanctus, Sanctus, Sanctus, Dóminus Deus Sábaoth.

Before they could begin the second verse, a scout galloped up. "Avars! In the hundreds, a half league distant."

Audeon leaped onto his horse and raised his lance high above his head. "Prepare for combat! Form columns!"

The footmen, numbering just over a hundred, formed ten across and deep.

"Shields high!"

They raised their large oval shields over their heads, forming a canopy against the Avar missiles they knew were coming. But Audeon delayed the order to advance.

"We should attack, Lord," Lebuin said. He was a solid but weathered-looking Frank. "I campaigned for ten years with Karolus. Your father would attack, now."

Audeon ignored the rebuff. "Lebuin, you are the commander of the horse for a reason. Think! The Avars count on our reckless charge so they can retreat and devour us with their arrows. Take the mounted *milites* into those trees and wait. I will advance the footmen into the open and form a square. They will surround us. No matter. Let them tire their ponies and waste their shafts. Then charge."

"But how will I know it is time to attack?"

"You just said you campaigned for ten years with Karolus. Surely you learned something from that. Attack when they appear weary of the game. Then, I'll launch the footmen."

He dismounted and handed the reins of his charger to Detleff. "I will fight on foot alongside the Franks. Go with Lebuin. I'll reclaim my horse after the Avars are scattered."

"Yes, Lord," Detleff replied.

Audeon could see he was skeptical.

"Go with God, Lord," Lebuin saluted and led his horsemen to their hiding spot.

Audeon addressed the footmen, "Franks! Be brave and trust in God's will. Heed my commands and maintain your positions. We shall let these devils from the East weary themselves. Then I will order the attack."

Audeon could see the men were surprised, but they obeyed. Their sergeants soon had them positioned behind a small rivulet that fed the Fulda. Although he did not show it, he felt nervous. He had never led men in battle. Yet he was the son of the greatest warrior of his age, now thrust with the awesome task of stopping the hardened warriors who threatened his father's empire and all of Christendom.

Father Thomas approached. "Are you all right, Lord?"

Audeon gulped and nodded. "Pray for me, father. Pray for Frankland."

A drumbeat of hooves began to shake the ground. The Avars came into sight, which meant the Franks were in bow range. Audeon watched the first volley of arrows darken the late afternoon sky. Fortunately, the sun was at their backs, so the square was darkened by the shadows.

Yet soon the *zhit...zhit... zhit* began, and arrow after arrow plunged into the heavy bossed shields of the footmen.

Waiofar, commander of the foot, called out in a voice that instilled strength and courage. "Stay close together. If your mate falls, hold his shield too. Stay strong…"

Audeon smiled. Waiofar knew how to coax the last measure of discipline from men accustomed to reckless action.

Audeon's throat went dry. Beneath the canopy of shields, the men panted, their anticipation mingled with the thought of a sudden steel tip plunging into bone and flesh, with no chance to strike back. But finally, the hooves of the Avar ponies began to slow, and the drumming of arrows faded. The men on the edge of the square had planted their shields in a wall, so the trick of firing low did not work. The advantage of a determined defense rather than an assault, Audeon thought.

At last, he sensed it was time. He made his way to the outer shields facing east and glanced between two of them. The Avars, hundreds of them, were in disarray, and several chiefs rode along the line, trying to decide how to break the square. Hundreds of arrows surrounded them, their feathered fletching waving in the breeze like thousands of bird tails.

They must be running short on arrows. "Waiofar! Form wedge and advance, shields high!"

Waiofar echoed the command, and soon stout legs began edging forward. He nodded towards Audeon. "This is how Franks should always wage battle, Lord."

The men trod through thousands of shafts that made the fields about them look like a wheat field of deadly stalks. Their shields bristled with as many shafts, making the wedge look like a porcupine.

The Avars regrouped and now, with their terrible swords flashing, they galloped at the wedge. They spread out to surround the footmen. The frenzied horsemen buzzed like a swarm of angry bees, which, coupled with the endless drumming of hooves, struck fear into the hearts of their enemies from the Urals to the Danube.

"Halt! Shield wall!" Waiofar ordered.

As one, they locked the shields, and now the wedge became an iron triangle.

"Sound the *Barritus*!" Audeon ordered.

Outnumbered almost ten to one, the Franks let loose their own intimidating war cry. It began as a low, ominous murmur, then slowly gathered into a terrifying bellow, like the sound of a stampeding elephant. The Avars rode up to the wall, and hundreds of sword blades struck madly at the shields. The Franks, for their part, plunged their spears into horse or rider as the opportunity arose.

Soon, scores of Avars lay dead or dying. By the dozen, more Avars broke off from the attack, sensing the hopelessness of breaking the triangle. Their chiefs rode madly back and forth to rally them and renew the charge. But the attacks grew smaller and less determined. Throughout the fray, the *Barritus* droned on—a dirge to the death of the hated Avars.

The *Barritus* was also the signal for Lebuin to strike.

"Form a line and lower spears," Lebuin ordered.

The mounted *milites* lifted their shields and trotted until they reached the wide-open spaces where the Avars were scattered.

Audeon sensed he had them. "Charge!"

The horses charged straight at the Avars, who were struggling to regroup. Despite their chiefs' orders, the Avars broke when they heard the thundering hooves and saw the glint of metal coming at them like a storm across the steppes. The Franks plowed through the few who dared remain. Spear tips pierced Avar mail, plunged through shields, and skewered more than two dozen. The Franks then galloped in pursuit, broadswords waving, cutting any stragglers to pieces.

Detleff rode up and handed Audeon the reins to his horse. Audeon mounted and nodded to Waiofar.

"Form line and move forward," Waiofar ordered.

As the *Barritus* grew louder with each moment, the wedge formed into a line, and as one, they stepped forward. The Franks cut and slashed with broadswords and jabbed with spears at any wounded Avars lying in their path. They moved with great deliberation toward the darkening towers of Fulda.

"You have achieved a great victory, Lord," Detleff said. "I'd say you broke a thousand of them. That is more than the *missus* faced."

Audeon paid no heed. Their work was just beginning.

***

The heavy ropes burned into Melchior's arms, legs, and midriff. He strained against the knots, which tightened with each move. The Avar khagan sat on a makeshift throne with Kristel at his side. Melchior tried to make sense of things. When he thrust his sword into the earth, all went black. He awoke trussed and bound in a chamber full of ranting Avar chiefs. He could not understand the babel, but their intentions were clear. They were deciding his fate, not his death, but how he would die. Several jumped around, demonstrating different ways of dispatching him. His stomach churned as he wondered how Kristel had come to be sitting next to him.

Finally, Dgno signaled for silence, and the hall fell still. Dgno spoke in Saxon, which Melchior understood. "Well, I finally have you where you should be, Lord Melchior, *Missus Dominicus*. Are you ready to meet your Christian God?"

"I defy you!" Melchior blurted. He felt foolish using a remark he probably remembered from some old American film. But then, it was what he felt.

"So you do," Dgno chuckled. "Regard my chiefs, Melchior. All veterans of a hundred skirmishes over twenty years. We have fought the Saxons. We have fought the Byzantines. We have fought the Mussulmen. We have fought the Slavs. We fought the Bavarians. We have fought the Lombards. We have fought your Franks. All have defied us, yet here we are. About to pillage the first of many Frank towns."

"We killed hundreds of your men. We killed hundreds of Saxons, and you, it seems, killed the rest. How do you suppose you will have enough to take on our great king-and-emperor?" Melchior demanded.

"My scouts tell me he is engaged in other places. That you were sent here as a diversion, well, this was my little diversion. I have another thousand warriors riding here, even as we speak."

"That's a lie," Melchior said. But he feared it was not a lie.

"It's no lie, Lord Melchior," Kristel purred. "The khagan is craftier than all the wise men of the west."

He looked in disgust as Kristel stroked Dgno's arm. She averted her eyes from his. *My God, what a fool I have been.*

"My brave queen struck you down, Melchior. She spared my warriors the trouble of subduing you. For that act of bravery and loyalty, she will ride at my side. I will take two wives. Udela will be my consort, while the girl they say is Karolus's offspring will be my second and bear my children."

Melchior could not believe his ears. "You have Genofeva?"

Dgno signaled, and from the recesses of the chamber, several men dragged the young girl before him. She looked defiant, not fearful.

"The Saxons held her, but we found her with the other maidens. Since she was already an Avar, she lives. The others provided a needed feast for my warriors' lust."

"I challenge you to combat!" Melchior bellowed. *My God, another mindless statement.*

Dgno smiled. "Normally, I would accept such an offer. Since the preferred weapon for the challenge is the bow, I would kill you in an instant. Even with my string finger missing."

Melchior looked once more at Kristel. She avoided his glare. *Was her earlier passion a ruse? A dream?*

Dgno stood and began pacing back and forth. "So... how should you die? Some of the chiefs want the darts to suck the lifeblood from you slowly. Others want arrows. A few want you to hack to pieces, while others want you torn apart by the ponies. So many ways. But I have decided on a plan."

Dgno once more seated himself by Udela. "You, Lord Melchior, so-called *Missus Dominicus*, will burn on a pyre of wood placed at the gate of the fort. We'll let the fat of your flesh help open a way into the fort where we will kill the soldiers and monks who are hiding there."

Dgno then rattled off a series of commands in the Avar tongue. Cries erupted as they dragged Melchior, chair and all, from the chamber.

Melchior saw Kristel stroking Dgno's arm and whispering to him. His heart churned with a mix of despair, loathing, and love. "Kristel! I forgive you for this, but do not betray Christendom to this creature of Satan."

His voice was drowned out by the thunderous cries of the Avars, excited by the prospect of roasting a hated victim before the eyes of his fellow Franks and making him the instrument of Frankish deaths. Melchior did not see the messenger whispering in Dgno's ear.

***

Stilicho watched from the safety of Fulda's fort. He yearned to be in the midst of the battle, giving orders and leading good Franks against a hated enemy. He also wondered who had performed such a feat. About one hundred Franks smashed many hundreds of savage horsemen in the open field.

"Dgno's secret force has not only been revealed, but it has also been destroyed," Stilicho said.

Baugulf grunted. "There are still almost half a thousand here."

"But Avars cannot hold a town. And if they do, we'll sally out and take them from behind."

"I'm not sure we'll be in time, Lord Stilicho."

"In time for what, Abbot?"

"Look."

The Avars had dragged Melchior, who was now spread-eagled on a great oak board. They raised the board so that Melchior presented a target with his arms and legs forming a great X.

"They will have target practice with Lord Melchior!" Stilicho could stand the waiting no longer. He donned his helmet, gripped his shield, and drew his broadsword. He descended the stairs. His men followed him, as did a few of the monks.

"Throw open the gates!" Stilicho commanded.

"No!" Baugulf commanded from above. We cannot risk losing the manuscripts to save one man. Even if it is the great *Missus Dominicus*."

"That man saved you from Lothar's evil scheme, and now you would watch the Avars make sport with him?"

"This is what Dgno wants… to lure you into opening the gates. I can't risk losing the manuscripts. The legacy of the church… and the world… is at stake."

Stilicho's face darkened. His Christian piety was gone, replaced by a savage bloodlust that traced back to the first pagan Franks emerging from the dark forests of the east.

"Open the gate!" he ordered.

Four of his men slid the great bolt and pushed open the great wooden gate, their shoulders high. Stilicho stepped out. He saw Melchior a quarter-furlong away. "I'm coming, *Dominus*!"

Stilicho rushed across the bridge. His five men followed with two of the armed monks.

A band of Avars galloped from a nearby stable, their ponies churning dust in the yard, obscuring Melchior. The Avars halted. The dust cloud slowly rose and wafted off into the late afternoon sky.

Stilicho could see Melchior. Then he saw Dgno spur his horse before him and halt.

"You are the great warrior, Stilicho?" Dgno asked.

"You know who I am."

"Surrender the fort, and I will let the *missus* you cherish die a quick death."

"I just saw your army destroyed by Franks. You must surrender to me."

Dgno's eyes shifted left to right in rapid succession. Stilicho could see that his comment made an impression on the crafty Avar.

"I still have hundreds of my best warriors in hand. As for the others, they just made sport as we often do. Most escaped and are regrouping. By dark, I'll have over one thousand men. Those outside will torment your Franks. Those with me will burn you out... after we kill the *missus* before your eyes. Look..."

Dgno drew his bow and notched an arrow at the missus so quickly that Stilicho scarcely saw it. The arrow flew with a *zhit*... striking Melchior in the shoulder. Stilicho cringed when he saw the blood pour from the wound. But Melchior did not cry out.

A true Frank...

"With your surrender, I can end this with a shot into his eye." Dgno smiled as he loosed another shaft, sending its point into Melchior's thigh.

Stilicho saw something moving across the courtyard. *Udela!*

He recognized the evil queen and witch from the descriptions he had heard. She wore her black leather garments and had her golden hair plaited down her back. *If I move quickly, I can kill this serpent of an Avar and the witch.*

Stilicho rushed at Dgno with his broadsword at the ready. "*Deus vult!*" His men followed behind.

Dgno's belly rumbled with laughter as he drew his bow. The arrow caught Stilicho in the chest, but his *brunia's* mail rings dulled the impact, and the point barely pierced his breastbone. With bold strides, he reached Dgno, but then a swarm of Avars on foot surrounded him and his followers. The Franks hacked and stabbed like bears pawing at a pack of snarling wolves. Avar after Avar fell to blows and thrusts. But soon, the numbers overwhelmed the Franks. One by one, Stilicho's brave followers fell. The Avars took the time to slice off ears and noses in a wild orgy of blood.

Stilicho had taken blow after blow, but finally sank to his knees, panting and heaving from exhaustion and frustration. The circle of buzzing Avars suddenly quieted and parted. He looked up into the face of Dgno, half-hidden by the bow aimed at him.

"The Khagan of the Avars can be merciful, brave Frank," Dgno said before he loosed his arrow.

***

Melchior viewed the carnage in rage and frustration. He tried to undo his bonds, even struggling to free his limbs, pierced by Avar shafts. When the throng of Avars parted, he both prayed and cursed for a way out. He prayed for the cross and the sword. Through tears and sweat-stained eyes that stung like briars, he watched the noble but simple Stilicho sink to his knees. He saw the laughing Dgno loosed an arrow that struck the brave Frank in his left eye, sending blood and gray matter squirting in all directions, as his torso flopped into the dust.

"God have mercy," Melchior whispered.

Melchior heard the Avars cheer as Dgno carved Stilicho's ears and nose from his body.

"Now let us dance the dance of victory," Dgno exulted.

With whoops and yells, the warriors surrounded him, waving their bows in the air in near delirium.

"God have mercy on Frankland," Melchior whispered.

Suddenly, a wet cloth wiped the sweat from his brow. Kisses covered his face.

"Kristel!"

"We have but moments, my love. The Avars will seek me and finish you once they are done brutalizing your Frank warrior. I struck you with a stone to save you, Matthaeus. Forgive me. But the Avars would have slain you then and there. I have been playing Dgno's game, but it is useless. He has found my power."

"Your power?"

"My stash of gunpowder. It was in a chest with Radka. The beasts killed her, and worse, when they took the Saxon camp. My powder was with her."

Melchior's mind raced for a way out. "How much?"

"Perhaps fifty pounds. Perhaps more. I don't really know."

She drew her dagger. For a split second, he thought she would plunge it into him. Instead, she gently cut the leather strips binding his hands and feet. Then she yanked the arrows from his limbs. He grimaced but did not cry out.

. "Where's the powder?"

"They secured it to the plank right under you. Once they filled you with arrows and relieved you of your ears and nose, they were going to carry this plank with you and the powder and blow the door."

"Does Dgno know how to use gunpowder?"

"No, but he knows I do. It's the only reason he keeps me alive."

"*Das Schwein...*" Melchior gently moved his limbs. "We can't let them do this."

"We just need time. A messenger informed Dgno that his other army, nearly a thousand strong under his best chieftain, was routed by a Frank force marching here."

"Audeon! Leading the second battle. They must be planning on striking tonight."

"That is what Dgno fears. Thus, the desperate gamble. He hoped to lure all the Franks from the fort, but only a handful challenged him."

Melchior laughed. "The rest are monks dressed as *milites*."

Kristel continued to wipe his face and stroke him tenderly. "Then they will slaughter them all if they blow the gate," she said.

Melchior stiffened. Darkness was still a few hours away. He realized there was only one way to stop Dgno.

"Reach under my tunic, Kristel," he said. "My right arm is stiff."

She did as he said. "What?"

"My talisman, the Ronson. And my cross. Kiss the cross."

"What?"

"Kiss the cross and swear to me you are not a witch and will become a follower of our Lord Jesus Christ."

"I will follow you wherever you go, Matthaeus... become whatever you are... my love."

She kissed the cross with a tenderness he did not expect. Then she kissed him on the lips with a passion he had only dreamed of in his worst nights in Canada. When she released him, she took the cross and kissed it again. "I pray your Lord Jesus protects us... protects you."

"Pray for Frankland, Kristel. It is our only hope in this world."

She kissed him again. They could hear the Avars' roars as they celebrated their khagan's triumph over a great Frankish warrior.

"Take my cross, Kristel," Melchior said. "God will protect you."

"I don't need it, Matthaeus." She reached deep into her bosom and pulled out a small white gold cross of fine handiwork. "It was my grandmother's, *Oma's*. She was very devout and gave it to me just before she died."

It was elegant white gold, finely engraved in German, "*Gott schuetz Dich.*" Made in the 19th century — not of this time, he noted.

"Then let us exchange crosses as we may never exchange rings."

She looked at him with surprise but did as he asked. He took her cross, and she took his. Then they handed them back. When she tucked her cross into her bosom, he kissed her one more time.

"Now go, my love."

"Go?"

"Escape and make your way to Audeon. You are the only hope Fulda has. Tell him to attack as soon as he hears the sound."

Kristel gave a suspicious look.

He smiled knowingly. "Tell him to wait for the hammer of Thor to strike."

She looked at him lovingly and began to weep. "I will... do as you command... Lord Melchior, *Missus Dominicus*."

She placed one last, tender kiss on his lips… then his forehead. Then she handed him her dagger. "You may need this when you make your escape. *Ich habe dich lieb, Matthaeus.*"

Before he could say anything, she bolted towards the shadows gathering in the courtyard. The sun was still just over the horizon, but the sky had clouded once more, and rain began to pelt the earth. *Good… the damp earth will slow the Avar ponies.*

Melchior knew what he had to do. He had to reach the powder and scatter it so the rain would soak it, robbing it of its power. He mused that God had a solution for everything. And despite man's mad scheming, it was usually right before us in nature. He slowly slid himself down from the oak planking that was to have been his bier and pyre.

"Melchior!" He heard the lizard-like voice of Dgno spit out his name. The khagan walked towards him with his sword in hand. Suddenly, one, then two Avar darts plunged into his chest. He staggered from the impact.

Dgno raised his hand to signal his men. "No more darts! I want to earn his ears and nose before we lash him to the gate with the witch's powder."

Dgno's blade stung like an adder's bite. He struck once, then twice. Melchior slid from side to side, but his legs and arms throbbed with pain. He gasped as blood oozed from the darts. He knew he had to get under the sword. When Dgno's blade flashed a third time, he moved with all his strength and grabbed the Avar's wrist. Dgno's fingers clutched his throat and squeezed with a grip as strong as a vice.

Melchior felt his windpipe going. He struggled desperately for air. The sweat and tears blinded him.

Dgno's lizard eyes bore into him. "Killing you with my hand brings much more pleasure than any blade could give. I hope it's the same for you, Melchior."

Melchior's eyes widened. He knew he was staring into the closest thing on earth to Satan.

"*Deus vult!*" He uttered with his last breath, plunging Kristel's dagger into Dgno's left armpit and through his heart. Just as the Canadians had taught him.

Eyes wide in disbelief, Dgno released his grip.

Melchior blurted in English, "Killing with the blade is more efficient."

Dgno staggered back. He fell forward with blood spurting into the rain-soaked dirt at Melchior's feet.

"Kill the Frank! Kill the Frank!" The chant rose from over a hundred angry voices.

Melchior did not understand their tongue, but he knew what they wanted.

The throng of crazed Avars charged him, swords flashing and darts streaming through the air. He ducked behind the oaken planks as the missiles flew at him. They began to hit, each sharpened point striking deep into the wood. He had but seconds. No dagger. It was in Dgno's side. He reached feverishly and found the sack of powder, securely stretched across the rear of the planks.

"*Verdammt!*" he exclaimed, in German. The sack was waterproof. He could see several Avars brandishing pitch torches. He realized it would take more rain than this to extinguish them. He glanced at the gate some a quarter-furlong away. They would have to drag this there to do any damage to the gate. He knew they had more than enough men... he knew.

Knowledge can be dangerous... But to whom? The Avars now swarmed around him. Darts flew. Another grazed his shoulder blade. He reached into his tunic and pulled out the cross, kissing it. He then did the same with his talisman. But then he flicked open the Ronson and let the spark fly. He smelled the alcohol and felt it on his fingers, just as he would at Aachen...

He flicked it again, and a tongue of flame erupted. *"Deus vult!"*

He touched the flame to the sack. The Avars began tugging at him, but he held on to the planking as only a desperate man can. Despite the pain in his limbs, he kicked and kicked. He smelled the sack begin to burn. *Steady now.* He held tight despite the tugging and the slashes of the Avar blades. With each slash, he held on tighter. He grew stronger. He smelled the powder as the Ronson's flame reached the sack, sparked, sputtered, hissed, and then flashed and boomed like a thunderclap from hell.

Chapter 26

Baugulf's crucifix chain dug deep into his fingers. He watched in horror as the Avars cut down Stilicho and his men, as if butchering sheep. In some ways, Baugulf felt that was just what happened, lambs to the slaughter... but lambs of God. Yet they were simple warriors doing their duty as Franks and Christians. Just as he had done his duty by securing the gate behind them. He had saved the fort and thus the manuscripts. A thousand years of knowledge and a direct link to God's word was no small prize to preserve for Christendom and the world.

"Pray for those brave men," he said.

Several of the monks already had their heads bowed in prayer. Not just to seek God's help, but to avoid watching the scene of carnage below. Baugulf knew most understood it was a portent of what would soon befall them.

"Look there, father," Brother Giffin said with a quaking voice. His finger pointed at the oak planking and where the body of Melchior lay bleeding. Who is that? Is that a woman?"

"That is no mere woman," Baugulf said calmly. "It must be Udela, the Saxon queen-witch, and consort to Dgno."

"She is going to kill the *missus*!" Giffin exclaimed.

The monks broke from their prayers, and all eyes fixed on the scene below.

"She will surely use her magic on him, the witch," several said.

"Pray not," Baugulf commanded. "Pray for God's help. It is the only recourse."

The monks all lowered their heads in prayer. All but Giffin, who, along with Baugulf, watched as the witch tended to Melchior.

"Is this some sort of spell she is preparing?"

"No, Brother Giffin, I do not believe so. They are talking and..."

"Is she breathing her evil charms into his body, Abbot? Is she stealing his soul?"

Baugulf stared intently. "Perhaps, Brother Giffin. But perhaps he is saving her soul. It works both ways, you know. The sacred can triumph over the profane."

"*Deus vult*," Giffin whispered.

"Exactly, Brother," Baugulf said. "If God wills it."

Griffin squinted. "She's leaving him. Running into the shadows. Running back to join the demons from whence she sprang."

"Perhaps not. Pray not, Brother Giffin." Baugulf focused more intently, seeing her steal onto an Avar horse. "Prayer is your only weapon in such matters."

"The Avars are attacking the *missus*, brother!"

The monks raised their eyes and watched as Melchior fought and killed Dgno, then frantically struggled against the scores of Avars who overwhelmed him. Melchior disappeared beneath the wooden planking. They watched the Avars tug madly at his feet.

"Pray for the *missus*," Baugulf said. "This may be your last time to beg God's intercession. For if they take him, they take the fort."

A terrific clap of thunder, like none they had ever heard, erupted in a huge flash, followed by a cloud of smoke. The ground and the fortress walls shook with the impact. Shards of planking and splinters of wood flew in all directions, as did the limbs torn from almost fifty Avars. A pair of hands flew through the air and landed on the battlements — burnt black but with fingers still displaying rings taken from victims long before.

The monks all fell supine on their bellies in prayer and supplication. Many held their ears. Others covered their eyes.

"The end of time! The end of time!" several whimpered.

Only Baugulf and Giffin stood in silence over what had just transpired. Pieces of the planking, along with clothing and flesh still burning, littered the courtyard.

As the last bit of Avar flesh slopped onto the muddy ground, Baugulf clasped his hands in prayer and spoke. "Melchior has saved the transcripts and history. Thanks be to God."

"Thanks be to God!" Giffin replied with a smile, slowly coming to his face.

The other monks rose to their feet, dropped their weapons, and clasped their hands in prayer as well. "Thanks be to God!"

***

"Lord, someone is approaching. On an Avar pony."

"A sole Avar would never approach us. Ride out and see who it is," Lebuin said.

A few minutes later, the *milites* returned, leading the Avar pony and its rider — Udela.

Audeon rode up. "Lebuin, I am told there are Avars about."

Lebuin shook his head. "I've never seen an Avar, nor any woman, as beautiful, lord."

Audeon looked at the prisoner and agreed with Lebuin. "Who... who are you? How did you ride here from Fulda, and on an Avar pony? An Avar would kill before giving up his mount."

"You know me as Udela, queen of the Saxons... former queen of the Saxons. Lord Melchior sent me."

"Melchior? Lord Melchior lives?"

"For now. But the Avars are torturing him and plan to use him to blast their way into the fort."

"Blast?" Audeon was trying hard to take it all in. "What do you mean? Blast?"

Udela shook her head. "Never mind. The situation is urgent. He said you should attack the Avars at the sound of Thor's hammer."

The sky suddenly erupted in what seemed to Audeon like a massive roll of thunder.

"Thor's hammer!" he exclaimed. "Lebuin, follow me with your men. Waiofar, follow in a column with the foot. We must fight our way into Fulda at all costs! The *missus* needs us!"

Audeon spurred his horse along the plain toward the river and the town. Detleff rode at his side. Lebuin followed, leading Kristel behind him on the Avar pony. When they reached the town, they found no Avars guarding the bridges. They rode down the narrow streets and passages until they reached the courtyard outside the fort. It was almost dark, and the stillness was uncanny.

"It's like the netherworld," Lebuin whispered to Audeon.

Audeon made no reply. He tried to take it all in. The stench of dead and burning flesh, smoking wood, and traces of another aroma he could not quite place.

"Where is your consort, Dgno, Queen Udela? Where is the *missus*?" Detleff asked.

She was crying. "I think Lord Melchior sent the Avars back to the hell that spawned them."

"Did he use magic? Did you use your magic?"

"No magic. Just the will of God. He was going to fight them while I summoned you. They planned to use him to take the fort. They slaughtered a small band of Franks who came out to rescue Lord Melchior."

Audeon and his men went through the courtyard, gathering the scattered body parts. They knew something terrible had happened. The gate of the fort opened, and several monks paraded out, carrying torches.

"Abbot Baugulf!" Audeon dismounted and took the monk's hand. "You are safe."

"Yes, thanks be to God. The situation seemed quite hopeless. The Avars had the *missus* prisoner. They slaughtered bold Stilicho and his brave men. The *missus* was near death when this woman intervened. We watched from the battlements."

"What did you and the *missus* do to wreak such havoc? To bring a thunderbolt down to slay the Avars?" Audeon asked.

"She used magic for sure," Lebuin said. "The more beautiful the witch, the stronger her powers."

"I'm a Christian, not a witch."

"The Saxons say you are."

"Perhaps I was a witch... once. But my Saxons are gone. In that, the serpent Dgno succeeded."

Several of the *milites* recoiled. Their piety was only overpowered by their superstition.

"But I pledged to Lord Melchior to live as a Christian." She reached into her tunic and pulled out her cross.

Father Thomas, who had just arrived with the footmen, spoke. "That is proof she is no witch."

Baugulf declared, "The bolt of thunder was the will of God and the hand of God. Did I not have all my monks praying for his divine intervention?"

"So, where is My Lord Melchior? Where is the *Missus Dominicus*?" Audeon asked.

"Dead, as are all the *Missi Dominici*," Waiofar said.

A tear came to Audeon's eyes. "He was the last of the *Missi Dominici*."

Udela had buried her hands in her face and was crying. "After finally finding him, I lose him. It is fit punishment."

"You loved him," Baugulf said. "You knew him. I could see it even with my tired old eyes. The way you both moved… together. Even facing death, your love was evident."

"I loved him. Yes… Did I know him…? I…don't…"

"I declare this woman no witch. I take her word that she is a Christian. Meanwhile, it is time to settle your men."

"No abbot. I would like you to baptize me."

"So, you have not been baptized, Christian?"

"I was, abbot. But not yet."

"You speak in riddles. But I shall baptize you. Then we'll say Mass in the monastery chapel. After that, Audeon, your men should eat and rest. For tomorrow, they must ensure the Avars have headed east. While my monks have much to clean and repair."

Audeon bowed. "As you wish, abbot. And tomorrow I will search for Lord Melchior."

"What do you mean?" Baugulf asked.

"I don't believe he's dead. Detleff and I will search. Lebuin will command in my absence."

"I'll ride with you," Udela said.

"Abbot, we found a girl hiding among the Avar things," Giffin said.

"A Saxon?"

"No, a Frank!" Giffin approached, pulling a young girl by the hand. Even in the dark of the courtyard, Audeon knew it was Genofeva.

He rushed to her and swept her into his arms. "Genofeva! I have searched half of Frankland for you!" He stroked her hair. "I can't believe it…"

"As the last of the Avars rushed from the thunderbolt, I made my escape and hid in the back of the stables," she said.

"But you were one of them, so Dgno said."

Everyone looked surprised.

"They had a ceremony… on the plains… they said I was an Avar and would marry the khagan when the time came. Then that awful Mallobaudes… he was in league with them…But I have always held myself a Frank and Christian."

"Well, it is good. And to be expected that the… daughter of the great Karolus would resist the Avars. I'm proud to call you… my sister."

Everyone gasped.

"The lady Genofeva is not your sister," Baugulf's mouth tightened. "For she is not the daughter of Karolus."

"What?" Audeon was in shock. A mix of emotions coursed through him.

"It was all a ruse by Lothar, whose daughter she is. And what lands he has left after his treachery, will go to her until she marries… or takes the veil. Now, off to Mass. We have much to thank God for."

They all followed the abbot and his monks in silence. Audeon stared into the darkness. He had lost a love—but gained a sister. Now he had gained a love and lost a sister. Suddenly, a small hand slipped into his.

"Let us praise God together," Genofeva said with a smile.

Part 3

The West's Awake

"The farther backward you can look, the farther forward you are likely to see."

-   Winston Churchill

Chapter 27

Carleton University, Ottawa, Canada, December 1959

A nurse whisked out of the dispensary, her starched skirt swirling. She barreled past the startled secretary. Huffing for breath, she threw open Doctor Evan MacKay's office door.

"He's awake! Doctor MacKay! He's awake!"

MacKay looked up and calmly nodded. He put down his pen, jammed a pack of cigarettes into his side pocket, and stepped into the reception area. "Anne, please find Captain Doolan. Ask him to meet me at the dispensary."

"Yes, Doctor. Something serious?"

"It seems our patient has revived."

He strode down the hallway towards the dispensary. A number of doctors and nurses lined the outer room. Several nodded approvingly as MacKay walked past them. He paused nervously before he entered the patient's room.

Brooke Costain sat next to a bed holding the patient's hand. A physician stood over the bed while a nurse scribbled frantically on a clipboard.

"He's coming to," Brooke mouthed silently.

The psychiatrist turned spymaster nodded approvingly.

After a few minutes of rapid-fire dictation to the nurse, the physician spoke, "I never thought we'd see this day, Evan. A man comes here with scarcely a normal physical or mental reading now seems to be returning to us."

"Prognosis for a full recovery, Bill?" MacKay had received permission to consult with Doctor William Cherry, considered among the nation's top physicians. He had known Cherry since their student days at McGill University's Faculty of Medicine.

Cherry shook his head. "Very difficult to say at this point, Evan. My only experience like this was with bomb blast victims during the war. Those who recovered were never the same, mentally or physically."

"What about spiritually?"

"I don't understand."

"This man was chosen to join us in no small part for his spiritual dimension."

"You mean the metaphysical?"

"Yes, and much more."

Cherry slapped at his white jacket pockets like a child looking for candy.

MacKay reached into his jacket and handed him the pack, with one butt neatly extended in offering.

Cherry grabbed the butt, twirling it with a flourish, then placed it between his lips and lit it with a plain lighter. "Dunhill... beauty, eh?" He took a long drag. "You won't join me?"

"You know me, Bill. I prefer a pipe. I carry the Dunhills to reward friends and bribe enemies."

"And which am I?"

"I'll let you decide."

They both laughed.

"Can I have a look?" MacKay asked.

"Of course, doctor," Cherry replied.

MacKay reached out and took Melchior's hand from Brooke. He ran his fingers up and down his arm. He felt the pulse...*weak, but stronger than before*. He felt his neck glands, then, using a stethoscope, listened to his heart and lungs. "How's his oxygen level?"

"We have checked all the basics, Evan," Cherry said.

"I am confirming and checking a few things myself."

"Like what?"

"Like his wounds."

"He has recovered nicely from the bullet wounds and the blast wounds."

MacKay looked at Brooke, then at Cherry. "I received the radiology report from Bill Coats, as well as a forensics report from J.P. Hanley over at SIU. There are some interesting anomalies."

Cherry puffed at his Dunhill. "Such as?"

MacKay pulled up Melchior's hospital gown and revealed a body covered with burns and scars. He began to point at several. "Sword wound, arrow penetration— and a blade cut. And trauma from the explosion."

"Well, you lit the pseudo-bomb over his head, and...."

MacKay glared at Cherry.

"Sorry, Evan. Please don't turn me in to the SIU."

"These are cut wounds, and you know it. As for the blast burns and trauma, forensics has established something quite curious."

"Can you tell me, Doctor?" Cherry rolled his eyes. "Or am I not cleared for it?"

"Another misspeak, and you won't be, Bill. This is quite serious stuff."

Cherry squished his Dunhill into a nearby ashtray. "You're right, Evan. I'm sorry."

"I know this operation has been stressful," MacKay glanced at Brooke. "On all of us. We've come to know this man. We chose him and brought him here for our own purposes. To advance science and to win this so-called Cold War without violence—at least of the physical sort."

"And are we winning?" Cherry asked. "Diefenbaker canceled the right's beloved Arrow aircraft, didn't they?"

MacKay knew from the SIU report that his old colleague was left-center. A "pinky," they called him, a patriotic Canadian but with some Soviet sympathies, as maybe one-third of the country was.

"You know that's something we can't discuss here," MacKay hesitated. "Should not discuss, in any event."

"Can we discuss why the School is now crawling with soldiers and plainclothes cops?"

"You know the answer, Bill." He could not let on that there was a connection between the controversial and abrupt cancellation of the Avro Aircraft's breakthrough design interceptor, the Arrow, and his project.

Brooke broke up the discussion. "His eyes are opening!"

"I knew it. There's no longer any physical reason he can't recover." Cherry went up to Melchior and signaled the nurse, who handed him smelling salts. Melchior winced, then opened his eyes. They fluttered, then seemed to scan the room.

"Can you hear me, Matt?" Brooke asked.

Melchior did not respond. He seemed to take her in, then shifted his gaze to MacKay. He began to raise his head, but then dropped it back onto the pillow and closed his eyes. He tried to speak, but though his lips formed words, nothing intelligible came out. However, MacKay thought he caught the meaning, and it startled him — *Deus vult*.

***

Captain Roger Doolan grabbed the thin sheaf of papers from his desk and tucked them into his worn leather briefcase.

"What is it, Captain?" Special Agent Todd Hadfield asked.

"MacKay – no time to explain. We've got to go."

"Should I ring up the Mounties?"

Doolan hesitated. He needed to control this case, which had gone beyond the understanding of mere detectives. "No. I think we have all the authority we need, right now. But bring your revolver."

Hadfield smiled and pulled back his worn gray suit jacket. "Never leave home without it."

Minutes later, they were speeding through the back streets of Ottawa, careful to avoid anyone linking the SIU agents to their destination, the secret annex to Carleton University known as the School.

They rode in silence until at last Doolan said, "Melchior is awake."

"I thought so. Is he speaking?"

"I don't know. I don't think so. But we'll soon find out."

Hadfield steered the sedan down the lane. He thrust his credentials out the window, and a military policeman signaled them in.

They met MacKay in his office. He was tugging at his pipe and leafing through papers. Doolan opened his briefcase and tossed the sheaf onto MacKay's desk. "These are the last reports from J.P. and the other labs."

MacKay's brow furrowed. "Including?"

"London and Washington."

"Good. Let's have a look." MacKay began to skim the reports page by page.

Doolan was amazed at how quickly he absorbed information. "How's Brooke handling this?" he asked.

Hadfield startled.

Doolan sensed his discomfort. He knew he had been one of her "hockey players." A boyfriend on every rink, people said. But he realized the usually free-spirited Brooke had changed. He knew she was fond of Melchior, despite the professional rules against falling in love with your source, suspect, and supervisor, whatever.

"As well as can be expected. Professionally, you really must put her in for a commendation. Her quick action saved this entire enterprise."

Doolan nodded. "I know. It's been nearly a month. I have time. But one such as this will be highly classified. Few will know."

"She will," MacKay said. He thumbed through the sheaf and stopped on the file of NOBLE, Patricia. MacKay put down the sheaf and placed his head in his hands.

"Are you all right?" Doolan knew the answer to his question. He knew how the report would be received.

"I... I don't think I can read this right now," MacKay said. "I feel sick to my stomach. I brought her into the operation. Now she's dead. Taking a bullet aimed at Melchior by an unknown Soviet assassin."

"Then I'll let Todd tell you what we found. He was the case agent. Where's your whisky?"

Doolan knew well where the whisky was and went and retrieved a bottle of Pinch from the cabinet. He found three glasses and poured each over two fingers, with a little extra for the doctor. *MacKay will need this. I know I do.*

"Take a sip, Doctor. captain's orders." Doolan tipped his glass and sipped, letting the slightly sweet blend caress his tongue before he swallowed.

When MacKay had taken a sip, Doolan nodded, and Hadfield began.

"I'll cut to the chase, Doctor," Hadfield said. "Patricia Noble was not who she seemed."

MacKay put his glass down. "Whatever do you mean?"

Doolan watched MacKay's movement for any nuance. He seemed genuinely surprised. That was good. They were not certain of the MacKay's connection. They needed more.

MacKay continued. "I have known her a long time... a very long time. She..."

"She what?" Doolan. "We already know you were once lovers."

MacKay sat back in his chair. "Tell me what you learned, gentlemen."

Doolan nodded at Hadfield.

Hadfield spoke very softly but very distinctly. "Patricia Noble was born Gulina Daria Grigorievna, near the city of Lviv in the Ukraine, a part of the Soviet Union. Seems she went by the name Dasha to her close friends."

MacKay straightened in his chair. "How on earth do you know this? How can you know this?"

"We have friends in Washington, Doctor. They have penetrated the Ukrainian world. Expats – mostly in New York, you know. Her fingerprints matched... well, that's all I can say. You'll have to trust our sources."

Hadfield looked at Doolan and then continued. "Date of birth around 1929."

"That's why she looked younger than her age," Doolan injected. "She was."

"I can't give out all the details, but she studied French, English, and European history — primarily medieval. It seems she came to the attention of the Lviv Residency, *Rezidentura,* of the Soviet Ministry of State Security, the MGB, in 1949. She had an affair with a young captain of the MGB. He recruited her, and they immigrated to the United States as anti-Communist refugees. They slipped through the American refugee center without too much trouble and began their new life in lower Manhattan. The so-called Lower East Side — a Ukrainian enclave."

"So how does she become Canadian?" MacKay asked.

Doolan could see he was genuinely surprised, upset, and hurt. *Good. Better this hurts, Evan.*

"She dies, apparently. Mysterious circumstances, but the husband managed an alibi. Truth was — they faked her death, and she appeared in various Canadian venues as Doctor Patricia Noble. The Soviets managed to "obtain" the death certificate of a Canadian baby of the same name. Money and certain cooperating Canadians enabled the rest of her bona fides to be established."

"Many of those folks are either dead or have fled behind the curtain," Doolan said. "But this is all pretty straightforward tradecraft. Easy to explain. Hard to execute. Harder to detect and neutralize."

"But you did," MacKay said. "How did you find out all this in a month?"

Doolan smiled. "We didn't. This case has been ongoing since February. Still, we moved it pretty quickly, if I do say so."

"How did you meet her, Doc?" Hadfield asked.

"Why do you ask? Am I under suspicion?"

Doolan pulled out a cigarette and lit it. "Doctor, you know that in programs such as yours, everyone is always under suspicion. We don't have polygraphs like the Americans. But we do have suspicions. I was put on this operation to find out who the possible Soviet mole was — who the Soviet mole, or moles, were."

"And you knew there was a mole? How? We just got wind of it last month." MacKay took another dram of the whisky. "You know... that's why we sped up the operation."

Doolan puffed a small cloud of smoke into the air. He smiled gently. "Surely you knew that was a ruse to flush things out."

MacKay took a deep breath. "You lads are clever. You should have gone to medical school and made something of yourselves."

"We actually like digging up moles and traitors, Doc," Hadfield said.

"And that's what you think I am?"

"Why do you think Brooke took such a liking to the kraut? She was to get close to him, to keep an eye on things," Hadfield said.

MacKay grabbed the bottle and poured himself another drink. "What else is in that file?"

S.W. O'Connell

"Well, you are cleared, Doc," Hadfield said. "But this Dasha was a dangerous bitch. Most men she met had something go wrong: suicide, divorce, disappearance, or death. And that doesn't count the Soviet moles who went east."

"We believe she was *an* illegal Resident in Canada, among other things. The CIA agrees. So do the chaps at MI6."

"Illegal Resident?"

"Spymaster of the non-declared Soviet agents. You know, operating undercover. We have accounted for almost all of them," Doolan said.

"Almost?"

"This is an art, as much as it is a science, Doctor. Much like your psychology and psychiatry. And some of the other disciplines you employed with Melchior. She was going to kill him, by the way."

"Patricia?"

"Dasha, yes."

"Nonsense! Perhaps she was what you say, but I knew her well enough to know she was no killer. She could not personally kill anyone. Not Patricia…"

Doolan shook his head. "I am afraid to say we found a syringe loaded with strychnine in her purse. There was strychnine in a glass of wine that Melchior declined. We found that later. One of the local police took a sly swig of it when his supervisor wasn't looking. He died. We kept that quiet, too."

"My God! But wait— it can't be true. A Soviet assassin shot at Melchior and missed. Killing Patricia."

"Wasn't a Soviet," Doolan said.

"Then who?"

"Can't say."

"The CIA?"

Doolan stared blankly.

"MI6?"

"You *were* once her lover, weren't you?"

"Something tells me you know the answer. I… I am ashamed of myself."

"Nonsense— she was beautiful and charming. And then trained to be that as well. Potent cocktail, eh? You never had a chance, Doc. No man she set her sights on ever did," Doolan said. "Why, even Melchior succumbed to her charms rather quickly."

"Are you saying she was shot by a jilted lover?"

"Let's talk about Matt. When will you be able to speak with him?" Hadfield asked.

"When he's ready," MacKay said. "He tried to mouth some words but then lapsed into sleep."

"What did he try to say?"

"Strange comment. I believe the words were, *Deus vult.*"

"Is that some sort of code?" Doolan asked.

"Sounds like Latin to me," Hadfield said.

"It is. It means God wills it," MacKay said.

"Wills what?" Doolan asked.

"That, Captain, is what I mean to find out. Assuming I am not under arrest for espionage, or murder, or treason."

"You dodged the trifecta, doc," Hadfield said.

S.W. O'Connell

Chapter 28

Melchior's finger twitched – just slightly. Brooke glanced at her watch. The dial read four o'clock. His fingers moved again, this time stroking her hand. He stirred, and to her surprise, he uttered a word before going quiet, "Kristel…"

Her heart sank. Brooke knew Kristel was his fiancée's name — the one who broke her promise to join him in Canada. She was the source of his ever-brooding presence. Brooke gently let go of his fingers. Doctor MacKay had said he must stir of his own accord. The smelling salts were a mistake.

Free of his fingers, she grabbed her cigarettes and lit one. It had been hours, and the first drag lifted her spirits. She paced, her high heels clicking across the darkened room. She thought of many things. Her role in the service. What she had made of her life. Of Melchior. How could she fall in love with someone so alien? She knew, of course, that was precisely the reason. He was like an original Cro-Magnon or even a Neanderthal. Primitive, innocent — yet worldly and earthy. But most of all, loyal. At least to the person he loved. Even if that person was not Brooke Costain. *The woman you love is some lucky woman, Matt.*

Brooke finished her last puff and fumbled in the darkness. She plopped into a nearby chair and stared out the curtains at the moonless Canadian winter night. The dim lamplight from the street seemed to be in a life-and-death struggle with the blackness. Her mind drifted back to the first time she saw him. Back to the training and their time together. Back to the desperate mission to accelerate the secret plan. Back to that awful night when the world came apart, in the middle of what was perhaps the most bizarre and exciting experiment in mankind — before the hit squad got to them.

***

Aachen, Germany, one month earlier

The ersatz bomb exploded into smoke and fire just as Melchior trailed off into unconsciousness. The blast stunned everyone and flung equipment in all directions. Brooke and the others were thrown to the ground.

MacKay crawled on his knees, covered in dust and debris, coughing. "That … that was a mistake. I don't think we needed a bomb."

The *crack* of rifle fire suddenly filled the night. One of the lights was shot out, spraying glass and hissing like a snake.

MacKay bent over Golden. "Get up, doctor. We have to move. He flipped the hypnotist over. Even in the dark and smoke, Brooke could see from his icy stare that he was dead."

A pair of dark silhouettes scurried along the edge of the woods just twenty yards off. "Champlain!" Brooke challenged.

S.W. O'Connell

When she received no response, she emptied her pistol at them. One of the figures fell. The other dropped to his knee, and a dull *crack, crack, crack* sprayed them. One of the technicians fell dead. Brooke reached for Melchior's Browning in the bag. Nervously, she took it off safety, chambered a round, and sprayed the 9mm Luger rounds at the shooter. She saw the figure fall, but in the dark, she couldn't tell whether he crawled off.

Doolan and one of the Princess Pats arrived, gasping for breath. "Hit squad," Doolan said. "It's a 'wet operation.' These are killers, and more are coming. We have to get out of here."

MacKay held a hand up. "Not until I can be sure he is gone."

Doolan looked down at Melchior's prostrate body. "If he wasn't killed by the blast or these bullets, you can load him up. But we're getting the hell out of here."

"I'll stay with Matt, no matter what." Brooke slammed the spare magazine into the Browning.

Doolan nodded at the soldier. "Get the doc and the others moving. I'll cover the approach. But be quick. If the bad guys don't get us, the German police will. My liaison only goes so far!"

As they loaded Matt into the lorry, Brooke realized the blast had scarred him badly and that he bled from several wounds. As the lorry bounced down the trail with guns blazing behind them, she bent over and gently kissed his forehead. *Hang in there, Matt. Please hang in there.*

The rest of the trip back was a blur. She recalled bumpy rides in the cold of night. Chaos when they returned to the Canadian airbase. They gave her no time to change or do the things a girl needed to do—followed by cold rations and hot tea. Then came the plane ride, sitting next to Matt and holding his hand. Scattered conversations between MacKay and Doolan. They knew something had gone wrong. *But what?* As she sat with Melchior, she paid little attention to the politics, the science, or the intrigue.

Brooke recalled even more chaos when they returned to the School at Carleton University. A hand-picked team of doctors and nurses came and went as they struggled to keep Matt alive. His wounds and burns were severe. No one knew what his mental state might be when he finally, if ever, revived. She left his side only to shower and change. She slept at his side or curled up in the chair as the medical professionals worked.

For the entire month, one thought occupied Brooke's mind: *God… please let him live… please let Matt live…*

***

"Kristel?" Melchior's voice broke the dark silence of the dispensary room. He opened his eyes to see darkness all around him. He wondered about the explosion, the filthy black powder she used, and the gunpowder from China.

"Kristel?" He moved his hands and felt the tube in his arm. *Where am I?*

He blinked. He felt his eyes stick at first, before opening and closing freely. The room was dark. He thought the Avars had secreted him in the bowels of the monastery. *But what of the arm?* He pulled the tube from his arm. The needle sent a sharp sting, but that was all. He heard the soft patter of footsteps. "Kristel? Jurchen? Weber? Zet? Audeon?"

He tried to sit up, but gentle hands pushed him back onto the bed. Melchior's mind once more raced with thoughts and images. Riding through Frankland. Leading armed men on a journey and into battle. Directing artillery and mortars against Bolshevik infantry. Snuffing silly *Ami Panzers*. Holding Patricia. Holding Kristel — Kristel — Udela. Snipers by a train... Avar arrows raining down. Explosions — artillery shells, mortar shells, gunfire, an *Ami* bomb. A Canadian bomb. Kristel's bomb...

"*Die Bomben!*" Melchior sat up panting heavily. This time, the arms could not hold him down.

"It's all right, Matt. It's all right, Matt," a woman's voice said softly. "It's me... It's Brooke Costain. You're safe. You're back at the School."

A light went on. "Can you see me, Matt?"

At first, the light blinded him. He slowly opened them. Melchior stared at her. He waited what seemed forever for the thoughts to clear in his mind and the focus to return. "*Ja, Ich sehe dich*... Brooke Costain."

He sat up in bed and looked around the room. His eyes went in and out of focus. He realized the woman spoke English. Melchior paused, then replied, "Where am I?"

"I told you. We're back in Ottawa. Safe. The Soviet and Stasi teams tried to take us out just as we launched you on your... your journey. So we had to break off and make a quick escape. Unfortunately, several of the team died. You were hurt too, Matt. But the doctors say you're on the road to recovery."

"This happened today? *Wo ist Kristel?* Where is Kristel?"

"No, Kristel, Matt. Just you. As I said, the journey was interrupted by the..."

"No!" Melchior exclaimed. "I made the journey. Just as planned. I was there. I was there."

"That's not possible. You had a dream, Matt. That's all. You've been in this room for almost a month. You probably had thousands of dreams. These are just what you recall. It's very common. You spoke sometimes."

The woman, who Melchior realized was very attractive, now looked very familiar, but... "*Kenne Ich dich?*"

"Excuse me?" she asked.

"Do I know you?"

"I certainly hope so, Matt. I have been by your side every minute, Doctor MacKay and the others would let me. Sometimes I slept on this chair. But I only left to shower and change or grab a bite."

Melchior now vaguely remembered the young woman who helped train him and who accompanied him to Aachen. "Why did you do this, Brooke?"

"My job, Matt. Protect you. Remember?"

He paused for a few moments, and the memories suddenly flooded back into his consciousness. He looked at her and smiled weakly. "I am sorry I put you in danger... that I inconvenienced you. A month, you say?"

"Almost."

A nurse came in. "I heard a cry. Is everything all right?"

Melchior closed his eyes and muttered as he began to lose consciousness again.

Brooke patted his hand. "Stay with me, Matt." She turned to the nurse. "Call Doctor MacKay. He should come as soon as possible. Tell him Matt was up and speaking. And send some help. We have to keep him from drifting off."

***

The clock on the wall showed eleven-thirty. The curtains were thrown open, and a soothing winter sun lit the room. Melchior bathed and changed gowns. He had also eaten, settling for a half-dozen eggs and a pile of American bacon with coffee, no ale or wine. Still, he devoured the food.

Brooke sat in her chair as Evan MacKay and Doctor Cherry examined him under the watchful eyes of Doolan and Hadfield. Melchior immediately recognized MacKay, but Doolan took longer. He had never met Hadfield and only vaguely recalled Cherry.

"How long must I stay in this room?" Melchior asked.

"Until Doctor Cherry clears you physically and I clear you," MacKay replied.

"Mentally. You were going to say mentally. Isn't that right, Doctor MacKay?"

"Well, I am a psychiatrist and head of this research project."

"Oh, so it's a research project now? It has taken me some time, but I've pieced all of this together. I remember when you brought me in here and began examining me, training me, vetting me. It was not at all about research then."

MacKay glanced at Cherry and then at Doolan.

Doolan nodded.

"That's right. This is the man who approves everything security. Well, you failed on that account, Captain Doolan," Melchior said.

"What do you mean, Mister Melchior?" Hadfield asked.

"I mean a squad of The Pats died because your security failed and the Bolsheviks or their *Stasi* dupes got to us."

Doolan turned red. "Why you…"

MacKay cut him off. "I'm afraid you are correct. But it was I who failed. And thus, the mission failed. The journey failed. I'm sorry for the dead, and your severe wounding. Those bullets were my responsibility."

"Failure? Bullets? The mission most certainly did not fail, *Herr Doktor*. In fact, I accomplished it."

The room buzzed with, "What did he say?"

"Huh?"

"He's not all there."

"Delusional."

MacKay signaled the others to silence. "What do you mean, Matt?"

Hadfield grabbed his pen and pad and began taking notes, as did Doctor Cherry.

"I mean precisely what I said. Your crazy, impossible plan succeeded. I made the journey. I returned to the year of Our Lord eight hundred and three. I went on my journey for Karolus, I mean, Charlemagne. And I succeeded in finding Udela."

The room grew heavy with anticipation.

Melchior saw a change in MacKay's expression. "You don't believe me. Well, that's to be expected. When one sets out to do the impossible, isn't it natural to disbelieve one's success?"

MacKay looked at him thoughtfully. "Very profound, Matt. Did you learn that in school? German medical school. Or during the war? Or here at our school?"

"I learned it from a monk. An abbot named Baugulf."

Hadfield blurted, "Say, that sounds like a character from a new novel I just finished by that Oxford Don. Have you been reading J.R.R. Tolkien?"

"Who?" Melchior replied. "I haven't read any books of the sort. Baugulf is the abbot of the monastery at Fulda."

"You mean was the abbot?" MacKay said.

"I mean, is. I was with him not long ago... very long ago, I suppose. But I was there."

"And how do you know this?" MacKay asked.

"Because it was real—is real. I saw the arrows and the savage tribes fighting Christian soldiers. I carried an *Epistola* from Karolus to the abbot. A message that held the fate of Christendom."

"I think you'll need to consign him to the loony bin, Doc," Hadfield said. "Captain, I see no need for SIU to get involved. The man's a loon. Plain and simple."

"At ease, Hadfield," Doolan said. "He might be right, Doctor MacKay."

"I... am the loon? You were the ones who arranged all this. And to my surprise, you were correct. The blast – I felt it momentarily but awoke in the same location, just one thousand years earlier."

"So, you're saying our metaphysics professor was correct after all?" MacKay asked. "That somehow, the physical, mental, and spiritual intersected because of what Teilhard calls radial energy?"

"Not somehow—through God's will. It is how everything happens, and anything is possible. I know that now."

MacKay glanced at Doolan and then at Brooke. "We had no idea of your religious and spiritual bent, Matt. I guess our assessment of you was off a bit."

Melchior smiled. "No, Doctor. What Brooke and the captain reported was quite accurate. I was a jaded agnostic at best, a bitter atheist at worst. But..."

"But what, Matt?" MacKay asked.

"I saw men who believed. I saw men who regarded God as their reason for being, not the other way around. Oh, these were not saintly men. Quite worldly – except for some of the monks and priests. But regardless, they understood man better than Western science, better than Bolshevik socialism, and of course, better than the pagan Nazis."

"Understood what, Matt?" MacKay asked.

"That they lived to serve God. And now I have learned as much. For that, I thank you and the Canadian government for sending me on this journey."

The room was still. Melchior looked from face to face, searching for disbelief, skepticism, and disdain. "You think I'm *verueckt*. Perhaps I am crazy. But it's reality. Take it for what it is worth. Your science was correct."

The room was silent. The worn soldier, Cold War tool, and medieval warrior bowed his head and clasped his hands together. He fought back tears welling in his eyes.

"I believe you, Matt," MacKay said.

Cherry frowned. Doolan and Hadfield looked at each other in disbelief. Brooke looked at Melchior, and he saw a smile as beautiful as he had ever seen on a woman or any person.

MacKay looked at Cherry. "We have indicators."

"What do you mean, Doc?" Hadfield asked.

Melchior glared at Hadfield. *Typical bull. Never off the case.*

"I have to echo Hadfield," Doolan said.

"The reports from radiology and your forensics. I have studied them and consulted them," Cherry said. "They show..."

"Show what?" Hadfield asked.

"Nothing. It's rather far-fetched," Cherry said. "Sorry, Evan. I am just looking out for your reputation." He glanced at Doolan. "And your clearance."

MacKay shook his head. "I told you. The reports corroborate that the wounds were not 20th-century gunshot wounds but ancient blade cuts and arrowhead piercings. A piece of the fletching was still in his leg. And we found the Carolingian sword tip. It closely matches the one we removed from his chest."

"How don't we know if the fletching wasn't a piece of a feather blown in there by the explosion?" Cherry asked.

"Now who's talking far-fetched?" MacKay said. "Besides, I have corroborating proof. The burn marks were not caused by the explosive device we built for the effort."

"What do you mean?" Doolan asked.

"I have a lab report that indicates traces of a very crude form of black powder. Ancient gunpowder. Matt was not injured in that explosion or in that firefight."

"So it did happen!" Brooke exclaimed.

MacKay nodded. "Yes, it did. Matt went on his journey. Here's more proof. The medics found these around his neck."

MacKay pulled a yellow envelope from his jacket and opened it. He removed two objects from inside and held them in front of Melchior.

"My amulet! The Ronson!"

"That means little, Doctor. The lighter was part of his kit," Doolan said.

"But it was included in the sack, which, by the way, disappeared after Brooke retrieved the Browning. But we also found this around his neck and secured it. The workmanship dates from the eighth century or thereabouts."

Melchior gasped. "That's the cross Father Thomas gave me. The last time I remember seeing it was when Kristel and I exchanged vows with our crosses — she had one from her grandmother."

"Then Kristel must be very old, eh, Matt?" Hadfield said.

"Say, wasn't Kristel the name of your fiancée in Germany?" Doolan asked.

Melchior nodded. "When I awoke in the year eight oh, three, I was immediately sent to seek out the evil queen of the Saxons—also reported to be a witch. Her name was Udela. She and others were part of a plot to destroy Christendom."

"And you broke it up, eh?" Hadfield said.

Melchior looked at Hadfield with contempt. "We're all here, aren't we... and nominally Christians?"

The room filled with sheepish glances.

"Go on, Matt. I believe you," Brooke said.

"Take good notes, Hadfield, and keep your trap shut," Doolan said.

Brooke gave Doolan a nod of appreciation.

"This seems to tell us something quite astounding," MacKay said. "Matt did transport back to the year eight oh three. Of that, we have both circumstantial and physical proof."

"I don't understand, Doctor," Brooke said.

"The blade wounds— the ancient powder burns and the Ronson and amulet. Physical phenomena fused with mental." MacKay looked at Melchior. "And perhaps even spiritual."

"So, the faux bomb caused a sort of chain reaction of spiritual, mental, and physical just as you theorized?" Cherry asked.

"Perhaps there was something else," MacKay said.

"What else?" Doolan asked.

"Something you're not even cleared for, Captain Doolan. A Top-Secret phenomenon that emerged from the Americans' Operation Paper Clip at the end of World War II. I did some work assessing the German scientists the Americans brought over to protect them from the Soviets."

"And exploit them," Cherry said.

Mackay nodded. "Yes—but their lives were saved, and we prevented a trove of scientific knowledge from falling into Stalin's grasp. I'd say that alone was worth it. In any case, I was sent to Wright-Patterson Air Base in Ohio, where the U.S. Air Force conducts much of its science and technology research. That's where I met him."

"Who?" Brooke asked.

"Professor Winfried Otto Schumann. Brilliant man. An electrical engineer with a doctorate in high-voltage technology. I maintained correspondence with him after he returned to Germany, to the Munich Electrophysical Institute. His most interesting discoveries have not yet been released to his institute—but he has discussed them with me."

"You?" Cherry asked.

"He was in rough shape after the war—psychologically speaking. So many scientists were. They, after all, used their knowledge and skills to perpetrate evil. So, Fritz—that's what I called Winnifred, turned to me for psychological help."

"You became his psychiatrist?" Cherry asked.

"Yes, but more importantly, his friend."

"How does Fritz figure into all this, Doc?" Doolan began taking notes.

"Please put the pen away. What I'm about to say cannot be recorded—not yet, at least. Fritz's research has exposed a phenomenon that just might explain things."

"What is that, Evan?" Cherry asked.

"Some twenty-two hundred or so thunderstorms batter our planet every moment. They cause flashes of lightning to strike the earth about three thousand times per minute."

"So, it was a lightning strike and not the explosive that sent Matt back in time?" Brooke asked.

"Good question, Brooke. Not sure yet. But Fritz discovered that lightning produces low-frequency electromagnetic waves that cover the planet. They reach up into the ionosphere, where they circle the Earth. The waves have crests and troughs that align in resonance to amplify the initial signal. The waves can affect a variety of things, such as radio transmissions and weather, and perhaps perturb things in ways we cannot yet understand."

"This is complicated, Doc. What's the point?" Doolan asked impatiently.

"I think I see why Schumann collaborated with you," Cherry said.

Mackay gave Cherry a knowing look. "We both believe the resonances, which is what he calls these waves, can affect the human mind. And perhaps the physical as well."

The medical school student in Melchior sent his thoughts in a thousand directions. "And the spiritual?"

MacKay ignored the question. "Just a theory right now, but I think the resonances are the missing link. The locations of both of your travels are near enough to bodies of water—rivers—for a trough to reach down from the ionosphere, and, given a certain confluence of events, make the intersection we believe happened. The result—time travel."

"Holy shit!" Doolan gasped.

"Again, just a theory. No one outside this room can know this, but the Avro program was canceled due to the impact of crest resonances on the aircraft. I can't tell you more than that."

"But he has been in our control the entire time," Doolan said. "Just when did he have time to go back and fight a war and return? And just what did he do there?"

"This has been an experiment from the start, Captain Doolan. I believe I can say with some certainty that he made the journey and returned to the exact moment he left. To us, it appeared as if he had never gone."

Melchior saw that Hadfield seemed convinced. "I think your bull here is skeptical. Truthfully, I know I went. I know it was real. But how did I return to the exact same time?"

MacKay took a breath and slowly slapped his pipe in his palm.

Melchior saw him at unease – Doctor Evan MacKay was rarely shaken. "What is it you're not telling us, *Herr Doktor*?"

MacKay let out a low sigh. "I swore I would not reveal this to anyone. I wouldn't include it in the official file."

"What are you holding back, Doc?" Doolan asked.

"No one knows this, but I have been in close correspondence with Father Etienne Pelletier at St. Regis College in Ottawa."

"A priest?" Cherry asked.

MacKay nodded. "Yes, a Jesuit priest. A scientist as well as a theologian. But unlike Teilhard, Father Pelletier remains unpublished, at least at the unclassified level. He has been contracted to research the preternatural aspect of the U.M. program. I'm the only one with read-on to his work and his findings."

Doolan leaned forward, and his face reddened. "Now wait a minute, Doc. I'm the security manager of this program. I don't..."

"You don't know anything of it. It's my compartment, Captain. Only Etienne and I are read on to it."

"But why?"

"Because if the Ministry got wind that I was working a religious angle, they'd sack me and end the program. They would never—could never accept that the answer to this is both in man's hands and out of man's hands."

"What is this priest working on?" Cherry asked.

"He is one of just a handful of experts the Catholic church has on the preternatural. I believe the U.M. is a preternatural phenomenon. There have been writings about this in the church for centuries."

"So this is a supernatural event?" Brooke asked.

Melchior sat in silence. But he knew at once MacKay was on to something.

"No, Brooke," MacKay said. "Etienne explained it using St. Thomas Aquinas's definition. According to Aquinas, the supernatural consists in God's unmediated actions—let's say miracles. The natural is what always happens or happens most of the time. We'll use science and technology as an example. But the preternatural is what happens rarely, by the agency of created beings—of rational men. According to Etienne's research, the U.M. is a preternatural phenomenon. That is, an extraordinary event caused by man's agency but with the help of God."

Cherry stifled a laugh. "You don't really?"

"I'm still unsure whether I believe it to be true. But I've read almost fifty papers by Etienne, including some from various Christian scholars and scientists. Many are quite old, and all point to this."

Melchior realized MacKay was right. *I would never have thought him capable of believing this. He is a very complex man.*

"One of his papers, in particular, drew me in. Drawing on St. Augustine, it described the Catholic view of time. Because God is beyond space and time, all things, wherever they are located in space and time, are equally present to him, and he is equally present to them and equally the cause of their being and reality. Thus, the Catholic ideas of purgatory and heaven exist without the time as we know it. Time is just a means of measure. An artificial construct of man."

"What does this have to do with Matt's journey?" Brooke asked.

MacKay's eyes softened. "A good question, Brooke. It means he returned to the moment he departed because all of these events occur concurrently. I mentioned St. Thomas Aquinas – as he put it, God lives in the nunc stans, the now that stands still."

"What about Einstein?" Cherry challenged. "The fourth dimension and all that?"

"Etienne's papers took on Einstein, whose ideas danced around what the ancient philosophers and the early medieval thinkers knew to be true. In the sixth century, the Roman philosopher Boethius addressed it in his writings. God possesses all of life and all of eternity at once. We, on the other hand, experience it in a moment-by-moment progression. It's how we experience time. But not how time is."

"I believe *Herr Doktor* is correct," Melchior said.

"So Matt entered the ninth century, experienced life there, but transited back to the moment he left?" Brooke asked.

"I tend to think he was in both simultaneously. That means he could be in others as well, even as we speak. But this is still all theory. We have a lot of work to do in this area."

MacKay drew his pipe from his other pocket and lit it. He also pulled the Dunhills out and offered them to everyone, including Melchior, for a smoke. "Now that we have established an informed theory of how this journey happened, Matt, tell us what happened in your own words."

Chapter 29

Melchior's words rolled out in a measured cadence. He needed to make sure they believed him. Several times, he had to fight back his emotions, especially when it came to Kristel and also when it came to the deaths of his men and the innocents.

Doolan had ordered Cherry from the room. But he let Brooke stay. To keep Melchior at ease.

When he finished, MacKay handed him another Dunhill. "So this Udela was Kristel, your lost fiancée?"

"At first, I didn't believe it possible. But then, as I learned, with God all things are possible. She was forced into the same sort of program by the Bolsheviks. She is no Communist. And she is no witch. I know her. She is good. Just brainwashed and programmed by the Soviets and East Germans. As I told you, she saved my life. We joined our crosses in a pledge of devotion just before the black powder exploded. I only pray to God that she got away. And that the Avars were destroyed along with their fiendish plot. At least that was my..."

"Plan?" Doolan asked.

"In such extremes, there are no plans," Melchior said.

Doolan nodded. "We'll have to spend some time later talking about everything Udela, that is, Kristel, revealed. Mainly about how the Soviets identified her, her training and handlers. We'll need all of that in greater detail."

"I know little more," Melchior said.

"Humor me, Mister Melchior. We bulls have our routines," Doolan said.

Melchior nodded. "*Dass glaube ich...* That I do believe."

"Yes—and we'll want to know whatever she might have revealed about how she went on her journey. Damned, how they caught on to this. Just like the atom bomb, I suppose," Doolan said.

"I suppose," Melchior said.

MacKay took a puff on his pipe and blew a ring into the air. "Tell us again about the plot, from the Soviet perspective."

Melchior shook his head. "Not much I know, doctor. Something about shifting the balance of power to the east. If the plot succeeded, there would be no Western Europe as a dominant cultural, economic, and geopolitical force."

"Why do you suppose they thought that would influence things in their favor?" Mackay asked.

"Ignorance of geography, Doctor MacKay. Their location at the center of Eurasia has put them in an interesting position. But as much as they struggle to overcome it, they cannot. They wanted Western Europe to develop slowly, hoping they in the east would leap past them. After all, they hoped to take Miklagard."

"Miklagard? What's that?" Doolan asked.

"Constantinople, Captain. Today known as Istanbul, but then the center of the Eastern Roman Empire. It's all tied together."

"Yes, of course," MacKay said. "Very sophisticated. But toying with history is risky."

Melchior shook his head. "You know, before I took this journey, I would have said the same thing. Now I would say that toying with God's will is risky."

"So what do you think happened after you returned to us?"

"I have no idea. I can only hope Kristel escaped the Avars. And that Karolus was informed of the plot. Although I don't know if I succeeded in quashing it."

"Give yourself more credit, Matt," MacKay said.

"What do you mean?"

"The West rose, in no small measure because your Karolus built his Christian empire. You succeeded in allowing that to happen."

Melchior gazed silently for a moment. "But it fell in just a few generations. Maybe that's all God needed for his plans to unfold."

"I suppose so," MacKay replied.

"What about Patricia?" Melchior suddenly said. "I had almost forgotten poor Patricia. You brought her into this scheme, and she died for it."

MacKay looked at Doolan.

"What?" Melchior sensed something was wrong. "I know she died at the hands of a Soviet assassin."

"Yes, Matt," MacKay said.

Melchior sensed they were holding something back. "Tell me the truth."

Doolan chose his words carefully. "Patricia, it turns out, was a Soviet agent. We believe the chief of their illegal network in Canada. She was poised to kill you when..."

"When what? What are you saying? Kill me? Ridiculous! Patricia was no communist!"

MacKay tapped his pipe against his knee. "We are saying that she was a dangerous enemy, and now she is gone."

"That can't be. She was a..."

"She was a Bolshevik agent, Mr. Melchior," Doolan said. "A top-notch one at that. She had a syringe full of strychnine on her. It was meant for you."

"But the shot. I saw her die." He looked at Brooke.

She lowered her eyes.

"She had us fooled, Matt. Do you think I would have brought her in to train you if I had known? Oh, they planned this well," MacKay said.

"We're still investigating how the Soviets knew who the leak is," Doolan said.

MacKay pulled his pipe from his mouth. "The fact that they used your fiancée Kristel, were, aware of this phenomenon, and successfully used it is of grave concern. Serious consequences will follow if they find someone else to send back, or forward, in time."

"We are planning countermeasures, though," Doolan said.

"So tell me, Matt," MacKay said. "Out there, you made mention of a leak, a mole. What made you say that? Think that?"

"Did you know something, suspect something?" Doolan asked.

"Perhaps you journeyed forward in time as well as back. Perhaps there are other secrets within you. Experiences you don't even know about, or don't recall, or don't want to recall."

Melchior lay back in his bed, closed his eyes, and sighed from exhaustion. "I recall one last thing. Kristel whispered it briefly while we were trying to escape the Avars. I had almost forgotten."

"Would you like to talk about it, Matt? Or we can discuss it later," MacKay said.

Doolan leaned forward. "I'd rather he discusses it now if you don't mind, Doc."

"It wasn't much. She overheard a comment from one of the Soviet bosses, a general and a commissar overseeing their program. You know, for political correctness?"

"I do," Doolan said. "What did she hear?"

"Just that their program had a direct link to something called *Lunnyy Vystrel.*"

"Great, that's Russian. Did she say what it meant?" Doolan had his pen on his pad.

"*Mondschuss.* She called it Moon Shot."

MacKay glanced at Doolan, who was scribbling madly.

"Does that mean anything?" Melchior asked.

"Depends," Doolan said. "Did she say any more?"

"Just that they want to go there before the west. They had sent another "universal mind" forward in time. Or so they thought. But when he returned, it was a man from the Caucasus region. They seemed to think they wouldn't make it in time. The west would beat them. And they hoped her journey would change what they called the trajectory of history."

"You remember quite a lot from such a brief conversation," MacKay said.

"It's funny how panic can sharpen the mind and the senses," Melchior said. "Does this mean anything?"

"I'm afraid we can't tell you whether it does or doesn't," Doolan said.

***

The keys clicked like a machine gun as MacKay typed his report. The metallic rattle of his hunt-and-peck style annoyed him, but he worked through it. He had let the secretary go home. His report was so highly classified that only he, Doolan, and the Chief of the Defense Staff could read the unabridged version. This was the report on Melchior's journey and the information he brought back, especially Moon Shot.

The abridged version, properly sanitized to protect sources and methods, would be released to the Prime Minister, the Minister of Defense, and the two major party leaders in Parliament. That version would omit any mention of Moon Shot. The Chief of Defense informed MacKay that the Moon Shot piece was going to be passed to a partner nation as a matter of high interest. Part of what the Chief referred to as an extremely compartmented bilateral agreement.

MacKay was taken from his work by a soft knock on the door.

"It's open."

Brooke stuck her head in the door. "May I come in?"

MacKay signaled to her to take a seat in the large, overstuffed leather chair. "You look beautiful, Brooke. Going anywhere special?"

"Thanks. I haven't had a chance to pamper myself in a long while. I am bringing Matt some dinner since he isn't cleared yet for release."

MacKay glanced down. He did not want to tell her the truth. Matthaeus Melchior would not be leaving the School for a very long time, if ever, for security reasons.

"I know this is hard on you. But your performance has been impressive. Don't tell him I told you, but Captain Doolan has recommended you for promotion to Special Agent."

Brooke's large eyes widened.

He noticed something. "You don't seem overjoyed."

"I'm sorry. I'm very grateful. But I've been doing a lot of thinking. What I've seen Matt go through has changed my idea of success. I wanted so badly to be the first woman in the SIU to make it as an investigator—a Special Agent. But after all of this..."

MacKay smiled. He liked her introspection.

"Did I say something funny, Doctor?"

"No, Brooke. It's just that I can see the maturity of thought in you. I think the strange case of Matthaeus Melchior has changed us all. Not the least of all, you."

"Strange? You make it all seem so odd. Yet it wasn't odd when we were shooting back at the hit teams. I'm sure Matt didn't think it odd when he fought Saxons and Avars on a mission for Her Majesty the Queen—as well as for Charlemagne."

"Bad choice of words on my part. Not odd... let's say extraordinary."

Brooke smiled. "I like extraordinary much better."

"Matt has changed the most. He was a cynic, almost devoid of human regard, post-war trauma and all. But now he is a man of faith. Not that his nose is in the Bible all day. He has asked for several religious works to read: City of God, Summa Theologiae, and several others. His cerebral and spiritual sides are going full bore."

Brooke's eyes welled with tears. "He's such a dear man. He's been through so much. I like him so much..."

"I'm glad you do, Brooke. He needs friends. I'm going home to my wife and children. After this, I'll hug them all the harder. Matthaeus Melchior has no one. The woman he loved and perhaps still loves is in another millennium. His comrades in both centuries are dead or wounded. Two homelands are gone, and Canada has not fully embraced him."

"What are you saying?"

"Nothing... Just go... keep him company. He may not know it yet. But you are the best friend, perhaps the only friend, he has in two millennia."

Epilogue

Fulda, 803 A.D.

The blare of a hundred battle trumpets heralded the host's arrival. A long column of mounted *milites* thundered down the mountain road and filled the valley. Baugulf counted the flapping pennons, numbering over a score.

"There are over five thousand, Abbot," Audeon said.

"Our lord king-and-emperor travels with a large *scara*. Let us bid him a royal Frank welcome. Your first official duty as Count of Fulda," Baugulf said with a smile.

"Will he meet the Saxon queen, Udela? I spent a fortnight with her searching for Melchior. I believe she is now a true Christian woman."

"That is, of course, your father's decision. She has taken the veil at a convent some leagues from here."

From the monastery chapel, the sound of the monks chanting the Te Deum filled the air, as if their throats were engaged in some sort of sonic battle.

"You said the bull he sent revealed his plan?" Audeon asked.

Baugulf pulled the scroll from under his sleeve. "The *Epistola de Litteris Colendis*" itself does not. It lays forth a way ahead for educating Christendom and the lands east. A way to civilize the pagans and bring God's peace to all."

"I don't understand," Audeon said. "I guess I'm after all but a simple Frank soldier. I have the *missus* to thank. Before I met him, I was but a callow boy. A bastard at that."

Baugulf smiled. "The message also revealed that the missus was sent to buy time until Karolus could come to grips with Widukind and the main Saxon army. Little did Karolus realize that Melchior had collided with a more sinister plot to topple Frankland. A greater danger than the mere armies of Widukind."

"Mere armies? A nation of savage enemies."

"Widukind and the pagan tribes were a large but simple threat, physical in nature and blunt in purpose, intent on killing Franks. Willehad and the heresy — the false promises of his strange and evil mix of heretical Christianity, Saxon paganism, and the unholy Avar beliefs – were much more insidious. Taken together, they posed a graver danger. They were poised to rob men of their faith in God and to substitute it with faith in man. That is not true faith. And without true faith, man serves no true purpose."

"Thank God our lord king-and-emperor sent the *missus*. Thank God, Frankland had a warrior such as Lord Melchior. A true Christian warrior. I'm so sorry I could not find a trace of him. Other than in the heart of Udela."

"You mean Postulant Udela," Baugulf said. "She has begun the process of dedicating herself to God." The abbot tucked the scroll safely into his sleeve. "Frankland will need many more like Melchior if Karolus's vision is to be realized. You said you believe the missus dominicus Melchior yet lives?"

S.W. O'Connell

Audeon nodded slowly as he stared at the column winding over the bridge. "I shall resume my search tomorrow, if Karolus will allow. I do believe, abbot, that Lord Melchior, the last of the *Missi Dominici*, yet lives..."

Baugulf's eyelids shut tight, and he intoned, "*Deus vult...*"

-The End-

Cast of Characters
(* = Historical Figure)

Aachen
Hauptmannn Matthaeus Melchior – Former medical student turned infantry officer
Faernerich Weber – German subaltern under Melchior
Kristel von und zu Zelinsky – Melchior's fiancée
Leutenant Norbert von und zu Zelinsky – Melchior's second-in-command, friend and Kristel's brother

Canada
Warrant Officer Gregory Coale – Special Agent, SIU
Doctor Bill Coats – Radiologist
Brooke Costain – Investigative Assistant, SIU
Doctor William Cherry – Physician and former classmate of Evan MacKay
Captain Roger Doolan – Officer with the Special Investigative Unit (SIU), Canadian Ministry of Defense (MOD)
Doctor Simon Field – Professor of Philosophy, Carleton University
Doctor John Golden – Psychologist and hypnotist
Gulina Daria (Dasha) Grigorievna – Soviet Agent
Warrant Officer Todd Hadfield – Special Agent, SIU
Sergeant John-Pierre Hanley – Forensics Chief, SIU
Captain Leander "Mac" MacConnell – Physician with Canadian Forces
Doctor Evan MacKay – Psychiatrist and Director of the Top-Secret UM Unit, Canadian MOD
Doctor Luc Martin – Professor of Physics
Matthaeus Melchior – Former medical student and Wehrmacht officer
Doctor Patricia Noble – Professor of History and expert on Carolingian period
Doctor Charles Norton – Psychiatrist with Canadian Forces
Professor Winfried Otto Schumann –   German physicist who predicted the Schumann resonances
Sergeant Tremblay – A Royal Canadian Mounted Police officer

Frankland
Alcuin of York – Renowned religious scholar from Britain and advisor to Karolus. *
Alager – Saxon war chief

Anfeald – Priest under Bishop Willehad
Anfelisia – Italian slave and waitress in the canteen
Angilram – Bishop of Aachen
Arbogast – Commander of the watch at Lothar's fort
Arnulf – Coadjutor of Aachen cathedral
Audeon – Frankish noble and illegitimate son of Charlemagne
Baugulf – Abbot of Fulda*
Bavo – Frankish warrior and farmer
Boso – Manager of the canteen in Lothar's stronghold
Bruno – Chief of the Issepi and chamberlain
Bayan I – First khagan of the Avar Khaganate between 562 and 602. *
Cassyon – Melchior's man-at-arms
Chlodwig – Warrior under Stilicho
Chrodegang – Son of Morloch
Detleff – Squire to Melchior
Father Derian – Saxon priest under Willehad
Dgno – Khagan of the Balaton Avars
Ducfred – Young Saxon messenger
Eberger – Chief of the Nabo
Enurchus – Frankish warrior under Count Lothar
Fromm – Danish warrior and follower of Melchior
Gaetani – Apulian archer and follower of Melchior
Genofeva – Daughter of Morloch
Gudrun – Mallobaudes's wife
Guntramn – Aging Frankish *milites*
Giffin – Benedictine brother guarding Fulda
Hartmut – Man-at-arms to Melchior
Hincmar – Frankish warrior and messenger from Lothar
Hrodger – Saxon warrior and war chief of the Haari
Irene – Byzantine (Eastern Roman) Empress*
Jurchen – Abbot and Melchior's guide
Karolus (Charlemagne) – King of the Franks and Lombards, and Holy Roman Emperor*
Lebuin – Frankish Commander of the Horse under Audeon
Pope Leo – Pontiff who crowned Charlemagne emperor of the Romans in December 800 AD*
Lothar – Count of Fulda and Lord of Karolus's domain on the Eastern March
Maiuel – Frankish warrior under Lothar
Mallobaudes – Frankish lord and Melchior's cousin
Father Mannix – Saxon priest
Maya – Bulgar bondswoman
Melchior – Frankish lord and last of Charlemagne's *Missi Dominici*, special envoys
Morloch – Ferry Master

Nithard – Lieutenant of Count Lothar
Osgar – Saxon and Haari assassin
Otmak – Avar retainer of Dgno
Brother Paul – Benedictine monk
Radka – Bulgar bondswoman
Richomeres – Frankish *milites*
Samo – Austrian Lord and enemy of Charlemagne*
Spad – Frankish hunter
Stilicho – Frankish lord and general
Tassilo – Duke of Bavaria*
Father Thomas – Irish priest and monk
Tilo – Chief of Saxones Eucii
Tuldila – Avar general
Udela – Witch-queen of renegade Saxon tribes
Udo – Deacon of the Cathedral at Aachen
Varna – Bulgar bondswoman and daughter of hetman
Vulmar – Exorcist
Wandregisel – Lieutenant of Count Lothar
Waiofar – Frankish Commander of the Foot under Audeon
Weid – Count and Lord of Koblenz*
Werinbert – son of Morloch
Wala – Frankish hunter
Widukind – Saxon war chief and rebel against Charlemagne*
Willehad – Bishop of Fulda

Gazetteer

Aachen – Also known as Aix la Chapelle, the site of Charlemagne's capital on today's German northwest border and the place the American army selected for their first attack on German territory in 1944.

Apulia – Puglia of modern Italy, the southeastern "heel" of the Italian peninsula.

Austrasia – The heart of Frankland (today western Germany).

Baden–Soellingen – Small German town nestled along the upper Rhine River.

Balaton – A Lake region in today's Hungary and home of Khagan Dgno's tribe.

Bavaria – Region in southern Germany

Carleton University – A major university in Ottawa, Canada.

Fulda – City on Frankland's eastern frontier (central Germany) and site of a Benedictine monastery that served as a base from which missionaries would accompany Charlemagne's armies in their political and military campaigns to fully conquer and convert pagan Saxony.

Koblenz – Imperial city on the Rhine.

Laugona – The Lahn River of modern Germany and a tributary of the Rhine.

Lombardy – Region in northern Italy.

Miklagard – Norse name for Constantinople, capital of the Byzantine Empire.

Neustrasia – Heart of Frankland (today eastern and central France).

Nordhausen (modern) – Site of Udela's fictional Saxon capital

Ottawa – Canadian capital.

Rome – Capital of the papal realm of central Italy and seat of the Holy See.

Rheine – Archaic spelling of the Rhine River, the major river running through the Frankland from the Alps to the North Sea.

Wiesek – A town near Giessen.

Glossary

Avars – Turkic tribe from the eastern plains who were renowned fighters and plunderers of central Europe.

Banner – Medieval term for a body of troops, no set number but less than a *Scara* and more than a *Cunei*.

Barritus – Roman war cry, a deep roar in unison using shields to channel the sound towards the enemy, adopted by the Franks.

Brunia – Body armor used by Frank *milites* made of either leather or leather with iron rings.

Coadjutor – An assistant to a bishop who managed the day-to-day life of a cathedral.

Cunei – Latin term used for Frankish army sub-unit of around fifty men.

"*Epistola de litteris colendis*" – Historical letter written by Alcuin of York for Karolus, sent to Abbot Baugulf of Fulda instructions on establishing schools and combating heresy and paganism to build a Christian realm. Believed penned between 800 AD and 804 AD.

Eucii – Small tribe of proto-Saxons, possibly an off-shoot of the Jutes.

Euduces – Saxon tribe.

Exercitus – Latin term used by Franks connoting an army.

Francisca – A battle-ax suitable for throwing or hacking. Originally a favorite of the Franks and believed to be the source of their name.

Franks – Germanic tribe that emerged in the 3rd century AD on the east bank of the Lower Rhine River. They would go on to form a version of the Western Roman Empire and set the foundation for the transition from the post-Roman period (so-called Dark Ages) to medieval Europe.

Furlong – A measure of distance equal to one-eighth of a mile.

Haari – Ancient Germanic *berzerkers*, crazed warriors whose frenzied mental state made them particularly fearsome.

Irminsul – Sacred tree of life to the pagan Saxons.

Issepi – Saxon tribe.

Khagan – An Avar king.

League – An obsolete unit of distance of variable length that varied from country to country and over time. Supposedly the distance a person could walk in one hour, for purposes of this tale, is about 2 ½ miles.

March – An archaic term for the frontier. Counts (or Margraves) who ruled the marches usually had special authority. The marches – the frontiers of Charlemagne's realm, lacked fixed borders and required active defense.

Milites – Latin term used for professional warriors within the Frankish military hierarchy, includes mounted and foot soldiers.

Missus Dominicus – Envoy of the lord, specially selected warriors empowered to act on behalf of the king-and-emperor.

Muhammadans – Archaic term for all Muslims of the period.

Nabo – Saxon tribe.

Patzinaks – Semi-nomadic Turkic people from Central Asia. But a separate khanate (nomadic kingdom) from the Avars.

Saxons – A warlike Germanic tribal grouping in north-central and northeast Germany. Besides invading England, they fought a series of wars against the Franks.

Scara – Latin term used by Franks to denote a unit of 5,000 -10,000 *milites*.

Seaxe – A long dagger of up to 22 inches. The traditional weapon of Saxons and believed a source for their name and adopted by Franks.

The Ring – Fortified encampment where the Avars stored the spoils from earlier campaigns.

Varangian Guard – Personal bodyguards of the Byzantine Emperor/Empress made up of Nordic warriors.

Warda – Locally raised Frankish soldiers, not milites.

Authors Notes

This story is a work of fiction. Yet some of the characters, places, and events are based on history or legend. Karolus, Charles the Great, otherwise known as Charlemagne, led the Franks of modern France and Germany in building a successor state to the great Roman Empire that his ancestors helped topple. He fought a series of wars to achieve this. His empire, although not long-lasting, laid the blueprint for a modern Europe centered on the nations of France, Germany, and Italy.

The Franks built a monastery at Fulda, the site of Saint Boniface's conversion of the first Germans. The Fulda monastery would become a great center of Christian learning. Baugulf was the abbot of Fulda during the period covered in this tale. He received the mysterious *Epistola de litteris colendis* from Charlemagne, who intended to strengthen Christianity and thus his empire. The exact contents of the letter remain a matter of some debate.

Charlemagne was a worldly man with many wives and concubines and many children, both legitimate and illegitimate. Yet his faith and commitment to Christianity and Christian learning were unquestionable. A virtual Camelot grew around his capital at Aachen (Aix-la-Chapelle), where Alcuin, Clement, and a group of learned monks thrived under Charlemagne's sponsorship.

The King of the Franks, Lombards, and Bavarians was crowned a new Roman Emperor by Pope Leo III at St. Peter's Basilica in Rome in 800 A.D. and adopted the title "Charles, most serene Augustus, crowned by God, great and pacific emperor, governing the Roman Empire."

Not just another warlord, Charlemagne introduced Jury Courts, revised the legal system, introduced new silver-based coinage, and reformed weights and measures. These reforms helped establish an economy that would bind his realm and enrich it, improving life in this world.

But he also advanced missionary enterprises and monastic reform. The overarching purpose of these efforts underpins this tale — forging the temporal and spiritual realms to combat evil and build a righteous realm under God. This was to be done through a mix of military power, diplomacy, and the establishment of a new Christian culture underpinned by religious education.

Charlemagne's goal was informed faith, not blind faith. No wonder his two favorite books were *The Bible* and Augustine's *City of God*. He wanted Christianity to be in this world, not just of the next. He sought a Christendom, a realm, that could fight the satanic forces that walked the earth.

In the political sphere, Charlemagne was a pivotal figure, taking the former Western Roman Empire and forging a new Holy Roman Empire that would be the forerunner of Europe. In that sense, he may well be the first European.

***

The term *Deus vult* is used throughout this work, predating its use during the First Crusade three centuries later. It is used, along with other terms, to show that Latin phrases were used in secular life, especially when referring to religious expression. For the purposes of this tale, it is meant to show the Carolingian acknowledgment of God's power and authority, not a battle cry, per se. One can also muse that the early crusaders borrowed it from earlier use. It has no connection to any so-called political movement today.

Widukind did exist. He was a great leader of the pagan Saxons who threatened Charlemagne's eastern marches, the frontiers of his realm. It took the Franks some fifteen years of warfare to subdue these savage fighters. The Saxons were the last large Germanic tribal group to accept Christianity. One wonders, though, how much pagan influence lingered. I stretched history a bit, for by the year 800 the great warrior finally submitted to Charlemagne and was baptized, disappearing into legend.

The Avars were a mysterious Turkic tribe of mounted warriors from the east who had fought numerous wars for and against various tribes and nations. By the time period covered in this tale, Charlemagne had reduced their power and seized their treasure trove — plunder from centuries of conquest and terror.

The *Missi Dominici* — envoys of the lord - also existed. One of Charlemagne's strategies aimed at the control and mastery of the lords, counts, and dukes who held sway over vast domains. Not to be confused with the paladins, his top level of noblemen, the *Missi Dominici* were warrior administrators and diplomats. Their role was to demonstrate Charlemagne's presence across the vast empire; communicate laws, both secular and religious; enforce those laws; and ensure the people were fairly taxed and properly schooled in orthodox Christianity. In some ways, they were the precursor to the Christian knights who would arise in medieval Europe. They had plenipotentiary power to rule for the lord (Charlemagne) and usually traveled with a small band of armed retainers and priests or monks.

The fictional queen Udela's use of magic was based on my hypothesis that Marco Polo was not the first to bring gunpowder from China to the West. After all, the Chinese used gunpowder centuries before Charlemagne's time, and Chinese skeletons have been found in Roman cemeteries in Britain. Anyone who could harness it would indeed have "magical" powers. Or perhaps it found its way back to the 9th century with Kristel.

***

The "science" of sending Melchior on his journey is fiction. But the idea of the intersection of the spiritual, mental, and physical is not. Pierre Teilhard de Chardin, S.J., was a French idealist philosopher and Jesuit priest who trained as a paleontologist and geologist. The ideas used to transport Melchior are inspired in part by his writings.

The project headed by Doctor MacKay was pure fiction, though it was based on certain programs, such as the US Army's Stargate Project during the Cold War. This program sought military members with the ability, among other things, to engage in remote viewing, the practice of seeking impressions about a distant or unseen target, purportedly "sensing" with the mind. The connection to Doctor MacKay's fictional experiment, which sought to fuse the physical, the spiritual, and the mental to transcend time and space, is intentionally vague, as such things are.

***

The story begins during the savage struggle for Aachen, America's first taste of what a desperate German Army would be like fighting on its own soil. This offers a preview of the good vs. evil struggle that follows, albeit through the eyes of those serving evil.

***

The Cold War was a real war. It included military combat (conventional and unconventional), an arms race, a technology race, and an espionage war. Although the United States and the Soviet Union were the main protagonists, a host of East Bloc and West Bloc nations participated in various ways and to varying degrees. East Germany was the key Soviet partner during much of the period. The United States had many more (and better) partners, both in political and intelligence matters as well as on the battlefield.

Walter Ulbricht was the Communist stooge who ruled the "German Democratic Republic" (East Germany) for the Soviets. State Security General Ivan Alexandrovich Serov was the head of the KGB from March 1954 to December 1958 and head of the GRU from 1958 to 1963.

The launch of SPUTNIK by the Soviets was a seminal event that sent a chill down the spine of the West, which always perceived itself as ahead in matters of technology.

This spurred the American Moonshot effort and the establishment of a joint US-Canadian partnership called the North American Air Defense System (NORAD).

The Canadian military's Special Investigative Unit existed during the Cold War but is not the same as the Canadian police unit of the same name. Working with the RCMP at home and its NATO partners abroad, the organization was key to protecting the Canadian Forces from espionage and other threats.

The Princess Patricia Regiment, nicknamed The Pats, Patricia's, and The Patricia's, plus a few juicy ones, is a real Canadian Forces unit that was stationed in Germany during the Cold War. It was the first Canadian regiment to arrive in France in World War I, fought in Italy and France and Germany in World War II, and was famed for fighting with distinction in the Korean War in the Battle of Kapyong (April 1951), where the 2nd Battalion held against overwhelming Chinese forces, earning the U.S. Presidential Unit Citation.

The Avro CF-105 Arrow was a cutting-edge fighter-interceptor developed by the Canadian aviation industry in the 1950s. The project was abruptly halted before a planned review in early 1959. Shortly thereafter, the assembly line, tooling, plans, and

S.W. O'Connell

existing airframes and engines were ordered destroyed. The circumstances surrounding this program's mysterious demise remain shrouded in Cold War mystery.

About the Author

S.W. O'Connell holds degrees in History (Fordham University) and International Relations (University of Southern California). He is a retired US Army intelligence officer who spent most of his service in counterintelligence. Most of his time was spent overseas with the US Army Europe and Allied Command Europe, but he also served a tour in the Pentagon and a stint at the John F. Kennedy Center for Special Warfare at Fort Bragg.

A native New Yorker, S.W. O'Connell settled in northern Virginia after returning from his last overseas tour. His long-standing love of history made it only natural that he would turn to the historical novel when he finally succumbed to a decades-long urge to write fiction.

As the author of the acclaimed Yankee Doodle Spies series, he has three published historical novels set during the American Revolutionary War.

Envoy of the Lord, his first foray into science fiction, is blended with historical fiction to produce a genre-bending tale that moves the mind, heart, and spirit.

www.ingramcontent.com/pod-product-compliance
Lightning Source LLC
Chambersburg PA
CBHW060411030726
47495CB00003B/531